The Return Trip

By

Michael Byrne

Acknowledgement

The idea for this novel emerged during a November 2016 trip across seven states to visit Tai Chi and *qigong* masters I'd met online, and whose lessons, conversations, and motivations informed the development of this story and some of the characters. I'm very thankful for the counsel of Bill Douglas in Kansas, Bruno Repetto in Nebraska, Lee Fife and Beth Rosenfeld in Colorado, Michael Paler in Colorado, Ray Abeyta in New Mexico, Justin Harris in Texas and David Lenkovitzki in Arkansas, whose practices I publicized in my blog, *The New Dharma Bums*. A special thanks goes to David Carr and the many experts who chime in with chats in his Facebook group, the *Kwoon*, a "classics" source of information for people around the world.

My Dharma Bums trip coincided with the election of Donald Trump, a seismic event that followed me all along the way, and was roiling Washington when I got home a month later. *The Return Trip* story, reported by the protagonist, journalist Ray James, covers the first nine months of the Trump presidency. Aside from the real political events and figures, and actual places along the route of the trip, all characters and their stories are fictional. However, the practice and philosophical underpinnings of the Taoist martial arts and traditional Chinese medicine are true to the best of my knowledge.

I began practicing Tai Chi in Great Falls, Va., in 1989 under the guidance of Warren Connor of The Tai Chi Center, a school founded by former CIA agent and martial artist Robert W. Smith, who wrote the essential primer, "Tai Chi," on the Yang-style form introduced into the United States by Professor Cheng Man-Ching in the 1960s. It is one of the countless books I've consulted over these many years of daily form practice, and continuing education through workshops and meet-ups, most documented in *The New Dharma Bums* or my other blog, *Keeping Time*. I'm grateful to all Tai Chi masters, past or present, who shared their insights with me, including Adam Mizner, whose Heaven Man Earth Internal Arts practice is a global phenomenon.

I'm thankful, as well, to National Nurses United and its organizer, the California Nurses Association, for their battles to improve the U.S. healthcare system – campaigns I was thrilled to support and publicize. Those values take root in *The Return Trip*, as does the work of doctors, nurses, and mental health counselors I've consulted over the years. I'm grateful, as well, to all the women and men I worked with during my 30-year career as an advocate for America's unions.

I'm indebted to the ideas and writing of Jack Kerouac, who set the tone for a generation of Beat writers to redefine literature in the 50's and 60's, and to the "new journalists" who took the baton from the Beats and ran with it. Norman Mailer, Tom Wolfe, Hunter Thompson, and others working even today engage readers by putting themselves at the heart of the stories they cover. Reporter Ray James of *The Return Trip* fancied himself among this group.

I was fortunate to work with two outstanding editors. Jennifer Sawyer Fisher, a literary editor with experience in publishing, provided an analysis in 2021 that convinced me to revise several sections and restructure the novel. Most importantly, I was challenged relentlessly on facts and prose by my wife, Terry, a copy chief at work and home. Your best critics are always the ones who love you the most. Thus, I owe everything to my family and friends.

About the Author

Michael Byrne was born and raised in Henderson, Kentucky, certain that he would grow up to write novels infused with love and squalor. Instead, he trained as a Chinese and Vietnamese linguist with the U.S. Air Force and wandered the Far East circuit before earning a master's degree in journalism at Indiana University. He worked as a writer and editor for newspapers from Florida to Virginia before moving to Washington, D.C., to advocate for unions as editor of the *AFL-CIO News* and *America@Work,* and as an executive in two Washington public relations firms developing communications strategies and campaigns for labor, education, and progressive political groups.

Byrne's interest in Chinese language and culture led to a 33-year pursuit of the Taoist martial arts, particularly Tai Chi and *qigong,* healthful breathing and internal energy exercises he practices every day at home in Reston, Va. He is inspired by his wife, Terry, and five amazing children.

The Return Trip is a first novel. He's been working on the second one for more than 20 years. Stay tuned.

1. A Cockeyed World

I remembered the late spring smells of the mountain, the chill, and running along the slippery path by Tunnel Creek, chasing George in all his youthful vigor, his flying hair, and I know exactly where I am, again, except I'm having trouble keeping up. Not the first time we've been on these mountain trails above the lake, and every time feels fresh and new, even now. But George is moving well ahead and quickly. I stop, grabbing my knees, studying the ground, inhaling the licorice mint bursting in rosy spectacle, invigorating enough to catch my breath, nature's smelling salts. Now I move faster, beginning to gain on George, and he's stopped. He turns and flashes his wide smile, excitement in his eyes.

"This way," he says and launches from the bank to the top of a fallen tree, two quick steps, then over to the other bank, off trail, rocky and overgrown. I follow, more tenuously, feeling the mossy slipperiness under my feet and land just short of the bank. Splash! My feet are wet and cold, but I plunge ahead because there's no stopping George. Before long, he has turned away from the stream, heading onto a rough trail, and I follow, pushing and kicking limbs and brambling out of my way. I don't need to rush now. George has slowed to a walk, almost creeping as he crouches along the trail. He turns and shushes my loud path-finding advance, and I stop. "Hush," he whispers. "We'll surprise them!"

Who? I want to ask, but I'm staring at his backside as he moves his crouch forward without a sound. My steps crunch twigs and brush, so I hang back, keeping him in view. The air is crisp, and I can feel the moisture spread from my feet up my legs to my hips and then my

1

chest. Damn! I'm not dressed for this. Every bramble in my way now attaches itself to my pants, and I can feel the clingy plants pull me down. I lurch ahead, noisier now, and see the clearing ahead as George stops, turns, and motions his hand, palm down. Be quiet. Slow down. I move slowly in his direction until I'm crouching directly behind him, looking over his shoulder.

Ahead, I see the lake and the snow-capped peaks beyond. Off to our right stand wood cabins, several below in a grove, and a main cabin nearest us, with a covered porch and swing, where two women sit talking earnestly. George suddenly springs to his feet and breaks into a trot, galloping across the field toward the cabin. I lunge to follow him, seeing the startled women rise and clutch their thick fleece robes at the sight of the running men. Now they're waving excitedly and crying in unison, "Geo-o-o-o-rge"! They leap from the wooden platform to greet us as others burst through the cabin door. This place, these people, our college Tahoe getaway!

The swingers are Meg and Stacy – George calls out their names as they jump into his arms, hugging his neck and planting kisses on both cheeks. I slow to a walk, feeling somewhat invisible as even those rushing off the porch are calling George's name. Leading the charge is Arthur, the perpetual graduate assistant, long brown hair gathered in a ponytail in the back and a beard that might charitably be described as unkempt. Behind him are two women, with another man trailing. I recognize one of the women as Holly, who fancies me, I think, but she's also yelling, "George!"

Finally, I notice that everyone appears to be naked beneath their uniform white robes as the straggler, a guy I vaguely remember as Ben ... or Barry, fumbles while donning his robe, leaving him mostly exposed as he draws near. Stacy has wrapped one leg around George's waist, displaying the alabaster curve of her naked hip, and Meg is pulling at the belt on his jeans. "Yabyum," she's muttering. "Yabyum." George gently pushes her away, extricating himself from the leglock, and greets Arthur and the others in turn. "The prodigal sons return," he says. Holly, meanwhile, has rediscovered me, appearing at my side, pressing her body against my hip.

Inside, George has eagerly shed his clothes and is standing naked by the fire, holding his hands toward the flames, "Gotta warm up the digits," he says. "Who said, 'yabyum'?" Meg rushes to own up to the suggestion, this time claiming George with a two-leg wrap, and they collapse on the cushions with Meg sprawled in his lap. George sits up with his legs folded beneath Meg's rump, which he holds with both hands. I'm aroused, vaguely remembering this sexual exercise – a Tibetan ritual, I think, tantric sex to meditate by. I don't remember the meditation, but Holly is reminding me of the physical sensation as she helps me out of my shirt and jeans. I'm doing my best lotus within minutes, and she's sitting on my lap, gyrating furiously. Arthur is hosting Stacy, and the other woman is squirming on Barry's lap.

Moans, whimpers, grunts, groans, and pleasure tones punctuate our revelry's rhapsody until, chillingly, there's a ruckus outside the door, which flies open for two frantic, breathless men screaming, "Fire! Fire!" The words don't register at first, Holly's warm vaginal caress of my genitals overriding cogent directions, however alarming. "Just over the hill, hurry! Blowing this way," the urgent voice cries. "We gotta get out of here!" Now Holly stops, disengaging, and I'm one of four semi-hard men leaping to our feet and grabbing robes, shoes, and other garments to follow our sentries out the door.

Flames are bursting along the hill line above the grove, licking trees on the slope, coming our way. "It's moving fast," George says,

3

still pulling on his hiking clothes as he skips away from the rolling forest fire. "Follow me!" he calls, retracing our jaunt across the field and toward Tunnel Creek. Arthur, Beth, and the rest of the gang are skipping along behind as I struggle to pull on my jeans and hiking shoes. The heat is on my neck as I scramble off the porch and immediately stumble and fall flat on my face. What?!

———

Oh, no! Groaning, I sit up and wipe the perspiration from my neck, and chest … the bed is soaked, but this is no fun wet dream, a fucking nightmare. Man, I'm whacked. Where am I? OK, my bedroom, just me, my perspiration and crazy dreams, an aching head, and general misery. "What the hell?" The dream is fading fast, but my erection points to sexual stimulation of some sort, naked women, coitus interruptus. And George! Was that George? The fog has thickened. I haven't seen him in years.

I can't get out of bed, just lie back into the dank sheets, pull a blanket over me, close my eyes, and think. What day? They run together. There was a party, or maybe it was just me. Something happened. Think: Empty bed, sweaty mess. My head is the only thing throbbing, the usual inflamed gray matter, less a few more cells. Alcohol certainly was involved.

Rolling over and sitting up, I grab my head, rub my face in my palms, and groan. The whisky bottle sits on the table, nearly empty, a glass half-full. The ceiling fan hums above. Jesus! What a headache! I trudge to the bathroom and put my hand against the facing wall to brace myself as the stream falls, yellower than usual, the acrid smell further insulting my senses, such as they are this morning. At least I'm awake, barely.

4

The phone rings, and I listen as my recorded voice invites my caller to speak. It's Jim Bradbury, my editor. "Ray? Where have you been? We were expecting you at the office last night for the vote count. Man, we've got to sort this out! There are a million stories in it. We need to talk about covering the reaction, what it means to California and local communities – and, you know, our readers. We got the 2 o'clock, so think about it."

I'm shaking, and it isn't just the alcohol. The big news of the evening is now screaming inside my head. We've apparently elected a reality television personality, a billionaire real estate mogul with a carnival bark, a self-absorbed buffoon. Donald Trump is president. It's a shocking development that kept me glued to my television screen and away from the working party at the *Chronicle* office. But booze didn't wash it away. Now, besides the pounding head, I've got a morbid sense of doom.

Jumping into the shower, I try to think it through, scrubbing my head ferociously. We must be the laughingstock of the world this morning. Holy crap! This guy will have control of the nuclear codes. He'll have the Red Phone. Maybe there's some mistake, and we'll fix it today. Nobody figured this would happen, none of the people I talked with up and down the Left Coast. They depend on me to make sense of how the news affects them. But what's the sense in this?

I can't think about it now. It's a world of shit, and I'm feeling it this morning. Is it morning? God, I don't even know. I towel off and turn on my cell phone. It dings and whistles. It's almost noon, and I've got voice messages and countless emails. Bradbury left a message on the cell, too.

I put on the coffee and whip up the easiest brunch, cereal with milk, sitting down to parse the messages. First, there's a call from Will Reynolds, a political consultant and pollster who lectures at Berkeley and is an occasional source. "Ray? Will. The Trump win is even worse than you think, according to the numbers I was looking at in the last weeks, and from the exit polls. We should talk. A lot of young people stayed home or voted for Jill Stein or Gary Johnson. Democrats should have seen this coming, particularly in Pennsylvania and Michigan. Reliable Democrats swung to Trump in the final days. You should see this. Call." Click. Note: Pass to Bradbury and Julie Bowers, political beat.

Cherry is next in the queue. Did I see her last night? I click on the message. "Are you OK, Ray-Ray? I was at the club when you called, but I didn't understand your message … you were talking kinda crazy. Everybody's upset about the election, baby. We gotta get over it. Come see me tonight. Frank is coming in, too." Click. Ah, Frank, this is a message from Frank, no doubt, with a new potion. Frank and I are devoted to the fiery exotic dancer Cherry Fine and certain mood-altering substances. I'm invited to a party tonight. I will need to bring cash.

The next call is from a number I don't recognize, from Los Angeles. I click on it. "Ray, it's Jay … Lee. Remember?" Yeah, Jay Lee wrote a New Age religion column for the *Chronicle*. I helped him get the job, talented kid who dropped out of sight. "It's been a while," his message continues. "Sorry I lost touch. I took a long trip, stayed with Taoist monks. But I'm back, got a new gig, a holistic wellness practice in LA, acupuncture and more, mind-body stuff. Pretty radical, I know. I have a new book and a workshop retreat in Big Sur, the Esalen Institute, early next year. Can you come down? I'm allowed a guest and can put you up. I just sent details to your *Chronicle* email. Come on down and get healthy; try out my *qi* healing. Call me." Click.

Definitely, I click on my calendar and add a note to next year, January 2017, "Week in Big Sur/Esalen. Get dates." Jay's sudden exit surprised me. He went to China to see relatives, according to my bartender at Bow Bow's. Jay Lee is a second-generation Chinese-American martial artist and "medicine man" – at least, that was his gig when I met him, chasing herbs in Chinatown. I championed him when he got religion and began to blog about it. They loved him at the *Chronicle*. Now he's practicing Chinese medicine? What exactly is "*qi* healing?" I'll need research, a trip to Chinatown.

The last call is from Mona, my daughter, the doctor. "Dad? I couldn't sleep. I can't believe this is happening to our country. What are we going to do? Trump! It's not just that he hates women, blacks, immigrants, and poor people; he'll try to kill Obamacare, then Medicaid, then Medicare. Nobody will go to the doctor, and everybody will suffer and die!" I laugh out loud. "I need to see you before you go back out on the road. It's important. Can you meet me for lunch Friday? How about Pier 23 at 1 o'clock? Call me." Click.

I make a note. More than Trump anxiety in Mona's tone. She has something on her mind beyond her usual concern about my physical and mental health, which has reached the stage of obsession, in my opinion. It's not like I've been a great dad or anything. When you look at the overall record, I may be one of the world's worst. I resisted from the beginning, abandoning Patricia before Mona was born. I refused to pay child support, too, denying she was mine. The paternity test settled the issue, but I wasn't happy about the responsibility, anything connected to her scheming mother, using me like she used so many others.

Eventually, Mona won me over. Patricia moved back East, and I got a chance to be a father, helping Mona with school and to buy a condo, my place now. She's a doctor in a busy emergency room in San Francisco and doing well; she even got a girlfriend to take care of her. Maddie turns out to be the best thing that ever happened to Mona. Madelyn Parker – Maddie – is a registered nurse who organizes nurses for the California Nurses Association, a smart cookie. I like her. She also helped organize Mona's life; they're a good match.

Cereal bowl deposited amid a collection in the sink, I hurry to get dressed for the hour-long BART ride from Berkeley to downtown San Francisco. Living in the Bay Area, you learn a lot about alternative lifestyles, particularly the LGBTQ varieties, which are all out with a vengeance – even the Q – making up lost time. Where I grew up in Massachusetts, calling someone a queer was about the worst insult. But the queers have reclaimed the word, and that's fine with me. San Francisco is rightly proud of helping give queer a good name with its festivals and public displays that flaunt sex of all sorts. In the city by the Bay, it's easy to love the diversity and the perversity of it all. Who are we to judge, really? As long as Mona is happy, I have no complaints.

Still, as a man who ducked and ran from fatherhood, I wonder if an absent father makes a girl more likely to seek affection and companionship with someone of her own gender. Or would the absent dad lead to the longing for a faithful man to love? Do fathers even matter? We keep moving the marker on the norms of American culture. The nuclear family used to be the basic fact of life; now it's something out of a Norman Rockwell painting.

Take this Trump character. He's on his third wife, third family, and brags about being able to assault women at will, "grabbing them by the pussy," he said out loud, on tape. But voters apparently elected this big Daddy Warbucks despite his ugly sense of privilege and power. Or maybe he was elected because he embodies the bad-ass daddy people want. That's depressing. Another kind of crazy.

The BART ride from Berkeley into town gives me time to figure out a storyline for the news budget meeting. I'll be late, 2:15 at best, the ETA I text to Bradbury. The immediate story is the public reaction to the election stunner, and Bradbury will press me about what people are saying because I'm the guy who's supposed to have an ear to the ground. That's what he said when he gave me the column – *The Vibe*, the name is all mine. He trusts my judgment for whatever reason – maybe because I get the story from real folks, not flacks.

I'm no political guy. I try to play it down the middle, just like when I was a reporter. Not that I'm objective, not fully. That's the first thing you learn in J-school: Recognize your biases. Everyone brings their experiences to the table. The key is to not jump to conclusions and show mature judgment. No political party has a corner on goodness or wisdom, and more than a few politicians have low-minded reasons for their decisions -- money, and position. I'm thankful for newfangled media tools that allow me to call out people when they're cruel or stupid, even if social media creates a slew of digital interruptions, including incessant email. That's life in the information biz in an Information Age, too much information. Sorting it all out is half my job.

And now we've got a president who campaigned against the establishments of both political parties, and voters apparently rewarded him for his anti-establishmentarianism, even if he communicates in one-syllable words and dog whistles on race and nativism. What are you thinking, America? That's what I have to figure out. How did we get here? Now what?

Emerging from the Transbay Tube, I'm still scratching my head when the phone rings; 303 area code, Colorado? I move to a corner of the car to take the call. "George?" His greeting is in Chinese Mandarin, with one of the few phrases he taught me. "*Wode pengyu, ni hao?*"

"*Hao*. I am well – or recovering, at least. *Ni hao?*" I look around the car to see if any Chinese speakers may have heard me mutilating their language. He wants to know if I've been sick. No, no, recovering from the election! I ask him if he's so isolated out in Colorado that he hasn't heard that a rich hotel magnate and reality TV host is now president of the United States and the country is open for business. That's a fucking nightmare.

"Sounds like business as usual, Ray. No big deal. We have more important things to talk about." Really? This has to be part of a longer conversation, I tell him. I'm in a rush. But George won't be deterred, rushing to evoke memories of our youthful expeditions, finding our bliss in the wilderness. "We need to pick up that thread, Ray. We missed something. Can you come see me?"

George confirms he's still in Boulder, teaching comparative literature and Asian philosophy at Naropa University. "The air is fresh, the water cool, the people warm and friendly. It's a good place to create." I rush off the BART at the City Center into a throng of dawdling pedestrians, skipping and bumping my way toward the office. I have to go, I insist. But he wants to thank me for sending the *Chronicle* review of his book. "It's nice to be read, even if it's only by reviewers," he says. I assure him that poetry will make a comeback and he'll be rediscovered, but I have to bid him a hurried goodbye, promising to carve out time for a visit to the mountains.

"Lao Tzu says a journey of a thousand miles begins under your feet," he adds, suggesting a route through Arizona and New Mexico, where he has friends "to guide and sustain you. I'll send you contacts. Now, go save the world. We'll work on saving you later."

Saving me? Those words ring in my ears as I scamper into the *Chronicle* building. I see little hope of my personal salvation, but I'm thrilled at the prospect of catching up with George. He hasn't been far from my mind since we left Stanford, as he wandered off to China for a decade of cultural immersion while I raced away from school with nary a second thought of education, luckily landing a reporting job at the *Chronicle* right away. I'm a storyteller with a low horizon, the daily news.

George helped me with one of my early pieces at the *Chronicle* – an investigative series on the banned Chinese movement, Falun Gong. The buzz in Chinatown was that the group was taking hold in the United States and around the world – with millions of people in China actively defying the law to practice what appears to be a simple health regimen. I called George, and he put me in touch with contacts in China, then the *Chronicle* let me follow the trail based on George's good information.

We've had little opportunity to get together since our school days, just quick phone conversations and sporadic emails. Now I'm suddenly following him in an erotic dream, and he's calling me out of the blue, asking me to join him in Colorado. Something important. Knowing George, there's a psychic hand at work. He's probably divining my trip using his *I Ching*, the Chinese *Book of Changes*, a game we used to play. The ancient oracle often foretells a journey that "brings great fortune," a good omen. A great fortune is hardly ever in the cards for newshounds like me. I rush upstairs to the conference room to get the latest news.

2. All the News That Fits Me

Jim Bradbury, the managing editor with the bushy walrus mustache and bald pate, is holding court. "Sorry I'm late," I say, waving and easing into a chair at the opposite end from Bradbury. He gives me a long look. "What about this guy Reynolds, the pollster?" he asks. "Is he a good source on the numbers?" I nod, explaining how he tracked the late movement to Trump and warned Democrats. "I think Julie also has used him as a source."

Julie Bowers, the political reporter, is typing notes on her laptop and nods a quick smile. "Also, a lot of people thought Hillary was going to run away with it, and her campaign may have bought the sure thing," Julie offers. She reports that local Democrats are stunned, seeing how Hillary clobbered Trump in California and lost the election.

This is my opening, with a germ of an idea born of sudden Colorado wanderlust. "Maybe we're missing a big part of the story here," I say, pointing out that only a slim majority of eligible voters bothered to go to the polls – the lowest in 20 years. So Trump won with fewer than a quarter of eligible votes – and he finished second to Clinton in the vote total.

"Yeah, that's democracy in America. The Electoral College rules," Bradbury says. "What's your point?"

I plunge ahead, explaining that the people on the sidelines are making a big statement, given the stakes raised in the campaign. We should try to understand why people turned away. Was it these candidates or something larger – maybe the political system, or

13

they're caught up in their own lives and don't want to get involved. What are they looking for? "I think there's a big story at the margins of the system," I conclude.

"How the hell do you find the margins?" Bradbury thunders.

"That's where Ray rolls, at the margins," comes a barb from wiseacre Sports Editor Tim Norris, prompting snickers around the table. I cut them off, flashing an exasperated look to Norris as I argue that we can't afford not to ask the questions. We may be missing something because we're focused on all the drama – and the absurdity – at the top. Reality TV things come easy to us, right? We're trying to find interesting angles. But the most interesting – and maybe the most important – could be hiding in plain sight.

"OK, give me a proposal," Bradbury says, rubbing his chin. "With specifics. No fishing expeditions. I know the margin is a big-ass area, but narrow it down a bit for me. An itinerary would be nice. Let's all get going. News is getting old. Web team, hang back. We need to talk about the exit poll graphics and the election database."

As we file out of the conference room, I fall in behind Norris, poking him in his muscular bicep and pointing out that the San Francisco 49ers are on the margins of being an NFL team. "Yeah, tell me about it," Norris says. "It's ugly out there." In fact, our office is on the margins, I tell him, right here at the edge of San Francisco's Tenderloin section. The margin is our territory, I announce my plan to start the post-election postmortem tonight at the Crazy Horse exotic dancing palace, and I invite him to join me.

"There you go, just like I said, Ray. You can have it. I'd rather watch Kaepernick pass the football for a miserable team than make empty passes at bargirls." Norris, recently married, isn't looking, but

I insist that I am. "Yeah, in all the wrong places," comes his retort. "I told you, e-Harmony worked for Clarissa and me."

I laugh and slap Norris sportingly on the back. That's not me, and I'm not looking for anything serious, just fun. I remind him I'm still available for the basketball games he organizes at the YMCA. "Sure you are, in your mind," he snorts. "But can you drag your old body up and down the court? The game may have passed you by."

I'm familiar with his abuse, so I wave a dismissal and turn toward my cubicle. Maybe half-court, I mutter to myself. No question, my body is sagging under the weight of age and self-abuse. But in my head, I'm still the high school shooting star who got a basketball scholarship to Stanford, albeit never to play with the team. It's an All-American memory for a guy who struggles through 18 holes of golf nowadays. Sure, a lot has to do with age, as I ramble into my 50s, but my energy level is way down.

I slump in front of my computer terminal and begin composing a proposal to explore the nation's political margins, a vast undertaking that stops me immediately. I need to focus. My mind is following my body out the window. I'm not sure how I did it just a decade earlier, climbing high in the Wudang mountains and chasing the Falun Gong story. It was invigorating – and not just the exercise. The hint of danger was in the air, Taoist monks quietly telling their stories about the purge and ongoing persecution of Falun Gong, with a translator George found for me. I was *alive*, chasing a hell of a story. Now I don't even know the story I'm chasing.

The phone rings. I pick up. "Hey, Ray, it's Frank. Will I see you tonight?" Absolutely, I tell him. He wasn't sure I got the message but wanted to let me know he's got something for me, "a little different, but better." Better is good, I tell him. I've really got the blues.

"Yeah, you and everybody else in this town – the ones I know anyway," Frank says. "This will cheer you up, for sure." Good news. My guess is that Frank has stocked up on sativa marijuana strains, the ones I like, those high in THC like Sour Diesel or a hybrid like Blue Dream – known cures for depression.

Frank found his way to pharmaceuticals after falling out of the Gulf War, a battlefield medic with a habit and a grievance. He also was a news source for me, strictly on background, with a story about the epidemic of PTSD among military veterans who return broken. Frank appeared in my story as an anonymous dealer who sees his drug business as a form of mercy for his brothers trying to cope with "The World" and is happily slouching toward legal pot sales. Not only does he put me in touch with people living on the streets or hiding out, but he also supplies me with the best and safest drugs available.

I try to keep my head down, but I've been taking risks my whole life as safely as I can. Yeah, I'm a bit of a stoner, but I'm no druggie. Recreational drugs are good, within reason, and I'm in high gear rationalizing the reasonableness of it. Nothing wrong with getting high if you play it safe. On a typical day, I can chill out with mildly psychotropic drugs like pot, maybe rev it up with a line or two of coke, then spice it with a margarita from the bar. Mostly I keep it away from work, except when my work is on the road, which is often. But I don't need a supervisor. Just stay on an even keel, and manage the dosage. Stop when I've had enough. Tweak it with a little coffee, or espresso. Dessert. A lovely woman. Everything in moderation, I figure, except for the lovely women.

But now I need to make a coherent case for a story about a disturbing trend in American democracy, with a travel budget that gets me to Boulder, Colorado, at least. Tall order. I'll need to break it up into a series of assignments focused on different kinds of people who have retreated from politics. Young people, for sure, and African-Americans. People who live in the shadows – illegal immigrants concerned about their families, homeless vets, the working poor. People have lost their faith in elected leaders, maybe lost whatever faith they had. Maybe it's a spiritual crisis.

I'm reminded of Jay Lee, the former *Chronicle* religion writer turned faith healer, and his workshop at the Esalen Institute. Bradbury will want to know about it. What is *qi* healing? I ask Google, learning that it involves the same energy as in *qigong*, like the Falun Gong exercises. Healers are able to channel the energy, using a "*qi* field" to transmit healing energy. Quite a feat if you can pull it off. Maybe Jay's a miracle worker.

Bradbury is wearing his usual gruff scowl when I walk into his office, but he breaks into a big smile when I tell him about the message from Jay Lee, "a good reporter, an ambassador to Chinatown," Bradbury recalls. "Some older readers complained that he didn't genuflect deeply enough to Christianity or Judaism, but the young people loved him, even the nonbelievers. He's a Buddhist, right?"

I'm not sure about his beliefs nowadays, I say, especially since he's practicing Chinese medicine. I hesitate to suggest he's a doctor since his credentials probably would be challenged by the U.S. medical community. But he has a business in Los Angeles, a holistic wellness center that treats patients with old-style Chinese cures – acupuncture, herbs, and a mysterious energy they call *qi*.

17

"No shit!" A look of bewilderment crosses Bradbury's brow. This is news. "That doesn't seem like a step up in the world. Is it even legit?"

I tell him that some Chinese medical practices are covered by insurance – like acupuncture. As I understand it, qi healing uses the same meridians of the body to channel qi energy for healing. I can find out more at the workshop Jay's planning in the new year at the Esalen Institute in Big Sur. He wants me to stay as his guest, but I'm thinking the newspaper may want to foot the bill because there will be a story or two coming out of it. It's natural for us, I tell him, "and maybe it'll also shed light on the electorate post-election."

Bradbury snorts. "Nice try, Ray. You still owe me a proposal for an exposé on the rise of the nonvoter as a determinant in national elections, or elections generally. I want to see where you go with that – and check to see if either party is working to reach these nonvoters or to disqualify them. But, yeah, use the company credit card to book the Esalen trip. Let me know when you nail down the dates. Give my best to Jay Lee."

I go back to noodling over my proposal on the margins that could lead to Colorado. This is going to take more imagination than I reckoned. I'll have to figure it out as I go along. For the record, I search the voting rates of towns and counties down the coast, cross them with economic and social data, read a few headlines, and plot a likely story from San Francisco to Los Angeles. It's a painstaking process, time-consuming but worth the trouble, even if half the story ideas won't pan out. The ball is rolling. I'm polishing this fabrication when Frank calls.

18

"Ray, are you still at work?" I look at the clock: 6:30. Yeah, but I'm checking out. Frank's not waiting for me at the club. He's downstairs, out front on Mission Street. I save the proposal and attach it to a message to Bradbury, warning that it's just a first draft and I'm working through the itinerary and details. Odd that Frank would come to meet me. I expected to see him at the Crazy Horse, only a few blocks away. Something's up. I grab my jacket and head to the elevator. Most of the reporters and top editors have left, including Bradbury, and the copy desk is cranking out the first edition. No one looks up as the elevator dings, and I retreat.

Frank is nowhere in sight as I exit the *Chronicle* offices. I walk to the curb and look left and right. Around the corner from 5th Street, a white stretch limo moves slowly onto Mission, pulling up to the curb in front of me. The rear window rolls down, and Frank pokes his head out, "A car for Mister James!" he shouts.

Nice ride, I tell him. "You're moving up in the world."

"Not exactly. Just hustling, finishing up my rounds, saving the best for last." He opens the door. "Come on in. You haven't met Gretchen." Sitting opposite Frank in the facing limousine seat is a dazzling blonde woman with dangling sapphire earrings and a string of pearls above her ample cleavage. I get in the car beside her and extend my hand. She grabs it with both hands and reaches over to kiss me on the cheek, emanating a fragrance of dewy rose petals. "Ray, I've heard so much about you. I finally get to meet you."

I look at Frank suspiciously. "Have you been making up stuff about me, Frank?" He wears his cockeyed grin. "Nothing but the truth, so help me, God," he says. "Gretchen is a business associate.

19

We only talk business. She digs your writing, particularly the piece on PTSD. We talked about how you and I talked about it."

Good to know. I measure Frank's "business partner" again, also apparently a dealer in pharmaceuticals, and not involved personally with him. And she likes my writing. "Very nice to meet you, Gretchen, and thank you. It's good to be read. Newspapers are fading into the sunset."

"Yeah," Gretchen sympathizes. "I mostly read the news online myself. We should save the trees." Well, there you go – the end is near. I point toward the six parallel lines of white powder on the table in front of Frank, asking what he's cooked up for us.

Frank's in his early 40s, but he's got a shock of gray hair in his dark beard, making him look older. He keeps his hair and beard trimmed neatly, like a businessman, which he is. "I think you know our girl Molly," he says. Of course, Ecstasy, MDMA, but I've only done the pills, I admit. "This is the different and better I was telling you about," Frank says. "I've got the pills for you, too, but we won't delay tonight. This'll go right to your head. Cherry's going to meet us after dinner. We're heading to the new Black Cat. Here, I brought a straw for each of you." Gretchen expertly snorts two lines of Molly, and I eagerly take my turn.

3. Group Therapy Fail

The Black Cat has been a San Francisco tradition for years in various locations. Now it's conveniently located in the Tenderloin and a new favorite hangout for me. The food isn't all that great, but the jazz blows alternately hot and cool, a good combo if you like jazz, which I do. Tonight it's the Black Cat Trio, the house band, with a guest female vocalist, a black woman lighting up "God Bless the Child."

Molly is kicking in, making me feel all warm and fuzzy and loving myself – loving everybody, really, and especially that jazz singer, who is giving me the chills. "She'll be glad to hear you like it," Frank says. "You don't recognize her, do you? You interviewed her for our story." He is smiling at my puzzled expression. "It's Annamarie. Remember the lawyer who helped get me extended health care with the class-action suit?" No, I wouldn't have recognized her singing the blues. I'll be damned. Annamarie … Scott, yes. She's really good, more than just a lawyer.

When Annamarie finishes her set, she joins our table and trades enthusiastic mutual admiration expressions with me, for our work, for the cause, the craft, and the art. I tell her how much I've been moved by her singing. "And you also move juries!" I add. She laughs, telling me she sang her way through law school and still has a few gigs, just for fun. She was a semi-finalist in the West region of "America's Got Talent" and is happy to have public service law to fall back on. I give her my card and propose we have lunch soon. She seems thrilled.

Cherry makes a splashy entrance at 9 o'clock, jiggling noisily to our table. "Is this the party?" she asks. My head tells me the party never really stops; it just keeps spinning around. We're soon back in the limo, and Cherry is fishing ice cubes into a glass and pouring drinks around – Johnny Walker Black on the rocks for me, she doesn't ask. "Come here, pretty dancer," I say as I pull her to my chest, and she lands in my lap. "We get to dance together tonight, Ray," she says. "I can show you my new moves." Oh, yes, please.

Frank gives us a Molly refresher and lights a joint. I ask about the price of Ecstasy and how much I can get. "The pills are 12 dollars each on the street, but a special deal for you. Twenty-five in this pillbox." He shakes the aluminum container for effect. "Just two hundred, and only for you. If you like it, there's more."

I quickly agree, counting out the bills and asking about the sativa. "Bonus leaf," he responds, sliding a small canister of the pot over in front of me. "We have a lot of this, different strains. Spread the word. We're ready for this shit to be legal; that's the good thing about the election – even though the state's gonna take a big cut. Listen," he pauses and points to me, "don't overdo it with Molly."

Sure, Frank. He knows me; I'm a survivor. No busts, no busted noggins, no code blues. I might get fucked up, but I keep it between the lines. Gotta stay in the game. "It's a writer's curse, isn't it, alcohol and drugs?" This question comes from Gretchen, who is leaning forward, elbows on her knees, listening to us. I laugh and agree. Literary history is full of drunks and addicts, many of them brilliant and creative beyond their contemporaries. Lots of losers, too. "Some didn't make it through their addictions," I add. "Some are lucky, like me … so far."

Frank returns the stash to his shoulder bag. "Let me know if Tim or any of your other buddies at the paper want in on anything." I'm sure they will. I'll spread the word, like always. I tell him about my coming road trip; I'll need some bennies and mild hallucinogens to help me merge into the passing landscape, especially good grass. Frank holds out his hand, and I shake it. "It will be arranged," he said. "Meanwhile, we're almost at the party, special invitation only. *You are invited!*"

"I think we've missed the naked yoga, but there's an after-election party," Cherry says brightly. "We're going to shake it up. Frank got us the reservations." Frank shrugs and grins. "I figured this would be perfect for you the night after Donald Trump was elected. Pussy grabbing is allowed."

"Oh, no, Frank!" objects Cherry, the woman who faces assault from drunken clods nearly every night she works. "There's only love in there," she insists. "No mean stuff. Naked yoga twist dancing, but only among consenting adults. Just don't hurt anybody."

"Not that I would hurt anybody, but I'm going to miss the fun," Frank says. "I've got a few more stops to make tonight. Cherry's got all the reservation info. Gretchen, I'm going to the Presidio after all, apparently. I may catch up with you later. Enjoy."

Cherry opens the door and pulls me out as we all laugh, feeling buoyant and bulletproof. Gretchen scoots over and out, clutching a large cloth bag I learn holds scotch, bourbon, and vodka, lubricant for the evening. We'll want to share.

I promise to call Frank tomorrow, even though I know he'll call me first. Cherry and Gretchen lead the way to the club door, where an overdressed Chippendale is checking IDs and reservations. I learn they don't accept single men, but single women are just fine. Our threesome is more than welcome, particularly along with the wad of cash that Gretchen deposits at the door. We enter and climb a flight of stairs, where a barely dressed woman points us to the sign-in book.

"For the bar," Gretchen tells the attendant, holding up the bag of liquor. We are directed to the corner bar, where a few patrons are serving themselves. I try to get my bearings while Gretchen fixes us drinks. On the next level, music is pumping, and strobe lights are flashing. I see the silhouettes of dancers, some of whom *do* appear to be nude. In my current hallucinatory state, I can't be sure.

Putting my arm around Cherry, I ask her what's her secret in taking off her clothes in front of strangers, being so bold. "Well, it helps to have a nice body … like you do, Ray!" Pfft! Hardly, I scoff. It's old and softening up nowadays. Cherry puts her arms around me, kisses me, and offers a smile. "You sell yourself short, lover boy. You're big and strong and beautiful. Everybody here wants a sugar daddy like you."

"Including me!" Gretchen exclaims. "But now let's get more comfortable." She has stashed the booze on the shelf and come around the bar to join us with our drinks, proposing a toast. Hoisting her glass, she declares, "Here's to threesomes!" We all drink to that, then head to the dance floor, finding a table on the outer rim. A few dancers are writhing in the buff, left over from the erotic yoga exercises, perhaps. Some are in underwear or negligees, but most are dressed. Women outnumber men by at least three to two, a promising arrangement.

Very exciting, ladies, I say. It's hard to tell who is dancing with whom and what the relationships are, if any. "Let's join them!" says Gretchen, grabbing our hands and pulling us out onto the dancefloor. The sound system is pumping out electronic music, and the dancers are bouncing and churning to the rhythms while multicolored lights

24

are spinning from a projector, reflecting off the glittering disco ball and giving the entire room an ethereal glow, no doubt exaggerated by the effects of the Ecstasy, which is well-named and well-appointed for this party scene. I've never felt better.

Cherry and Gretchen look absolutely stunning – Cherry, with her long red hair falling halfway down her back, gathered in the front with side braids that fall past her ears over her shoulders, pointing to the open bodice that offers peekaboo breasts as she dances; Gretchen with her blonde hair cut in a bob falling casually above her neck and over her eyes, bejeweled as I mentioned, and a slinky blue dress that hugs her curves all the way down. Everyone is looking at them, I'm sure.

I move into Gretchen, grinding my body along her hip and shoulder. As she turns to me, Cherry presses her breasts against Gretchen's back, running her hands down the sides of her hips and to her front nether region, rubbing me at the same time. "Mmmmmm, Gretchen sandwich," Cherry coos to us both, then spins off and around behind me. I turn to face her for another step in the dance, sliding under her, feeling Gretchen's arms immediately around my waist, hands rubbing my cock, which is straining against my jeans. I've been sandwiched. Lovely. I hope this never stops.

Even the electronica music is growing on me as it pulses with my body, pumping blood to all my extremities. My mind is racing, bouncing with the beats as I circle Cherry and Gretchen, and then it's a woman I don't know, one of the naked ones, and she leans in and unbuttons my shirt, then twists away. Then there''s a black man, very svelte and smooth, with amazing moves, dancing into my space to let me know he could fit into whatever plans we have. Eventually, I lose track of Cherry and Gretchen, but each new encounter is promising

25

as orgiastic music sends me into fantasyland. Finally, Gretchen makes her way back to our dance, grabs my arm, and pulls me off the floor.

I happily follow Gretchen to our table, where a bucket of champagne has appeared, with four glasses and a bowl of fruit. "Surprise! Did you order champagne, Ray?" she asks. It wasn't me, I say. Maybe the money that Gretchen handed the attendant is paying for it. Maybe she's the money-woman behind Frank's operation. Are you the banker? I ask her. She smiles and shakes her head. "Maybe there are some banks involved, but it's import-export. I know people." She grabs the bottle, studying the label. "Real champagne, too, from Champagne," pronouncing the French region.

I'm gnawing on the fruit, my mind still whirling out on the dancefloor. Did we lose Cherry? "She's right over there. Oh, you missed it!" Gretchen is pointing to a small circular stage at the other end of the floor. "It was crazy. Cherry just went into her dancing act – except it was double time with the trance music, shaking and shedding. When she was down to her G-string, a couple of guys hoisted her up on that little stage. But she's gone …."

"I'm here!" Cherry walks up, cheeks flushed and still out of breath, a silk Oriental-style robe covering up. She has a friend, a slim Asian woman dressed to the nines of Chinese style – a red dragon-pattern silk satin dress that falls to her ankles and buttons at the collar, totally formal and seemingly out of place. Cherry's introduction proves me wrong. "This is Mimi, one of the owners of the club. She used to work with me at Crazy Horse! Mimi, this is Ray and Gretchen. They are first-timers here."

"Ah, virgins!" Mimi says, flashing a toothsome hostess smile. "Welcome to the Twist party. We hope you're having as good a time

26

as Cherry is. She turned one end of the dance floor into a den of oglers, and many ran off to the play area. Have you been upstairs?" Obviously, the "virgins" haven't, and Mimi cheerfully agrees to give us a tour. "And, yes, it's okay to watch, or hide out, whatever you want to do. Only one rule: Be nice. Respect other people. Always take no for an answer."

She leads us down a hallway and up a short flight of stairs to the vast play area, lined with ample and colorful beds and curtains – to draw or not to draw, and it appears that few areas are fully enclosed. From our vantage point, we can see a mass of indistinct moving flesh, assorted love-making entanglements. Moans and gasps compete with the pulsating music down the hall, but no one seems to notice stimuli outside their immediate circles.

"We try not to talk much on this level," Mimi says. "You don't want to spoil someone's moment with idle chatter. You can't invite yourself into a party, but you may get an invitation if you hang around. You are expected to tell any potential partner about STDs. You'll find condoms everywhere. I'm going to leave you here. Feel free to wander and get comfortable."

We bid her adieu and turn toward the mass of moaning humanity. I like to watch, I tell Cherry, but I hope we find our own playground soon. She squeezes my hand, turns me to her, and begins unbuttoning my shirt. "Let's go ahead and get comfortable, Ray-Ray. You need to loosen that belt, and drop those jeans. Here, I brought a bag for our clothes. The lockers are just behind us."

Cherry has already shimmied out of her robe, and Gretchen takes the cue, dropping her dress to the floor and stepping out of it. Two beautiful women standing nude before me; I fumble with buttons and zipper, yielding to their hands stripping me. Soon we are but three in a sea of naked people, and I'm feeling a bit more natural.

With my arms around the waists of my lovely consorts, we search for a place to light. The first encounter is a group of four, maybe two couples, although it is hard to discern two separate couples – unless the man and woman sharing a blowjob on the other man is a couple, and the woman sitting on the face of the blown man is his mate. No room for us, so we move on.

We come to an expansive playland with two beds and two loveseats where a woman is on her hands and knees, attending one man with her mouth while another man fucks her from behind. On the loveseat facing us, two women sit stroking each other, smiling as they watch us watch them. Cherry and Gretchen find my cock almost simultaneously. "Shall we stop and play?" Gretchen asks hoarsely. Of course.

We walk over to the loveseat, where the two women stand up, join in a group hug, and kiss all around and around with gentle strokes. We are meeting Jenny and Grace and soon are joined in an eight-way huddle bunch by George, Ian, and Gloria, all "devoted pansexual" lovers who love that we joined them.

This is where my memory gets a bit clouded, so bear with me while I try to sort out how it goes down. It begins, I remember, with me going down on everybody – and by that, I mean I just go down on my knees in the middle of the huddle because I've touched Gretchen between her legs. She feels so wet and hot to my touch that I sink to get a closer look and taste. Another lovely snatch is right there, too, I think it's Grace, and I'm touching and licking her too. Then I find a big cock sticking in my face and give it a little tug in admiration as I rise up through the humanity and find Cherry's beautiful lips hungrily pressing against mine, and someone has my dick in their mouth. And I get sick.

With all the excitement, it doesn't seem like a big deal at first, but I'm having trouble breathing. I push Cherry away and put my hand on my brow. I am sweating, my head hurts, and I feel dizzy. My whole body hurts. I grab my chest. Whatever expression I have on my face alarms Cherry, who cries out. "Ray! Are you okay? Ray!" My legs give out, and I don't remember what happens after that until I see Mimi's face hovering above mine with a look of concern. Behind her, I see Cherry, Gretchen, and other naked people with knitted brows. I'm on my back with a dull throb in my head and a sharp pain in my arm. I try to speak but can't get the words out of my mouth.

"Just relax for a minute, Mr. James," Mimi purrs, a smile coming over her face. "I think you probably had a mild heart attack. Luckily you were here because I'm trained as a nurse. I gave you a drug that dissolves blood clots, and it appears to have worked – at least for now. You need to follow up with your doctor. Okay?" She strokes my forehead with a cool hand, and I try to return her smile. Obviously, the club has taken precautions to avoid having clients die on them, and I'm very grateful. Mimi appears as an angel of mercy. I'm spared.

Cherry called Frank, and he's returning with the car. She and Gretchen get me dressed and down the stairs into the lounge area, where they sit on each side of me, holding my hands, heads on my shoulders. "Poor baby," Cherry whispers. Mimi has gotten me water, crackers, and fruit and is waiting with us, asking me questions about my job and family, making sure I'm past danger.

I hear Frank's voice. "What's going on?" His face is flushed, and he's out of breath after bounding up the stairs. It's my fault, I tell him. I ruined the evening. I think I may be getting too old for this. "No!" Cherry cries. "It was just a little episode, baby. You'll be back better than new."

"I certainly hope so, Mr. James," Mimi says. "Please get better and come back to see us. You're always welcome!"

"Yeah, you'll be okay, partner," Frank says. "It's the damned election. It'll get better."

4. Mona: The Doctor in Charge

Mona was growing increasingly angry as she listened to Ray tell about his heart attack, trying to minimize its importance and impact on his life – on her life. He didn't say what he was doing and where he was but admitted to drinking and probably overexerting himself. "You don't take care of yourself, Dad! You're killing yourself," she said, pointing to the Bloody Mary he ordered before she and Maddie arrived at this bayside table on Fisherman's Wharf. Gray skies cast a dull shadow over the choppy bay, reflecting the dark mood at their table.

"You've just received a warning, loud and clear," Mona continued. "Now, what are you going to do about it? It won't get better until you change your behavior and protect your health." Ray nodded, admitting sheepishly he was lucky that immediate treatment was available, with a clot-dissolving drug and an experienced nurse, and that his regular physician, Dr. Newman, had scheduled a series of tests. Mona sighed. This isn't how she expected their conversation to go when she called for this meeting to talk about life changes – not just the Trump election, which is life-changing enough. She and Maddie have news. But the first topic on the agenda is her father's heart attack.

Mona had seen her share of heart attack victims at the emergency room, and she saw her father fitting the profile – heavy drinking, probably taking other drugs, too, based on behavior she thinks is peculiar at best. He pushes himself too hard with his work schedule, sleeps odd hours, if at all, and must be surviving on roadside fast food and gin joints—all part of a recipe for heart attack.

The AMA Code of Medical Ethics prohibited her from treating a member of her immediate family, but she can steer her wayward father toward proper treatment. Having referred patients to Dr. Newman, Mona is sure he'll be happy to discuss the test results with her and how she can help influence her father's bad behavior, the primary threat to his health. Faced now with a lecture from his "family doctor," he sounded penitent as he promised to get a thorough checkup and to follow Dr. Newman's advice.

Maddie, who'd been listening quietly as Mona pressed her father on the unexpected health news, rushed in to offer her support. "You've got the right attitude, Mr. James," she said. "There's medicine you can take, and you'll have to watch your diet, get regular cardio exercise, and manage your stress, which won't be easy in the age of Trump."

Ray grabbed his chest in mock agitation, shaking his head. "I know they're just going to give me more drugs. It's the American way," he said. "We've got a health care system intent on selling me things I don't need, especially expensive drugs. I'm leery of every prescription."

"You're right, Mr. …. Dad, sorry," Maddie said, laughing as she remembered his admonition not to use a formal title for dear old dad. But this was a serious topic for her. "We've been calling out Big Pharma and the medical industry profiteering on sick people, driving up the cost of health care. It's a story that's not told enough in the media."

Ray chuckled, asking Maddie if she was bringing the nurses' union public relations to the table. Maddie didn't deny it, but she was warming up to the topic, determined to persuade the *Chronicle* to write about people losing health care or being unable to afford it. "I can get contact information for nurses all across the country who can help put health care on the front burner in the sick new age of Donald Trump," she told him. It's not his beat, Ray said. "You should be talking to George Stevens, our healthcare reporter."

"Our communication folks talk to Stevens," Maddie said. "He covers the process, which is boring and not moving anyone to action. But you write about regular people who depend on the health care system to work for them. You can make it real, the real-life public drama. Our nurses are on the front lines."

Ray sat back in his chair, studying Maddie's intense expression and returning an understanding smile. Does the union have nurses in Colorado? he asked. "Sure," Maddie said. "We've got national affiliates all the way to the East Coast." Ray agreed to think about it since he was looking for good post-election story ideas and soon would be hitting the road. Mona objected to any road trip before he got a clean bill of health, warning that many highway deaths occur when drivers suffer heart attacks. He dismissed the idea with a wave of a hand but promised he'd be careful – "a model of good health" – before getting back to his traveling job.

"Dad, we're asking you to please stay home for a while," Mona told him as she reached across the table and took his hand. "Maddie and I have decided to make it official, to get married, and also to have a child." Ray looked stunned, then suddenly jubilant. He let out a whoop, rose, and quickly walked around the table, stooping and leaning into hugs, embracing both women. "Terrific!" he exclaimed. "I've been waiting for the announcement of a wedding, but the baby is a shock – a grandchild! I'm so happy for you .... and me."

Maddie, who had been fretting about how Ray would take the news, was ebullient seeing the reaction, explaining how she and Mona decided to use the Pacific Sperm Bank and that Mona would bear the child. "Ramona and I have a deal on our parental duties – I'm the nurse, and she gets to nurse," Maddie joked. "In the initial division of labor, she gets the labor." Ray laughed. "There'll be plenty of labor for two moms, I'm sure," he said.

Mona proudly announced she was eager to carry on the James genes and James name, which elicited only a shrug and a tight smile from the patriarch. "I'm thrilled and look forward to watching the baby grow," he said, "but don't count on much help from the James gene. I hope it doesn't hurt." Mona pooh-poohed his negativity, proclaiming her love for the name and for him.

"I've done some research on the James family tree, so you know," Ray said. "We are descended from a family of wanderers, going all the way back to England's Norman conquest. Our forebearers fled Wales in cramped boats in the 1600s and never made much of the name in Massachusetts, just kept their heads down and survived until hard living wore them out, usually at an early age."

Maddie responded in disbelief. "What about Henry James, the author, and his brother, the psychologist, William, famous people," she said. No traceable connection, Ray responded. "It appears their family traipsed the highlands before landing in New York, never to cross paths with the lowland Jameses." Ray had earned a newspaper byline for the name, for what that's worth, and wasn't overly concerned about not having some grand James tradition to carry on. "Nothing matters but the future, so cheers to you ladies and our child-to-be," he said.

Two weeks went by before Mona got a look at Ray's test results, along with a briefing from Dr. Newman, seeking her help as she expected. "Your dad has some important decisions to make, and you can help." The news wasn't all bad, and Dr. Newman gave Ray the good news first when he called him in, along with Mona. His heart and valves would be fine with the maintenance drugs, but the doctor wanted to perform an angioplasty to implant a stent to fortify the damaged artery. He also wanted to add a new blood pressure medicine to the statin Ray was taking for cholesterol. And he prescribed regular procedures to screen for colorectal and gastrointestinal cancers going forward. "Pain in the ass," Ray grumbled.

"The worst news," Dr. Newman proclaimed as he pulled up images on his computer screen, "is that your liver is on the verge of failure, Mr. James. You have a fatty liver working overtime to process what you're eating and drinking." He pointed to dark ridges on the image and said, "This is scarring here – cirrhosis from all the alcohol. Early stages, but irreversible."

Startled by this announcement, Ray glanced at Mona, who shook her head, biting her lip. "You have to quit drinking, Dad, or you'll die. It's a real threat." Ray looked into his daughter's moist, pleading eyes and squeezed her hand, saying nothing.

"There are no guarantees," Dr. Newman said, "but continuing to drink would be suicide. As I said, the scarring is irreversible, but you can still get years out of your liver if you stop poisoning it." Dr. Newman had been pacing the office, stroking his gray beard as he talked. "You have other risk factors, including unhealthy food," he continued. "Your glucose readings have tipped into the Type 2 diabetes range. You need to cut the sugar."

Mona reminded her father that he quit smoking cigarettes when she came to live with him, and he could quit drinking, too. Ray shrugged, "It's not that easy. Fewer people smoke nowadays, but drinking is different. It's how I meet people, how I greet people, where I go, and what I do. It goes with food and most of the fun. It's part of my proudly bohemian lifestyle. I don't know many people who don't drink."

"You need to meet some, Mr. James," Dr. Newman said. "There are groups out there with people trying to overcome addiction. I can give you referrals – not just AA but other groups that aren't religious. And I can prescribe drugs to help you get past the cravings."

Ray quickly agreed to the proposition of taking drugs to stop using drugs, opting for naltrexone, an opioid antagonist that blocks endorphins in the brain, making drinking less pleasurable. Mona objected. "That takes too long, Dad," she said. "You should take Antabuse, which works right away. It makes you sick if you drink. You have an immediate incentive to quit."

"No, I'm not ready for that," Ray said. "Surely I can drag my soused liver through a couple more months." Mona shook her head sadly. This was not the attitude adjustment necessary for her father to survive himself.

5. Slow Walk to Rehab

I'm checking out options on WebMD when Norris pokes his head into my cubicle. "Three-on-three half-court tournament at the gym, James. Do you still have that shot?" I beg off, telling him my ticker's acting up, trying to be careful, but promise I'll be back on the court with the new year. By the way, there's a new supply of goodies making the rounds, and I'm taking orders. "Great!" Norris exclaims. "Let me make a couple of calls, and I'll get back to you."

I go back to researching heart attacks and treatment. Yeah, I should definitely rejoin the gym, plug in regular cardio work, and maybe start the day with a swim. Shit! Who the hell am I kidding? I'm not getting up early to jump in a pool.

The question of my mortality has never been an issue before, just a fact of life, nothing pressing. But time is a cruel mistress pushing you to that steep precipice where the end is near, and you sense the regrets of your life – in my case, so many – and you don't want to leave on those terms. I feel a moment of panic. Can we renegotiate? No, I'm on my own. What will I make of this fleeting life? I'm not ready to die.

Bradbury calls. "We need to discuss your post-election series," he says sternly, and I gather from his tone he's not happy with my preliminary analysis. No matter. I'm not going to lay out a detailed plan, and he knows it. We're just brainstorming floating ideas. It's the process. As I enter his office, I broach the immediate "important issue we need to discuss before we get to the election project."

"What's more important than explaining to our readers what happened with the fucking presidential election?" he asks, waving his arms. "That's all anyone is talking about. That's all anyone cares about." I tell him about the heart attack, apparently mild, and how the doctors are running multiple tests on me and want to perform minor surgery. Bradbury's expression turns glum, then pitiful, as I tell him I will need to slow down for a while.

"Oh, no," he says, putting his head in his hands and massaging his temples. "What happened? Did you go to the hospital?" I explain that it was a mild episode, and a nurse treated me at the scene. I'm under my doctor's care. "How much time do you think you'll need?" Bradbury asks, with a tone of resignation and what I'll presume is concern. I tell him I'll probably need a month to sort it out -- through the holidays, at least. I promise to continue my research on the nonvoter story and handle local stories, maybe some editing if he needs me, but I will have to stay off the road for a while.

"Okay," Bradbury sits back in his chair and considers his options. He knows he wasn't going to get anything out of me right away, anyway, and multiple reporters are working official channels. "Your health is paramount," he says. "Keep me posted. Give me the paperwork to sign for human resources, and go take care of yourself."

That was easy. No drama. Even before I get the test results, I've got time off to recuperate. Now I have to construct a six-week program to get back in the pink. Mona will want to help me with that. My cell phone rings, a number I don't recognize. I pick up the melodic voice of Annamarie Scott, who asks, "Are you okay?" Frank had briefed her about my heart incident, thankfully not in explicit detail. "He told me you passed out after I saw you," she says. "He was worried about you, and so am I." I'm feeling much better, I tell her, even negotiated time off to recuperate. "That's good," she says. "Getting away from the office helps. In fact, maybe you can break away this evening and join me for dinner, my treat."

No, that would be my treat, I tell her, but we can negotiate that later. Her laugh is a cool burst, like a jazz expression. She doesn't resist. "Fine!" she exclaims. "I know you reporters like to pay your own way to avoid the appearance of a conflict. Right?"

I predict no conflict and express excitement at the chance to meet. The rendezvous will be at the Bazaar Café, near her neighborhood south of the Presidio. It's open mic night with a few old friends singing along. "Maybe we can do a duet," she offers, and I quickly demur: I want to hear her sing, not create a spectacle. We make plans to meet in 30 minutes. I pack up and grab a taxi.

Annamarie is sitting off to the side of the stage listening to a young man singing and playing an acoustic guitar when I arrive at a lively bar scene, conversations rising and falling around the halting tenor of the tunesmith, performing an original song, I learn later. I watch Annamarie's rapt attention as she smiles and nods in rhythm, and I approach as she rises to applaud. She turns and greets me with a hug.

"I hope this seat is okay," Annamarie says, holding my hand as she gestures with the other to the chair beside her. "If anyone plugs in an electric instrument, we can move back." I can take it, I assure her, asking if she brought her electric guitar. She points to the piano on the other side of the stage. "They let me play and sing, too," she says. "It's a lark for me. I've always performed, from the early days growing up in Oakland."

Annamarie has a medium-dark complexion and wears her hair in corn rows gathered on top of her head, some falling loosely down her neck. Her red lipstick accentuates her burgundy pantsuit, a fashionable office choice that also works in this joint. She orders a salmon salad. I order a bowl of soup, a chicken panini, and a bottle of chardonnay for the table—two relatively healthy meals in one day.

I ask how the legal gig is going as I pour the wine, learning that she is still in the public defender's office, despite several offers to join law firms and earn a better salary. "The justice part of lawyering is more interesting to me than the money part; not really a career girl, I guess. Volunteering to help with the PTSD class-action suit put the law in focus for me. Victims fall through the cracks if they don't have money to hire lawyers. I feel like I made a difference for Frank, and that's the whole point." I know Frank is grateful, I assure her, as are a lot of other veterans.

A young black man has taken the stage, and Annamarie turns to watch him. He says his name is Jimmy, and he comes with a beatbox and a rap for us. He speaks in a quiet voice and slowly turns up the volume. First, the beat, the rhythm, then the rhyme, rising in that unmistakable cadence, the attitude of hip-hop poetry that is almost derivative now. Jimmy is in the flow, bouncing with the rhyme. I turn on my recorder, enjoying how he raps the sadness and anger, joining Annamarie and the smattering of audience members in applause when he's done.

Annamarie waves at Jimmy as he leaves the stage; he smiles and walks over to our table. "Hi, Jimmy. I loved that one," Annamarie says. "This is Ray James, a music critic with the *San Francisco Chronicle*. Ray, Jimmy Morris."

I laugh at the introduction and hurry to puncture Morris's expectations. Music is not my beat, I assure him. Everybody's a critic,

40

though, right? I tell him I like his rap and suggest that we talk later "about where your music comes from." I hand him my card, and he walks away, smiling as he studies it. I'll get a call, I'm sure.

Annamarie is suddenly on her feet, turning to ascend the stage and sending a small smile to me over her shoulder. She sits down at the piano and adjusts the mic, launching into "What a Wonderful World," her sweet departure from the familiar growly Louis Armstrong's version. Again, Annamarie makes a song her own, and I'm enraptured, this time without drugs, except wine and infatuation. Her jazz piano is a perfect accompaniment for the cool, clear voice matching the beauty of the rainbow in the sky with her jazzy accompaniment, lending cool clarity to the simple expression of love among all people. What a wonderful world, indeed.

I'm on my feet applauding enthusiastically at the end of the song, Annemarie feigning embarrassment. "Thank you to my devoted fan," she says, then launches into "At Last," the Etta James classic. Mesmerized and counting on a few more songs, I order a cocktail. I'm already picturing myself as her agent, exposing her talent in exchange for a recording contract. She sighs when I suggest it. "I sent a demo to a few studios, but the market for female jazz singers may have peaked long ago," she says. "I had the offer to join a local band as a backup singer, but it was a dead-end."

I tell her she just needs a good press agent, and I volunteer my services to promote her, only half-jokingly. I want to help her get a bigger audience. Annamarie laughs. "Well, I don't want to take you away from the critical issues of the day," she says. "I'll just let you know when I'm taking the stage, and you can bring more audience."

Good deal, an ongoing date as long as Anne Marie is performing, and I'm thinking about my standard haunts to pitch this beautiful jazz singer, doing a bit of unofficial public relations to keep it going. Unfortunately, this enchanted evening is slipping away, confirmed by a glance at my phone. I've got a date to start fasting in a half-hour and a final round of medical tests before the stent procedure. I make apologies for a hasty exit, the last thing I want.

Annamarie covers my hand with hers and gives it a little squeeze. "Your health is the most important thing," she says. "Get rest. Be well." I'm startled by this intensity, her shining eyes, that smile, showing genuine concern. She is a revelation, this gorgeous dark woman in a business suit. I stammer as I thank her for her kindness and offer to share a cab.

"I live just three blocks away," she says, inviting me to walk her home. Lovely. I grab our coats and wrap her against the November chill. A cool mist floats up from the bay, enveloping us as we walk, obscuring the street lamps. "Brrrr ....," Annamarie shivers, and I put my arm around her. Her apartment comes too soon, the basement floor of a three-story row house. She turns to face me, taking both my hands. "I would invite you in for a drink if you weren't on curfew," she says, once again disarming me with her smile.

I stammer, asking for a rain check. She presses up and kisses me on the lips, lingering for a precious second. "Please get better and come see me again." Annamarie is in my head all the way home and keeps me awake a while longer. I feel thoroughly intoxicated.

I call her the next day to set a date. I can't wait to see her again. But a change of mood, she's having a bad day and snaps at me, then apologizes. "I'm sorry, Ray. So much going on," she says. "I get caught up in other peoples' lives, trying to defend them or help them – and it's crazy, particularly when children are involved." She explains that she's representing a drug-addicted couple who abandoned their kids and were gone for days. "They were found overdosed in a parking lot. The paramedics revived them with Narcan. Now they're on trial for criminal abuse of their kids, and I've got to defend them. It's horrible."

Not so horrible if you're looking for a good hook to the opioid crisis, millions of people dead, families shattered, and addiction poisoning communities, happening right here in the heart of San Francisco. I commiserate and ask for details – discreetly, of course. It's a story that I should tell, the survivors' stories. If it runs in the *Chronicle*, we put public pressure on politicians to turn it around to save lives. Annamarie listens morosely as I make this case.

"I feel so frustrated seeing it in court, not being able to protect the kids," she says. "It's hard to understand the mind of junkies who don't care about their kids, who won't even fight for custody. They don't want them, and they shouldn't have them, ever!" I try to soothe this angry, fired-up Annamarie, praising her inspirational work, her crusade for justice.

I say we're in league, journalists and public defenders, insisting on the rights of the weakest among us – especially when it comes to free speech, the highest law, and the right to know. She sighs again as she yields to my argument. Yes, she'll provide more information and help set up interviews. We're going to help each other, a compact.

I admit to Annamarie I'm battling substance abuse myself, using naltrexone, similar to Narcan, to suppress my urge to drink. My doctor recommends it, along with group therapy. I'm planning a trip to Big

Sur for a wellness workshop early next year, and will write a column about the treatment. Annamarie is excited to hear this news. "Wow! That sounds great!" she raves. "I do yoga – for stress and to feel better. I can't wait to read your wellness news."

She doesn't have to wait for the story, I say, inviting her to come with me as my guest and meet my friend Jay Lee, who has developed a wellness program around Chinese medicine. I'm not sure about yoga, but I know he teaches *qigong*, which may be similar. Annamarie doesn't commit, but she's intrigued. We make a date for dinner, and other affairs over the next few weeks, including visits to her basement apartment for video games and dinner. I don't get to stay, unfortunately, but I'm cheered by the mutual affection, the heightening of infatuation. I can already feel it.

6. *The Vibe:* Howl Now

By **Raymond James**, *San Francisco Chronicle*, Nov. 25, 2016

In a city of 870,000 people of all races from all places, beliefs and disbeliefs, persuasions and orientations, you expect a certain amount of aberrant behavior. Donald Trump, for example, collected almost 10 per cent of the San Francisco vote running on a platform promoting "America first" white nationalism and immigrant-bashing. That should be no contest for Democrat Hillary Clinton in a city that celebrates diversity and tolerance. She won 87 percent of the vote despite some defections on the Left. San Franciscans overwhelmingly oppose the politics and persona of Donald Trump, and you can expect the city to be in the vanguard of the resistance ahead.

In fact, San Francisco may be Trump's worst nightmare – a mixing bowl like no other, Asians and Hispanics rising, women dominating, a vibrant community of lesbian, gay, bisexual, transsexual, and other queer people, out and leading the way in a new high-tech economy that challenges the old ways and the old money, Trump's world. He was a target of Occupy SF in 2012 when demonstrators surrounded 555 California Street, the old Bank of America Center, where Trump holds a 30 percent stake. Trump is making money off the iconic San Francisco building every day and may carry those profits into his presidency, if it comes to that. It was enough to turn out San Francisco voters in record numbers this year, with mail ballots pushing the participation rate to 81 percent. Compare that with barely half of the registered voters casting ballots nationwide.

Can we even see what happened in this presidential election from our vantage point here on the West Coast? How did a majority of electors apparently pick a New York real estate mogul who stokes hate against immigrants and minorities? Is this some other America? Do people out there think that this rich businessman who stands to make billions of dollars on this deal while rewarding his rich friends along the way is really going to help them? No, it doesn't make sense. Maybe we can't blame voters for making this unlikely decision, since only one-quarter of all registered voters voted for Trump. Maybe the answer lies with the millions of people who simply didn't vote, the real majority.

I found a local guy who didn't vote, and he had a lot to say. Listen:

"My vote doesn't matter, man," said Jimmy Morris, dribbling the basketball once, then firing a jump shot from about 20 feet out. Swish. I rebound and toss the ball back. "The future doesn't matter?" I ask. We're shooting around at the Koret Health and Recreation gym at the University of San Francisco. Morris is a student majoring in English literature and a poet with a musical bent. "My future," he said, "is not being decided by bureaucrats in Washington, DC, or even in San Francisco. I decide my future. I don't count on the man, the powers that be. They don't care about me. Democracy is a myth."

Morris is a young black man, 24, who voted for the first time in 2012, for Barack Obama. The four years since have left him disappointed in the political process that hogties action, that covers up the truth, he says. He doesn't hate Hillary like the "lock-her-up" crowd at Trump rallies, and he isn't like the 3 percent of San Franciscans who cast their lot with the Libertarians or the Greens or the 2,000 voters who wrote in the name of Democratic Socialist

Bernie Sanders. Morris says no one speaks for him – at least, no one with any traction in the political arena.

If anyone would feel marginalized in San Francisco, it would be Morris and other African-Americans who have been pushed to the sidelines in San Francisco, a vanishing minority where others are rising. Back in 1970, one in seven residents was black. Today, it's one in 20, about 38,000 people. The population decline may have its roots in the burgeoning tech sector, which has changed the character of the job market. More and more tech openings have gone to other residents, especially Asian newcomers, and more black families moved away.

Morris bemoans the loss of black neighborhoods and the musical culture that nurtured him growing up – the jazz clubs in the Fillmore area near USF are nearly gone, replaced by upscale shops. "It's like we're being wiped off the map," he said with a measure of bitterness in his voice. "Most of my family moved to Oakland or down to LA, and I'll probably move on after this gig."

This anger is reflected in Morris's poetry, on display the night before at the Bazaar Café's open-mic stage, where he brought his boom box and wowed the small crowd with several original works, slammed with a musical beat, a rap that moved from sadness to anger to defiance. The alienation he feels comes through loud and clear in this one, called "I Rise Alone."

"Daddy long-gone came then split and shit

An' me supposed to clean up the mess

I'm just wastin' here more or less

Sweet sister crying, but I grit and spit

It out; just another day gone

I rise alone."

Morris's declaration of independence belies the fact that he's studying at USF with the help of scholarships and grants, including a federal Pell Grant. But he's not feeling the black privilege, up here on his own. So he's got his back up and ready to fight his way out as if there's nobody who wants to see him succeed.

"The professors are great, and I've got no beef with other students," he said. "I feel like a freak, though, me and some of the other black students, not knowing if we should fit in or not. My beef, really, is with the system. It's not all black and white. The system is created so power is all at the top, built on the backs of most of us, and most of us don't realize it. We need to open the eyes of people who don't see it."

The way Morris sees it, San Francisco ought to lead a cultural revolution with music, art, and poetry that expresses ideals worthy of America, the ideas of liberty and justice, and peace. Ultimately, he sees himself fitting right into the city's parade of cultural revolutionaries, trying to change the world.

"I'm collecting all my poems under the title, *Howl Now* – you know, after the Allen Ginsberg poem," he said. "He introduced it with a reading not far from here, Six Galleries, now gone, just like the beatniks. The beatniks died, and the hippies were born right here, and they died too. I think they both fucked up by making it all so white. You know? They listened to jazz and tried to write with the bop, but they didn't get it. They missed the culture, the spirit that moves you, the beat, beat, beat. They needed black people to make it real. We got our own grievances, you know."

Out there in the hinterlands, a lot of people have pulled away from the government, and from participating in democracy. They've got grievances, as Jimmy Morris says; the political system doesn't seem to work for them.

7. Black Magic Woman

Looking for a home-grown example for my first post-election *Vibe* at the margins of San Francisco, I figured marginalized and underrepresented Jimmy Morris would do, even as Bradbury grumbled and called it "a stretch" before grudgingly sending it along to the copy desk. Granted, Jimmy represents a small group and may not connect with the broader readership in the Bay Area, but he's got a compelling story. Plus, he serves my purpose of connecting with the voluptuous public defender and jazz singer Annamarie Scott. She called immediately, thanking me for calling attention to the plight of young blacks in San Francisco and beyond.

"Jimmy needs for people to listen to him; you heard it, it's part of his anger," she says. "You've helped raise his voice. It means a lot to him and to me." Annamarie explains how she helped Jimmy get his scholarship as a trustee at USF, where she got her law degree. "I understand what it's like to be the only black girl in a class, to be slighted. Jimmy could be a star if he perseveres. Your article gives him a boost."

Those words are the impetus for another *Vibe* a week later with details from Annamarie – about young victims of the opioid epidemic featuring Helen, 10, who calls 911 when her overdosed parents don't return home, and she and her brothers, ages 6 and 4, are abandoned hungry and filthy. Besides the court case, I work with other sources – first responders and nurses who witness the human cost close up and the state child protection system that tries to place abandoned children. As Veronica Adams of the state Department of Social Services tells me, the tragedy is a lifetime for children. An excerpt:

Helen may have served as a buffer, maybe buffeted too. She is stoic and sad, not saying much, Adams says, probably hiding a variety of abuse she's endured at the hands of her parents and their drug-addict friends. Without guidance, she has invented herself amid the squalor, blending in, steeling herself with a tough veneer that may mean trouble later on, Adams predicts. The children almost certainly won't stay together in the foster care system. "There will be trauma in the separation, especially for the boys," she said. "They both show signs of addiction. Their mother probably was using when she was pregnant."

The mother, Melanie Trent, dropped out of high school when she got pregnant with Helen, then found herself living on the streets and in shelters with the baby, unattached and floating, "Depending on the Kindness of Strangers," she wrote on the cardboard sign she wielded at the corner of Turk and Hyde in the Tenderloin section of San Francisco, perhaps appealing to literary as well as humanitarian sensibilities. Then, in 2013, she moved in with Luke Savage, the father of the boys, who worked as an auto mechanic and tow truck operator before an injury led to disability and long-term dependence on pain pills. Even before he hooked up with Trent, he was in a downward spiral with opioids. Before long, drugs took over their lives.

In court last week, where the couple entered into a plea agreement that included forfeiting the children, Trent was inconsolable at the table, crying throughout the brief hearing. At the end, when Circuit Court Judge Greg Allen asked them if they had anything to say, Savage just shook his head. Trent stood, wiping her tears and taking deep breaths to quiet the sobs, expressing her sense of loss. "I'm so sorry. All I ever really cared about was my babies, but I couldn't ... I wasn't good enough ... I'm so sorry," she said haltingly before bursting into tears again.

"She's really tore up," Savage told me as he awaited transfer to the state prison in Stockton. Trent was already on her way to the Federal Correctional Institute in Dublin, California, and both will have access to drug treatment and counseling as part of their sentences – five years for Savage and three for Trent. "We just weren't right, you know, to have kids," he said. "We tried to do it, but it's hard. We didn't have any money ... for them ..." his voice trailed off, thinking about the little money and where it went. "We took what we needed. I'm not proud of it."

It was Savage's back pain and a doctor's prescription for Vicodin that started it all, he said, and the fentanyl patches. Addiction slipped up on him. When the insurance ran out, he was in a bind, the pain overcoming common sense and regular dignity. He found out that he and Melanie could get heroin cheaper, especially when it was cut with fentanyl. It didn't take much to get wasted, to forget the pain. This wasn't their first overdose. "We're lucky to be alive," he said. "I need to get my life right, get back with Melanie ... and maybe the kids."

No, that's probably not going to happen, that getting-back-with-the-kids part. Adams says her agency will place Helen and her brothers in stable family situations as soon as possible. "They have a lot to forget," she said. "No going back." They've just begun to figure out that their parents aren't coming back, a prospect that frightens the boys more than it does Helen, Adams says. She seems relieved.

I get a chance for a brief encounter with Helen in the waiting room outside Adams's office, introduced as "my friend Ray, who is writing a story about growing up in a messy house," an unlikely story that

52

nevertheless draws immediate interest from the young girl. "I could tell you about that," she said. "It stinks."

"What do you hope for in a new home?" I ask her, seeing just the hint of a smile in her eyes. "I want a room just for me," she said, "with a door."

Annamarie says she burst into tears when she read about Helen, who just wants to be alone but needs to find people who love her. "You tell the story so well," she says. "It touches me, the way you write. Thank you for making people realize how hurtful addiction is to families. I'm proud of you for speaking out for the children."

Bradbury isn't so charitable. The piece is "maudlin," he says, and I need to get back on the road and away from all the "bleeding hearts" in San Francisco and start looking at the big picture, including the perpetrators of these heinous crimes against children. That's an outlier sentiment, I'm sure, but I assure him I'm on the lookout for a story focused on the perps, the opioid drug dealers. That's the pharmaceutical companies, right? Bradbury snorts.

Not that I'll be able to get the goods on them. Big Pharma is a prime advertiser – in the *Chronicle* and everywhere. It's the American addiction, money for something, the corporate influence game. All institutions, including newspapers, depend on it. I'm perhaps the most dependent of all, even dipping into the black market for my favorites. Doping products are everywhere.

What I *can* get, what I really want, is a date with Annamarie Scott, and my latest columns may have done the trick. She asks if she can come to visit me in Berkeley, where she was an undergraduate before moving over to USF to study law. She has friends and former teachers here, she says, and insists on showing me the Berkeley Botanical

53

Gardens, located at the edge of the campus. I'm all too happy to stop and smell the flowers with Annamarie.

It's just after noon when she rings my bell. I buzz her up and turn on the music. A few minutes later, she is knocking softly on my door. I welcome her with a hug and kiss, then admire her at arms' length and release a soft whistle. She's wearing what appears to be a buckskin skirt with fringe at the bottom falling below her knees, with a matching vest covering her white blouse. On her feet are boots that rise about mid-calf. Her cornrows are tied in pigtails. I tell her she looks like a modern-day Annie Oakley.

"Just my hiking clothes," she says, then spotting the plates on the table. "You've got food – you cooked!" I tell her I just rustled up some grub, something fit for a cowgirl. I enjoy Annamarie's high-energy patter through lunch – from moon landings to space travel to Martian settlements to hydroponic gardens to Venus fly traps to black widow spiders to the roach motel she found stashed behind the kitchen trash can. "Why do you use glue strips to torture bugs to death?" she asks. I accuse her of rushing to defend the "underbug," even though there are billions of them, and they're taking over.

We agree to take the discussion outdoors, where insects rightly belong. I propose that we commemorate Annamarie going back to school by smoking a bowl, and pull a small pipe from my stash drawer. "No, not for me," she says with a dismissive wave. "I'm saving my warm breath for the flowers … you know, photosynthesis. We don't want to foul our carbon dioxide."

I roll my eyes, and she laughs. "I don't mean to sound like a health nut, and sometimes the grass is greener. It sure was during my undergraduate years here," she says. "But you should be careful with your heart. We'll be walking three or four miles, some hills."

Perfect, I say. I load the bowl and take a hit; good for my heart, I announce. "My stress test was a piece of cake. I need more exercise, not less." I grab my jacket and escort her down the stairs, avoiding the elevator to make my point.

The sun is still high in the cloudless sky as we set out across campus, and I reckon we'll have at least three hours in the garden before it closes. Annamarie is joyfully tripping down memory lane, introducing each building to me as if they are old friends, each holding some essential chapter of her history as an earnest student rising. As we greet UC-Berkeley students along the walk, I'm reminded that Annamarie is not too far removed from their milieu, while I must appear to be one of their frumpy professors.

She wants to give me the full story on the school's library complex and the collection of Mark Twain's papers, but I cut her off to confess that I've seen the papers at the invitation of my daughter, who studied here, acknowledging for the first time that I'm old enough to be her father. She appears surprised – and intrigued as I tell her how I bought the condo for Mona, then moved back to Berkeley when Mona graduated and began studying medicine at UCSF – now happily self-sufficient as an emergency room doctor in San Francisco.

"Excellent! I hope you listen to her advice," Annamarie says. I assure her I'm not wanting for medical advice from the family doctor. We're approaching Sather Tower, the famous Campanile, just as the bells toll for 2 o'clock. We abandon the path and wander through a well-pruned field toward the dense garden ahead. As we draw near, I can see trees that definitely are not native. "What is that?" I ask, pointing to a group of odd-looking trees. "Baobabs, out of Africa," Annamarie says. "We'll swing back around to Africa. Let's start with the desert and work our way up to green."

Just past the entrance to the garden, we pass a variety of cactus and desert bushes on one side and California redwoods, oaks, and wildflowers on the other. There are few visitors at this hour, so we're behind the crowd, no push. Annamarie plots a course that will take us through an exotic world tour in a few hours through North America, South America, Australia, Asia, and Africa. She invites me to take photos of the flowers and birds, and I angle for the photos that include my lovely companion.

The plants are cool and the air is fresh, an elixir for a tender heart, and Annamarie's ebullience helps elevate my mood as she pulls me along from plant to plant, reading each description aloud to me as if she is a tour guide. I'm not much interested in all the specifics of the plants, but I have fun playing the eager student, feigning rapt attention and cracking wise.

When we discover the herbs in the Asian section, where sprouts of *mahuang* and *jinchong* pose as sure cures for what ails you, I seize the opening to remind her of Jay Lee's upcoming Esalen Institute workshop on holistic health and Chinese medicine, based on cultivating internal energy, called *qi*. "Oh, yes," she says. "That's like *"prana"* in yoga, right? We have breathing exercises, pranayama."

Perfect. That's just like *qigong*; Jay Lee will teach breathing lessons at his workshop. I take both her hands and kiss her softly, proposing that we take our breathing lessons together. Annamarie is excited by the prospect of adventure in Big Sur, radiating new warmth as she clings to my arm. We wander past Australian and South American plants, which serve to stimulate her wanderlust.

"I've always had my nose in books," she says. "Growing up in Oakland, then going to school and working here, I've never really left the Bay Area, except for a few road trips. We drove to Yosemite once and down to LA and to Vegas, but that's it. I've heard the Big Sur drive is magnificent."

I rave about the drive down Route 1, two-lane blacktop that winds along the coast. I assure her that she can enjoy the heady sense of danger without fear, with an experienced and cautious driver. The company even gave me a car to work the road, my dedicated beat.

"I envy you," she says. "You've been all over, a man of the world. I'm just getting started. Some people want me to run for state delegate, which might get me as far as Sacramento, anyway."

I'm flabbergasted, thrilled by the prospect, telling her she would make a great candidate. Can I break the news? "Wait! No! You can't report that!" She is startled. "I forgot who I'm talking to here!" I laugh and assure her that I can keep a secret, but she has to promise me that she will call me first when there's something to announce.

We have walked into the heart of Asia, where the path splits a bamboo grove and a gorgeous Japanese pool. "Here, I think you'll like this," she says, pulling me along a path beside the pool that is adorned with bonsai plants and trees, broad and hugging the ground. At the far side of the pool, we come to a small grove of what Annamarie says are weeping maple trees, also with branches sweeping low to the ground but more colorful and much larger than the bonsai varieties.

57

"Come," Annamarie says, crooking her finger at me and then walking to the largest of the trees, lifting a branch, and crawling under. I follow her. Although the tree spreads wide, we still have to crouch under the limbs, which sprout almost immediately from the trunk close to the ground. I peer through the branches to see the path on the other side of the pond and the bamboo grove beyond. We are comfortably ensconced as part of the floral environment.

It's the best view in the garden, I say, turning to Annamarie, who is reclining on several of the low limbs, legs spread like the tree, making me smile. I lean over to kiss her waiting lips, and she's ready, pulling me down on her. I am between her legs, grabbing a branch with my left hand to steady myself, grabbing a vest button with my right, playing buttons for just a moment before she helps, and I'm nuzzling her breast and reaching below the fringe to find her naked and wet. I sink to my knees and bury my face between her legs. She squirms against my mouth and tongue, moaning as I explore all the soft contours, kissing and nibbling my way. Delicious flower, a slight caramel accent from the tree. I'm like a bear discovering honey.

I hear talking along the path and pause, but she whispers, "Don't stop," and I obediently continue my oral worship while stealing a glance at the gaggle of students walking past the pool. I can see them clearly, and they could certainly see the moving huddle of us if they stop to stare, their presence heightening the excitement and daring of our public lovemaking. I unbuckle and push my jeans down to my knees while teasing Annamarie with my tongue. As their voices fade, Annamarie pulls my head up to her and kisses me hungrily on the lips, reaching down to guide me inside her.

The sensation is like nothing I've felt before, with her straddling the limbs to create a pelvic tilt. She is alternately squeezing and stroking my cock as I move inside her. I grab the limbs above her head to gain more leverage and thrust, digging my feet into the moist earth. The branches of the tree are shaking in rhythmic bursts that correspond to our love-making, our excitations floating on the wind like birdsong. I can feel the warm heat of Annamarie's body as she gasps and moans into my ear. Slowing my thrusts, I hold and circle inside her, feeling her body shudder again and again, and then I release as she clings to my neck. I'm not nearly so quiet, and I catch my breath, snuggling against her neck.

I tell her she's extraordinary, that she even made me sing. She laughs and pulls my head up, kissing me with mingling tongues. "And you thrilled me to the end," she says.

Africa holds less interest in leaving the garden than it did going in, so we walk slowly past the baobabs and marula trees, eyes mostly on each other as we talk about the places I've been and the things she wants to see and do. If I hadn't just made love to her, I might have felt like her professor, sharing a lesson while walking across campus. Instead, I feel like her champion, her protector. I'm thinking about how much I want to show her the places I've been and to do new things with her.

Annamarie has a court appearance early the next morning, so she begs off my dinner invitation, and we walk directly to the train station. I pop the question: Will she come to meet my daughter, Mona, and her wife, Maddie, when they get married next month? Annamarie doesn't hesitate. "Yes!" she proclaims. "I would love to. Should I wear my Berkeley colors?"

Sure, I laugh. Anything will do. Mona doesn't stand on ceremony. It's a civil marriage performed at City Hall. "I like her already,"

Annamarie says. "They sound like the perfect modern couple." Soon-to-be modern threesome, I say, planning a baby, with Mona bearing it.

"Wow, very cool!" Annamarie says. "You're a surprising man, Mr. James." I smile and take her in my arms for a parting embrace. I'll take "surprising" as a moderate romantic overture from a woman not entirely enamored by the prospect of romancing a grandfather-to-be. I've got her attention, at least.

8. Annamarie: Modern Love

Annamarie Scott, at 32, was ready for a change of scenery, new goals, and a bigger arena to play in. She's not unhappy with her job as a righteous public defender with a sidelight of occasional performances in jazz clubs – all satisfying work, even fun. But the clock was ticking. She could feel it in her bones. She'd been playing it safe all her life, for the most part, and was now ready to take a few more chances, to step out of her comfort zone. She was excited by the twin prospects, perhaps related, of running for state office and finding adventure with newspaper columnist Ray James. He might not be the safe choice, but there was an opportunity as well as adventure in hooking up with the guy who told front-page stories that help her clients and friends, and perhaps her own political career.

Also exciting for Annamarie was the prospect of modern love in the family, on display at City Hall as she and Ray arrived for the wedding of Dr. Ramona James and her bride, Madelyn Parker, RN, and she was eager to meet them. She and Ray were early so as not to miss what promised to be no more than a 10-minute civil ceremony in the spectacular Rotunda. Ray seemed visibly nervous to her, ill-at-ease wearing a tie for the occasion, apparently a rarity. Annamarie was dressed a bit more elegantly than her usual button-downed legal counsellor outfit, with a lavender taffeta dress beneath a dressy white jacket. She wondered if the brides also would wear white.

They climbed the grand staircase and entered the Rotunda under the ornate dome, which cast magnificent light in all corners of the huge public space. "The lighting should be good for the wedding photos," said Ray, whose contribution to the cheap wedding was a first-rate *Chronicle* photographer with a freelance sideline. Annamarie was drawn to the mayor's office, including the busts of former mayors George Moscone, Dianne Feinstein, and Willie Brown. "San Francisco loves its mayors – after they're gone," Ray offered cynically. She wondered aloud if he was going to be an antagonist, with such low esteem for political leaders, but he laughed it off. "It's the nature of my profession," he said.

Ray's phone rang; it was Mona. She'd just entered the building with Maddie and friends, alerting her father that the ceremony was not in the Rotunda but on the mayor's balcony across the way. "We're here," Ray said, taking Annamarie's hand and leading her down the short flight of stairs to the balcony, where chairs were set up in several rows. "I can see you!" he said. "You look fantastic."

Ray pointed to Mona and Maddie below at the foot of the grand staircase, and to his photographer buddy Fred Simmons, who danced around the brides and entourage as he snapped digital photos. The brides both were dressed in stylish business suits, although Mona's included a pleated skirt rather than slacks. They had a gaggle of friends with them, three of whom were dressed in scrubs, perhaps just taking a break from hospital work. Mona turned and waved. "I've told Mona nothing about you except that I'm bringing a friend," Ray told Annamarie. "Just be you, and she'll love you."

A well-robed woman had joined them, a justice of the peace, and they all ascended the stairs and walked down the hall toward the balcony. Annamarie and Ray retreated to the hallway to greet them. Mona wore a serene expression with a gentle smile that changed little when Ray introduced her to Annamarie. Maddie was more animated, warmly greeting Annamarie and offering Ray a jocular half-hug. "Thanks for coming, Dad," she said.

The ceremony amounted to little more than the vows, but Annamarie was joyous seeing the big smile on Ray's face as he watched his daughter with an obvious sense of satisfaction, hearing in her voice the self-confident woman who knew her mind and was comfortable being who she was. Mona and Maddie sealed the marriage with a kiss, to Annamarie's delight, as she squeezed Ray's arm and extended a tissue to him. He waved it off with a smile.

The mood turned from solemn to celebratory as they moved to the reception on the fourth floor, where Maddie and Mona had rented a room and sprung for hors d'oeuvres, beer, and wine. After a congratulatory round of hugs, Ray introduced the *Chronicle* photographer, who smiled and waved as he shot the celebration.

Annamarie was struck by the contrasts between the brides even as they jibed in motion and conversation. Mona was the reserved one, tall and thin with dark hair worn in a loose bun and penetrating hazel eyes. Maddie was forward and direct, short and muscular, not fat, with light brown hair, closely cropped. Mona seemed almost quiet in manner, yielding easily in conversation, while Maddie was more commanding verbally, speaking quickly in deliberate, complete sentences. They seemed perfectly at ease with each other, in synch, soulmates.

Mona didn't take long to turn her focus to her dad's new girlfriend. "Annamarie, thank you so much for coming. How do you know my father?" she asked mischievously. Annamarie laughed and clung to Ray's arm. "He's my champion," she said, flashing a bright smile. "He writes such nice things about the San Francisco public defender in the *Chronicle*. I think we're on the same team – at least, that's what he says."

"Annamarie is very talented, very smart," Ray said. "The Democrats are trying to get her to run for state Assembly." Annamarie pinched Ray's arm and objected. "That's just some talk," she said. "I have no plans to run for office. I like being a public defender."

Mona's mouth flew open and grew into a broad smile. "Maddie, come here!" she cried, motioning to her bride holding court in a huddle of enthusiastic scrub-clad nurses. "We have our candidate!" Maddie came quickly as Mona, beaming, announced, "It appears we have a political soulmate. Annamarie is running for state delegate. I think the nurses' union will want to help her get elected." Maddie agreed quickly, with the qualification that "we'll have to educate you on the health care issues first, but I'm sure you would be our champion, right?"

"Oh, yeah," Annamarie testified. "I'm on the side of angels and nurses – and doctors."

"Let's talk it over, then," Mona said. "Maddie and I are celebrating this evening by taking the ferry to Sausalito, with dinner on the boardwalk there. We would love it if you joined us, right Maddie?"

Maddie added her enthusiastic approval, and Annamarie's excitement was palpable. "Thank you so much," she said, "but I don't think I'm ready for political office. I have a lot of work to do now."

The possibilities were exalted in conversation as the boisterous wedding party boarded the ferry to Sausalito. Ray trailed after, smiling sheepishly and perhaps considering that he was the odd person out in this discussion, although he nodded and smiled while squinting against the wind-swept retreat of the golden city on the hill, glistening in the afternoon sun. "Look at that!" he called out to

64

Annamarie. "It's easy to see how the Chinese transliterated San Francisco as *Zhou Jin Shan*, Old Gold Mountain."

Annamarie and her new friends finally yielded to Ray's discomfort, agreeing to retreat from the rail of the boat, with the wind lashing their faces, and retire to the warm confines of the cabin where they could better hear one another. Mona was talking nonstop, excited, face flushed, all smiles. Ray put his arm around her and remarked, "You already seem to love married life, my dear," he said.

"Oh, so many things to love about today, Dad, beginning with the wedding, of course," Mona said. "But here's breaking news: This morning, I decided to take a job at Children's Hospital in Oakland, more regular hours and closer to home."

Ray was quick to congratulate her. "That's great!" he exclaimed. "I'm so happy you're escaping the trauma in the emergency room! Will you be working as a pediatrician?

"Yes! I aced the test, so I'm certified to care for kids," Mona said. "I'll be able to do research on grandbabies." Ray hooted gleefully, hugging his daughter. Beaming, Annamarie put her arms around both of them. "Thank you for letting me be a part of this great day," she said softly. "A beautiful wedding ... with planned parenthood. Very cool."

The joyful celebration of the wedding party continued through dinner, spilling out of the Sausalito restaurant and onto a returning ferry, where the mood remained high. The conversation was giddy as even Ray, warmed by the spirits, happily joined them outside along the rail as they enjoyed the night air and flickering light show along the San Francisco waterfront.

After they said goodbye to the newlyweds, Ray hailed a cab and offered to take Annamarie to her apartment, but she demurred, suggesting they go to his condo instead. "No court cases tomorrow," she said, her mood elevated by the ceremony as she pumped him for information about their upcoming Big Sur trip. "We're all set," Ray told her. "I made reservations for 'me and my girlfriend' to make sure we got a room together. I needed to discourage Jay Lee from booking us in a three-person room, with him the third."

Annamarie laughed. "We're definitely not ready for a threesome," she said, hugging his arm as they entered his place. Ray offered to fix her a nightcap, but she wrestled him away from the bar. "I'll save you from demon rum, and we can explore the contours of that king-sized bed you were bragging about," she said.

And so they did, a long night into morning with passionate and uninhibited lovemaking and free exchange of body fluids. Lovers in and out, over and under, nice and easy, hard and sticky, all over the bed and around it, too. At some point, Ray retired to the bathroom for a long time, by Annamarie's calculation, and came back newly excited, his breath heavy and wet as he made love to her with his mouth. It seemed to go on for hours, with periodic bouts of mouth-to-mouth resuscitation. Just before dawn, Annamarie drifted into sleep as Ray spooned her behind, his penis not yielding to the gentle motions of sleep. Eventually, he would fall asleep.

9. Slow Walk to Rehab Redux

Life with Annamarie gets much more complicated when I'm back in the office with the new year. A tip from Maddie led to possibly the opportunity of Annamarie's political life – legislative assistant to Oakland Mayor Libby Schaaf. I'd like to take credit for introducing them, and getting the ball rolling, but instead, I'm cursing myself for letting opportunity get in the way of love. Now that Annamarie is plugged into a busy city administration besieged in the wake of the "Ghost Ship" warehouse fire that killed 36 young artists, musicians, and concertgoers in early December, she has no time for me. She's working on rules and sanctions to improve building and fire inspection systems and reporting. It'll get worse when the inevitable civil suits are filed. Trial by fire for public defender Annamarie Scott, stepping up in class. She's guaranteed a week off for our Big Sur adventure, so I'm biding my time.

I missed all the holiday parties closing out the disastrous 2016, avoiding ostentatious good cheer and celebrating alone, half-heartedly. The angioplasty was inconvenient but not a big pain, even as it gave me a convenient excuse to stay off the road until the Big Sur trip. I served my health furlough from work as if it were a sentence to solitary confinement – with periodic filial and conjugal visits, not related. The medical diagnosis hasn't fully penetrated my consciousness, which continues to be tempered by various psychotropic drugs lubricated with alcohol. I still take naltrexone daily and continue to enjoy my favorite beverages. I may increase the dosage of the drug, or maybe not. I feel pretty good.

Here in the newsroom, the journos are atwitter with the coming Trump presidency, the inauguration spectacle, and the protests that have formed around the event. I listen impassively to the chatter: Some are excited about a potential confrontation in the streets, while some are morose over the same, sensing imminent doom with an impetuous, unprepared president. There appears to be no middle ground of disinterested observers in this newsroom, which I attribute to the function of the media itself being a political target of the incoming administration, the "fake news media." Yes, we will have stories galore.

The biggest story now is the mass of women charging up the hill, taking on Trump and his policies. The Women's March on Washington, which began with a Facebook post in Hawaii, has spread to hundreds of cities around the world, including several in the Bay Area. Newsroom odds-makers are taking bets on the possibility of confrontation with Trumpeters at the barricades, perhaps not giving enough respect to the powerful movement of women scorned.

The best medicine for me, I think, is to get back on the road, start talking with people, and get my bearings. Six weeks of medical leave is a long pit stop. And now I return to the track only to discover I've lost my regular wheels. The company car is kaput, Bradbury says. No replacement until the spring. I'm fretting about the hassle of renting a car to Big Sur next month and the logistics of getting Annamarie back to Oakland before I drive to LA as I sit through the morning news budget meeting. Bradbury is gruffly moving the discussion around the table.

"A pro-life march ahead of the women's march?" he's asking Julie, the political reporter.

"Yeah, pre-scheduled," she says. "The organizers tried to join as co-sponsors of the women's march but were told they weren't welcome."

"That's a story, isn't it?" Bradbury wants to know. "It's part of the story, but I don't think it's a headline," Julie says. "It doesn't really compete with a hundred thousand people protesting Trump around the Civic Center. At least one supervisor is speaking, Jane Kim, and women representing a bunch of community groups. Then a candlelight march."

"OK, we're going to put our best Bay Area face on the national story, with good local people and images," Bradbury says. "Photogs, video, we need everybody on it, January 21st, all day, plan accordingly. Julie, you've got the main story, and Lou," motioning to Lou Murray, the news editor, "will feed you the wire and regional reports." He pauses and looks my way, "Ray, you should be on the scene talking with the people in the crowd. I'll be assigning at least three reporters to the grounds. Let's hear from Bay Area demonstrators, including pro-life and pro-Trump counter-demonstrations. Everybody get close, but don't get hurt."

Bradbury knows I'm not going anywhere for a while, so he has, in effect, just given me notice not to call in sick. A doctor's note won't do. But I'm feeling much better, certainly healthy enough to wade into a crowd of women, even if they're only hot under the collar. I corner Julie after the meeting to walk through the people and events on parade, looking for an angle.

Julie was my lover for a while, an affair of convenience, as many office romances prove to be. She's married now to Dale Cannon, a political consultant and a continuing source of information. We get along, no hard feelings, barely a feeling at all, just respect. She's good. I'm glad she's on the *Chronicle* team. I tell her I'm not really looking for community organizers or leading voices in the women's and LGBTQ groups, the usual suspects. I'm looking for "someone not so well known, maybe off the grid a bit."

This draws a laugh from Julie. "You're still looking for the nonvoters who gave us Trump, aren't you?" she asks. "This is a crowd of angry Hillary voters!" True, I admit, but there could be some lurker there – a Russian, maybe. Their fingerprints are all over this election, I tell her. Putin ordered it, according to a leak to the *Times*. Everybody's looking for a good leak when the world is going to hell.

It's a predicament that journalists face in January 2017, bearing witness to a curious political transformation of a nation under the influence of a self-absorbed, Twitter-happy reality TV personality, and we can't help but laugh at the situation. Who knows what will happen? Julie is cheered by women gathering strength. "This is how the revolution begins," she says, promising to send more information before abruptly turning on her heel and hurrying away.

Not likely, I think, as I study the schedule and speakers Julie sends me. Women were supposed to decide the election, to push Hillary over the top, but 62 percent of non-college white women voted for Trump. The white women assembling in San Francisco for the march are mostly a different demographic – well-educated activists and professionals flying rainbow flags and wearing their grievances across their chests. And they will be in the minority among all the ethnic groups. Diversity is the city's strength. I'm Googling names to ID people of color as agents of change when Mona calls.

I greet her enthusiastically as "Doctor James," assuring her that I've been taking all my medicine and that I feel great. "Now the truth, Dad," Mona says. "Have you been sticking to a healthy diet, and have you stopped drinking?" I'm eating better and drinking less, I say, a dodge she won't let pass, so I hurry to turn the conversation to my pressing work assignment, asking if she and Maddie will attend the Women's March in San Francisco.

"There will be people from the nurses' union in San Francisco, for sure," Mona says, "but Maddie and I are marching in Oakland. We're sponsoring several young medical students – 'Dreamers,' you know, who are in danger of being deported by the spiteful Trump regime." Dreamers, I know, are illegal immigrants brought into the country as children, about 3.6 million of them, who now are trying to win a pathway to citizenship. Trump has threatened to kill the Obama-era plan that protects them. These are people who are truly on the margin of the political system, and I'm interested.

A broad immigrant rights coalition, including the nurses' union, is sponsoring Dreamers and marching in both the San Francisco and Oakland rallies, Mona tells me. They're also offering scholarships and mentoring, a hand up from community groups, including Bay Area high schools and colleges. "The Dreamers are victims of the Trump nightmare," Mona says. "They don't really have any other country, and they should have a voice. Talk to Maria Vega. She's pre-med at Berkeley and very well-spoken. I'll be marching with her and her friends." Sounds good. I thank her for the info and advice and obliquely promise to be a better patient and dad.

I'm finding it hard to focus on the plight of the Dreamers or any of the collateral damage from the brave new world of Trump America, consumed as I am with the concurrent personal dilemmas of physical

71

deterioration and personal awakening. Just as things are looking up for me, with a new girlfriend who both thrills and intrigues me, and the promise of a reunion with my longtime friend and soulmate, George, I face ominous reminders of my mortality and the imperative to clean up my act. The trip to Big Sur, and Jay Lee's holistic treatment, loom large.

I call George to tell him about my medical setback. My daughter, the doctor, says I've got to change my way of living or die, apparently. My heart is weak, and my liver is on the ropes. This comes as no surprise to my old friend, who warned me about my college-era party circuit revelry. "I knew there was something," he says. "I could feel it. You have many reasons to get on the road. The journey will be therapeutic."

Therapy, in fact, is on the schedule, I say, telling George about Jay's holistic health seminar and my immersion into Chinese medicine for the edification of my reading public. He surprises me with the news that he knows Jay Lee. "We met at a Taoist meditation retreat in Salt Lake City a few years back, and I read his blog. We keep in touch." I had compartmentalized these relationships without thinking about the connectivity. George is a lifelong student of China, so of course, he follows fellow travelers. I ask if he understands *qi* healing.

"I've met those who claim to be *qi* healers, and I suppose it's possible to transmit *qi* energy to heal others," George says. "*Qi* is a powerful energy, misunderstood by the West. I try to channel it through *qigong*, through meditation. It works for self-healing. Jay Lee will be good for you, Ray, for whatever ails you."

George wants me to stop on the way to Big Sur and see our former professor at Stanford, Al Cross, who now runs a drug counseling program in Carmel. Cross was an English lit teacher who kept us entertained; absent-mindedly stoned, we assumed, and flamingly gay. "Now he's straight as an arrow ... well, he's still gay, married to a Chilean writer," George says. "But he's off drugs, in fact, a bona fide behavioral therapist." He gives me Cross's contact information and promises to call him ahead of my visit.

Mona expects substance-abuse counseling, so why not Al Cross? At least for now. I remember Cross as an easy "A," a professor who seemed to have a crush on George. He flirted with me, too, or perhaps I misjudged his gregarious nature and the sly double entendre of his personal notes. I was in awe of his encyclopedic knowledge and command of American literature, which allowed him to quote liberally from great authors, even as responses to questions. Other than that, he wasn't my type.

I'm sure Annamarie will enjoy Cross's repartee, but the sojourn does create a complication. I don't want to tell her about my latest diagnosis, the collapsing liver, afraid that it may scare her away. Not that a mild heart attack isn't scary enough. I'll strike the heroic pose of a man seeking guidance from a substance-abuse counselor, an old friend, to develop strategies to improve his health, determined to give up drinking.

As I stare at my computer terminal, considering my options, I hear the loud challenge: "Are you ready to run?" That's Norton, the sports editor, standing with his hands and nose pressed to the top of my cubicle, looking like a reprise of the Kilroy cartoon character. I laugh at the image in my head. No, of course not, I protest good-naturedly. But I want to play. I'll be on the wing; just feed me the ball.

73

"Basketball doesn't work like that, James, not anymore," Norton retorts. "The days of the two-handed set shot are gone. You have to run and jump, work to get your own shot."

This is the day I promised to get back on the court with Norton and the lunchtime basketball gang, and I'm determined to pull it off. Easy does it, I tell myself as I change into shorts and a T-shirt in the locker room at the Y. I take the time to stretch before hitting the court, then introduce myself to the regular players by apologizing about recent surgery and my intention to take it easy, just trying to work myself back into shape. There's only nine players, so I'm assigned to the team that appears to be weakest. The preliminary shoot-around convinces me that I could surprise these youngsters – if nobody guards me.

But I'm good for only 30 minutes, a couple of baskets. The other guys are mostly younger and in great shape, and my own level of play falls far below the standard I hope to achieve as an aging shooting star. But it's my first time out in years, so I'm cheered by the fact I'm still standing – fragile ankles, knees, and all. I bow out and promise to do better next time, stretch for a few minutes, and hit the shower.

I'll pay tomorrow for this little exercise; I can feel it already. Muscle memory doesn't accommodate the rigor and pain of realizing a healthier, active body. The naked body staring back at me from the locker-room mirror reveals the atrophy and flaccidity inherent in years of ass-sitting. Not a pretty picture, this slumped and paunchy flexing man. I must retrain the muscles, and cut the fat. I've got a lot of work to do, and I'll start with an attitude adjustment. Pulling on my office clothes, I grab an Ecstasy tablet from my gym bag and self-medicate, chasing it with the icy fruit water provided at the locker room exit. Instantly, I feel better.

10. Chasing the Dream

Frank calls, frustrated that he's unable to reach Annamarie and figuring I know why she's not answering her phone. "The Sheba jazz band is looking for a singer, a steady gig," Frank says. "She would really light up the place." No doubt, but don't count on it, I say. She won't return my calls either, and I haven't seen her all week. Her new job is sucking the fun out of her.

Frank didn't get the message about the new job, an opportunity that she couldn't pass up, I tell him. But he doesn't agree. "Lawyers are a dime a dozen," he says. "Annamarie is a major talent." She's also very ambitious and really good at lawyering work. She's promised to take a break with me; I tell him about the three-day workshop in Big Sur and my conundrum without the company car. I'll either have to rent or hitchhike, I say.

"I might be able to help you out," Frank says. "Are you available tonight? I'll be hanging at the Crazy Horse." Oh, yeah, perfect. I've missed seeing my Cherry delight, and I have a little business for Frank, as usual. The prospects make me tingle, or maybe it's Molly I'm feeling, but I'm ready to go. I can't wait until tonight. In fact, I'm literally itching to move, rubbing my hands, massaging my temples, foot tap-tap-tapping.

Damn, I've got to go, I think and think, looking for an angle to escape the newsroom clatter. Eventually, I flee, mumbling quick goodbyes to cubicle-mates as I head to the elevator, standing, waiting, watching, ding, waiting, an eternity. Out in the street, walking down Mission, walking, circling blocks, looking for an Irish pub. The Tenderloin is crawling with them, I'm thinking, and a couple of blocks later, I'm sitting on a bar stool swilling a Guinness, yakking it up with some guy who's just been laid off from a job in the Embarcadero and is drinking part of his last and fatter paycheck. "Life goes on," he says, and indeed it does for most people until it doesn't. I have another beer, mesmerized by the stoic beauty of two elegantly dressed young women across the bar talking softly and conspiratorially, heads close together, not looking around at any of the eligible men making eyes at them, and I am clearly in that group. Are they lovers or family, dealmakers or lawbreakers? I invent a few circumstances that brought them here, their secret identities, and settle on the notion that they are spying on me, averting their eyes while I stare at them. Suddenly, the woman with wild Carol Kane hair raises her eyes and looks straight at me, coolly, with no smile, no warmth, a challenge. I smile wanly and turn away, sigh, drop a healthy wad of bills on the bar, salute the bartender, swing around on the barstool, and stagger toward the door. I'm sure I don't need any complications right now.

The Crazy Horse is a few blocks away, and I pull my collar up against the cool Bay breeze, which slaps me around enough to convince me I'm sober, just a little jagged. I fish around in my pocket for the vape device Frank got for me, loaded with a hybrid strain of cannabis, and fire it up; time for a couple of tokes before I get to the club. I'll be chill.

A slim Asian woman I don't recognize is straddling the pole on the stage when I walk in, performing to a tinny canned torch song. She points a high heel in my direction, then swings the leg out and around the pole, finishing the pivot with her back to me, both legs pointed away from the pole, her body held almost perpendicular, then lowers her legs slowly to the stage in a magnificent display of balance and strength. I can't move from my perch just inside the door, admiring the athletic grace and erotic beauty as she spins around the pole with her legs spread apart, inviting, welcome to the club.

It takes a while to get my eyes accustomed to the dim room and bright attraction. I edge my way to the bar, greeting regular dancer-hostesses Ginger and Vicky, and bartender Ross – all very happy to see me. "Frank's all the way down on the right," Ross says, pouring me a scotch over ice. "How do you like Vu Du, the new dancer? She can move!" She truly lives up to her name, I say, unable to take my eyes off the charismatic dancer prancing naked across the stage as I sidle down the aisle toward Frank's booth.

I call out a greeting to Frank before I see he has company … It's Gretchen. She looks fabulous, and I tell her so, asking if she'll be dancing here tonight. "Ha!" she says, takes my hand, and offers her lips for a kiss that she quickly breaks into a smile. "This is not my game," she says, "but I do like to watch, you know. I'm here for you because Frank said you could use our help."

"We fly into the Monterey airport a couple of times a week," Frank says. "Gretchen is an excellent pilot. She has her own plane." I offer a wide-eyed look at Gretchen, and she laughs at my dumbfounded expression.

"I dreamed of flying and got an appointment to the Air Force Academy," she says. "But after I graduated, they wouldn't let me in pilots' school, gave me a bullshit excuse, so I quit, took them to court. I got the training and the pilot's license anyway, and I don't have to put up with the military bullshit."

Gretchen describes her aircraft in elaborate detail – all I remember is that it's a Cessna Skyhawk, a four-passenger turboprop, that she's flown all over California and Nevada. "After a while, it's just like getting in your car and driving to the store," she says, "but there's less traffic – particularly at our altitude."

"It would cut your travel time from over two hours to about 30 minutes," Frank says. "And you don't have to drive. Leave the flying to us."

They convince me easily enough. The *Chronicle* doesn't care how I get there, as long as it's not too expensive. I'll have to pay to satisfy my employer, I say, assuming the rate will be reasonable. "You would be my guest, and I will bill whatever you say," Gretchen says, returning my smile. "We're flying to Monterey regardless. We just need to arrange a time that works for you."

I'll firm up the details once I know the travel schedule and talk with Annamarie to make sure she's on board. I'm assuming she'll warm to a trip with Frank and his amazing business partner, although he hasn't shared the nature of his business with her. Frank makes no secret about his intention to set up cannabis shops when the recreational use of the drug is legalized in 2018, so she may be on to his work in the underground economy.

Vu Du is leaving the stage, and Penny, a brunette dancer, and Cherry's good friend, takes her place on the stage. Where's Cherry? I ask, looking around the dingy bar.

"Oh, I thought you'd heard," Frank says. "She dropped this gig. Her webcam is taking off, plus she's got some video jobs with Elite Models. Cherry has a standing invitation to come dance anytime she wants, so maybe we can get a command performance." Elite Models. Isn't that a porn outfit? I ask. "Not sure," Frank says. "You'll have to ask her, same cell number. She'd love to hear from you."

78

I'm suddenly out of my comfort zone in a club I've haunted for years. Cherry kept me coming back – and Frank, of course. I met them at about the same time. But the Crazy Horse will not be the same without Cherry, I'm thinking as Vu Du suddenly appears at my shoulder, now wearing a thong and a thin T-shirt over her perky breasts. She's carrying a tray with refills for all our drinks. "Hi, I'm Vu," she says, smiling as she replaces our drinks.

I tell her how impressed we are with her acrobatic dancing and ask if she trained as a gymnast. "A little in high school, but not a serious competitor," she says. "Balance and strength training help a dance routine, though."

"I'll say," Gretchen chimes in. "You've made quite a transition from uneven bars to the pole and from the floor exercise to … what? Really getting down on stage. That was fun to watch."

I scoot over in my seat and invite Vu to join us, which she does, beaming at the rave reviews. "Thank you so much!" she says. "It's hard to know what people think, you know, unless they're putting bills in my garter." I apologize for coming in late, pull a $20 bill from my money clip and rub it along Vu's leg, ostensibly looking for a garter. She giggles. "I only wear it on stage," she says, squeezing my hand and lifting the bill at the same time. "Thank you. You missed a lot of it. I can give you a private dance if you like." I confess that I would like that, maybe later. I know this drill and the price of champagne and a "dance" from Cherry.

We learn that exotic dancing defrays Vu's costs at San Francisco State University, where she majors in business and also provides income for her elderly parents, "boat people" from Vietnam, she tells us. Born in San Francisco, Vu is an American by birth and doesn't fit into my "Dreamers" narrative, which I'm carrying with me and mentally revising as I go. Gretchen wonders why a business major works here and not some job she can put on her resumé.

"The money is good," Vu says. "Great, actually, for a temp job with a four-hour night shift. Primarily, though, because I like it. It really turns me on to do the show for a bunch of hot guys – and girls, too. The club makes sure the clients here are cool. So far, it's all good." Gretchen gets it. "It's easy money," she says. "But a smart woman could make a lot of money doing business with her own erotic enterprise. You think about that?"

Vu's eyes and mouth are wide open, with a smile forming. "No, you're *way* ahead of me!" she says. "I just come here to dance." She laughs. "But sure, maybe women would do a better job with this business." Gretchen agrees. They trade ideas about female-centric erotic art in film and on stage as Frank and I listen attentively, aroused. We get a titillating lesson on what turns on Gretchen and Vu, which is edifying enough. They both say they want to have a club that pairs men and women dancing erotically together, attracting couples. "Maybe with a high-stepping group chorus line?" Frank jokes.

Vu soon excuses herself to attend another table as Penny exits stage left and a new girl sashays to the pole. I promise to send Frank my best schedule for the Monterey flight and thank Gretchen profusely for the lift and for being a friend. The *Chronicle* will reimburse her, I promise. "It's a pleasure," she says. "It's the most exhilarating feeling – flying, almost as good as sex. I'm looking forward to seeing Annamarie again. Do you think she'll remember me?" Frank and I respond simultaneously: "Sure!" "Oh, yeah!" People don't forget Gretchen.

As Frank and Gretchen depart, I consider Vu Du and the prospect of a lap dance and possibly a happy ending in a dark corner of the club, with champagne and lipstick. She stirs my passions, no doubt, and she's ready and willing. But I think about the other Vu Du, probably with a different name, a child of poor immigrants stripping her way through college, And I'm reminded of Dreamer Maria Vega, whom I'm meeting in the morning as she prepares for a march of defiance against a president who epitomizes white male privilege. And I have my own dream to consummate with my public defender girlfriend. So much work to do. I slide out of the booth and head to the door, waving to the bartender as I go.

11. Thinking into the Box

Annamarie is gripping my thigh so tightly I'm numb. I place my hand on top of hers, patting her gently and telling her to relax; we're almost there, pointing out the city snuggled against the bay. I click on the camera app and focus on several shots of the Pacific washing along picturesque Monterey Bay, wowing at the view. Annamarie's eyes are closed, a grimace on her face.

"We'll be touching down at the airport in no time," Gretchen says. "Easy as pie, Annamarie." She's still stylish in a flight suit, shouting an encouraging word to her extra-nervous passenger. Frank is sitting beside her, looking back at Annamarie with mild concern. She had agreed to the flight plan grudgingly, having never flown before. The experience itself, with the turboprop engine and air noise whistling through the cabin as we chugged along 6,000 feet above land and sea, has flipped her stomach.

"I'm a little airsick," Annamarie says. "I'm glad we're almost there." I give her a reassuring hug for the umpteenth time this short trip, telling her she'll look back fondly on this adventure and that next time will be a breeze. Annamarie, recovering her balance, tells Gretchen the flight "was very smooth. I'm just a little queasy, being a first-timer."

Gretchen says she understands, and that's why she's being gentle. "These light aircraft really are easier to control. We'll be down in no time. If you close your eyes, you may not even notice we've landed."

"I was planning to do just that," Annamarie says wryly as we begin our descent toward the Monterey airport. "It's a good thing we're going to a wellness retreat. I need some kind of medicine to cure this upset stomach."

"It could be worse," Frank says. "Your first flight could have been flying at 35,000 feet in a pressurized cabin, with your ears popping and your nose smelling farts."

"Ha! That was you, wasn't it, Frank?" Annamarie asks accusingly, and we laugh. "I *am* thankful we're almost there."

A text from Al Cross comes chirping to my phone. He just got to the airport. At least the Professor's timing is good, even if Mother Nature is playing havoc with the rest of our trip. Cross now is part of our emergency arrangements to get to Big Sur. The dilapidated bridge over Pfeiffer Canyon was just condemned and closed, and torrential coastal rains are causing mudslides along the narrow road. Jay had called to warn me, offering to meet us on the south side of the canyon. Annamarie and I decide to hike the canyon, with Professor Cross delivering us to the north side of the bridge.

So our airplane ride to Monterey is the easy first leg, just a preliminary part of the adventure I hope draws Annamarie closer to me even as it complicates my *Chronicle* travel voucher. Complimenting Gretchen for the smooth and picaresque ride, I propose a $200 check to cover the air taxi ride from San Francisco to Monterey, based on going rates.

"Perfect," she says. "I can also take your company credit card – see, I'm set up like a road taxi," she says, pointing to a scanner on the dash. "It's $200 for you, no charge for Annamarie. If you want a return flight, just let me know your schedule. I'm always in and out of here."

Watching Gretchen's blonde ponytail swing as she commands the aircraft, leaning into the approach to the airport, I find myself visualizing her naked, in heat, aroused by memories of her athletic, bisexual lovemaking. And now, the high-flying businesswoman. Even sitting here beside my paramour, I'm thrilled by Gretchen. I don't mean to compare her with Annamarie, but it occurs to me, weighing their attractions. Equally beautiful, equally brilliant. I allow my mind to linger on a fantasy, bringing Gretchen and Annamarie to bed. Gretchen eases the plane onto the runway. Annamarie rests her head on my shoulder as we roll smoothly onto the taxiway.

After arriving at the general aviation terminal, we say hurried goodbyes to Frank and Gretchen, then catch a shuttle to the main terminal where Cross is waiting, reading a book, naturally. I call to him as we approach, supposing that he finally has discovered the Great American Novel. The Professor has a big smile as he rises from his seat to greet us, holding up the cover of the book for us to see. "Canadian," he says. He's rereading *The Handmaid's Tale*, "preparing for the new dystopia." I grasp his limp hand firmly and clap him lightly on the shoulder.

I introduce him to "my friend, Annamarie Scott, lawyer, jazz singer, and my beautiful muse." Annamarie looks at me sharply, an amused smile as she greets Cross. "Are you part of the Mayday resistance?" she asks, referring to the rebel forces in the novel. "Women are going to need all the help we can get to protect us from the evil pussy grabber."

"*Nolite te bastardes carborundorum,*" Al says, and Annamarie raises her hand for a high-five salute. "Don't let the bastards grind you down," she agrees, and I'm pleased to see everyone on the same page. "I hope you brought some rugged wear for the Pfeiffer Canyon crossing," Cross says, pointing to my backpack." He says he's happy to shuttle us to the bridge but offers this elliptical caution: " 'It is good to have an end to journey toward; but it is the journey that matters, in the end.' " Of course, he's resorting to literary quotes, and I guess Lao Tzu, from *Tao De Ching*.

"Close," he says. "Ursula Le Guin, channeling Chinese philosophy as she imagined new worlds. It's good to see you," he adds. "I'm glad to help with your trip, and I look forward to talking with you about the addiction. I understand what you're going through."

The professor leads us to his car, and I climb in the back seat with the backpacks. I marvel at how good our host looks. He's still a short man with long hair thinning on top but bushy on the chin, gray but better groomed nowadays. His complexion is no longer pasty and splotchy but a healthy-looking pink. The biggest difference is the loss of at least 50 pounds. No longer roly-poly, with a belly straining the buttons of his shirt or vest, Cross is a man who wears his body well in his early-60s. I ask him his secret to staying young.

From my perch in the back, I see the professor's eyes crinkle into a smile through the rear-view mirror. "You can live to be a hundred if you give up all the things that make you want to live to be a hundred,'" he said. I know that one: It's Woody Allen. "I thought you'd get it," he laughs. "But seriously, it's amazing what happens when you stop putting poison in your body. I discovered that even common foods are poisonous, especially processed food, and I've shaped up my diet. Of course, the drugs were the worst – the smack, the speed, the booze. No more poison."

Annamarie, sitting beside Cross, is listening intently. "Did you quit all the poisons at once, Professor Cross, or did you conquer them one by one?"

"I couldn't conquer anything, young lady," Cross says. "I needed a lot of help – old friends and relatives who intervened, who forced me into rehab to detox from the heroin and meth. George was the instigator," he glances at me through the mirror. "That detox saved my life, thanks to George. He stayed in touch with people who knew me. I was a mess, suspended from teaching, living in a crack house, and shooting up. George organized an intervention and saved my life."

Cross's struggles continued after his rehab program, particularly with alcohol abuse and an eating disorder. He finally found his equilibrium with stability in his personal life and the perfect husband. "You will understand my secret soon," he says. "Ricardo is cooking for us."

Ricardo Cortez appears to be in his late-40s, with specks of gray in his dark hair, trim and athletic, with a very firm handshake. He's wearing an apron when he greets us at the door of the stone cottage in Carmel's tony residential section. We learn Ricardo inherited the home from his father, Roberto, a writer and photographer who emigrated from Chile.

"Besides being an excellent cook," Cross is telling us, "Ricardo is a personal trainer and massage therapist. Plus, he's one of the most well-read men I've met – in several languages. We are good for each other."

Watching Ricardo circle the kitchen appliances, expertly juggling the pots and pans, I understand his point. I ask Cross if massage therapy helps to stay off drugs and alcohol. "Massage helps my body feel better, so part of the solution, sure," he says. "But it's a combination of physical activity, particularly cardio-vascular. Keep the body moving and breathing, and you'll have little use for self-destructive behavior."

Annamarie is impressed. "That sounds insanely simple, Professor," she says. "But I'm sure you have other self-regulation controls – sleep, diet, natural stimulation … "

"That's right, Annamarie," Al says. "What we have to do, to prevent substance abuse and addiction, is to create new habits and recreate the daily schedule. My approach to recovery is thoroughly scientific – modify behavior by applying the principles of behavioral psychology. At a practical level, it's amazing how adding tennis and biking to your day can build fortitude."

I can't help but laugh at my old free-spirited literature professor extolling the virtues of building "Skinner boxes" to reinforce good non-drinking behavior and punish bad drinking behavior. I ask him if he remembers, many years ago, when I submitted a book review of B.F. Skinner's *Walden Two*, which puts Skinner's theories of operant conditioning into practice. Cross had dismissed it as unworthy of a college book review, a sophomoric and clumsy literary attempt by a nonliterary psychologist.

When I remind Cross of his long-ago response to my review, he slaps the table and laughs uproariously, beaming at me and our memory. "You taught me something!" He proclaims. "It doesn't have to be a literary classic to be a valuable read. There is a simple truth in behavioral psychology. Positive reinforcement works. But I wouldn't call it a box, a Skinner box."

The professor cites a 1970s laboratory study of rats given a choice between regular water and cocaine water. They kept coming back for the drug until they were dead. And the same choice was given to rats in a lush cage with lots of things to do, colored balls, tunnels, friends, and good rat food. Those rats lived long and healthy lives, just sampling the cocaine water, nothing more.

"You should think about your own 'Rat Park,' filled with activity that makes you happy, that provides the incentives for you to make good choices," the professor continued. "Find alternative drinks, food, refreshments, activity. Reward yourself. "

I complain that much of my job is spent hunched over a laptop computer, taking notes, drafting articles, sending emails, and tweeting – or staring and poking at the small screen I keep in my pocket. What's the remedy for that?

" 'Tis in ourselves that we are thus or thus. Our bodies are our gardens to which our wills are gardeners,'" the professor says, to which Annamarie quickly responds, "Shakespeare." "Indeed," Cross says, "*Othello*. You get an 'A,' Annamarie." Then, to me, "Ray, we need to have a longer, candid discussion about this later on, after dinner."

We rise and follow him into the dining room, where Ricardo has laid out a sumptuous feast of small proportions – "Tapas!" Annamarie exclaims. "You like it, I hope," Ricardo says. "I love the Spanish style; very healthy. And delicious." We all agree it looks and smells divine. Ricardo is beaming. He encourages us to try the jicama, citrus, and watercress salad to start, with tapas portions. "More to come," he says. "That aroma is the shrimp and chicken paella casserole up next."

88

I'm thinking how much better the meal would taste with a jug of sangria, but it appears that water is the only drink we will have. Once again, I forget myself. Ricardo joins us at the table and encourages us to sample everything, providing commentary on the preparation. I compliment him on his good taste and culinary skill. Cross's secret is on the table: He has a partner who incentivizes good habits.

"We have synergy," as Cross explains it. "It helps to have a stable relationship. For you, it may be harder on the road, just you and your thoughts, unmoored. You have to figure that out, Ray. It appears you have help with Annamarie here with you. She is part of your support network."

"Absolutely!" That's Annamarie, quickly agreeing. "How do you feel about tapering off a bad habit – drinking less, trying to moderate alcohol use, for example?" she asks.

"Maybe that works for some people, but I don't think it will for Ray," Cross says, "based on what I hear from George. "He's concerned, and so am I. And I can help."

I'm irritated that Annamarie has hijacked the conversation to illuminate my half-measured attempt to shake alcohol, and I offer a standard excuse: It's difficult to let go of a pleasure that has been an essential part of my life.

"That's right. It's hard," Al says. "You are physically addicted – probably to more substances than alcohol, if George is right. 'Every form of addiction is bad, no matter whether the narcotic is alcohol, morphine or idealism.' (Pause) Carl Jung. The idea is to create positive energy, and overpower your destructive habit with a series of positive steps. Your addiction won't go away by itself."

"I'm taking a drug – naltrexone – that presumably makes alcohol less pleasurable, that eventually makes me not drink," I say.

"I'm not sure you can wait, Ray, with your liver," Cross says, and I cringe. Keeping the liver diagnosis under wraps isn't working. Cross has gotten the report from George. Without looking at Annamarie, I agree with the key point – that I intend to quit altogether. My flesh is weak, and my first inclination is to rely on drugs. I admit it. But I'm ready to learn strategies to put my id in its place.

We retire to the library, which passes as a living room in the cottage. It's teeming with literary gravity, from heavy-bound volumes to art prints hung elegantly in thoughtful repose. At entry, a lithograph with the image of Gabriel Garcia Márquez and the quote from *Love in the Time of Cholera*, "Take advantage of it now, while you are young, and suffer all you can, because these things don't last your whole life." Ricardo's voice, I decide, listening as he bangs and cleans with gusto. It must be quite a trip to live with a life coach at the top of his game.

"I remember you and George were the driven ones, the two boys I was certain would write and create," Cross is saying. "You have tied your talents to the public story, Ray. I read your articles."

The professor wants to know how drinking fits into my life as a journalist, and I launch into an extended soliloquy on the party mixers, the lunches, and dinners, the bar meetings, the general cultivation of sources, and alcohol's traditional role in that. That's just one end of it. There's also the family of working stiffs pouring out frustrations in after-hours cantinas. It's all part of the same daily brew.

Cross, who's nodding as he listens to me talk about my drinking life, smiles and extends an accusatory finger at me. "I think what you have covered is your own part in stirring that brew," he says. "You seem to be setting the rules of the road as much as following a well-worn path."

Annamarie appears to enjoy this reproach, snorting. "Bob Woodward found Deep Throat in a parking garage, Ray," she says. "Maybe you're looking in all the wrong places." I feel the color rush to my face. It's true. I haven't tried anything else. But I insist that drinking has been as much a part of my work and profession as it has been a part of my personal life. It's no easy chore for me to divorce myself from it.

Cross reaches over and touches my arm, smiling. "When thought becomes excessively painful, action is the finest remedy," he says, pausing to see if his students will provide the source before saying, "Salman Rushdie." He rises from his seat, walks to the middle of the room, turns, and faces me. "First of all, you have to be realistic," he says. "You have romanticized a drinking life that you find compelling and comfortable, even though it's neurotic and dangerous. Once you accept the proposition that you'll quit, then you will."

Ricardo has joined us, sitting beside Al and listening intently. "For me, it's simple," he says. "Physical activity improves your mood and outlook, replacing that little endorphin kick you get from alcohol or opioids. It fills the need and gives you even more."

I'm eager to agree with this Latin Adonis, angular and powerful, sleek and graceful, his muscles and poise visible in every movement. I'd pick him to be on my team any day. I tell them I'm going back to the gym and trying to stick to it. But is that enough? I'm not so sure.

"The most important thing," Cross says, "you have to beat the addiction, shut it down. Focus on that. You need a clear mind and a clear plan. Physical activity fits into your schedule, but it's just part of your day. Think about how you can develop good habits to fill your day, things you like to do or will grow into."

I wonder if drugs fit into the equation for things that make you feel good. Some drugs make you feel better, some improve your performance, and some help control blood pressure and diabetes. Herbs like cannabis are being prescribed by doctors here in California for all kinds of ailments, I point out. "I think drugs are overprescribed," Ricardo says. "It's the easy fix that hurts everybody in the long run. Drugs are overrunning neighborhoods. Terrible."

"We can't write off drugs that save people's lives or keep them alive," Cross interjects. "And some herbs are the perfect alternatives to substances that can be harmful. I'm sure Ricardo will agree there are good alternatives to table salt and refined sugar …."

"Yes, of course," Ricardo says, waving a hand, but Cross quickly qualifies his statement. "You need to do your research," he says. "You must be judicious." Cross reaches across the table to touch my arm. "I took the liberty of writing up some suggestions for alternative activities and substances, all healthy," he says. "Also, some ideas about reinforcing good habits and building new ones. I'll email it to you."

I'll need some help, for sure, I'm thinking as I cling to Annamarie later that night in exquisitely slow and languid lovemaking, quietly desperate to the end. Will she be able to help me create an alternative universe from the one I've been living all my life? Maybe I should make her my first new good habit. Maybe she already is.

12. One Good Habit

Annamarie seems unusually quiet as we drive down Route 1 toward the bridge. Ricardo is behind the wheel, and Professor Cross is beside him, turned in his seat to face me in the back. The windshield wipers are timed to flick off a light but steady drizzle that foretells a messy canyon ahead. Annamarie is listening and watching as the professor patiently responds to the old student's questions about the finer points of self-control.

"Think about willpower a little differently," Cross is saying. "It's not just about you gritting your teeth and steeling yourself against your cravings. It's about building a support system – people who support you and your goals. That's the value of AA and therapy groups, social networks that reinforce the value of not drinking."

I'm not sure I have time for formal meetings, I say. I'm on the road, moving around, living out of a suitcase – or backpack, in this case, with a bag packed and ready to ship, depending on which way I'm going after Big Sur – hopefully south to LA. "There's AA and rational recovery meetings happening all across the country, in many cities," Cross says. "Google it, schedule it, you won't regret it. You'll meet new people and get more perspective – maybe even for your writing."

I chuckle at the professor's cagy argumentation. He might as well have ended that last sentence with "checkmate." I can't win this one, especially if he insists on expanding the discussion beyond the adequacy of my anemic willpower. Once again, it comes down to my determination to pump myself up, with a little help from my friends. Cross wants to know if I got his email suggestions, and I nod. "Just tailor it to fit your routine, not take everything literally," he says. "It's just a guide. You have to fill the time, consciously build a healthier lifestyle."

"Send me a copy of the email, Ray, so I can see how to help," Annamarie finally speaks up, albeit curtly. I happily agree and quickly forward the email to her, suggesting we'll have time to talk it through on the trip. She smiles wanly. "The adventure continues," she says. "Thank you, Professor, for your hospitality and your counsel. I can see you are a good teacher – you care about your students."

"My pleasure," he says, looking earnestly at me. "It's a challenge, but you can do it. I have faith in you, Ray. Give my best to George. … Look, there's the bridge." We're within view of the warning sign and blockade. "Do you know where you will enter the canyon?"

We don't have a clue. The plan is to explore and find a path of least resistance. As Ricardo pulls up, we see a young couple emerge from the side of the road, coming up from the canyon – a man and a woman, both with backpacks and empty canvas bags slung over their shoulders. I get out of the car and wave to the hikers, putting on my ball cap to shield the light rain. I ask if they know the best trail over to Big Sur.

The man, with a full beard and long hair pulled back in a ponytail, leads his companion over to our car. We learn that his name is Joey, but it is Susan who's apparently the trailblazer of the pair. She's thin, also with long hair in a ponytail, wearing wire-rim glasses, and a big smile.

"It's not really a trail," she tells us. "You have to make your own trail, pretty much. They say we'll have a footpath eventually, but now we just hack our way back to civilization. The park people say they want to study all the wildlife before they start cutting a trail."

"Yeah, you'll be fined, too, if they catch you hiking through the state park," Joey says. "So keep your heads down."

I'm surprised by this news, given the nature of the emergency. The damaged bridge essentially cuts off an area dependent on tourism. But it's California, so the environment holds its weight with the economy – probably more than equally. Joey and Susan turn out to be tourists themselves, hiking the canyon two days ago to visit friends, then hiking back out. They say Big Sur residents are getting desperate, and many are walking out to pick up supplies, see a doctor or visit friends.

"We delivered supplies to our friends and stayed to party," Joey says. "They really know how to throw a disaster," he laughs. Ricardo offers the couple a ride back, which they happily accept, and we disembark from the car, tugging on our jackets and gathering our own supplies for the hike. "The stream at the bottom of the canyon is about knee-deep in places," Joey warns. "It's narrow enough at some points to jump, but you might get wet."

"Sounds like fun!" Annamarie says. We say our goodbyes to Professor Cross and Ricardo, with promises to keep in touch, then walk to the point where the hikers had emerged. There are no signs of a trail, just brambles and brush.

I lead the way, holding branches for Annamarie. The thicket is less tangled below the highway line as we begin our descent through overgrown shrubs entwining the oaks and redwoods, but the tall grass is slick. We'll have to trample our way. I don't last long in the lead as Annamarie rushes ahead to get a better view – and vantage point for

95

photos. From here, we can see the far side of the canyon, where the crumbling bridge ends and Route 1 resumes. I protest any photos of me stumbling around.

"Just recording the intrepid reporter's historical trek through Pfeiffer Canyon," she laughs. "But mostly, you are the background for the plants and birds." Ah, my history in a nutshell. I warn her to watch out for snakes. She pooh-poohs me and rushes ahead; rattlesnakes beware. The brush is beaten down in places, and we're finding better footing. Now the expedition leader, Annamarie turns periodically to see if I'm keeping up; finally, I grab her for an embrace, kissing her gently on the lips. I'm feeling frisky thinking about our romp in the Botanical Garden, but Annamarie pushes away and pushes on.

Lead on, Annie Oakley; I grumble and follow her down the hill. I'm not so eager to rush to the other side of the canyon and the steep and slippery ascent to the top and a waiting Jay Lee. There's a two-hour window, and I'm sure we can make it.

Just as Joey suggested, the stream cutting through the canyon poses a challenge to cross. We walk along the muddy bank several hundred yards, then turn around and cover the same distance in the other direction, looking for a narrower passage. I find a spot where I think we might be able to leap onto the stones that line the other bank, but Annamarie has a better idea.

"I've got a towel in my bag," she says. "Let's roll up our jeans and wade the stream. We can carry our shoes and socks with us."

That makes sense, I tell her, then watch as she girds to ford the stream – water just above her knees at its deepest. I'm gauging the distance to the other side and thinking my long legs and decent

Caucasian hops could carry me across without getting wet. Once Annamarie is sitting on the bank drying her feet, I retreat along a clearing at a bend in the stream, then turn and call out, "Geronimo!"

I take four bounding steps, then plant my left foot to leap across the stream. I have my eyes on a layer of stones and pebbles at the edge of the far bank, but I can see as I extend my right leg that I'm going to fall a bit short. My foot hits a submerged stone at the water's edge, and I feel my ankle turn just before I feel the sharp pain shooting into my brain. I pitch forward to land face down on the bank, cursing as I fall.

"Are you all right?" Annamarie has rushed over, but I am oblivious to anything but the searing pain, a minute to writhe and clutch my ankle. A familiar pain, a sprain. I'm wet and mortified, but I'll be able to limp on. Annamarie is unlacing my boot, and I help her get it off. She opens her backpack and pulls out a first-aid kit, and I'm about to get an instant ice pack pressed against my ankle. "We've got gauze to wrap it," she says. "We'll have to slow down."

She was on top of it, like everything she does, and I am like a child being led through the canyon. I've definitely lost my swagger, bumbling through the woods. While she holds the ice pack to my ankle, I unzip my backpack and pull out the flask of Johnny Walker black, uncap it, and take a healthy swig. I'll need medicine for this, I say.

"I don't think that's what the doctor ordered," Annamarie says sharply. "I wonder if you're taking seriously the quest you are on – you know, to save your life."

I sigh, recap the flask, and return it to the backpack as I protest. It's all I have for pain right now, I plead. I do have some weed and mild hallucinogens. But I need pain relief, at least for this moment. I'm going to give up alcohol, I promise. Annamarie is quiet, stewing, as she turns the ice pack over to me. She pulls out the gauze from her bag, then expertly wraps the ankle. I press the boot on gingerly and rise to my feet. She has a grip on my arm.

"You didn't tell me about the cirrhosis, Ray," she says icily. "I found that out from Mona. I texted her this morning after hearing the professor. She was surprised I didn't know about it, and so am I."

Busted. I make my excuses and apologize as profusely as I can, owning up to my vanity and insensitivity in not telling her immediately, how I planned to tell her everything on this trip, and how I needed her help. Her look makes my words feel lame, but I punctuate them with my most heartfelt and genuine expressions of endearment, as honestly as I can muster. I put my arms around her and tell her directly.

"Annamarie, I love you," I say. "My liver will last many years if I can stop drinking, and I will. It's a struggle for me, a real shock to my system, but I can do it with your help." She returns the embrace and buries her face into my shoulder. "OK," she says softly. "The first thing we need to do is get rid of that flask and its contents."

I retrieve the flask and hand it over. Annamarie uncaps it and pours the golden elixir into the stream. Then she throws the flask as far as she can into the brush. "There," she says. "I feel better about our adventure already." I am thankful for her forgiveness and also thankful I didn't share the other flask of vodka inside the zippered pocket of my backpack. I'm sure I'll need it at some point.

I test the injured ankle, with Annamarie at my elbow, walking along the creek, looking for a pathway up the hill to the road above, following the plane of the failing bridge. Once we get a foothold through the brush, Annamarie reorients me slightly to the right as we climb the hill. She drops in behind me as I move gingerly upward, balancing and pulling myself along with the limbs of trees and shrubs.

Progress is much slower going up, being careful with the muddy banks, although the rain has stopped. The pain in my ankle has subsided, and it's responding well to my cautious weight-bearing. I find a fallen tree limb, about 5-feet long and sturdy, steadying myself as we climb the hill. We've been traveling for less than an hour, easily on pace to meet Jay at the top – barring another bad decision on my part. What was I trying to prove, anyway? That I'm still able to jump wide streams after all these miles? Damn! I can feel the rising tension from Annamarie, even with the momentary reconciliation.

Calling to Annamarie and motioning to a fallen tree, I suggest we stop for a minute or two. I use my stick to sweep through the grass and prod the log, propping my backpack against it, assuring her there are no snakes or fire ants. She slips off her backpack but stays standing. I sit and massage my leg, apologizing for being a klutz.

She shakes her head and shrugs. "What do you hope to accomplish in Big Sur?" she asks softly. "What's your plan?" I don't have an actual plan except to enjoy the time with her and still do my assignment. The story will dominate much of my time, gathering information and writing. But Annamarie has no restrictions. She's registered for the workshop and can wander off to pursue her own interests. My invitation for her to be off on her own doesn't inspire her.

"I'm interested in how you plan to use the experience to help you get control of your drinking problem," Annamarie says. "Have you read Professor Cross's suggestions for creating new good habits to replace destructive ones?"

No, I haven't gotten to it, I admit. It was just yesterday. But I'm looking at this four-day workshop as an opportunity to learn how to treat my addictions. The Professor's advice will be relevant. Annamarie is ahead of me, as usual, having taken "a quick look." She describes the first exercise: "Write down your core values, things you really care about. Then, across from those values, write down specific actions that are in accord with your values. He says these actions should be driving forces in your life."

Sounds reasonable, I say. I'll want to think about the values piece before I fill up my post-drinking schedule, I tell her. Annamarie grunts an agreement and holds out her hand to me. "Are we ready?" I take her hand and lean on the makeshift walking stick as I pull myself up and grab my backpack. I'm ready, even if I'm stung by her sharp jabs at my commitment. Well, I asked for her help, and she weighed in. That's the good news. If she's also dishing a healthy dose of criticism with her prescription, it tells me I've got a lot of work to do this week to repair the rift I'm feeling with my lover.

While the going is progressively tougher as we climb, the vision of the top salves my ankle as I stumble along. Annamarie, patient and considerate of my distress, is pointing out hazards and wonders along the trail, in her element in the wilds of Earth, a place to me that is just boyhood memories. Her youthful vigor lends a sense of rejuvenation, even as our chasm of ages yawns back at me. I'm determined to step up my game.

We'll have lots of good exercise this trip, I remind her. Breathing exercises, *qigong*. … I gasp … Yoga, for sure. … Breathe … Tai chi and other martial arts, how Jay got started. … pant … I'm exhausted just thinking about it. Annamarie looks back at me, smiling cheerfully. "It seems like the break we both need," she says, and I grab her hand and squeeze it, happy to get her mind back on her own well-being.

Deep breath. I can see what appears to be clearing up ahead, and I hear a voice, maybe a radio? Civilization! I'm breathing hard as I pull myself up a step with my walking stick. Annamarie puts her hand on my elbow to steady me. "Poor Ray," she says, and I hear the genuine sympathy in her voice. "We need to get you off your foot and soak the ankle. You're a trooper for gutting it out."

No, I'm an idiot for trying to jump the stream, and I'm paying the price for my stupidity. But I know that Annamarie's prescription is exactly right, and I'm grateful to have this beautiful and attentive young woman caring about me. And again, I am struck with a vague sense of guilt, the same feeling I sometimes get with Mona, that I am not worthy of affection. It's a mixed emotion, and I'm not sure whether this feeling comes with either berating or congratulating the lone wolf in me. I'm in conflict with myself, one of me.

Annamarie is the first to reach the top, leaping the last few steps to pull back the shrubs and expose the abandoned two-lane blacktop. Hobbling up, I lean on my stick, surveying the scene. A Lexus luxury sedan is parked down and across the road, probably Jay's car, is my guess. I ring up his number as we start walking. "I see you!" he answers, and the car door opens. "What happened to your leg?"

I wave. Sprained ankle, I explain into the phone. Jay is walking quickly toward us, different from the man I remember – that edgy and intense young martial artist, almost in a defensive crouch when he moved. Now, as he rushes to me with his hand extended and a big smile, I'm struck by his tall, upright air of self-assurance, his maturity, his jet-black hair longer, pulled back in a ponytail, skin still smooth, bright eyes masking his 40ish years. Jay has found his groove and wears it well.

I compliment his rock-star haircut, grasping his hand for a hearty handshake, then an embrace. "Chen warrior haircut," he corrects me gently, "and this is Annamarie?" I introduce her as a "public interest attorney and good friend" who is interested in the healing power of *qi*, and its applications in yoga. Jay takes her hand and bows without letting go of me. "You are in the right place for *qi* and prana," he tells her. "Many enlightened teachers and students here, energy for all." He turns to me to ask about my injury, and I assure him it will be fine, with temporary discomfort and minor restrictions from a mild ankle sprain. No running, though.

"You are also in the right place, with a Chinese doctor to help you," Jay says. "Let's get in the car and get your shoe off." I limp over to the car and climb into the back seat, propping my foot on the seat. He helps me with the laces, and I gingerly pull off the shoe, emitting a soft whistle through clenched teeth. Without removing the wrap, Jay touches the foot gently; palm stretched along the sole, fingers to toes, then cups the heel, his middle finger gently pressing against the space behind my swollen ankle. Gradually he increases the pressure until finally, I wince. He holds it there, and my pain subsides, feeling only the pressure to that point of my foot.

Is this *qi* healing? I ask. "Acupressure," Jay says, seeming to increase the pressure slightly. "If I had my needles, we could touch all the points with acupuncture. Same principle, more points. It is a mild sprain, and this provides immediate relief for the pain.

Annamarie, will you put pressure here while I drive?" She eagerly agrees to minister to my foot, asking where exactly to apply pressure. "It's in the well behind the ankle," Jay says. "It's a little swollen, so be gentle at first. The pressure is sending signals to the brain that counter the pain. He needs to feel it. We'll still want to soak it when we get to the Institute."

Annamarie applies her cool hand to my fevered joint, and I'm immediately transported to an erotic place as she is situated, smiling at me and pressing her finger into my flesh. "Does this hurt?" she asks. Not enough, I say, but I love looking at her while she caresses my body part. Annamarie's smile widens as she pushes harder into my foot. Ouch!

Jay takes us first to the Nepenthe restaurant, a Big Sur landmark and tourist attraction that provides breathtaking views of the Pacific coastline. We have the restaurant to ourselves, except for the forlorn staff that cheers when we walk through the door. My ankle already is feeling better as we make our way to a table with a fabulous view. Annamarie has the Green Goddess salad, naturally, and Jay has a veggie burger. I'm famished, so I go for the filet mignon, and imagine that I could chase it with several glasses of Cabernet.

Annamarie is lively, vivacious, and fresh, no doubt cheered by the overlook and adventure but also charmed by Jay, as I suspected she would be. He is telling her the story of how I helped him become a columnist, promoting his writing in the newspaper. "I had started a blog for my temple, explaining the global search for meaning, about spiritualism in all its many faces, and the *Chronicle* liked it," he says.

"Ray was reading Buddhist blogs?" Annamarie asks, eying me mischievously. I knew Jay before the blogs, I explain, when he was the meanest kid in Chinatown. He was a martial arts fighter who hung out at bars, even though he was a teenager. It was quite a transformation, I recall, a revelation to watch Jay win a Kungfu match. And then he's inviting me to meet a grandmaster at his temple.

"The martial arts isn't really about fighting," Jay says, "even though I competed. I was finding my way to spirituality, my Temple teaching me about the *qi* in the universe, and human potential, my potential. I learned to channel energy through *taijiquan*. You will see. I will introduce the principles and practices tomorrow. You will learn the power of *qi*," Jay promised, "and how it can be used."

13. Jay Lee: Just Breathe

Jay Lee had dissolved all thoughts as he sat quietly in the corner of his cabin, breathing slowly into his abdomen, then slowly out through his nose, releasing the slight tension in his neck and sensing the energy circulating through his body, the *qi* he channels for internal serenity and expresses for healing, or for defending himself. In this meditative state, Jay wasn't thinking any of this, just doing, and being. He was focusing on nothing except a black hole of serenity, a loose connection to existence, little else. A gentle rap on his door brought him back to the moment. He opened his eyes. "Yes?" he answered calmly.

"Shifu Lee, your students. They are gathering on the grounds." The voice was of his assistant, May-Lee Chen. "We have light rain and wind," she said.

"Good. Perfect," Jay Lee responded. "I'll be right there." He rose in one motion and grabbed a windbreaker as he moved toward the door and quickly out into the gentle breeze and sea spray. *Feng shui,* he said to himself. What could be better?

He was well aware that this Big Sur workshop was his national coming-out party and counted on the revival of an old friendship with Ray James to provide the platform and a narrative to elevate his ideas to the masses, to celebrate a new book and his already-booming LA wellness practice into the mainstream of the American health craze. He looked forward to renewing their relationship – but now, as the teacher, exposing James to the unique Chinese approach to mind and body balance, and naturally good health.

Jay stopped at the Lodge for a quick bowl of rice pudding, chasing it with green tea before adjourning to the grassy oval overlooking the Pacific Ocean, where his charges were stretching and bouncing to stay warm. Everyone followed his dress instructions, wearing loose-fitting but warm sweats or flannels, some with rain jackets against the morning mist. Ominous clouds loomed off the coast, but the sea air was sweet. "Welcome, everyone," Jay said as he strode to the front of the group, his back to the sea. "Our first exercise is simply to stand, breathe and listen."

Ray and Annamarie were positioned near the front and far right of the class. Ray waved to Jay with his phone recorder, which he turned on and slid into his jacket pocket. Everyone introduced themselves one at a time – acupuncturists and massage therapists, an osteopath and a graphic artist, martial arts and yoga instructors, two authors, an actor, and a Silicon Valley exec, girlfriends, boyfriends, seekers. Ray announced he was there both as a participant and as a journalist writing a story, which caused a brief stir.

Jay introduced May-Lee, his bouncy, smiling assistant, who was dressed in colorful hospital scrubs. She will conduct the session on acupressure massage and acupuncture, Jay said. "Today, we're going to start with the basics, our breath, the energy in our bodies, how to improve it and move it, a process that will make you healthier and wiser. And, if you teach others, perhaps also wealthier," he added.

Demonstrating the gentle stretching routine, reaching high and out and back and down to the ground, Jay Lee noticed that Ray was gingerly favoring his sprained ankle and might be disguising other infirmities with his earnest grunts. Beside him, Annamarie was striking with her yoga-supple body in motion. She was well prepared for this workshop, Jay surmised. Ray will need work.

"First, if you don't know, the secret of our practice is breathing, breath, *qi*, *q-i*, pronounced *chee*," Jay said. "It also means energy, the invisible vital force, and it is the core value of this course. Many of you know it, have studied it, and know there's no real equivalent in English. It's a 2,000-year-old idea that's central to Chinese culture, as basic as *yin* and *yang*, and practiced in Chinese medicine and Chinese martial arts. Our most important lesson here is learning breathing exercises called *qigong*, energy work. This is where we begin."

Jay demonstrated the "Bear" posture – head erect, as if on a string extended from the crown, chin in, body straight with knees slightly bent, feet shoulder-width apart, arms hanging away from the body, palms facing to the back. The feet should be firmly planted, sensing the Earth through the "bubbling well" in the arch of the foot, he said, "the starting point of the kidney meridian, as our acupuncturists know." He advised them to keep their tongues against the roofs of their mouths, behind their teeth, to help the *qi* flow.

The group should breathe "slowly and deeply, softly and evenly," in and out of their bellies – the lower part of their lungs – keeping eyes open slightly and sensing a calming of their minds, slowing the racing of their hearts. "You have already lowered your blood pressure," Jay said after a few full breaths. "Now let's see if we can lower the *qi*." He instructed the group to stay relaxed, breathe lower, and send their energy into a single point, about two inches below their belly buttons. "This is called the lower *dantian*," he said. "You should feel *qi* flowing into your *dantian* … focus your mind there."

As they continued breathing through this lower place, inhaling into the belly, exhaling out, Jay and May-Lee moved through the congregation, adjusting their postures. It appeared everyone was in need of adjustment, Ray as much as any. May-Lee placed her fingers on his chin, pushing it back, and straightening his neck. She widened Annamarie's stance slightly and pulled her arms away from her body. They continued the standing exercise for about 10 minutes before Jay and May-Lee returned to the front of the class.

"When you breathe steadily and gently into your bellies, see it in your minds," Jay said, pointing to his head. "Your breath and *qi* are moving inside your body, massaging your organs, your heart, liver, bladder, kidneys, intestines, blood vessels, nerve endings. Visualize it first, then feel it inside, get in touch with your *qi*. Focus your mind, *yi;* it's called in Chinese, 'intention.' You control how you move the energy in your body."

Jay switched to breathing along a microcosmic orbit, a form of reverse breathing he called the "self-winding wheel of the law." "Inhale up your spine to the top of your head and exhale down the front, through your organs to the *dantian*; feel the energy inside you as you repeat. If you have an ache or an itch, send the *qi* there."

After 10 to 15 minutes with this exercise, Jay invited everyone to take a break, and he made a beeline to Ray, making sure he was getting the story correctly, introducing him to a prized student, a martial arts expert and Hollywood stunt man. "This is Marcel," he said. "He's an actor with several action film credits who has been training with me for a while. You might recognize him if he wore his cowboy hat."

Marcel chuckled and shook his head as he gripped Ray's hand. "I've had my share of saloon brawls and corral shootouts, that's for sure," he said. "It pays pretty well." Marcel, in his early 40s with thinning hair combed straight back, passes for a much younger man with his trim physique and energetic manner. He said he stumbled upon the "Way of Qi" thinking it was affiliated with Jet Li, the Kungfu film star. "I found out that Jay Lee is better, trains the inner fighter, you know, and the inner lover too. You'll see."

Marcel's companion, Serena Gonzales, was a Tai Chi teacher who operated a beachside martial arts studio in Santa Monica. Lean and athletic, with black hair stylishly short, she had Chinese characters tattooed on the back of her neck. "Marcel and I will be helping with Jay's Tai Chi training tomorrow," she told Ray. "You'll like that."

Jay Lee led his reporter friend on through the crowd, introducing him to the osteopath, Dr. William Reilly of Los Angeles, who's "surveying a number of alternative medicine techniques," he said, and an author, Margaret Ferguson from Carmel ("I like to discover interesting people and ideas at Esalen"). He introduced the Silicon Valley business executive, Chaz Logan, accompanied by two female "business associates," as a benefactor who believed in the Way of Qi. "Master Lee should get more exposure, opportunities to train many people," Chaz said. "He brings ancient wisdom to our modern life."

The group tour came full circle back to Annamarie, who was listening intently as yoga instructor Jenny McNamara discussed the similarities between *qigong* and yoga – "both help open the meridian system, allow the energy to flow," Jenny said. Annamarie turned to Ray to announce, "I want to catch a yoga class tomorrow. Want to join me?" Ray said he needed to stick with Jay Lee's main program.

Jay Lee smiled and bowed, then returned to the front as the light mist from the Pacific was turning into a steady drizzle, prompting an outbreak of additional raingear and head coverings. Jay assured his faithful that only a few more exercises stood between them and the lunch break, with indoor work through the afternoon.

"Now," he said, "let's feel the wind, tap into the energy outside our bodies, to the *qi* in our universe." He led a series of two-minute breathing exercises called "bone marrow washing," which sought to "bring this external energy into our bodies and down through our structure to the Earth, cleansing us and rooting us to the Earth. The wind and rain flow through us and strengthens us. We're grounded here above the sea."

After a while, the surge of wind and rain uprooted the hardy students, and they beat a hasty retreat into the Lodge to dry out and talk it out during lunch. Jay had promised he would sit for an interview with Ray, who had only one basic question: "How did you get here, personally, from the time we worked together at the *Chronicle?*" Jay Lee greeted the query with a slight smile and a two-word response: "*Fengshui,*" he said without elaboration. Ray shrugged. "You rearranged your environment? I don't get it," he said.

Jay shook his head and grimaced. "You've got the wrong idea about *fengshui,*" he said. "It's not about flower arrangements. It's about harmonizing with the world you live in. *Fengshui* is what just hit us in the face out on the lawn. It translates as wind-water, *fengshui.* We were drawing energy from natural forces. There is power in *fengshui.*"

"Remember Grandmaster Yun from my former temple? I took you to meet him," Jay Lee continued. "We didn't talk specifically about his Buddhist sect, but it focused on *fengshui,* how to use *qi* in daily living." Ray shook his head, confused. "I thought all the Buddhist temples were the same," he said. "You never wrote about your own temple, not like this. I remember the meditation pieces, the survey on the nature of prayer, how religion creates communities,

110

examples of how spiritualism affects how we behave toward others and the world we live in."

"My Chinese medicine started with *fengshui*, is what I mean," Jay said. "I wasn't thinking about healing at first. I wanted to understand and use the energy I felt with *qigong* and *fengshui*, and I came to realize I hadn't even scratched the surface of *qi*." In fact, Jay had stumbled onto only two of the eight divisions of Traditional Chinese Medicine and was nonplussed to discover he'd only just begun to understand it all.

"I sort of lost my religion at that point, realizing I had so much to learn," he said, recalling that he stopped writing and started reading more, took off two years to live in Taiwan at a Taoist temple, "meditating and digging deep for understanding." He returned not to San Francisco but to Los Angeles, enrolling at Yo San University and earning a degree in Chinese medicine. "I'm a certified doctor of ancient rituals," he said with a laugh. "And I've learned to teach."

That's how he met George Bayer at the Lake Tahoe retreat. Jay was beginning a new blog, which turned into his book, on sale here, complimentary to working press, of course. He remembered George fondly. "The man has poetry in his heart, how he approaches Chinese culture and philosophy," Jay said. "His style is reminiscent of the ancient Chinese poets, but he has created a unique form, merging East and West."

Jay had texted May-Lee, who showed up with a copy of the book, *Breathe In. Breathe Out: A Guide to Cultivating Qi for Health*. He agreed to a longer interview at the end of the workshop to answer questions and clarify the finer points of Chinese medicine and the philosophy behind it. "Western doctors and scientists will tell you that

Chinese medicine is fake and doesn't stand up to the scientific method. But I know that it works. Maybe someday Western science will catch up to us."

The afternoon session was held at one of the institute's larger yurts, the portable and sturdy tent structures that facilitate small gatherings. May-Lee opened the session with a description of meridian points, where acupressure and acupuncture practitioners work their magic. "These acupressure points can relieve pain or save you from yourself," she said. "See this point, P6, *nei guan*, ..." she touched a point about two inches above the crease in her wrist, palm, and little finger side ... "pressure here can reduce cravings, whether alcohol and drugs or food – even chocolate." She had everyone's attention, including Ray and Annamarie, who were probing their inner arms to press the point.

"It also helps to press *nei guan* if you want to counter nausea or upset stomach or if you suffer from panic attacks," Jay Lee added as he moved to the front of the class. "If you slide your fingers down to the wrist crease, to H7, *shen men*, you press here if you're nervous or irritable or if you need to focus your mind for a project." These acupressure points can help you start the day by tapping specific points of the body on both sides, he said, bending from the waist to touch a point between his big toe and second toe. "This is an important acupressure point to sedate or to relieve pain, but that's not what we want here. There's a point on the outside of the foot, between the little toe and the next toe, which stimulates and moves the *qi*."

Jay Lee held up the first two fingers of each hand, with the other two fingers folded below the thumb, "sword fingers," he said, then starting at the feet, he tapped various points maybe half a dozen times each using both hands and sword fingers, rhythmically, one after the other on both sides of the body. His students followed along, watching as he moved next to points on the inside of his legs, just above the ankles, and then to points on the outside, just below the knee. Moving up to inside the leg, about mid-thigh, and then to the buttocks and above, over the kidneys. Then to the chest, just below the clavicles, on the shoulders, around the ears, temples, crown, forehead, below the nose, and on the chin.

"Now relax," Jay said, "sink into the bear posture, breathe into your belly. We go back to the microcosmic orbit, the little meditation from the morning. We are moving our breath up the *du mai* channel at our back, a *yang* meridian, and down the *ren mai* channel of our front, a *yin* meridian." The circle is unbroken between these two meridians, *yin* to *yang* to *yin* to *yang* and on, *qi* flowing freely; he added, "Sink into the microcosm of your being, relaxing your shoulders, relaxing your minds, gently breathing, calm but energized."

He coached the group through about five minutes more of breathing and sinking, relaxing and releasing, then directed their attention outward to his flip chart. Pointing to the Tai Chi symbol of *yin* and *yang* together, forming a circle, and said, "this philosophy of *taiji* is at the heart of Chinese culture, for more than 2,000 years. It means 'supreme ultimate,' and is part of Chinese Buddhism, Taoism, even Confucianism. The "supreme ultimate" physical expression of Tai Chi is *taijiquan*, the internal martial art that mobilizes *qi* to balance *yin* and *yang* for fighting – and also healing. It is your best practice, your best *qigong*. Developed as a martial art, it is also the way to good health, to internal energy."

Marcel and Serena took their positions on the side closest to Ray and Annamarie, and another couple stood on the other side of the formation, Jay Lee introducing them as "Tai Chi teachers who can help guide you as you turn toward them in our circle of Tai Chi movement." They started with the Bear posture, relaxing, eyes aware but not watching. "Your weight mostly will be on either one side or the other," Jay said. "Step out empty, separating *yin* and *yang*, except for the beginning, the commencement."

Jay Lee led the class through a series of movements called "Grasp Sparrow's Tail," ward off left, ward off right, roll back, press, and push, with weight shifting from one foot to the other. "Then we load our back right foot with all our weight, form a dangling 'hook' with our right hands and use it to balance a 90-degree pivot, stepping out empty with our left foot, heel down first, weight shifting slowly forward 70 percent into 'Single Whip,'" he said. Jay drilled these first few postures many times over the next hour or so, forcing Ray to the sidelines to nurse his ankle, which he took as an opportunity to observe and take photographs.

Taijiquan, by most accounts, was developed by elders in China's Chen Village in the early 1800s and adapted by the Yang, Sun, and Wu families for different styles but with the same principles. Jay taught a short form of the Yang style introduced to the United States by Cheng Man-Ching, a Chinese doctor, artist, and poet who migrated from Taiwan to New York City in the mid-1960s.

As he demonstrated the movements, Jay commanded the entire space, flowing through the form like a ballet dancer in slow motion, balanced and rhythmic. Announcing the different postures as he moved through them, he urged students to continue training with Tai Chi, to find a good teacher, or become one themselves. Then, he dismissed the session with an invitation to gather again in two hours to "focus on touch and sensitivity training, starting with *tuina*

114

massage. This is massage not for aching muscles but for moving *qi*. We will explore and open blockages for good *qi* flow."

Jay Lee adjourned the class for a break, urging everyone to return at 6 o'clock, when they would meet at the Aldous Huxley room in the Lodge, and advising them to "wear loose clothing." Annamarie was excitedly rubbing her hands and beaming as she and Ray approached their new wellness master. "This gets better and better," she said. "Meditation, workout, massage." Jay bowed and shook their hands. "We've only just begun," he said.

14. A Sensitive Man

Pleased that Annamarie is enjoying herself, I propose we take a quick walk to explore the grounds, aiming to find the hot tub carved into the cliff overlooking the Pacific. First, we grab a snack and freshen up, and I manage medicine in a pill and a bowl, determined to turn this adventure into a full-on trip. You need to get your head right if you're heading to the Aldous Huxley room.

Aldous Huxley got his room at Esalen before Alan Watts, Abraham Maslow, and others because Huxley, the celebrated author of *Brave New World* and *Doors of Perception,* inspired Michael Murphy and Dick Price to market the Human Potential Movement as an Esalen brand. For 50 years, New Age gurus like Jay Lee have held forth in the yurts of Esalen, shining light on the next wave. And here we are again, even if the current wave is thousands of years old. What is old is new again.

Tuina massage, for example, the "healing art of fingers and strength," dates back at least 2,300 years, Jay tells us. But it's more than fingers that Jay and May-Lee apply, adding oomph with elbows, knees, and feet as they press to promote healing and *qi* flow. We're encouraged to relax and talk about how our bodies feel. What needs *qi* energy? Only 10 of us gather for this evening's session, getting comfortable with mats, pillows, and pressure. Jay gives my diagnosis special attention, starting with my ankle and leading to persistent pressure on my feet. I ask if he's a reflexologist.

"You remember I talked about the 'bubbling well,' the acupuncture point for the kidneys and also a pathway to the Earth?" he asks as he presses into my foot, and I nod. "An acupressure point for the liver is just over toward the little toe, still in the arch." I feel him press both spots, one after the other. "It wouldn't hurt you to see a reflexologist," he says. "You would benefit."

I chuckle my thanks and relax as Jay continues kneading or "vibrating" various points of my body, moving up from my feet but also passing his hands slowly over my body, apparently sensing his way through to my *qi* flow. "What do *you* feel?" I ask him, but he only smiles and turns the question back to me. "You say you want to fix unhealthy urges," he says, taking my wrist and pressing firmly on the point May-Lee called P2, *nei guan*. "This is a prompt, a trigger, a nudge for the mind. Is your mind able to respond?"

Jay continues. "Chinese medicine has different answers for you, and we will cover them all, herbal remedies too. But the most important Chinese medicine is meditation and *qigong*, including *taijiquan*. Train your mind every day. This is your intention."

The solution to my consumption problem keeps coming back to my weak mind, the lack-of-controller. The similarity between the recommendations of my Chinese doctor with a metaphysical approach and the advice of my drug counsellor with a systematic behavioral approach is striking. I need to train my mind to move my body toward internal energy and vitality on the one hand and external health and fitness on the other. Each has its own set of tools to accomplish the task. A kind of East-West *yin-yang* connection.

I understand I've got to do the work, like Mona says, and I rely on the immediate inspiration of the luscious and loving Annamarie, undergoing May-Lee's diagnosis and treatment on a nearby mat. Later, after making love to the sounds of the surf clatter and wind whoosh along the cliffs below, we lay sleepily entwined, walking

117

back our day, thinking about the next. We're comfortably ensconced in a private cabin overlooking the sea, courtesy of Jay Lee's premium pass. Snuggling against my neck, Annamarie softly expresses her sorrow that she will miss part of the morning session on herbal remedies. "I'm heading to yoga at 10," she says, "so you are my resource on herbs." Yes, happy to serve.

But our best-laid plans dissolve with the morning mist, and the insistent vibration of Annamarie's phone as the sun glints on clouds hanging ominously over the sea. On the second buzzing, she picks it up. "Hello," she says groggily, then listens quietly. I'm watching her as she sits up and looks around at me, seeing that I'm awake, shakes her head, and sighs. She rises and walks slowly into the bathroom, closing the door, and leaving me to think the worst.

It's not the worst, but it's bad enough. Annamarie is being recalled to work – an emergency for the City of Oakland that requires her negotiating skills immediately. She won't tell me more but promises to give me the scoop when it's ready for release, which obviously doesn't satisfy the newshound in me. Later, I learn that Annamarie helped negotiate a settlement in a $66 million lawsuit brought by a young woman at the center of an Oakland police department sex abuse scandal, with a payout of less than $1 million. But I didn't learn it from Annamarie.

Her route out of Big Sur is much easier than our route in. The city arranges for Esalen to fly her to Monterey in the institute's helicopter shuttle and a waiting car to take her to Oakland. We are forced into a hurried goodbye as I delay my session with Jay to see her off. "This is all too brief and sudden," she says regretfully, giving me a soft kiss that lingers on the tip of my mind as I hurry to catch up with my *qi* group, which is just breaking from warm-up exercises.

Jay invites us to sit on the mats and listen, and ideally to take notes. I take a copy of the illustrated booklet distributed by May-Lee, "Your Body in Balance," and move to my regular perch, where I see him talking with Marcel and Serena, the Santa Monica Tai Chi instructor. They nod at Jay's instructions and take places at the rear of our group. I turn on my recorder as Jay begins:

"Herbal remedies are a Chinese medicine tradition, and I know many of you have your own herbal treatments. Acupuncturists and *tuina* masseurs often prescribe herbs as part of their treatments, and martial artists have their jows for muscle aches. I'll give you information about herbal applications and recipes. But you should remember that it's your diet, not the herbs, that's most important for healing your body. Good nutrition is essential to good health and a primary focus of Chinese medicine."

Herbs can help, he says, opening channels for *qi* energy by improving digestion and other functions. He cites ginger, peppermint, fennel, and cumin, as well as milk thistle for liver cleansing, and gingko, which he says helps with circulation and is used to improve memory. "Herbs have proven uses, but they are not magic potions," Jay says, holding up a copy of the brochure we received. "The herbs and foods described here, if ingested wisely, help to balance your body. This is an ongoing process, not a cure."

That's all Jay says about herbs, just points to a guide with descriptions and recipes and cautions us not to overuse them. Herbs serve to spice and elevate the main course, food in a balanced diet, he says, picking up a pointer and futzing with a flip chart. He flips to a list labeled, How to Eat. "Number one rule for a healthy, balanced body: Eat food that's good for you. That means more grains, vegetables, and fruits, less fats, sodium, and refined sugar. Number 1 Rule."

Simple enough, I'm thinking, and the full list seems mostly common sense:

No. 2. Don't eat more than you need.

No. 3. Eat at regular times.

No. 4. Wait until you've digested before eating again.

"No. 5," Jay concludes: "Don't hold anything in. Excuse yourself whenever necessary," a final rule punctuated by someone in the back of the room with a fart sound and a comic, "Excuse me!" We are all amused, including Jay. "When you've got to go, you should go," he says with a sly grin. "Hopefully, excuse yourself first." He puts the pointer down, holds up his hands, spreads outward toward us, and then briefly rubs them together. When he separates them, one is balled into a fist and the other open, palm facing the fist. "*Yang*," he says, raising his fist. "*Yin*," he says, raising his open palm.

Slowly he brings the fist to the palm and closes the hand on it. "*Taiji*," he says, holding up the ball of fists. "The supreme ultimate, bringing *yin* and *yang* together. The supreme ultimate of your health is to balance *yin* and *yang* in nutrition and digestion, with mindful consumption of food and herbs." He points to a chart in our booklet listing foods as having either *yang* or *yin* energy, as well as recipes that take advantage of seasonal foods. "We can balance *yin* and *yang* with good eating, or we can eat poorly and mess up our insides," he says. "We're going to drill deeper into the question of balance later. For now, don't forget to balance your lunch. As always, vegetables should be the main course, with some protein and carbohydrates on the side."

I look around for a luncheon companion, deciding to approach Marcel and his Tai Chi accomplice, who are huddled near the door. He and Serena confirm they would be demonstrating Tai Chi in the afternoon. "Do you know *tuishou*," she asks, "push hands?" No, I confess my ignorance of anything related to martial arts, wondering if we are going to engage in fighting. She laughs, "No, we're going to see if you're a sensitive man."

I puzzle over this comment as we walk toward the Lodge for lunch. The spring drizzle continues, but the gulls are swooping and calling along the coastline, lending a cheery note to the dreary day. Serena is talking about the sunny push-hands competition on the beach, which she organizes in Santa Monica. Marcel, a regular competition winner, helps promote her event.

"At Serena's place, it's more like a beach party than a competition," Marcel says. "And push hands really isn't a competition, even if you keep score. It's a learning exercise. You'll see."

We balance our lunch (burgers all around) with a conversation about the miserable weather and California's inevitable slide into the Pacific Ocean. "It's all this rain," Serena says. "Some LA neighborhoods are flooded, my sister called, and this road ...," she trails off, and Marcel picks up the thought ... "A mudslide on Highway 1 could strand us here," he says. "We've already got the bridge out in one direction."

Marcel asks about Anne Marie, and I explain her sudden flight. We're not totally trapped, and it's not so bad in this misty paradise –

and it promises to get better, we discover a few minutes later, with news from Jay. "We're moving the *tuina* massage this evening to the bathhouse, down by the hot tub," he announces, drawing immediate support from our table. "Marcel and I were the only ones in the tub last night," Serena says, "the weather was so bad."

"It will be clear tonight, I'm told," Jay says, turning to me. "I'm leaving early tomorrow afternoon, Ray, if you're still looking for a ride to LA. The institute is cutting all workshops short with the bad weather. We'll finish up in the morning."

Besides the weather emergency, Jay clearly is eager to move on and happy to take me away. But first, he demonstrates why he is regarded as the charismatic "master" to my new Tai Chi friends, easily pushing them around in front of our class. But that isn't the point of his instruction. Serena offered a clue: Jay wants us to get in touch with our feelings.

"We have worked to move *qi* through our bodies, to remove blockages, and to draw *qi* energy into our bodies from our environment," Jay reminds his class. "Now we are going to feel inside the body of others," he pauses dramatically, looking around the room a moment at the inevitable titters, before concluding, "no, not with sexual organs, dirty minds, but using our higher senses." Laughter.

To begin, Jay insists, we must "get our minds right with our bodies," an adjustment that requires what seems like an hour of standing meditation (*zhanzhuang*), with gentle moving *qigong* exercises (*jibengong*). "Calm your mind, relax your shoulders, feel the tension dissolving into the Earth," Jay intones. "We want to be *song*, the Chinese word, thoroughly relaxed, releasing, receptive, *yin*."

Once we've reached an adequate state of relaxation, Jay again leads us through the beginning Tai Chi postures, the series called "Grasp Sparrow's Tail" – Ward Off (left and right), Roll Back, Press, and Push – but this time he is introducing names for the energy (*jin*) expended with each movement. "*Peng, Lu, Ji,* and *An,*" he says. "*Peng,* ward off, is an explosive exchange of energy, absorbing incoming and pushing back. With *Lu,* rollback, we are pulling energy in and redirecting it. *Ji* energy, press, allows us to connect, to stick to and neutralize our opponent. *An,* push, is pushing down and through your opponent."

Calling Marcel to the front, Jay demonstrates how to incorporate these four *jins* into a push-hands exercise he calls "Four Directions," Standing basically toe to toe, right feet forward, the two men move in unison through the four directions, connecting loosely by hands and arms in steady motion, back and forth, gently feeling through the movements of *peng, lu, ji* and *an.* Jay talks as he sticks to Marcel through the exercise, "Now we come to perhaps the most important *jin* of all, *tingjin,*" he says, explaining how this "listening" energy allows us to feel inside a partner's body, to find their center balance and then to use the other *jins* to uproot them.

Jay has us pair off with different partners, and Serena is the first to guide me patiently through the exercise. We start off with a push to the right ward-off, then roll back, press, push, repeat. I feel Serena push into me, then yield, then back into me, and I see in her eyes that she's in me, right in my center down to my root, such as it is. I have no clue where her center is, based on this light touch and looking into her sparkling green eyes, which make me feel something, at least, and keep me interested in this monotonous little dance. Obviously, I'm thinking too much as Serena sends me sprawling.

"Whoa!" I say, looking up at her from the floor. "You were barely touching me, but I couldn't move. You bowled me over." Jay has joined us, smiling broadly as he gives me a hand up. He turns to Serena and bows, fist into the palm in the martial arts *yin-yang* salute. "Will you tell Mr. James what happened?" he asks. She bows.

"I found his center right away, and he wasn't concentrating on his balance, on sinking," Serena says. "It was a teaching moment; I hope you don't mind, *Shifu* Lee," using the Chinese honorific meaning teacher. "I think Mr. James should be more sensitive."

I feel my face flush, and Jay pats my arm reassuringly. "The Tai Chi classics say you must 'invest in loss,' so you're learning well," he says, then calls everyone to gather around. Continuing to rub his hands together, he instructs his charges to do the same. We rub our hands easily at first and then more vigorously, imitating Jay. After nearly a minute, he stops rubbing and holds his open hands a few inches apart, and we follow his lead.

"Do you feel that?" Jay asks. "You have created a field from static electricity, and you should be able to feel it." He opens and closes the space between his hands, and we again follow, feeling the sensation of static electricity. "*Qi* energy feels something like this, when you can summon it to your fingertips – to heal or to defend yourself. You have to work to bring the energy to the surface, and work harder to transmit it."

Push hands, he explains, allows two partners to feel the energy transfer, working together to cultivate your *qi* energy and bring it to bear on your partner, and the world around you. "You learn to be sensitive to each other, to feel and transfer *qi* energy, for good or ill."

We play push hands, rotating partners often, and I begin to feel the different energies, stronger in the practiced players. Jay likened the sensation to different "frequencies" you have to tune in to, a wave image that helps me get a sense of it, if not the real thing. I need a lot of work. The energy-exchange process at least brings me closer to my instant classmates as we prepare for a final celebration before class is dismissed.

I'm immediately drawn to Jenny McGregor, the yoga instructor chatting earlier with Annamarie and who now seems eager to spend time with me in the hot tub. Meanwhile, our osteopath Dr. Reilly wants to share a bottle of scotch and primo weed, an offer I can't refuse. "Maybe a few hits," I tell Reilly and join him for a while before bugging out with a drink in hand, returning to my seaside accommodations to work on my story for the *Chronicle*, but first to call Annamarie. No answer, so I leave a message.

I call Bradbury and tell him that Jay sends his regards and that we're breaking tomorrow and heading down to LA. I listen to his critique of my travel schedule and a brief lecture about the "company dime," and promise to send a draft in the morning. Another deadline blown, I'm sure. Two hours later, the rough draft is mostly still in my head, pending answers from Jay and a writing spark.

I wander down to the bathhouse, my mind foggy and body aching. The bathhouse and hot springs are in the spotlight of a warm sun's retreat across the Pacific, shimmering along the water. I stand under a shower for a few minutes, then grab a Terrycloth robe and head into the hall, now a *tuina* massage center, with Jay and May-Lee assisted by several other masseuses, each working over pliant bodies covered with sheets. *Tuina* usually is performed with loose garments or with

125

covers. I slide along the wall and slip out the door onto the sundeck. Sounds of merriment come from the hot tub.

Chaz Logan of Silicon Valley fame is celebrating with a bottle of champagne, passing it around in plastic cups. Marcel and Serena are here, along with the Carmel writer, Margaret, the graphic artist, Jaime Martinez, and two women, Ginny and Marcia, Chaz's girlfriends, apparently. They are all sublimely unselfconsciously naked. I drop my robe and ease into the steamy water, taking Serena's proffered hand to steady my step. What are we celebrating? I ask.

Chaz pours me a drink. "We are celebrating my retirement," he says, launching into his success story: Google will buy his start-up game program for $52 million, adding it to its developing virtual reality systems. Chaz also gets a minority board position at Google with a six-figure annual salary and a "golden parachute" pension plan. "I am now a man of means," he said. "Next stop, Las Vegas!" That announcement draws cheers from Ginny and Marcia, whom I learn have regular jobs as showgirls on the Vegas strip when they're not taking extravagant vacations with benefactors like Chaz. "I've been lucky all my life," he says. "So I keep rolling."

It's not all luck, I learn. Chaz has a team of financial wizards managing to grow his accounts, and he's always had the means to while away the time with fun and games in Jamaica, Tokyo, and Marseilles, among other destinations he touts. "I am on a worldwide quest for a fountain of youth," says the slight but sinewy tycoon, probably in his late 30s or early 40s. "Workshops like this keep me focused." He takes Tai Chi seriously, easily pushing me off my root during push-hands exercises earlier. As with all trained internal martial artists, his force is bigger than his body.

Ginny fishes a joint out of her bag and asks if anyone has a light. Marcel quickly rises and jumps out of the tub, retrieving a lighter from his slacks nearby. As he climbs back in, I look up and come head-to-head with his enormous penis. Even flaccid, Marcel's package hangs ponderously between his legs. Ginny is staring agape as she takes the lighter from him. Marcel sits down quickly, winking at the smiling Serena.

I wonder aloud if Marcel doubled as Dirk Diggler, the hung stud in "Boogie Nights." He laughs and shakes his head. "That wasn't even real," he says. "I just do bit parts in the big movies, action stunts mostly; that's my body-double act. The gold is in adult films, especially gay porn." Smiling, he adds, "That's not me, but I may play that in the movies."

The well-massaged group begins to trickle in as the joint makes its round. A few people have bathing suits, but most join in the buff. Jenny comes directly to me after stripping, grabbing my hand, and massaging between the fingers and thumb, purring, "You missed all the bodywork, a chance to unbundle those nerves, Mr. James," she says sternly, making me smile. I tell her about the session we had with Jay and May-Lee last night, which was good as far as it went, but I was hoping to learn partner massage. Jenny puts her arm around my neck, presses her breast into my chest, and kisses me softly, an unmistakable signal that I won't be alone in my seaside bungalow tonight, if I choose her company.

There must be 20 of us gathered in the hot tub, not an uncomfortable number but cozy. Jay and May-Lee are the last ones in, he in the altogether and she in a one-piece swimsuit. Jay invites us all to gather in a circle against the tub's walls and join hands.

127

"We have many water treatments in the Chinese medicine tradition," Jay says. "We have much power now, with so many of us here, to concentrate *qi* energy and dissolve barriers. First, we must synch our breathing. Remember, breathe slowly and deeply into your belly. Follow me."

Holding hands with Jenny on my left and May-Lee on my right, in a circle of *qi* energy, we focus our breathing in unison, relaxing and sinking into the warm and turgid water, guided by Jay's soft "breathe in … breathe out." After a few minutes, he asks us to squeeze our partners' hands in unison, "squeeze … release," matching our syncopated breathing. "We are pulsing," Jay says, and, indeed, we seem to have become one integrated, pulsating organism, the magic potion *qi* lubricating our insides and, perhaps coincidentally, giving me an erection.

15. The Limits of Limitation

Pulsing in a hot tub with 20 mostly naked people is an obvious starting point for *The Vibe* about Jay Lee's journey from Chinatown street fighter to *Chronicle* religion writer to Hollywood minister of holistic health. I rush back to the cabin to draft the column that evening, reluctantly pushing Jenny away, because the story is begging to tumble out. I call it "Doctor Qi," and try mightily to explain the invisible energy Jay says he mobilizes to heal, and how *qi* exercises and mindful eating would help anyone.

"We can all live much more healthful lives if we slow down, relax and work on the mind-body connection, the energy inside us," is a nut-graph quote from Jay. "I offer common-sense advice on how to live better and longer. Who doesn't want that?"

I reacquaint *Chronicle* readers with Jay's offbeat spiritualism column, connecting his training in *fengshui* to the esoteric Buddhist temple, where he was "attuned" to be a "clearer," able to remove bad energy in the home and work environments, and tell how his quest to mobilize *qi* led him to Taiwan and eventually to Yo San University and a degree in Traditional Chinese Medicine. "When I was in Chinatown, I would laugh at the old people practicing *taiji* in Portsmouth Square until one of them threw me across the square," Jay said. "They created great power with such a soft exercise. *Neigong*, internal work. I wanted to learn more, and I did."

Jay learned that his spiritual beliefs, rising from his Buddhist *fengshui* temple, and his physical experiences with the invisible energy, *qi*, were connected, and he believed it to be a unifying force in the universe. "The tradition goes back thousands of years when people drew guidance from mystical forces like the stars or the five elements," he says. "*Qi* is in all these things, and it is inside us all. We can tap into this energy if we practice."

I reported that Jay's practice at Way of *Qi* included not only internal medical and martial arts practices, *qigong,* and Tai Chi, but also a full nutrition program with herbal treatments. "Western medicine recognizes the value of *qigong* and *taiji* to relieve stress and lower blood pressure," he says, "but they do more. These exercises can empower you."

I close the column with a blurb on how to get Jay's book, but I'm too weary to send it. I save it for the morning, collapsing in the lonely bed for a few hours before our final exercises, at the crack of dawn. I sleep fitfully despite my fatigue, dreaming about being alone and running in the forest – naked, of course. Bristles, thorns, burrs, bugs, body on fire. I'm wet with blood and suddenly in the middle of a pack of wild animals, lion nostrils flaring at the smell of torn flesh, jackals baring teeth, coyotes nipping at my heels. I awake in a panic, jumping out of the soaked bed and rushing to the mirror to check for lacerations. Only the usual scraggly suspect struggling to focus returns the gaze.

The shower slaps me to my senses, and I shave the fuzzy image from the mirror before I hurry down to Jay's morning reveille, a shot of wind and rain blowing from the sea, braced for another day. Farewell, *fengshui.* Now Chinese Doctor Qi salves my wounds with a series of *qigong* exercises called "Eight Brocades," each intended to provide energy and relief to particular internal organs or musculoskeletal issues.

The formal lesson complete, Jay also carves out a social hour for fond farewells, a chance to plan future flings. Chaz invites me to "come to win" with him in Las Vegas, enticement enough for me to get his contact information. Jenny, sticking close to the end, wants me to visit her at her studio in Palo Alto, "and bring Annamarie," she adds, and I think she means it, probably as interested in my paramour as she is in me, and why not?

The rain is less invigorating and more troublesome as we navigate Route 1, heading south out of Esalen in the afternoon. Jay wants to get to LA by 7 o'clock, optimistic thinking given these driving conditions and rush-hour traffic near the city. Fortunately for the two of us, May-Lee is handling the driving chores, apparently enjoying the slow-going along the mountainside overlooking the sea, which Jay casts as a perilous sign. "Water above the earth above the water. Not a good place to be," he muses; I marvel at the moody scene of choppy gray sea as we wind along the craggy course. Wary of the mudslide warnings, May-Lee turns away from the coast and heads inland toward Route 5.

I'm not able to get in touch with Annamarie – no response to my phone messages and emails, except for a terse "Covered up" text response that comes this morning as we prepare for our brief warmup and *qigong* workout. I shake off the distraction to finish *The Vibe* on Doctor Qi, who is sitting beside me in the back seat, also working on his laptop supported by a pop-up tray table and built-in wi-fi, his regular portable office. I quiz him to clarify a few points and finally send the draft along with several mediocre photos, which is not my strong suit, even with smartphone technology. The accompanying email promising more later won't satisfy Bradbury, but it will buy time.

As I close my laptop and sit back in the seat, I see that Jay is watching me, smiling and nodding. "Now, enough about me," he says. "Let's talk about you." I snort. Nothing to talk about. I'm a survivor, I say, just trying to keep up. Jay nods. "Time does that to us all," he says. "Is that your goal? To just survive?"

I'm nodding with him now. "Nobody here gets out alive," I say, quoting the Doors' Jim Morrison, which became his epitaph when he died soon after he wrote it. I tell him I'm not a religious man; I don't worry about heaven or hell. Just enjoy myself, my friends, especially now, with Annamarie. I need some time with her. My family is tiny, just my daughter and her wife. "Did I tell you Mona got married?" I ask. "And she's going to have a baby. So there are more good reasons to survive."

Jay remembers Mona as a high schooler, but I've told him about her medical mission to change my bad habits, particularly alcohol. I admit it's important for me to have someone who really cares about me, especially now. It's time for me to come to terms with my health, with my life, really. I thank Jay for his help and for showing me the way, the Tao. I admit I have a long way to go.

"Not as far as you think," Jay says. "But you do have to work at it." He suggests we consult the Oracle before I get too far along, pointing to his laptop. The computer? He turns it so I can see the *I Ching* online site with a digital coin toss. "A technological upgrade to the ancient *Book of Changes*," he says.

I confess general ignorance of the process, describing a fleeting memory of a long-ago drug-fueled ritual in college with George, my guide to Asian mysticism and other exotic cultural fads. It involved a thick book and three oversized coins, but I remember little else. As

Jay explains it, the Oracle is determined by building a hexagram with lines that are *yin* or *yang* (or changing one to the other) based on coin tosses. There are 64 hexagram combinations, each with meanings expressed in haiku-like verse forms, usually cryptic and often eerily prescient.

He points to the Enter key so I can "toss" the coins – heads equal three points, and tails equals two. With three coins, the possible combinations are 6-7-8-9, with 7 being yang and 8 yin, 6 is yin that changes to yang, and 9 is yang that changes to yin. The changing lines become important when reading the judgment. At the end of six rolls, I've built the hexagram No. 60. *Chieh*/Limitation

 The top trigram is water (*k'an*), and the lower is a lake (*tui*).

I read the text aloud:

"JUDGMENT

LIMITATION. Success.

Galling limitation must not be persevered in."

Jay interprets for me. "There is a danger of overflowing water over the lake," he said. "Success comes from setting limits. But, as the last line states, you must be careful not to hurt yourself. There are limits even on limitations. Let's see how it describes the image." He reads from the screen:

"THE IMAGE

Water over lake: the image of LIMITATION.

Thus the superior man

Creates number and measure,

And examines the nature of virtue and correct conduct."

I nod and agree that it makes sense to me. I need to set specific limits, number and measure – on my drinking, obviously – and try to live a more virtuous life. "Virtue is whatever good you mean, doing your duty, whatever it is," Jay says. "'Correct conduct' is acting within the limitations you set."

I move down to the changing lines – in my case, the second line, a *yang*, changes to a *yin*, and the fifth line, also a *yang*, changes to a *yin*. I read from the screen:

"Nine in the second place means

Not going out of the gate and the courtyard

Brings misfortune.

"You're on the road, so this is good," Jay says. "I think it's more than that, though. I believe it indicates you have a big chance right now, and you don't want to miss it. There's an added sense of urgency." This jibes with my notion that I have an important journey ahead of me and I'm on the right track. I read the final line judgment:

"Nine in the fifth place means:

Sweet limitation brings good fortune.

Going brings esteem.

"I think that's clear," Jay says. "If you make good decisions establishing limits, and refocusing your life, you will be admired and emulated. Maybe you'll write a book about it – or maybe I will!" We playfully spar over who will have the rights to my story, such as it is, and I am reminded of what initially attracted me to Jay when we first met – his sense of humor and ready banter. He enjoys verbal sparring as much as the physical challenges of martial arts. And he's a worthy opponent.

How is it that a man of medicine – even the Chinese variety – is helping me consult the fortune teller in the *I Ching*? I ask jokingly. His response is earnest. "The cosmology of the *I Ching* is the Taoist perception of the universe and our place in it. The healing arts also are based on the idea that we have the ability to tap into the stuff of the universe, *qi*. You must practice *qigong*, meditate, and balance body and mind. That is the Way."

Jay's Way of *Qi* holistic health mantra is beginning to work its way into my subconscious after just a few days of practice, and I'm seeing the possibilities – *qigong* and Tai Chi, meditation, nutrition, therapeutic massage, good vibrations for the heart and liver and a shot of internal energy to keep everything in balance. He's showing me a good way to go, but I fret over what is certainly a steep climb. Where do I go from here? I ask him.

"If you are ready, then you take your first step, find a teacher," Jay says, reaching into his computer bag, pulling out a video disk, and passing it to me. "I'm your first teacher, but you need another. Follow these video lessons, and we'll see." He promises to pass along useful Internet links and introduce me to Los Angeles teachers and students. I want to follow up with some of his Hollywood clients to explore the potential for *qigong* and Tai Chi as coping mechanisms in the age of Trump. I'll need the stars to sell the story to Bradbury, I'm sure, but Jay still resists putting me on to his clients. Surely some Hollywood ingénue would like to appear in the *San Francisco Chronicle*, I argue. He agrees to make a few inquiries.

As if on cue, my phone rings, and Bradbury is on the line. He got the file I sent him and wants to know what happened to my native cynicism. "Are you buying his bullshit?" he asks. I tell him Jay's sitting right beside me and sends his best, asking if I should put him on the speaker. Bradbury curses softly and mutters the affirmative, and I comply with a nod to Jay. "You're on," I say.

"Hello, Jay, Bradbury here. Congratulations on the book! I knew you had it in you, but I didn't think you'd be writing as a doctor of Chinese medicine."

Jay returns the greeting, smiling at me. "We all are looking for our dharma, you know, finding our dreams, Mr. Bradbury. I was lucky to learn so much from you and my other editors at the *Chronicle*." Bradbury is pleased to hear of his role in Jay's success and asks him a few genial questions about his life in LA: Is he settled down? (Yes, but no family or love interest.) How does he promote his business? (Mostly word-of-mouth and "sometimes my friends want to write stories about me," eliciting nervous laughter all around.) How does the local community accept his Chinese medicine practice? (Lots of clients, demand even in far-out places like Esalen.)

"It's a wellness practice," Jay says. "Staying well is what people care about where I live, in West Hollywood, especially movie stars; they want to live forever. Ray has been pumping me for names and phone numbers." I smile at Jay appreciatively and interrupt to tell Bradbury I'm still negotiating. But the newspaper editor has little time for Hollywood, quickly saying his goodbyes to Jay and suggesting he and I have more to discuss. I take him off the speaker.

"Three things," he says curtly. "Give me a paragraph, sentence, something, an insert for the Jay story that suggests his spiel may be a

136

little off the wall rather than definitely the next big thing. Maybe talk to a regular doctor for a quote." Got it, I say. "Second, get off Jay as soon as you can and move on to the news, maybe follow up on your column on the Dreamers. There's a 'Day Without Immigrants' action down there. They shut down parts of LA this week to protest Trump's border wall. Or see how motorists in Smog City feel about climate-change denier Scott Pruitt being approved to head the EPA. Something real."

I sigh, glancing sidelong at Jay, who's studying his computer screen. "You're right," I say. "With the rising health care costs, Jay's holistic remedies may be cost-effective alternatives for many." Jay smiles without looking up, and Bradbury grumbles and curses. I tell him I'll find a follow-up to the opioid story in LA. It's a big port of entry for fentanyl, which is killing a lot of people. I'll look around.

"Yeah, do that; look around," Bradbury says. "The big news is your car is ready. It's a used Chevy Cruze, built for economy, like usual. So the rental in LA should be your last one. You can fly back after this assignment."

I have my marching orders and a ride that's in the opposite direction of my planned route. First things first. I create a new email to Bradbury, subject: Devil's Advocate, and draft a qualifier, suggested as the penultimate paragraph:

Traditional Chinese medicine is viewed skeptically by Western physicians, although acupuncture is recognized as an effective procedure by the American Medical Association, as well as by many health insurers. As health care costs have risen recently, many patients have sought alternative remedies that treat the whole individual, not just their body parts.

137

I read it over and send it, closing my laptop. Jay smiles and does the same. I propose a toast to celebrate our reunion, plus Jay's book and my escape from the clutches of my nitpicky editor. I pull out my canteen, still with a couple of swigs therein, and offer it to Jay. He is shaking his head, a thin smile on his face. "So, you're not really serious about quitting the booze," he states matter-of-factly. I pull the canteen back with a shrug, sticking to my alibis, explaining how the naltrexone is helping me manage my cravings and how I'm drawing down my drinking habit. He's not impressed.

"Haven't you been listening?" Jay asks. "You manage your cravings. You control your impulses. You are not using your mind, your spirit You are letting your body do what it wants."

The logic of Jay's sharp retort is undeniable, affirming not only what Al Cross told me but also what I already know in my heart. I can only fool myself for so long, right? Maybe I was anticipating and hoping for his reaction. In any case, I feel a sense of relief. I sigh, roll down the window and toss the canteen far into the brush whizzing by. I smile sheepishly and admit that he's right and I'm setting a new course. "No turning back."

Jay pulls out two bottles of water he's carrying in his bag, giving one to me. "Let's toast to limitation, to setting boundaries that absorb what helps you, like this water, and repel what hurts." I take the bottle, uncap it and hold it out to Jay in a salute, thanking him for teaching me how to take control of my feckless mind. We laugh and take a long drink. I'm hopeful my feckless mind doesn't kick back, but for the moment, I'm flush with fortitude as the cool water settles into my gut.

16. Kicking Back

A cacophony of annoying banging and braying pierces my warm bubble of slumber. I roll over to smash the offending LA morning banter, a screaming digital clock radio alarm beside my bed. I turn off the glad chatters and peer through fuzzy eyeballs at the dial; 7:30, way too early. I roll back and pull the covers up over my head. Where am I?

Can't be a hangover, no alcohol for days. Something akin to a hangover that throttles consciousness while spinning random ideas through my head, like a crazy roulette spinning, spinning, hypnotic spiral. The overstimulated brain and body rebel against lovely herbs and pills, the constant play with mind and body. Off stage, behind the curtain, sleep. Zzzzz, into the soothing ether … Do-do-do-do, do-do-do. Do do-do … My phone. Damn. I left it on. It's on the table; I fumble for it, and give a hoarse "hello."

"Are you coming down?" A woman's voice, May-Lee Chen, Jay's assistant. She's here! Right, morning meditation. It's coming back to me why I picked The Standard, a hotel close to Jay's studio. Way of *Qi* has a deal to provide morning meditation exercises, mostly *qigong*, for the guests. It's part of my story, and a wake-up call I can use this morning. "I'll be right down," I say, suddenly awake, jumping out of bed and into the bathroom. No-fuss dressing. Swimming trunks and a T-shirt. Poolside play in LA.

May-Lee still has that radiant smile, a virtue of *qi*, I decide. She is dressed in a loose white silk blouse and pants, standing among a group of about 10 guests, including two other men. I wave, walking across the blue Astroturf pool deck, checking out my morning mates, especially an exotic beauty who smiles as she watches me approach. I fall in beside her at the rear of the group and introduce myself. "I am Wei-Lin Chen, May-Lee's sister," she says, looking like a Hollywood starlet in a pale pink blouse that barely covers her lean, toned body and skimpy bikini. Thrilled to meet her, seriously. As we begin our stretching and gentle qigong, it's clear that Wei-Lin is no novice at the art, and I admire her graceful movements and calm demeanor, trying to catch her eye with a smile.

As our taskmistress moves from the gentle to grander *jibengong* movements, taking us down into knee bends and up to reach the sky, I remember Jay's instruction, using my breath to sink the *qi* to the *dantian* while also circulating it through my body, staying balanced, relaxed. The physical sensation is exhilarating, I admit, without any pharmaceuticals or herbs, before breakfast, chasing away the confusion of the morning, the fog of sleep. Even the scent of chlorine is an invigorating addition to the sweet morning air, not yet fully fouled by sluggishly rising humanity. I can feel the sun's warm embrace, absorb the energy, think good thoughts, cast off the bad, and imagine the fullness of my limitations, and the wellbeing that lies along this path.

The group breaks up after an hour of the morning retreat, and most jump into the pool for a swim or splash. I join the Chen sisters and ask about life in LA., learning that Wei-Lin is not a fan of the city but enjoys traveling – as a professional dancer, accounting for her graceful poolside movements. Her show, a traditional Chinese dance troupe that portrays the drama of 2,000 years of Chinese history, is sold out in an LA finale this evening, but Wei-Lin will get me a ticket if I come. I promise to attend, pleasing both sisters.

"Maybe you should have *tuina* massage this morning for pressure points to relieve anxieties and cravings," May-Lee suggests, and I quickly agree. She leads me to a portable massage table, and I slide onto it face down; May-Lee asks me to roll over. Wei-Lin is sitting beside us, I see, as I spin around. May-Lee covers my legs and torso with a towel and begins again at my feet, magic fingers against those pressure points at the bottom of my feet, sending sensation to the top of my head. I close my eyes and feel the energy, the opening of the meridians. Suddenly, another set of magic fingers touch my left hand, raising my arm, and pressing into the palm and wrist, moving up the arm. Wei-Lin has brought her energy to the *qi* party. She leans hard against my shoulder, rolls up my neck, then cups my head gently as she moves above it, massaging the neck and shoulder muscles from behind. May-Lee is now at my other arm, and they're going around the world on me. I feel as if I'm lifted to a higher plane.

"This morning, I got my first taste of nirvana," I tell Jay later over lunch, describing the acupressure massage with May-Lee and Wei-Lin, and the exhilarating feeling I had in moving and storing *qi*. I think I'm beginning to get this. Jay is cheered by my assessment but cautions against overconfidence.

"It takes many years of practice," he says "If you devote yourself, it will pay off in the long run – you'll have a longer run, in fact. But you have to work." I assure him I'm committed to doing the work and deeply grateful for his help. He has come back into my life at a critical time, when I was dangling off a cliff, hanging by my fingernails, I say, and he rescued me.

"Very melodramatic," Jay says wryly. "Are you sure you've got a good grip now?" I treat the question as rhetorical, returning his smile with a shrug. "I want you to meet Zhou," he says. "He's a friend, a Tai Chi brother, and more, a source – unidentified, of course – who can give you information about fentanyl traffic. Can you take a little trip to the other side of town?" I've moved to the edge of my seat, surprised and intrigued by Jay's offer. Of course, I want to meet "Joe," I say, hearing an English nickname and not realizing it's a Chinese surname until later. I'm wondering what Jay knows about the black market in the powerful opioid fentanyl, formulated to tranquilize elephants.

Whatever he knows, Jay's not talking about it. He makes two phone calls, the first in Chinese to a man I later learn is called "Lou Guy," and a second call to Marcel, who within 45 minutes pulls up outside the restaurant in a baby blue Thunderbird convertible. He greets me like an old friend, a brother of the hot tub, happily reliving the adventure of performing an ancient Taoist water tradition in a modern whirlpool aesthetic. We're in a boisterous mood as he drives toward downtown, away from Hollywood with the top down.

"Koreatown," Marcel says as we drive slowly through a festive street scene by mid-afternoon, young people milling on every corner, boom boxes blaring K-Pop, "party central for many Asians." We pick up Lou Guy in front of a club that vibrates with funk music and is patrolled by black-clad ninjas with nunchucks hanging from their belts. Lou Guy eyes me warily as Marcel makes the introductions, climbs into the back seat and nods a curt hello, and briefly bares a tooth-gapped smile.

The ride is taking us into deep downtown, past the Staples Center and the glittering office towers into a seedier skid row section, where homeless men and women lounge on the sidewalks, attached to their bags of worldly possessions, some wandering glassy-eyed along the streets, talking to themselves or yelling at others. Several people are passed out, or sleeping, curled up in doorways, or up against a fence. Most are just sitting, sad. Marcel whips his car into a public parking garage with security guards walking the perimeter. He raises the ragtop and locks it up before we descend into the street.

Leading the way, Marcel is jut-jawed and sure-footed, his head on a swivel, taking in everything, his body balanced for any trouble. I kick a plastic syringe to the curb and sidestep a used condom, reminders to keep my head up. I look to see Lou Guy behind me, on a swivel at the waist, ready to get my back if need be. Marcel turns abruptly around a corner, and I fall in line, feeling like a running back escorted to the goal line by a couple of burly blockers.

Our destination is a gray, nondescript building – except for the American flag flying above the roof. A security guard sits on a bench near the entrance, eyeballing but not stopping us as Marcel leads us through the door. I get a quick glance at the indistinct legend above: United States Health and Human Services, Los Angeles Branch. Another guard is perched inside amid a mass of pungent people, looking homeless and destitute. Three lines snake to the counter, where patient pen-pushers and typewriters record vital statistics before dispensing drug antidotes, food stamps, or other relief services. They're making a list, checking it against other lists, keeping tabs. Behind the counter sit three desk jockeys, all gazing intently at their computer screens. Marcel walks to the end of the counter and calls to one of them. "Hey, Jim," he says. "We're here to see Mr. Zhou." Jim jumps up with a smile and opens the gate, his eyes sweeping our faces as he greets us cheerfully. We follow him down a long corridor past doors all shut except for the last one, where Jim knocks lightly.

"Come in," Zhou says, rising from behind a desk and coming directly to me, extending his hand. "Mr. James, please come in and have a seat," he says, turning away from the disinvited blocking backs, who are led away by Jim. Zhou is escorting me to a spacious seating area with Wi-Fi hookups and work tables. In the anteroom, I see a full conference table and audiovisual set-up. Zhou is no average Joe, clearly, and this is no ordinary administrative office of a federal agency downgraded to where health means cutting human services, especially the health care services known as "Obamacare."

"I'm not authorized to tell you anything, Mr. James, but this is important to me," Zhou says, getting right to the point as we sit. "You must protect my identity." I assure him I'm duty-bound to never reveal a source, no matter what, apparently mollifying him. Zhou has closely cropped black hair and a wispy Fu Manchu moustache that makes his thin face look slightly sinister, like the man in black in a Hong Kong martial arts film. And Zhou does, indeed, carry himself like a Kungfu fighter nimbly at ease in a government office wearing a Western suit. "I'm prepared to help you expose a fentanyl trafficking ring because that may be the best way to stop it," he says.

First of all, I want to know who he is, specifically, and how I know what he says is reliable. Zhou leans back in his chair and considers me for a moment, a smile playing on his lips. "You can say that I'm an intelligence analyst for a federal agency with a three-letter acronym," he says finally, and I snort. He continues: "Soon you will know I am reliable because I'm going to give you documents and lead you to a perpetrator, who will be arrested." Now it's my turn to lean back in my chair, mouth open but not saying anything. He laughs.

"No, we're not setting this up for you," he said. "The bust was in process when Jay Lee called, so we're expediting. I'm expediting. We're adjusting for an opportunity to stop, or slow, the traffic."

I learn that Zhou first met Jay Lee in Taiwan, when they were both studying Tai Chi. "I wasn't a serious student back then," he says, "just wanted to get high. Jay rescued me; he showed me the Way – the *Tao*, you know." Zhou's family had fled China with Chiang Kai-shek when Mao Zedong led the Communists to power in 1949, and he was a ready recruit for U.S. citizenship and undercover work to help his new country. "Because of Jay, I'm in a place where I can make a difference. I'm on a mission. And maybe so are you."

Zhou gets up from his seat and walks toward the desk, turning to me to say, "Let me show you something." I rise and follow him. He sits in front of the computer and clicks on a spreadsheet on his desktop, then invites me to sit down. It appears to be a statement on letterhead from the Bank of Communications, out of Shanghai, printed in both Chinese and English. But the text itself is in Chinese. I don't read Chinese, I tell him. Zhou clicks on a tab that shows the translation.

"It's a transfer of $500,000 U.S. dollars to the account of Xu Quan Xi, in LA's Cathay Bank," Zhou says. "Miss Xu has used this money to fund a series of 'grow houses' in greater LA, like hundreds of others across California cultivating marijuana, but these are also covering a fentanyl operation." The houses are owned by other Chinese nationals, part of a global drug ring. LA is just one port, but we're being swamped. "That means it's cheap on the streets, where it's being mixed with heroin and other drugs sold in small baggies," he says. "People are dying."

This much I know, having chased down national and state statistics and talked with emergency room nurses and emergency responders. But I heard that most fentanyl was moving in the mail, rather than through U.S. ports. And I'm surprised to hear that a government-run bank in China is underwriting a drug operation in the United States.

"Lots of money moves through China nowadays, and the Chinese are big players in the global economy," Zhou says, explaining how drug lords and crime families use banks worldwide to finance the drug trade – with government acquiescence if not outright protection. China, he says, has risen in a century from a feudal and myopic Middle Kingdom – the literal translation of its name, *Zhongguo*, places it at the center of the world – to a high-tech global competitor. After centuries of relative isolation, China today is benefiting more than any nation from global integration, Zhou says.

"Who's to say this is not the third act in the Opium Wars?" he asks. "Look at the history. China was trounced twice by Western powers with guns and opium, with the Brits helping to run the drug through India." But it's about more than opium, Zhou continues; it's about power, who owns the future. He asks if I've heard of the Boxer Rebellion? I shrug, and he rushes on: "That was the final straw at the beginning of the 20th century, when a popular rebellion against Western armies and missionaries brought down the Qing dynasty." It was led by a secret society of martial artists, the boxers, who thought their Kungfu could defeat anyone. Their swords were no match for U.S. Marines, and the missionaries won. "But the Boxers made China fight," Zhou declares, "and they're still fighting."

It makes sense to me that the Chinese would fight outsiders who came in blazing with guns and foreign-devil religion, but the idea of

146

China getting payback by fomenting a drug-trade war seems far-fetched. "It's not government policy," Zhou says, turning back to the computer. "Cartels and crime families are bigger than governments, anyway. Look at Miss Xu, one of the foot soldiers in the war. We've been watching her, and her associates for a while." He pulls up a live camera view of a home front hidden behind a wall and lush garden. He clicks again, and we see four interior rooms, presumably in the house behind the wall. "There she is," Zhou points to a slight figure silhouetted in the kitchen window, busying herself at the sink.

I learn a lot about Miss Xu over the next few hours as she prepares for what Zhou describes as a meeting with her property owners to discuss neighborhood issues, including delivery schedules and inventory. She is a vice president of her neighborhood association, above reproach in her community, but the gathering this evening is with her other community of business associates. This meeting will be interrupted by a squad of DEA agents, a raid, and I'm invited to watch. I've never had news handed to me so graciously before, and I'm naturally suspicious of the set-up.

To prepare, I'm handed a stack of documents I can review but not keep. I'm allowed to take photos with my phone and make notes. A dossier on Miss Xu is included, as well as an intelligence summary of the Xu drug operation, and two bills of lading from Chinese freighters delivering to LA, with line items circled in red, marked "FEN CVR" to indicate drug package disguises, Zhou tells me. He has left me to my paperwork, stepping out of the office and closing the door. I check the time, suddenly realizing that I will miss the dance performance with the lovely Wei-Lin Chen. I try to call Jay but have no signal or Wi-Fi availability; everything must be securely hard-wired out of here. I have to take a break.

I don't see Zhou on my way out, but I wave to Jim, telling him I'll be back. Marcel and Lou Guy are sitting ramrod-straight on a bench outside the office building, nonchalantly rotating their heads this way and that, even when they see me. Marcel prepares to rise, but I tell him to relax; I'll be here for a couple of hours. They should just chill, grab a sandwich, or something. Marcel confers with Lou Guy, and they make plans for dinner, but they won't leave until I'm safely in the building. We are, after all, surrounded by a wandering herd of desperate-looking humans milling around. I excuse myself to walk out of earshot but within their line of sight to make my phone calls.

Jay promises to pass along my regrets to Wei-Lin for missing her performance and my hopes for a return engagement sometime in the near future. He apologizes for being unable to convince any of his movie star clients to chat with a reporter for the San Francisco *Chronicle*, no matter how cool and accommodating I might be. But it could change. That's fine. Hollywood can wait. I'm on to something here, I tell him.

I call Annamarie next, but again it goes directly to voice mail. I leave another message, trying not to sound too forlorn. Call me, please. Mona will be at the medical center, so I dash off a quick text message to her: "I'm getting better, body and mind. See you soon!" No idea how soon. Finally, I send a terse note to Bradbury: "Perp story in the works."

17. Turning the Page

The moment of truth comes with Morning Meditation, a poison pen letter delivered in person by Jay Lee, who thinks he's bringing glad tidings. Maybe poison pen is too harsh. It's a Dear John gut-punch that sends me straight to the poolside bar, cheerily open at 10 a.m. A stiff drink is just what's needed for a wounded heart, no matter what the doctor says. I order a Ginger Moon, a fancy concoction with mezcal and something fruity, breakfast of champions. I've always thought of myself as a champion, sort of, at least not some self-centered old brute with lust in his loins and venom in his veins. Something like that. I spread the letter on the bar and search for the exact words that Annamarie used to diss me, to write me out of her life. Here's a pertinent part:

"I came to the conclusion, after much soul-searching, that we are not compatible – not just because of our age difference, which is a barrier nonetheless. This is much more basic: It's about love. I am ready for it, but I don't think you are. The more I thought about it, the more I came to wonder how much you care about me. Like forcing me to fly, for the first time ever, in a small airplane over the ocean – I was terrified! You must have known, even as you gave me little choice. Was that just so I could see Gretchen fly? We saved maybe two hours when we could have enjoyed getting to know each other better on a leisurely drive to Carmel. What's the hurry, Ray?

"I have so many questions about you, about who you are. You haven't been honest with me – lugging that canteen through the gorge. I know you had another one, too, because I found it in your bag. Yeah, you made me curious, and I was right to be suspicious.

The fact is you're not even being honest with yourself – about drinking, for sure. That vision I had of a valiant knight riding in with his mighty pen to right wrongs has been tarnished by a sobering image of an insincere man who is conflicted about himself and me. I'm not sure where I stand, or how I fit with you. As an ornament, maybe. ..."

It goes on. I fold the letter and stuff it back into the envelope that Jay delivered – sent to his Way of *Qi* address. Jay made a special appearance for the morning exercises, but held on to the big news until after he led us through the "8 Brocades," the *qigong* movements to strengthen internal organs, with special emphasis on the liver and kidneys, just for me. I take a long swig of the Ginger Moon. Jay couldn't know the emotional bomb he carried in his bag, this toxic missive from my erstwhile paramour. Extra *qigong* for the heart, please. How do I softly breathe away the pain of lost love? Grief is already hardening into shame. She doesn't *love* me? She doesn't love *me*? Whatever it is, the deepest affection or the basest pride, it hurts. Whatever internal energy we were stoking with Jay's exercises, it's been scattered by this emotional wallop.

I can't forget the energy Annamarie radiates, and not just the sexual energy drawn up through the branches of a spreading maple tree and right to my core. I'm reminded of the radiance in her smile, the allure in her voice, the brilliant conversation and argumentation, the self-assured good sense of herself. Gone. And I'm feeling the emptiness, drawing energy from tequila, through a straw, which I know is not the way to imbibe early in the day, if at all, and especially if you're giving up imbibing, which I must. Someday. Today I've got to reconnoiter, to figure out where I am – and maybe who I am, if I'm anything like the person Annamarie sees. Despicable man.

150

She dangled the proposition that we continue as friends, get to know each other better, build trust, to … what? The cynical journalist in me sees a ploy by a wannabe politician to stroke the press, to keep me on the line for public relations. I order another Ginger Moon, trying to wash away the bitter taste of rejection. I need time to sort it out, to get over the bronze goddess of my dreams, to recognize the calculating woman who still seems to have her hooks in me. Stupid man.

The phone rings, Jay calling. I grunt a sad hello, and he picks up on the vibe. "Hey, I've got good news," he said. "You're invited! The show is going on to Las Vegas, and Wei-Lin left a ticket for you. You could use a trip to Vegas, no?"

"Yes," I admit quickly. That's the right direction, a good way station, but Sin City? Won't I need spiritual support? Maybe Wei-Lin can help me find the local temple, I suggest to Jay, and he erupts in laughter. "Your body is your temple; the power is inside you," he says. But Jay isn't worried about my struggles with self-destructive behavior. He's more interested in my recent adventures with the feds and the fentanyl drug ring, and how my story is coming. Already filed, part of a big package, being lawyered, probably will run tomorrow.

Jay has a specific suggestion: I should follow the drug story. The Chinese invest big time in Las Vegas, gaming too. Financial and cultural exchange, plus casinos in Macau owned by the same companies. "Follow the money. That's what Deep Throat told Bob Woodward, right?" It's always the money, I say. Jay makes a date for me to meet with Zhou that afternoon, with another assist from Marcel, who will pick me up in an hour. I should dress for the beach and beachside entertainment. Jay is like a conductor orchestrating this exposition for his soloist, the journalist, who might otherwise be

151

calling his own tune. But I need a story to sell the Vegas trip, and Bradbury is pushing drugs, figuratively. So what the hell, tell me more.

Marcel doesn't tell me much, only that we're heading to Serena Gonzales's Tai Chi studio in Santa Monica and that Jay promises to join us later. There will be push-hands play on the beach, an exciting prospect for Marcel, who wants to make sure I understand the difference between pushing on level ground and beach sand, and particularly against those who are moving rather than using the fixed stance we practiced in Big Sur. Since I am a virtual novice at the game, I listen intently, trying to make sense of his instruction. Being tossed into the sand isn't so bad, I think.

Serena greets me like an old friend with a hug and a kiss on the cheek. We wander down to the beach, where several push matches are underway. Serena takes me by the hand and guides me to an open spot. "Let's see what you remember," she says, taking me through the *peng-lu-ji-an* Four Directions sequence in the fixed stance, encouraging me to sense inside her body, down to her feet, to feel her root. This time I manage to avoid the distractions of dancing with a pretty girl, concentrating on the balance in my body and hers, and she is smiling appreciatively just before she sends me sprawling in the sand.

"You've been practicing," she says with a big smile as she extends her hand, which I take with a smaller, rueful smile, admitting that I've done little practice except for morning meditation with Jay and May-Lee, mostly *qigong* and standing exercises. This is the first time since Big Sur that I've touched hands with anyone. I need a lot of work, so thanks for the lesson.

"Standing is a good place to start, better than push hands," the voice from the sidelines belongs to Zhou, who has wandered up without me noticing, like the stealthy spy he is. I extend a hand and greet him as Mr. Zhou. He suggests we take a walk, and we begin a slow amble past the expanse of sunbathers lounging in the sand. I fit in, with my bathing suit, Hawaiian shirt, and wide-brimmed hat; Zhou looks a bit suspicious, I conclude, even as he plays nondescript in gray sweatpants and Tai-Chi T-shirt, another cool LA Asian guy ready for beach action. It's something in the way he moves that betrays his disguise, including how his eyes behind sunglasses sweep the scene along the boardwalk and shop windows above us as he speaks. And, how he speaks: "This will be the last time you see me for a while, although I may contact you. People will be looking at me after the *Chronicle* piece runs."

I start to protest, but he shushes me. "It's inevitable, and it's a risk I take," he says. "We must be careful." I agree. Zhou nods and gives me the minutes-long briefing on the Las Vegas drug market, where opioids take a backseat to party drugs like methamphetamine, Ecstasy, and cocaine. Fentanyl is a problem because middlemen are using it to cut other drugs, particularly cocaine and heroin, but only a trickle of overdoses compared with other cities. Drug use is part of the party in Sin City, and you smell it now that the voters put pot on a legal track. This is all good news to me, the casual recreational drug user, and I wonder if a DEA stakeout might help me replenish my stash. I ask if I'll be walking into a bust in Las Vegas.

"No, nothing planned," Zhou says. "But maybe you can walk into a story." He tells me about two sisters who run a Mexican food market on the west side of the city, a family market that's a cover for drug sales. The DEA has been watching the women on their trips to San

Diego, where they connect with runners from the Sinaloa Cartel. Some marijuana, but mostly cocaine, meth, and fentanyl, which the cartel is getting from China or manufacturing itself before moving it to Vegas and other cities. "The sisters are just local marketers, worth more in our sights than in jail right now," Zhou says. "We're looking upstream. They're headed for trouble, though. You may want to poke around Valenzuela's Market on the west side. Be careful."

Zhou promises more information and a contact in Vegas after I get to the city. He taps me on the shoulder, mutters a quick "stay cool," turns on his heel, and strides off down the beach. I watch his quick retreat and instinctively look around for watchers, seeing only the usual lounging beach life. I haven't had my first bowl today, and I'm already looking over my shoulder. Stay cool; good advice.

Walking slowly back to the hand pushers, I enjoy the sun and breeze that wafts off the Pacific but can't get away from the bug in my brain, Annamarie punctuating each sentence in the shame-on-me, point-by-point-by-painstaking point. A response has begun to bubble up in my brain, but working these ideas through my fingers will be a chore. No crying, just some explanation and an abject apology about the flight to Monterey. My idea of a fabulous adventure for the rising Oakland star was misbegotten and idiotic. I am trying to change, but I agree we should move on, and stay in touch. Damn!

As I approach, I notice a group has gathered around two competitors; one of whom I see immediately is Marcel because he comes flying backward onto the sand in front of me. I reach down to give him a hand, but Marcel springs to his feet, smiling sheepishly as he jumps back into the circle. In the middle is Jay Lee, hands on his hips and a big smile on his face. I catch his eye immediately, and he waves. "How about you, big boy?" he calls, and I make a show of running into the circle, then stop and bow, fist into palm in Chinese martial arts fashion. "Teach me, master," I say. Jay bows in return.

"Okay, grasshopper, assume the position," Jay says, offering a forearm to press. I try to push it through his body, but he disappears behind a soft roll back that directs me away from him. I adjust quickly to cover my flank, but not quickly enough, as Jay easily sends me off balance, but catching my wrist to prevent a fall. "Relax, stop tensing," Jay says. "You have to listen, feel my center, be *song*, release, then turn it back."

This is the *peng jin*, internal strength, that Tai Chi teaches you, Jay explains. Using his deft touch, he demonstrates how he uses this force to "stick" to me – essentially, preventing me from moving, controlling my center of gravity so that I am easily pushed and pulled by his fingertips. I am powerless to resist, except to eventually take a fall, away from his grasp. I roll away farther and rise, bowing again. As I catch my breath, I ask if this *qi* power he uses to dominate is the same *qi* power he uses to heal.

Jay nods. "Yes, good medicine and good self-defense," he says, "same coin, flip sides." He offers his arm again, and I approach cautiously, mindfully sinking and setting my feet in the sand, touching him gently and trying to sense his internal movement, his center. "Good," Jay says, answering my gentle touch with a slight movement of his own as we work through the Four Directions push-hands exercise. He quickly draws me off balance and dispatches me with a move I feel and do not see. I look up from the seat of my bathing suit and smile ruefully.

"Invest in loss, as the old masters say. It will come," Jay says, inviting others into the ring with him, controlling each with his soft touch. He appears to have some superpower, this *peng jin*, that allows him to dominate other people, not just physically but personally as well. Later, at a dim sum restaurant on Sunset Boulevard, I ask Jay how a traveling man can hope to learn a complicated martial art like Tai Chi without steady training. "The martial art is not the first thing," he says. "The goal is internal power, building your body, coordinating with your mind. Meditation. I gave you step-by-step instructions – DVDs and online links. You practice. Next time, come back and bounce Serena into the ocean."

This draws a big laugh, especially from Serena, who has joined us at the restaurant, along with Marcel. "You will do well, I'm sure," Serena says, "but don't get too cocky!" Naturally, I'm fantasizing about Serena, I admit it, licking my emotional wounds and wondering if I would find comfort with this warrior princess who so enjoys dominating me. But, alas, I can't compete with Marcel, sitting there smiling, hard and stoic as she rubs against him. Jay leans forward and lowers his voice with a question for me, a seemingly conspiratorial tone.

"Remember the first time we met, in Chinatown, in Portsmouth Square? You walked right up, just butted in when I was sparring." I vaguely remember and nod. "You asked me a question. Do you remember?" I scratch my chin and shake my head. I may have been looking for drugs, in that neighborhood, maybe chasing a story. "You asked me where you could find the Falun Gong headquarters," Jay says with a grin. "I told you there's no such thing." I was asking that of several people, trying to confirm the rumors. I didn't know Jay then, and I don't remember asking him about Falun Gong.

"I didn't tell you the whole truth," Jay says. "I was learning Falun Gong then, as part of my *qigong* training with the temple. I didn't want to draw attention because of the Chinese agents. Beijing has a long arm, especially in Chinatown."

People were fearful, I'd heard in my reporting – not only in China, where Falun Gong practitioners were actively persecuted, but also in the United States, where the pressure is more subtle. I guarded the identities of many sources, which was a problem with the lawyers. But Bradbury went to bat for me, and I got enough human rights and foreign policy experts to weigh in to get the story published. George was a big help in finding contacts in China, but I never got a good source out of Chinatown, just rumors. Even though the series was well publicized, Jay never mentioned it when he worked at the *Chronicle*.

"You are still on the road to discovering Falun Gong," Jay says, "catching up with Wei-Lin and Shen Yun, sponsored by the Falun Dafa Association. They have chapters in cities across the United States and around the world." There's no actual Falun Gong headquarters, except founder Li Hongzhi's hideaway in rural New York, apparently heavily guarded because of threats to his life. But Falun Dafa followers are in many cities, connecting through a news operation, *The Epoch Times*, and their cultural jewel, Shen Yun, as they build support for the spiritual movement around the world. "I'm not a member of the group, but I'm sympathetic," Jay says. "May-Lee and Wei-Lin are devoted."

He also has some advice for me in Las Vegas. I should book a room at the Lucky Dragon, a new hotel-casino that caters to Asian clientele and where Wei-Lin and the Shen Yun troupe are staying. "I'm sending Lou Guy to keep you out of trouble," Jay says. "He knows all the Shen Yun people and the Chinese agents who poke around. They won't mess with him." Marcel, who leans in when we start talking about Las Vegas, agrees that Lou Guy would be a good guide and guard, but that he – Marcel – should go along to provide additional back-up. "Suit yourself," Jay says. I resist lightly, insisting that I can take care of myself, but I'm not unhappy to be running again with my blocking backs. Why should I argue with a friendly security detail?

Serena invites me to Marcel's beach condo for "libations and sensations," an invitation I can't refuse. After all, we've all been naked together. Perhaps we'll make home movies, I'm thinking wishfully after a day of drowning my sorrows. But I don't stay late. My Las Vegas card is filling up. I send a text message to Chaz Logan, letting him know I'm on the way, to take him up on his invitation to come party and win. But first, I will need to check in with Bradbury, who is still expecting me to fly back to San Francisco and pick up my new old car. I know he's happy with the fentanyl bust story, so I expect to get a flier. Hell, boss, Vegas is full of stories.

18. *The Vibe*: Chinese Connection

By Raymond James, San Francisco Chronicle, March 14, 2017

LOS ANGELES – The takedown of Chinese drug smugglers in Los Angeles this week was more than just the latest shot in the war on opioids, a scourge here as in many American communities. The arrests of six Chinese nationals and seizure of nearly 100 kilos of fentanyl and related synthetic drugs also have rekindled decades-old hostility between the United States and China over the drug trade. But unlike the Opium Wars of the 1800s, the drugs aren't coming from Western nations. They're coming from China.

Questions about China's role in the drug trade are being raised because the alleged ringleader of this operation is the daughter of the director of the Shanghai Port, who is also a high official in China's Communist Party. Like many successful Chinese young people, Xu Quanxi fit in well not only in LA's Asian community, but as an officer in the local professional women's organization and the president of her local home owners' association.

In fact, by all appearances, Xu Quanxi was the new face of China – a UCLA-educated businesswoman helping to open new trade routes with the United States. As a vice president of Hai Nan Imports, a Shanghai-based clearinghouse for apparel destined for U.S. markets, the young woman known as Sue Kee at UCLA, now 34, was leading a surge of new business between our two countries.

But today, Sue Kee sits at the LA County Jail facing charges of conspiracy, money laundering, and drug trafficking after DEA agents raided her Beverly Grove residence and five other houses where marijuana and fentanyl were being processed and stored. Agents were examining computers and other records seized at Ms. Xu's house. Several Chinese-flagged merchant ships have been searched at the Port of Los Angeles as part of the investigation.

"Much of the fentanyl and its analogues coming into LA are from China, very potent and pure," said a federal agent who spoke under condition of anonymity. "We've stepped up our intercepts of international mail going directly to homes, but now it's coming in bulk, in container ships. They've upped the ante, working with gangs in this country."

Fentanyl is driving the opioid epidemic in this country today because inexperienced handlers are mixing it with other drugs, said Professor Victor O'Malley at UCLA Medical Laboratories. "There's a glut of it on the market, along with cheap heroin. It's also being mixed with cocaine, and pressed into tablets. It's prescribed by the millionth of a gram, and just two milligrams can kill you."

Now there are even more potent analogues like carfentanil and acrylfentanyl, also mostly manufactured in China, O'Malley added. And many amateur chemists are in the line of distribution, mixing dangerously, especially among Mexican cartels.

Ms. Xu and her alleged co-conspirators, all Chinese nationals who have lived in the United States for years, are accused of importing and receiving the drugs, and packaging them for wholesalers via regular parcel services. The Hai Nan apparel packaging flew under the radar. The Shanghai-based company had no comment, but the Chinese embassy pledged its cooperation with the investigation. China has classified fentanyl as a dangerous drug and restricts it domestically, while serving as the world's top export manufacturer of the drug.

This is not the first bust of Chinese nationals involved in drug smuggling and dealing in the United States, but it may be the most consequential with the involvement of Ms. Xu. Her father, Xu Fanhao, is the director of the Shanghai International Port Group and leads the regional political operation. A U.S. State Department spokeswoman acknowledged that "the Chinese government expressed concern for the well-being of its citizens, and we assured them they will get a fair trial. But these are serious charges. We expect cooperation."

Since China is a command economy, suspicions naturally arise about Beijing's role in what appears to be a multimillion-dollar operation with government footprints, including the Shanghai Port Group and its link to the prime suspect. The massive haul, just a drop in the bucket in the flood of opioids to the U.S. market, was estimated at 100 kilos of fentanyl, worth close to $750 million on the streets. While controlling access inside the country, China seems to follow a policy of uncontrolled trade in dangerous drugs.

"The Chinese have been on the other side of this drug crisis," said Frank Litton, an associate professor of history at Berkeley. "In the 1800s, Western traders introduced opium into the Chinese market, which created a generation of Chinese addicts. The Chinese resisted with two Opium Wars but were overcome by Western firepower." Litton's new book, "The Middle Kingdom Strikes Back," documents how China has emerged from those almost medieval days into an economic powerhouse. "China is demonstrating that it won't be pushed around anymore and may be ready to open a new front in the Opium Wars," Litton said.

China's role in the growing U.S. opioid crisis is expected to be a topic of conversation when Chinese Premier Xi Jinping visits with

President Trump at his Mar-a-Lago, Florida, resort next month. But while Trump has criticized China's trade and monetary policies, he's had little comment on the illegal drug trade. Members of Congress have urged the administration to declare a national public health emergency over the flood of opioids on the market, and the dramatic rise in drug overdoses.

Meanwhile, Ms. Xu and her alleged accomplices sit in the LA County jail awaiting a trial date, denied bail because they're considered flight risks.

19. Lou Guy: Rights and Wrong

Lou Guy might be more aptly renamed "Lucky Guy," given his flight from tortured prisoner to a Kungfu champion and Hollywood motion picture stuntman. But he will tell you he made his own fortune. Against all odds, he persevered and won.

It was 1999 when the young farmer, born Yang Jinxiang, was arrested for protesting in Tiananmen Square, the site of student-led pro-democracy demonstrations crushed by Chinese forces a decade earlier. The regime had banned the Falun Gong exercises Yang and his family practiced religiously, meditations designed to help them become happier and more virtuous people. Yang was among thousands of Chinese swept up in the arrests.

For this act of conscience, Yang was thrown into a Chinese "re-education-through-labor" prison, or *laogai*, a fancy name for a network of brutal forced labor camps not unlike the Russian gulag, and in recent years used against the minority Uyghurs in Western China. Few escape *laogai* lockups, but Yang fought his way out, and he's fighting still – now with a new name, Lou Guy, given to him by an Australian fight promoter who misheard him tell the story of beating the *laogai*. Lou Guy is proud to keep the Anglo name as an incentive, a badge of honor for a fighter and a patriot who recently became a naturalized citizen of the United States.

He's also a proud member of the Screen Actors Guild, thanks to Marcel, who watched Lou Guy dominate in a UFC competition in Los Angeles and lured him away from the Australian promoter. "You can make better money pretending to kill people instead of beating up on them in a ring," Marcel told him after the match. Lou Guy's screen credits not only drew attention in Hollywood, but also in the tightknit Falun Gong community, where the Lou Guy legend grew. But he had no use for the limelight. His focus remained on his persecutors, who continued to shadow Falun Gong activities.

"They follow us now," Lou Guy told Marcel as they drove through Death Valley toward Las Vegas. "China agents all around. We be ready."

Marcel shrugged and nodded his agreement. He'll be ready, too. He knew the story and understood Lou Guy's caution as well as the deep animosity he felt toward his former captors. Marcel had seen the scars – the one across his cheek is there for everyone to see, along with the separated collarbone, one of many fractures Lou Guy suffered at the hands of his brutal tormentors. "They can't touch you, Lou," he said. "You're in a free country with laws that defend you. We just need to protect our reporter, you know, and the show."

"China try to kill show," Lou Guy said. "Try to kill Falun Dafa, but we fight." Marcel nods. "Definitely," he said. "But we'll see. I think we'll be okay."

At the Lucky Dragon, they caught up with Ray, who flew in from LA with plenty of time to check in and relax in the lounge with cocktails by the early afternoon. Marcel was certain Jay Lee wouldn't approve of Ray breaking training so radically, but it wasn't his place to speak, or to judge. Jay Lee depended on them to look out for his friend.

Ray had the *Las Vegas Sun* open on his table when they arrived but was reading the San Francisco newspaper on his phone, admiring the Page 1 placement of his column, accompanied by a longer piece about the bust. "What do you make of this, Lou Guy?" he asked.

164

"China is shipping dangerous drugs into this country, and the Chinese government is looking away."

"They are killers," Lou Guy said tersely. "You know?" Ray nodded, returning to the story. "That's why I come to America," Lou Guy continued. "Home of brave, and free. You are not afraid to fight bad guys. China leaders bad guys."

"Well, President Xi is coming here next week – to Donald Trump's Florida resort – and they're going to talk about trade, is what I understand," Ray said. "They haven't really talked about anything else – not about drugs, not about human rights, and you know the Xi regime is not very nice."

"Very bad," Lou Guy agreed. "I think your president will fight them, too." Ray groaned. "No," he said. "I think it's just about the money. He's working for the rich people who want to make money off China." Lou Guy shook his head vigorously, but did not respond. He wanted to think the best about his new country and its leaders.

"China leaders kill people," he repeated. "If you do not agree, they kill you, torture you first." He raced ahead in his broken English, telling about his harrowing escape from the clutches of the *laogai*. "We road crew, I slip away, hide in forest. I break chain with rock, hide for many weeks, eat from farmer's field like animal. I tell him about *laogai*. He hide me and help me find ride to Hong Kong. I lucky, go to Australia, learn martial art, fight back."

Marcel interrupted to continue the story. "Lou Guy was a martial arts champion, the best in Asia, after a few years working with the Australian," he said. "Jay Lee saw him in Taiwan, and later I watched him beat the crap out of some poor Mexican dude at the Berkshire House. I told him he ought to be in pictures!"

165

Lou Guy shrugged, "Every fight, I fight them. In *laogai*, they cut out body parts, organs, sell for medical. I hear terrible things. But I am alive, stronger."

Ray wanted to know more about the organ harvesting of prisoners. "I heard about that when I was investigating for the *Chronicle*," he said, but only had anecdotal evidence from human rights groups. "You're the first victim of the prison camps I've met. Can you verify that people were killed for their organs?"

"I never see," Lou Guy said. "But I believe. They strip, beat, starve us. They say is 'reeducation.' That mean no peace, until you die. Is why I come to America, for freedom, and fight for my people, because America is good."

Good thoughts for the American president as he prepares to meet with the man who rules China with an iron fist. But Ray was skeptical that any such noble thoughts crossed Trump's mind. "Some Americans are better than others," he said, his gaze wandering to the middle of the lobby, where a statuesque brunette beauty is shimmying toward their table. She smiled broadly as she drew nearer, as if she had found old friends. She walked directly to Ray and kissed him on the cheek.

"Do you remember me?" she asked. "I'm Ginny, from the hot tub." Now Marcel is on his feet, with a big smile on her face. "Hi Ginny," he said. "I remember you." Her jaw drops as she notices Marcel. "Yes! Who could forget you? Hello!" She took his hand and also kissed him on the cheek. "I'm Marcel," he said, smiling broadly.

Ray, recovering himself, embraced Ginny again, asking about Chaz. "He's in the car, waiting out front, hoping you will join him for dinner and games," Ginny said. "Did you get the message?" No messages were waiting for him when he checked in this afternoon. "We talked about meeting tonight at the Bellagio, at his suite. But I'm ready for dinner and whatever else he's cooking up," he said.

Ray assured Marcel and Lou Guy that he would be in good hands, and that they should check into the hotel and relax. "Let's talk in the morning. I'm supposed to have tea with Wei-Lin here. You should join us." They agreed, and Ginny hugged Marcel again before she and Ray headed to the door and a waiting limousine.

20. High-Stakes Games

The Lucky Dragon, like most hotels in Las Vegas, funnels its customers into the adjoining casino, the payoff for the ubiquitous and unctuous hospitality, which includes free drinks from roving, slinking cocktail waitresses – a trap, if you don't know. When Marcel and Lou Guy arrive, I'm sitting in the lobby swilling a Bloody Mary and reading a *Las Vegas Sun* report about an FBI investigation of Trump's ties to Russia. Something's very fishy about this president, ready to square off against NATO allies while promising a trade war with China, an immigration war with Mexico, and a new partnership with Russia. So many crazy things are going on right now, not just Trump's erratic leadership.

The bust of Chinese drug smugglers in LA was too big for me and my little column, so Bradbury sent in reinforcements. Veteran reporter Fred Gleese handled the news story – I turn over the photos and assure Bradbury my source won't talk to anyone but me, but grudgingly agree to give up Zhou's name to Bradbury, who abides by the same vow of silence. I don't mention Jay's connection.

My bodyguard, Lou Guy, thinks fentanyl is just another weapon of the brutal Chinese regime, and that Trump is an ally of the Chinese people who will strike down the autocrats who run the country. I forgive him for his naivete: He doesn't really know the American players, nor the system, even though he passed the citizenship test. Let him live his American Dream. I've got my own American dream here, catching up with Silicon Valley playboy Chaz Logan.

"I'm glad you called," Chaz says. "I've been thinking about you and catching up on my reading – the *Chronicle*, I mean. Nowadays, I mostly just read investor news and tech stuff, but I enjoyed your profile of Jay Lee. And then today, the drug thing with the Chinese, the fentanyl. It seems like you write about anything and everything. What is '*The Vibe*'?"

Once again, I try to put into words the inexplicably wide latitude I'm given to punctuate the news by telling stories from the road, maybe off the beaten path, presenting the considered perspective of a wandering scribe on the people he meets. But right now, I lament, it's all Trump all the time. He casts this huge, ugly shadow over the course of events, interrupting regular life and sucking the oxygen out of rooms.

Chaz wants to set me straight about Trump, once we're talking over grilled steaks at The Top of the World, the restaurant on the 106th floor of the Stratosphere Casino. "You've got him all wrong," he says. "He's a showman. You have to let him run the show." To emphasize, Chaz sweeps his arm along the skyline of the glittering city that spins slowly through the 360-degree rotational view. "Presenting … the future," he says. "My Internet media game is going great, thanks to Trump. The guy is stoking all the channels, a fucking Tweeter-in-Chief." Chaz's voice rises as he waves his arms in glee. "The market's taking off, and it'll get even better when he cuts taxes on investments so we can create wealth for everyone."

I snort and shake my head. It's the old "trickle-down economics" extolled by the investor class to stimulate their game, based on the supply-side ruse that pumping up investments creates growth and more abundance for everyone. I complain that investors benefit a thousand times more than the "trickled-on masses," an expression that produces a howl from Chaz. I'm amused that Chaz would be so eager to defend Trump to me, maybe thinking his laissez-faire notions

169

should be prime feature material for *The Vibe* in the *Chronicle*? Bay Area folks wouldn't be too hospitable to a pro-Trump, reward-the-rich platform, I'm sure. But I'm a guest, all ears and a little mouth. Fortunately, he doesn't press it, cheerfully suggesting that we continue talking and comparing notes as events develop.

The conversation turns to gaming, Chaz's favorite pastime. "It's just like the market. If you make smart bets, you win," he says, again pointing to Trump, calling him "one of the smartest bettors." I counter that Trump lost millions with his casinos in Atlantic City, declaring bankruptcy four times to get out from under them. Does that make him smart? Yes, in the eyes of the investor class, Chaz argues, because he "knows when to fold them," turning losses into gains. "Then, when he opened his Las Vegas hotel, he focused on the luxury accommodations, including timeshares, and skipped the casino," he says. "Casinos are across the street, and everywhere. He's a smart man."

I concede that Wall Street may be irrationally exuberant about him, and swallow my conviction that a businessman who makes billions gaming the system is not the kind of guy we need as president. Why press the point now? The steak is delicious, the wine sensational, and the spinning view of Las Vegas intoxicating, so let it roll. Chaz is determined to show me a good time, and I'm willing to endure some proselytizing along the way.

He proposes that I join him and his friends in a risk-free, high-stakes game of Texas Hold'em poker. He'll set up a "play money account" for me, essentially staking me $200,000 to play in a game that requires a $15,000 buy-in and $100 minimum bets. "You can keep your winnings, and I'll write off your losses," Chaz tells me, advising me to play conservatively. "You should learn the players before you do anything rash."

What's in it for him? I want to know. "An audience," he says, "a journalist who will listen. We get a bad rap – the financial sector, international investing, and global trade. Trump understands, even if he's coarse, crude, and unnecessarily flamboyant." I laugh at how even Trump's supporters acknowledge the bad and ugly of their guy. It's an intriguing prospect, taking the pulse of the turbo-capitalist set at a high-stakes poker game in Las Vegas. That could be *The Vibe* for the ages. I'm in.

Chaz wants me to agree to ground rules: Everyone at the table is anonymous, and he gets the final say on the copy. That seems like a reasonable price to pay for a pile of funny money and a free ride with high rollers in Las Vegas, but I intend to hang on to my final say. Chaz will get a chance to see the column before it's printed, I promise, and we will negotiate any changes. Meanwhile, the limousine is back to pick us up, equipped with Ginny and Cynthia, a greeter from the Bellagio, our next stop, and a meeting with the players.

Chaz's penthouse suite offers another breathtaking view of the city, and is furnished with a bartender, chef, and waiter who set us up with cocktails and hors d'oeuvres. The introductions start with Robert Loving, the only other American-born player besides Chaz. Loving is a self-made millionaire communications guru, trading in image-building and influence-peddling worldwide. Franz Leonhardt is a multinational financier, German-born but without permanent residence – unless the bank accounts in the Caymans are home. He is an original instigator of this group, a consultant who helps corporations and individuals, including each of these poker players, shelter wealth.

The other two players are the most intriguing to me, one Chinese and one Russian, earnest new money in the international capitalist game. Han Xingjing is an investment banker leading a Chinese buying spree on U.S. property, apparently with the blessing and possible guidance from Beijing, and is the primary investor in the Lucky Dragon. Alexei Bredkoff may be the richest player in the room, an oligarch who's made billions in oil and gas, reportedly with a pipeline to the Kremlin. Like Chaz, he is proficient at martial arts – in his case, a Russian fighting style called Systema. He looks rough and ready in middle age, a player in the Russian crime syndicate, no doubt, but with a Loving spit-shine, he wears doing business and pleasure in cities around the world. I learn that Loving also recently signed on with Han to do PR and communications strategy for Chinese global investment.

Chaz announces that I've agreed to keep identities private and allow for a review before airing our game and conversation. The multimillionaires and billionaires nod while eyeballing me suspiciously. While the article has hardly taken shape in my head, I tell them I'm keen to understand how global industry and finance fit in with the political news of the day, particularly the Trump presidency. I ask what they expect out of the Trump administration, and what they hope he will achieve. Besides their general approval of the new president, they provide a remarkably consistent and upbeat projection for the evolution of our planet, species, societies, and cultures, for their class.

As we move down to the casino, where Chaz has arranged a private room, Loving, the communications guru, takes the lead in establishing the preferred message frame for the article, how wealthy investors essentially provide for the common good, stoking the economic engine that feeds the world. They should be rewarded by governments, not taxed to death. Trump is presented as a shining example. Dapper in a summer suit, with a diamond stud in his ear, Loving continues to direct the table chatter in his disarming drawl, trying to ensure that *The Vibe* is in tune with the narrative he's orchestrating. I wonder if he knows I'm on to him.

My fantasy poker game ends abruptly after about two hours when a hotel attendant summons me to an urgent phone call. Gretchen, my fetching flying friend, sounds near tears, or past tears, upset but audibly relieved to hear my voice. "It's Frank, Ray. He's in jail. I don't know what to do." Gretchen tracked me down through my office, and then the Lucky Dragon desk, which mysteriously now has my message from Chaz. And she's surprised to find me in the same city. She flew into Las Vegas the previous day in what was to be a quick in and out. "We didn't know you were here. Frank went to pick up, you know, then didn't show for our meeting," she says. "I find out he's in the Las Vegas jail."

I tell her to stay put at the airport hotel, her refuge last night, and return to the betting parlor to ease my way out of the game. I'm down $35,000, not good but not catastrophic, and Chaz is all smiles as I push the additional chips in front of him and say my goodbyes. "Our games will continue," he promises.

Back in the lobby, I call Jay, reminding him of my series on PTSD and the Gulf War veterans, one of whom is languishing in jail over a misunderstanding. Jay puts me on hold for a few minutes, then patches in Zhou, who sounds angry. "What do you know about Frank O'Connor?" he asks.

I know he's a good man, I say. I know he rescued a lot of wounded Americans in Iraq, as a medic, and he earned a Purple Heart and commendations for his heroism under fire. I know he's dealt with PTSD since returning to the States, and being in jail is setting him back big time. Zhou is silent for a moment. "We have video of O'Connor picking up bundles of cocaine, MDMA, and marijuana," he says. "It's the second time he's visited the Valenzuela sisters in the past three months, so it looks like a regular run. This guy is supplying drugs to a lot of people in the Bay Area. He's no hero."

Now I'm the one who falls silent, with a sigh, before making my best case for Frank, who is not a dangerous drug dealer but a strong opponent of opioids, for example. He's seen how they kill people. He's a businessman who plans to sell pot legally next year. That's his dream. He's got no prior arrests, and this bust could really hurt him.

Not hearing any sympathy from the drug police, I fret about finding a lawyer for Frank. Annamarie comes to mind immediately, but she's not doing criminal court anymore – and I'm not too keen on talking with her at this moment. Frank, too, won't want her involved. After Zhou signs off, rather coolly, Jay suggests Jerry Chang, an associate in a Las Vegas firm that handles criminal cases. "He knows the players and can give you an honest assessment," Jay says. "I will connect you."

I call Gretchen, who sounds almost cheerful now, shed of those anxieties she's passed along to me, her fixer. I tell her to meet me at the hotel bar so we can talk it through, and I grab a taxi. In short order, I'm sitting at a corner of the Four Seasons hotel bar, sipping a double scotch. Gretchen comes down looking sloppily luscious in what appears to be pajama bottoms and a T-shirt, UCONN the legend across her chest. I stand for a long embrace, reassure her that

174

everything will be all right, and then proceed to give her the bad news without sugarcoating.

The feds have the goods on Frank, I say bluntly. He was holding when they picked him up, and they've got video of the buy. Gretchen's mouth flies open at the mention of video, and I reach out for her hand to reassure her as the anxieties return to knit her brow. Gretchen is the strong one, the kind of person who would plow right through military brass to get a chance to fly, or walk away with head held high. Now she's worried not about herself, but someone she cares about, and she's shaken.

My phone rings. It's Jerry Chang, introducing himself and announcing he can't get Frank out of jail tonight but should be able to do so tomorrow – with a secured bail bond, to be negotiated. We agree to meet in the morning at the Lucky Dragon.

"We can use my plane, if we need property to secure the bail," Gretchen offers, resolving one possible problem. She is slumped on her stool, one elbow on the bar supporting her head, weary and beaten down. I get close and wrap both arms around her, inviting her to take one of the Ecstasy tabs I brought, if she wants a lift. I feel her body stiffen, then relax against me. "I'm so tired," she says. "This has been the day from hell. Tomorrow is another day." I promise to call her in the morning when I hear from Chang, and kiss her goodnight.

And suddenly, I'm alone at the bar, not so sure of myself after all, scrolling through a mountain of messages on my smartphone. I reschedule Wei-Lin for a late lunch. I've got messages from Bradbury and a series of directives from Mona, all delivered in loving, daughterly tones.

Bradbury bought the Las Vegas trip to extend my search for the Chinese drug connection, even if I don't have a solid lead. I figure my story resides somewhere at the junction of the Sinaloa Cowboy smugglers and the local drug market. Eventually, I'll have to make a few calls, take a trip to the West Side, and see if I can sniff out the wrongdoing, but for now, I'm excited about the bright lights at party central. I check my phone and pick up Bradbury's last email. "Book a flight back home through Vegas," he writes. "I need you back here next week." That won't happen, but I play along. At some point, I'll have to cash in vacation time.

21. The Man and Caesar's Ghost

Frank is in no mood to play ball after spending the night in jail. Gretchen and I hear his angry voice as we arrive at the Las Vegas courthouse to meet attorney Jerry Chang, who is catching the brunt of Frank's rage. "You mean become a rat?" Frank demands, fuming. "I'm not gonna do that!"

Gretchen and I each embrace Frank in turn before we sit down at the small table in the corner of a room usually reserved for marriages, but love is not in the air. Chang, meeting Frank for the first time, is working to defuse his furious client, staying calm, smiling, and shaking his head gently. He has just delivered a plea bargain proposal from federal prosecutors and isn't prepared for such an immediate and vociferous reaction. He rushes to better explain the offer.

"Listen, Frank," the young lawyer says, "the feds are willing to drop the charges if you agree to help them stop opioid drug distribution – heroin, fentanyl, oxycodone, stuff like that. You don't mess with that stuff anyway, right? But you know people who do. A lot of people are dying, and families are getting hurt. Think about it."

Chang points out that the government has incontrovertible evidence that Frank bought large quantities of illegal drugs – enough, in fact, to send him to prison for 20 years. But if he accepts the deal, nothing prevents him from continuing his work in the recreational drug trade. He can still apply for a pot license and set up a shop. All he has to do is report the bad stuff. "You'll need to keep your nose clean," he says, smiling.

Frank sits back and sighs, strokes his beard and turns to me, a look of resignation. I shrug and nod slightly, a "what-the-hell-can-you-do?" look of affirmation, for what it's worth. Frank gives Gretchen a tight smile before turning back to Chang. "I'm not gonna wear any wires," he declares. That hasn't come up and shouldn't be a problem, Chang says. "You'll get a contact in the Bay Area, and all you have to do is check in with information on opioid traffic. You can't dodge it, though. They can throw the book at you."

"Take it, Frank." That's Gretchen's voice. "Stay out of jail, and let's keep working." Frank snorts and casts a sidelong smile at Gretchen. Case dismissed. It's all over but for the paperwork. Chang's a smart lawyer, and Jay gets credit for bringing him to the table. But Chang had help, a reluctant DEA prosecution, and Zhou obviously was listening and doing me a favor, I'm sure of it. I owe him a thank-you and a good turn, which I expect he will suggest in due course. I'm a guy with a megaphone, after all.

Frank and Gretchen decide to lay over in Las Vegas for a few days, for rest and relaxation but mostly to regroup. Frank estimates he lost $10,000 cash, plus the drugs and the business for them. It puts a chink in his business plan, but he can recover. He may not be a man of means yet, but he is a man of resources. He calls in some chits to pay Chang's fee and pulls $2,000 from a rainy-day fund for the craps table, where he figures to regain his equilibrium. "Time to change my luck," he says, inviting me to join him. "The odds are good in craps. If you get on a roll, you can rake in a lot of dough." I promise to catch up with him and Gretchen later, after tea with Wei-Lin.

Gretchen and Frank have grown closer; I can tell by the way she looks at him and hangs on to his arm. Before, they seemed more reserved, maintaining a professional distance, partners. Now they're in synch, sharing intimacies, moving together, or so it seems. This new co-conspiracy might strengthen their relationship, or just the opposite. I tell them about my split with Annamarie, and how poor communication contributed to the demise of the relationship. They're sympathetic about the sudden break-up, but say it probably is for the best. Gretchen urges me to move on to new adventures, and Frank agrees.

"Don't look back," he says. "Maybe she's playing you a little bit. You were her ticket to getting in the public eye. And you helped her get a new job. I bet she'll still be calling on you, too. You're the man, right?" Yeah, right.

Annamarie is a million miles away now, or might as well be. Whatever I thought was going to happen never will, and I'm back to my lonesome road-self staring across the Las Vegas skyline from another elegant perch. Like the Stratosphere's Top of the World, Mandarin Oriental's Tea Lounge in the Waldorf Astoria provides a broad view of the glittering desert jewel. I'm sitting on a love seat staring at the Stratosphere's tower on the north end of town, squinting to see the gyrating floor where Chaz and I dined yesterday. He has been texting me insistently since early morning, seeking a follow-up meeting – wanting to talk through my article, and get a peek at it. Nothing doing yet, I tell him. He gives me a rundown on the game, winners, and losers. But everybody wins when they play, he says. All I know for sure – and I don't tell him this – is my plan to file it for Tax Day, April 15, hanging the tale on those who can afford to cheat the system and still keep winning the game.

Wei-Lin interrupts my reverie with a gentle touch on the shoulder, jolting me to my feet. Marcel and Lou Guy stand smiling behind her.

Wei-Lin is a vision of loveliness, immediately lightening my mood. I finally get to see the beautiful dancer with the magic touch.

We order a round of teas and scones, sandwiches for Marcel and me, and dessert for Lou Guy. Wei-Lin won't break training the day of the performance; if ever, her delicate and supple body is immune to the lure of the feast. She is intent on preparing me for the show, the elaborate staging of tales from ancient Chinese history, the creation of a rich culture bestowed by divine beings now savaged by the Communist tyrants. Shen Yun is translated as "the beauty of divine beings dancing," Wei-Lin says, but the beauty is interrupted on stage by violent attacks by government thugs against Falun Gong believers, a purge portrayed as part of a deliberate materialist plan to destroy the spiritual foundation of Chinese culture, all the old teachings, from Buddhism and Taoism to Confucianism.

Wei-Lin says she plays many roles and is proud of one in particular, a goddess trapped in a mountain, as punishment by the other gods for loving a human. "My son becomes a great fighter, comes and rescues me." Lou Guy interrupts to proudly announce he has played the Taoist master who teaches the young demigod to fight, though he is no dancer. His favorite scene, he relates comically in pidgin English, involves Wei-Lin as a young Falun Gong follower jailed and beaten by thugs in Red Guard coats. "Wei-Lin is good acting; fall down but fight back," Lou Guy says, raising his hands in a fighting posture.

"We are still fighting," Wei-Lin says, laughing at Lou Guy's description. "Falun Dafa is under attack all the time, here and everywhere. We tell a story of divine Chinese culture, our inspiration, and what the Communists want to destroy. Our music and dance are part of the beauty, the history. You will see," she says, reaching over and squeezing my hand, to my delight.

Wei-Lin and May-Lee practiced Falun Gong in China, the young and dutiful daughters of Li Hongzhi acolytes who joined the early protests in Tiananmen Square against the government ban. Eventually, the family fled China to escape the purge. Good fortune and LA relatives led them to Jay, who took them in as students and assistants. He also had a hand in getting Wei-Lin the gig with the start-up Shen Yun in 2006, when she was only 18. "I retire soon," she says of the demanding dance performances conducted by Shen Yun troupes around the world, "and maybe join May-Lee and Jay.

Falun Gong believers see the end of an era, a time of moral decline, Wei-Lin says, when a change in the dharma demands the teachings of Buddha be heard. "We teach with art and music – the Chinese word for healing comes from the word for music." Wei-Lin's ardor for the show quickly wins me as her eyes gleam with the telling. Could she be a cure for the Annamarie blues still gnawing at my bones? Tonight, I'll be sitting beside May-Lee, who is flying in for the show. Then we're invited to an after-party with the cast.

When Wei-Lin departs for rehearsal, I excuse myself from Marcel and Lou Guy, assuring them I'm safe in the casino with my friends, Frank and Gretchen. Descending to the Vegas Strip, I join the mass of wanderers on the boulevard, walking through the poker story in my head. Once I can sit down in front of a keyboard, it will spill out of me, I'm sure. I fish out my vape and fire it up, just another guy on the Strip sucking on an electronic device, mellowing an alcohol bluster with a blast of cannabis, casino-cool enough but not too fucked up to score.

I've got to pace myself, I'm thinking as I walk into Casino Royale and search for the craps table where Frank and Gretchen should be rolling. This is where the working class gambles, a camouflaged Best Western in the heart of the Strip, nestled between Harrah's and The Venetian, across from the Mirage. It's Frank's kind of place, especially after getting shot down. Safe bets. Cheap rooms, $1 drinks, and $3 craps tables. I search for my friends amid the boisterous players.

I see Gretchen first, the gorgeous woman drawing stares from men all across the room. Her blond locks are piled up high on her head, evening gown plunging between her breasts, proudly on display as she leans over the table. Now I see Frank, a pinched face bearing the strains of the moment. He's rolling as I walk up. "Seven!" cries the stickman, "Line away, pay the Don't." I move forward to see how Frank has played it, but I can tell by the look on his face and the single expletive, "Damn!" His chips, stacked on the Pass Line, are swept away by the stickman, who rewards the "Don't Pass" bettors with their winnings.

Frank, spotting me as I walk up to the table, shakes his head and gives me a grim smile. He pushes his chips to the box man, cashing out, and stands to pocket the remainder. Gretchen drapes her arm around his shoulder and kisses him lightly on the cheek, comforting him with the press of her body, a fine consolation prize in the eyes of the gamblers around the table. He takes his lady by the arm and guides her toward me. "Time to find another table, maybe another house," he says, and I agree. The night is young. It will come back around. We saunter off to the bar and order drinks, and I parcel out three tabs of Ecstasy, another positive attitude adjustment.

182

Frank wants to play the sports book at Caesars Palace, which plugs sports bettors into massive, comfy chairs arranged coliseum-style in front of big-screened sporting attractions. His favorite college basketball team, Gonzaga, has just beaten South Carolina, and he wants to get in on the betting for Oregon against North Carolina in the second game of the NCAA Final Four. Plus, he knows the horses at Santa Anita Park and figures to make a few other smart bets along the way. He won't even miss me when I wander off to the Smith Center and Shen Yen. Gretchen waves her good-sport goodbye, taking her Molly high to the spa for a massage.

I call Marcel and invite my bodyguards to meet us at Caesars for sports play before Shen Yun plays, then I plug in beside Frank for the easy-chair surround multiplex, like toggling into a massive video game, which it is. Young people gather in the e-sports arena at the Luxor, testing their reflexes against a machine. Here we're counting on the competence and integrity of mortal players, human and animal, playing the odds to win fortunes on the backs of the mighty gladiators of the modern games. March Madness, which is dribbling into April, is the game of the moment.

Molly is pulling my mind in a million directions, none close to the big board in front of me. I persuade Frank to take a walk for a smoke and vape. He's all for medication, but shakes off my THC-rich sativa in favor of the indica he carries to steady his nerves, a special import he gets through a medical dispensary. Ah, the irony: My friend the dealer trades in exotic strains of marijuana grown all over California and the world, but he pays extra for his prescription pot to stake a legal claim to the drug that presumably provides an alibi for possession. It's not nearly enough to dissuade the feds when they finally catch him holding more than medical marijuana.

"I need to mellow out, slow down my brain a little bit," Frank says, as we exit the hotel through the Forum Shops onto the promenade leading past the fountains shooting sparkling water high into the air. "This bust, man, it hurts my brain, like I'm at war, just thinking name, rank, and serial number, ready for the torture, with the cops, just trying to shut out everything, and then …," pause, a quick hit from his vape and a crooked smile … "then you sprung me. How'd you do that?" he asks.

It wasn't me, I protest, but Gretchen has filtered the story for him. We wander along the path between the mist of blowing fountains and the massive Roman columns, faux famous statues, and neatly manicured hedges that give Caesars Palace its unique footprint, an ancient theme in a cavalcade of gaudy theme parks that define Las Vegas. In evoking an ancient culture that fell under the weight of its lavish decadence, the Caesars Entertainment group has perhaps provided an apt metaphor for this glitzy city, where the grand promises of great riches, reflected in the ornate architecture of old Rome, cloaks the reality of all the losers by the wayside.

They call it Caesars to suggest that all players are royalty here, but big winners run the show. People like Frank, looking to recoup and get back in the game, are easy prey for the gamekeepers. He's cursing his luck as we reach the end of the fountains, the statue of the Goddess of Victory, headless but winged. "It's like the universe is trying to tell me something," he says, then zones out on that heavy thought. It runs in cycles, I tell him. If he keeps his eyes open, and stays in the game, he can catch the next big wave. "This shit's not for me," Frank says. "We're flying out of Vegas tomorrow, and I hope I never see it again." I sympathize and agree. "When your forces are scattered, you retreat.

No blame," I say, misquoting ancient wisdom from the *I Ching*, or maybe it's *The Art of War*. It's a comforting philosophy.

My phone rings. Marcel and Lou Guy are wandering through the Roman haunts searching for me. I direct them to exit toward the fountain area, through the shops' entrance. Caesars Palace is a little city of towers and courtyards, a "Garden of the Gods" pool complex, and its own Coliseum. It's easy to get lost on the way to the Forum. My imminent departure makes Frank even more resolute to leave town, so he's eager to collect Gretchen and return to their hotel. "I feel like I'm going backwards," he says. "I should just chuck this, go back to school, become a doc, and distribute drugs legally."

We're walking back toward the Shops entrance, oblivious to the few workers and tourists wandering past, Frank studying the ground as he grumbles something about the "war in the streets," and I'm listening half-heartedly but fretting with him, both of us feeling the glow of Ecstasy, in the zone. Four workmen, dressed for gardening and general maintenance, idling in the hedgerow by the second fountain, hardly in our sights, suddenly erupt into an assault force, hurtling toward Frank and me. There's no time to react, only to take the blows. I see clubs, shovels bared and swung, feel the collapse of muscle and bone, pressure, then nothing.

22. Something Happened

Slowly and spasmodically, I awake, over a period of days, I later learn, struggling to respond to the images of faces, friends, and strangers hovering over me – even family. Sweet Wei-Lin, knit brow and tears, surely touching my hand, although I can't feel it. She is a regular face and presence, comfort through the haze, but I'm not sure she's real; among all the images, some crazy nightmares, naked in the streets, at a party. Maybe a glimmer of glamorous Gretchen, also with tears? All the beautiful women, but not Annamarie, not even in my dreams. Did I dream her? The girl of my dreams, is gone. Memory fades in and out, not seeing, not hearing. Jay appears as a mystical figure in robes, surely a dream, strong and silent, with Marcel at his side, with a pinched face, and a bandaged arm. None of it is real, deep inside my head. What's wrong with me? I can't move, can't wake up. Where am I?

When I finally come to my senses, mostly alert, I'm looking into the loving face of my daughter, the doctor, her eyes widening with excitement at my open eyes – or eye, I realize, something over my left eye, my face. I'm groggy and numb, not feeling my body at all. Nor is my tongue working as I try to greet Mona, who puts her hand to my face, a thrill to feel; I smile, and she speaks:

"Relax, dad, you're going to be okay, but you still have to get your head examined, just like I always said," is what I hear, my smart-aleck daughter trying to cheer me up, but she's being serious. I'll be tested for a concussion and other possible brain damage. I have a broken cheekbone and fractured orbital bone, both of which were carefully reconstructed while I was unconscious, for almost three days now.

We don't know yet about the vision in my left eye, but Dr. James is consulting on my care and assures me I'm in the best hands. I'm lucky to be alive after being clobbered in the side of my head with the face of a shovel, she says, expanding on a prognosis I do not hear, nor do I remember much of this. It all becomes painfully evident over the next several bouts of semi-consciousness.

Jay is leaning over my bed, hand on my arm, talking excitedly to me, and the fog seems to be lifting. Mona is at the foot of the bed, Wei-Lin standing behind Jay, craning her neck slightly to get a better view of me, wanting to catch my eye, and that becomes my wake-up call. "Hello, Jay," I say with a rasp and a slight cough. Mona leans in, smiling. They are all thrilled to see me awake. Jay is still talking excitedly. "We need to talk about Frank," he says, and suddenly I remember. Frank and I were walking by the fountains at Caesars Palace. "Wha?" I demand, searching the fog. Jay says he will fill me in, and asks for a moment alone with me. Wei-Lin and Mona leave without question.

Jay gives it to me straight: Frank didn't make it. One of the gang members stuck a six-inch blade between Frank's ribs, slicing his heart. I'm crushed by this news, sputtering a protest but unable to speak. Frank was a good friend and a personal hero, a guy who risked his life to save others, and came home to nightmares and the pressure of post-traumatic stress. A survivor. But he didn't survive this attack. I'm cursing the petty thieves who mug a couple of casual gamblers, not exactly rich guys. Jay puts his hand on my shoulder. "It was a hit," he says. "Las Vegas police are investigating the murder as a drug gang assassination." The suspects are identified as Southerners (*Sureños*), local gang members who work with the Sinaloa cartel. The ringleader wielding the knife apparently is the younger brother of the Valenzuela sisters. All are still at large.

"Zhou thinks they were suspicious of Frank when he got picked up, then released right away," Jay explains. "You weren't on the hit list, but you're a witness now. You need to be careful." He tells me that Zhou is upset and feels partially responsible for Frank's death, having allowed him back on the streets without considering he might be at risk. He is offering "witness protection" for me, a place to stay in Arizona to rest and recover, away from the Las Vegas drug gang. Mona enters and announces that I've had enough excitement for the day and sends my guests away. I hardly notice their departure as I fade into the oblivion of opiated sleep.

Mona greets me at my next awakening with the first solid food I've had in a while, and I begin to feel more like myself, still groggy but not as sore as I will be later. They're going to test my eye today, Mona tells me, and I'll undergo a series of tests on my brain and neural system. But first, she wants to give me her own cognitive test, a deliberative conversation that is both personal and probative. I smile when I realize, after about 10 minutes, that her primary intention is to find out what happened between Annamarie and me, and what she can do to put it back together. My daughter the matchmaker. I assure her that we both have moved on.

"Annamarie was devastated by the news about Frank, and she's worried about you," Mona says. "I called her when I found out about the attack. I asked her to come with me, but she said she didn't think you'd want to see her and, in any case, you need a doctor and not a lawyer. I know she cares about you, Dad." I chuckle and reach out for Mona's hand, pulling her down so I can kiss her cheek. Thanks for thinking about lonesome me, I say, but I'm better off by myself. It's clear to me that, as much as I enjoyed hanging out with Annamarie, we're very different people – not to mention miles apart in the times of our lives. "She's up and coming, and I'm over the hill."

Mona sighs and shakes her head, her pat response to my cynicism. "You haven't noticed yet, but I've been gaining weight," she says, patting her abdomen. Oh my! I'm gobsmacked, mouth agape, managing to utter a thin, crackling question: baby? "Your granddaughter," she confirms, "in about five months, September." She kisses me on the good cheek. "She'll enjoy visiting you in your rocking chair." I manage a smile with my groan at Mona's joke, if it's a joke. She pages the nurse's desk to retrieve my breakfast tray and prepare me for tests. "You should know that several people have been trying to contact you, including your boss at the *Chronicle*." Ah, Bradbury, of course. It's not like me to go more than a few days without checking in. "You got these from the office," she says, gesturing at a spray of flowers by the window. "Also, your friend George contacted the hospital. He's been trying to get in touch. I think he talked with Jay."

I learn the attackers took my phone, along with all my money and plastic. I have a lot to sort out. Mona contacted my bank in San Francisco to stop any run on my account, and did as much as she could to cancel my credit cards, including calling the *Chronicle* about my company card. I'm temporarily without a driver's license until California issues a replacement. Zhou's offer of an Arizona retreat, temporary sanctuary, is more appealing as I learn about my situation.

My left eye will recover, although it's still blurry, and I don't have any measurable brain damage. But I'm told the doctors want to keep me under observation for the concussion and swelling, at least for a few days. I'm eager to get out of the hospital so I can self-medicate –

189

get off the pain-killers as soon as possible, except for alcohol. I need a drink, and a bowl of grass to steady my nerves. I set up a temporary office in bed as Mona gets me a new phone and retrieves my computer and effects from the hotel.

First, I need to negotiate with Bradbury. He's in a generous mood, feeling sorry for the victim of a mugging, a reporter on the wrong side of the story. I tell him I'm going to have to slow down, that I'm working on a *Vibe* for him, but otherwise will need to take a sabbatical, for at least two months. Medical leave should cover it, and I'll extend it if I must. Bradbury agrees to all my requests, including a stipend to cover the costs of travel during my convalescence.

I feel enormous relief after negotiating the holiday from the *Chronicle*, on my conditions, even if the deadline-tested, work-a-day reporter in me feels a momentary sense of panic at the uncertainty of time unbound by an appointed schedule. Now, at least, the pressure of work and deadlines won't slow down my trip to the mountains. Only my health can do that. The first chore is to get back on my feet. I call George, who's relieved to hear my voice and sympathetic about the loss of my friend. He wants me to focus on getting up and getting healthy. Again, he knows more than I expect.

"You're going to Arizona to visit Mo Williams," he says. "He will help you get oriented." George talked with Jay and apparently is part of the plot cooking up the sanctuary for me, whether it's "witness protection" or something else. He reminds me that I have Mo's contact information in an email he sent months ago when he suggested traveling through the Southwest to get to his perch in the mountains. "Mo is expecting you, but let him know when you will arrive," George says.

190

I'm ready to go, feeling trapped in the hospital room, but Mona insists I complete a full battery of neurological tests before I can escape. I'm working with a nurse-practitioner who is testing my reflexes and balance when Wei-Lin arrives with Marcel and Lou Guy, standing on one foot, balancing beside my bed. Wei-Lin walks straight to me and greets me with an embrace, her body presses against me through my thin gown, and she quickly pulls away, embarrassed. I kiss her forehead as I maneuver to sit on the edge of the bed, pleased more than embarrassed by the rising heat between my legs. I'm relieved she isn't repulsed by my bandages and swells, and that I'm otherwise working okay. She has come to say goodbye – the Shen Yun troupe is returning to LA that evening. I apologize for missing the show and promise to catch up with her again.

Marcel confirms my fuzzy memory of his bandaged arm; the bandage now compacts across a two-inch gash on the inside bicep and is hidden under his sleeve. "I got slashed a little before the bastards ran away," he says. Marcel and Lou Guy came running when they saw Frank and I were under attack, but the damage was already done. They got me to the hospital, though, maybe saving my life. I'm indebted to them, and to Jay, who took out this little insurance policy on me, for reasons I can't fathom. Frank's brutal assassination and the attack on me have left me more than a little insecure, thankful for a security detail.

Frank's father came from Oakland to claim his body, but I hear nothing from his business partner and lover, my good friend Gretchen. I've been calling her since I was semi-alert and got the new phone, leaving voice messages and texts. She has not visited, Mona says. No response makes me nervous, and fearful for her safety. This trip blew up in her face, and she must be shell-shocked, probably took off to

191

find her own safe haven. She checked out of the hotel, and no one at the airport will tell me about private airplane traffic in and out of Las Vegas. Marcel volunteers to search, and I'm embarrassed about how little I know about her. She attended Air Force Academy; she's from back East, maybe Connecticut, she has a California pilot's license, flying out of San Francisco, and she's blonde and beautiful. Gretchen LaPorte. Last known location: the spa at Caesars Palace. That's all I know, except she must be shaken now. She was shaking before.

As loopy as I am with the painkillers and the mind-numbing depression of losing Frank, feeling little, I'm increasingly grateful for the outgoing friendship of Jay. He's an old acquaintance who is treating me like a dear friend, and I appreciate it. I say as much when he arrives at the hospital to say goodbye. He's going back to LA, taking Wei-Lin and Lou Guy with him, but assigning Marcel to stay and drive me to Flagstaff. He's been more than a good friend, I tell him, and I can't thank him enough for his help – not only for his guidance but also for the other friends who are looking out for me.

Jay takes my hand, presses firmly, and bows. "Of course! We are friends," he says. "I've always respected you from the beginning. I appreciate you for listening, for telling my story, the story of the Way of *Qi*."

I shake my head, not wanting to acknowledge that my human interest column served to promote his business or his book. He earned free media, I tell him, because of his ideas and the people who follow him. Also, his savvy public relations didn't hurt. I'm grateful he stuck with me, I tell him. He nods his head and beams a broad smile. "No need," he says. "My wish is that you are well and back on your way."

Back on my way. I'm mulling these words that Jay leaves me before departing for the airport with Wei-Lin and Lou Guy. The first order of the "way" is to finish the high-stakes poker *Vibe*, which pours out in an hour of hammering intensely on my keyboard. It's a simple story with broad implications for public policy and American democracy. I polish the tale and ship it off to Bradbury, flagging the Tax Day hook – oh, hell; that's tomorrow. I've lost time, and now I'm on my way to who knows what. No more columns for a while, so I can let go of the Trump obsession sweeping the news media and concentrate on the journey at hand. I have to get my legs under me, then I'm off to Colorado, stopping first at an Arizona ranch. It's not a road I've traveled before, and I've got a new outlook – off the beat but back on the road.

A text comes dinging over my phone, from a number I don't recognize: "New Ray? G. Mirage 824." Instantly I know it's Gretchen, and my heart is in my throat. I must go to her. I use my Mona pass to get out of the hospital immediately, although I'm required to hear out Dr. James's personal prescription for healthful activity and diet, low-salt, and no stress. No hard physical exercise for a week and a program of physical therapy – and drugs, of course. A few pain pills, and an antibiotic. She gives me the contact information of a nurse at Flagstaff Medical Center, a friend of Maddie's, who will help if I need it. And she gives stern orders not to drink alcohol or take other drugs. Such a sweetheart, with love in her eyes, and a plea in her voice as she prepares to fly back to Oakland. I'll be okay, I tell her. My doctor is the best.

Grabbing a taxi to The Mirage, two small bags in tow, I'm expecting to spend the night, maybe longer. Gretchen and I both need the comfort of knowing we're okay, even if brutal reality has slammed us against a wall. I text her when I arrive at the hotel and ignore the Do Not Disturb sign on 824, knocking softly. She opens the door immediately, frantically, a wild look in her eyes, a sharp cry of "Oh!" and she's in my arms, sobbing against my shoulder. I hold her close, feeling the emotional release from her body.

I look around at the disheveled room, clothes everywhere, the bed unmade and rumpled. A half-empty vodka bottle sits on the desk, along with an open laptop computer and clutter that includes, I find out soon enough, a small mirror lined with white powder. Cocaine. Gretchen has been strung out for days on coke and pills, mostly alone in this room, now wearing only a pajamas top and panties, afraid to go out, ordering room service, and ducking the maids. She tried to call Frank, but someone else answered, with a Spanish accent. She freaked out, stopped using her phone, and bought another one in the hotel AT&T shop. She didn't know if my messages, from a different phone, were real.

"I only just found out about Frank," she says, her face streaked with tears and snot. I wipe them away with my fingers as she stammers, her chest heaving with sobs. "Just a small thing in the paper, just his name, nothing about you," she sobs. "I thought you might be dead, too. Are you okay?" She's looking at me with her bloodshot, unfocused eyes and touching me gently on the face as if seeing my bandaged cheek for the first time.

Tell me what happened," she demands. "I heard the sirens, saw police, didn't know what was going on. I tried calling and texting. Nothing …" I put my arms around her and hold her against my chest. I tell her about the attack, how they came at us too fast, and we couldn't do anything. I take a deep breath before continuing with the truth: They targeted Frank because it was their drug deal gone wrong, afraid he might give them up. They meant to take him out, and they did. I was just in the way.

Gretchen sinks her face into my shoulder, her arms around my neck, sobbing loudly and moaning. She pulls away suddenly, crying out, "We never should have come here." Turning, she walks across the room to the kitchenette, pulls down two glasses, and pours the vodka unceremoniously, straight up, handing one to me. I take it and hold it up to her, offering a toast to Frank, that we carry him with us forever. She smiles through her tears, shudders, and clinks my glass. "That his memory never dies."

We talk about Frank for hours, it seems, punctuated by several trips to the magic mirror, seeking a high that might lift us up to his level, or to whatever level we need to feel him with us, and we credit him for our high, not the coke. To Gretchen, Frank was a warrior who suited her sense of adventure. She was already in the business, running drugs up and down the coast, when she met him, and immediately suggested the partnership – her idea, she says, recognizing how well-connected Frank was, how they got along. She thought they were headed to a legit cannabis business, and maybe a dream home together. Now, suddenly untethered by the loss of her anchor, the pilot feels like she's lost control of her aircraft, hurtling to a crash.

I hold on tight, reel her back in, and tell her that Frank wouldn't want us to despair. Even in his darkest moments, the PTSD panic attacks, he kept his head above it all, looking for a way out. I tell her about his last words to me, about going back to school for a medical degree. He was always looking for the next chapter, and he'd want her to do the same. As I softly coo the possibilities, I'm fighting off the lurking thought that I had responsibility for Frank's death. If only

195

I'd known you were coming here, I mutter; maybe I keep him away from that market. Words are lost on Gretchen, who has settled into a restless sleep on my shoulder, moaning into my ear.

23. Home on the Range

The outline of the far rim of the Grand Canyon is as far as I can see from my vantage point beside Gretchen, so I squint through the binoculars and grumble. Our plane is restricted in altitude and distance from the natural treasure carved into the Colorado Plateau over centuries, a beautiful sight if I could only see. We can't get close. Federal rules allow similar aircraft licenses to tour within the canyon airspace, but my suggestion that Gretchen join the fleet and make easy money flying over grand scenery draws an unenthusiastic harrumph from her. Otherwise, she offers little conversation of her own.

I marvel at the high-desert plateau with its magnificent rugged landscape, a Western Adventureland that cloaks the sad history of European conquest, and the subjugation of the Native American tribes who still view these majestic mountain ridges as their shrines, even as they are cloistered in settlements on what was their land. A ruggedly beautiful and sad monument to the survival-of-the-fittest ethos that underpins life on Earth, even among the highest form, if that is what we are. At least we have a conscience about it. Some of us do.

.As we lean away from the Colorado River and toward the Flagstaff airport, I set the binoculars down and consider my grim pilot. Getting my bearings with Gretchen may be the most difficult part of the trip. I slept fitfully, if at all, I can't remember, still smarting from the blow to the face and head, and not getting any smarter with the blow we snorted first thing in the morning, remembering a quick sexual liaison, a release at least for me. I don't know about Gretchen. I don't think she was really there, her eyes unfocused as she floundered and clutched at me, like a wounded animal, clinging and pulling me down on her, hungrily nibbling at my lips, stroking my back and butt, frantically going through the motions to get higher, to thrill, to feel … It's over in a flash, and we sink back into semi-consciousness, drifting in and out of sleep until the dawn beckons us to fly away.

I call Marcel first thing to relieve him of his duty to chauffeur me to Flagstaff, but he plans to join me anyway. He has a special connection to Mo Williams, who trains martial arts combat and stunt horse riding, "all the adventure stuff," Marcel says. Staying on this assignment suits him just fine, but he warns me that I should be prepared to work. "Mo will drill you," he says, and I complain about my delicate condition. I may not be ready for full-on drilling. What did George say? Mo Williams will get me back on track? Help me get my bearings? Reorient me? Is there a drill to clear a hammered head? I need medicine, like the stuff Gretchen is holding, treats to last us a week or two. Relief.

Mo Williams is serious medicine; I will find out soon enough. He's a wiry, intense man in his mid- to late-50s, with a worn and weathered face, but a young, trim body, muscular and sinewy, with power and purpose. Peering from below the brim of his cowboy hat, Mo could be from central casting as a cowboy, or a herd-riding Marine officer, which he was, with duty stations around the world – he suggests diplomatic, or intelligence assignments, and I imagine CIA, maybe with a "license to kill," a la James Bond. Mo could tangle with Bond, or anybody. He's an unlikely comrade for my peace-loving friend George, a contradiction I aim to resolve.

Mo is waiting for us at the airport, leaning against his pickup truck when we walk out of the terminal, his arms crossed, hawk eyes studying the entrance. I had emailed him an approximate time of arrival, and he watched us land, surprised and impressed by the pilot who brought it in so softly. Gretchen is pleased by his lavish praise, smiling for perhaps the first time today. I introduce her as a good friend, as well as my pilot, and tell Mo we are both grieving over the loss of a dear friend and partner without offering other information. Mo shrugs. He probably already knows about Frank, if Zhou is in on this, definitely about me and my aborted journey. He doesn't know about Gretchen, though, and he's all charm and conversation as we drive southeast to his ranch, the Diamond M.

We've got a 30-minute drive southeast from the airport, giving Mo plenty of time to give us an abridged and redacted life story, including his recent preoccupations of range riding and Kungfu fighting. His first love, he says, is teaching martial arts, and he insists he will improve my fighting skills while also giving me the full run of his healthy stable of appaloosas and quarter horses. That's our first stop at the ranch, for introductions to the frisky horses, all seemingly ready to hit the high-mountain trails, which is how Mo maintains his public business, horseback riding, and trail adventures. Most of his income is from contracts with military and police units – from local Arizona city cops to federal border agents and Texas Rangers, who get two-week training tours at the Diamond M, a perk reserved for top officers. After his longwinded introduction, Mo finally turns to Gretchen and confesses to the complications her arrival presents to him and his ranch operation.

"We have the bunkhouse – that's where I was gonna put Ray and Marcel," Mo says with a sheepish grin, pointing to a cabin just off the stables, a line camp built originally for buckeroos. "A couple of hands live there regular, and a Texas Ranger trainee is here for another week. All men, though." He offers to clear out a room for Gretchen in the main house, but she politely declines. Maybe she's warming to the idea of roughing it in a bunkhouse with a few cowboys. I'm extinguishing thoughts of further intimacies with her.

Not that we have much of a relationship, two people trying desperately to make sense of disintegrating worlds. I'm healing in multiple ways, and so is Gretchen. I can see it in her sad eyes. We share a deep scar, the loss of a man we both loved, even if my relationship with Frank was more superficial. I admired him. I wanted him to do more than survive. I wanted him to win. His loss darkens whatever vision I had of this trip, once so noble and bold, a pause and renewal of ideals and friendship, getting reoriented. Now it seems more like a doomed flight of fancy, brutally interrupted by death and near-death. For all my bravado, I'm as vulnerable as Gretchen. We are both traumatized survivors clinging to each other, not sure of where we are or where we're going.

Bellows of baying and barking fill the air as we round the camp cabin corner, and Mo raises his arms and beams at the thunder. "It's Spike and Ginger for the welcome!" he cries, pointing toward the ranch house at the top of the hill. We can see the animals scamper our way, two big German shepherds leaping long and powerfully, racing toward us. I feel Gretchen recoil against me, the tremble of apprehension I immediately share. They are, indeed, police dogs in training, we learn. Mo runs out to greet them with the master's hearty rubs and pats, assuring them even as they continue their loud and insistent barking, even baring a flash of teeth at us, good dogs, Mo assures us, and he's got them well in hand. "Spike and Ginger react heroically to contraband as well as to bad people, but they can separate the two when the two are separated. So, I'll need to hold the goods while you're here. This is strictly a drug-free zone."

We comply; what else can we do? Gretchen rummages through her bag and brings it all out, the pot and coke, my last two Ecstasy tabs, and a few bennies. Plus, a new flask I brought along, just a taste of whisky, what St. Bernard might bring if I'm in peril on the cliff. I get to keep my prescription drugs, statin, naltrexone, and a few Percocet tablets. Mo gives them back to me and says they're the last ones I'll need, but I'm not convinced. I feel a major withdrawal headache coming on. I'm determined to tough it out, even if Gretchen is making other plans.

"I'm getting out of here in the morning," she announces the first time we're alone. "Are you coming?" We're walking down the hill away from the stables, puffing on cigarettes we bummed from Carlos, one of the ranch hands. Tobacco apparently passes the cowboy sniff test as Spike and Ginger show little interest as we walk toward the stand of Ponderosa pines along the road. I try to dissuade Gretchen from leaving, suggesting we need a few more days to get our bearings, but she's sure she doesn't want to be here, not like this. "I thought it was a retreat, but it's a fucking war," she says, comparing Mo's cavalier treatment of her to the treatment she received at the hands of Air Force brass when she graduated from the Academy. "I don't have to fight this one," she says in a resolute, if tremulous, voice.

I stop and take Gretchen's hands, searching her face for a sign she is okay. Her lips are trembling, her face flushed, but her gaze is steady, her eyes fiery and determined. She will keep fighting. I hug her and promise to be there for her, whatever she needs. We stand in an embrace for minutes, rocking back and forth. Whispering into her ear, I ask where she will go, and she shudders. "I have to go face the ghosts in our apartment, then call some of my people." That's the plan, to get back in circulation, to work and forget. Not a bad plan for me, too, when I get to the end of this road, wherever it takes me.

The loud clanging of a bell interrupts our conversation, an alarm from the ranch house; we're laughing at Mo's promise to ring the dinner bell. This was the real thing. We're in no hurry, though, trudging up the hill, me holding her by the hand. We see the big bell when we get closer – actually, a miniature version of the Liberty Bell, without cracks, mounted on a wooden platform and hanging from a rod that rotates with the turn of a handle. Mo says he uses the bell like the commandant of his fort, calling meetings and signaling changes in exercises and schedule, keeping a tight rein on his operation.

We meet Fernando, the older brother of Carlos and another resident of the bunkhouse, a regular hand even before Mo bought the ranch and now Mo's right-hand man. At his other hand is Sparrow, a young Native American woman, maybe mid-30s, who lives in the main house and seems familiar with Mo, perhaps intimate, although neither provides the visual clue. He introduces her as "my partner, the one who actually manages the ranch." Sparrow's name comes from growing up on the Navajo reservation north of Flagstaff, she says.

"I was called Little Bird, *diné bizaad*, a nickname many give baby girls, from our stories," she says. "My English teacher called me Sparrow, and so now that is me." Sparrow is the true mistress of the horses, organizing the riding classes and schedules, collecting fees, and paying the hands. She also cooked this meal, presumably with help from Mo, who is wearing a soiled apron and wielding a spatula when we arrive in the dining hall, a sunroom set off from the kitchen.

The visiting Texas Ranger is Doug McCoy, a tall, angular man of about 35 who wears a large and prominent mustache made bushier by fronting an otherwise shaven head. He greets us with a jocular laugh and smile, and appears to be smitten by Gretchen, who doesn't give him half a chance. She's in no mood to socialize with even the irregulars in Mo's Army. I'm the buffer, sitting between them at the table, quizzing Doug about his work with the Rangers. He complains that he's been given too many drug-interdiction assignments and not enough time to confront violent criminals. "The politicians just trot us out for show sometimes," he says. That's not so bad, I assure him, because those shows support his work. We exchange cards.

Mo and Sparrow have whipped up a scrumptious Southwestern treat with enchiladas, chili, and grilled beef and vegetables, with salsa, guacamole, cheese, and corn tortillas, maybe not the best thing on the stomach of the recently comatose and liquid-fed, but the taste is superb. I try to moderate, not quite filling my plate, discarding the jalapeños, but find myself making a second trip to the serving table, Mo suddenly appearing at my elbow to make sure I get plenty. Fattening me up for the kill, maybe. The foreboding about the coming "drills" rumble in my subconscious. I've never felt so physically insecure. Maybe Marcel's arrival tomorrow will fortify me.

My phone is buzzing in my pocket. I take a quick look, don't recognize the number, 928, Flagstaff area code. Who do I know here? I let it roll over to voice mail, and return to the table to talk with Mo, who sits across from me with Sparrow at his side. My chance, finally, to figure out why George has twice guided me to Mo's ranch, and what Mo knows about me. I tell him about my physical woes, being an invalid recovering from a brutal blow to the head. "George tells me your training will help me recover, but I worry about the physicality," I say. Mo laughs off my concern. "There's minimum physical contact for you, but you can watch how Marcel and Doug play. They'll be doing the play acting. You ... all work, no play."

Mo has no doubt about me, he says, because George vouches for me. That's all he needs to know. "We met in Beijing," he says. "He saved my life, even if he doesn't admit it." The Chinese were ready to arrest Mo on well-founded espionage charges, he suggests, and George got word to Mo at the U.S. embassy. He also helped arrange a quick exit to Hong Kong, through pro-democracy student contacts. "George stayed away from politics, at least publicly. But he was close to Chinese academics who pushed reform. He speaks their language, in more ways than one."

Mo's narrow escape convinced him to get off the world stage and start his Diamond M ventures. "George visited me here once, and we even trained a little," Mo says, "but he's more into *qigong* and meditation." They originally met in a Beijing park where Tai Chi players gather to practice the forms, meeting afterward for lunch at the Bridge Café, a hangout for students. Now, he says, "George's friend is my friend."

Mo's plan is to work individually with me while guiding Doug and Marcel on their programs – in Doug's case, it's advanced training in Bagua and Xing Yi, internal martial arts that focus on attack more than defense, which is the hallmark of Tai Chi. "They're all about building internal power," Mo says. "That's the first step, sink the *qi*, and condition the body to absorb and explode the power," Mo raises his shoulders, elbows, and hands sharply and puffs up his torso, as if releasing energy, accidentally striking Sparrow in the demonstration. She responds with an intentional blow that visibly moves Mo in his seat. "Sorry!" he cries, and even Gretchen is enjoying a laugh. Don't push Sparrow; I make a mental note.

Later, as Gretchen and I try to get settled into a corner bunk, I listen to the voice message: "Hello, Mister James. This is Holly Newman from the Flagstaff Medical Center. I'm calling to let you know that we have received your lab results from Las Vegas and would like to consult with you, along with Doctor Ramona James. Please call me back so we can schedule an appointment. I'm at extension 42."

I dial the number. How the hell is Mona in Flagstaff? She's not here, Nurse Holly tells me, but she wants to be Skyped into the consultation when I schedule the appointment. Holly is friendly and chatty, eager to tell me about her work with Maddie on nurse safe-staffing legislation in Arizona. She hasn't talked with Mona but understands that she wants to change my medicine and make sure I have an adequate supply. Sorry, Mo, doctor's orders. I schedule an appointment for early morning, after I see off Gretchen at the airport.

That evening, as we settle in the bunkhouse, Gretchen's anger at Mo and this hostile cowboy environment is replaced by quiet sadness and resignation as she cuddles with me on the lower bunk, sighing and whispering softly in my ear, "I feel like Frank is here, still, with us," and I hug her close. We are both exhausted, and I figure we may drift into sleep like this, but eventually, I'll climb to the top bunk to give us more sleeping space. For now, I assure her that Frank is, indeed, right here with us, because we are holding him here. It's a comforting thought, that our friends never leave us, even if I don't really believe it. I don't know what Gretchen believes, but I know what she wants to hear. Anyone who touches us, we carry them with us forever, I say, and she hugs me back. I run my fingers softly down

205

the small of her back, feeling her tingle and shudder against me. We both want to believe it.

Again, the phone buzz interrupts. I reach over to pick up the phone from the floor, where it's charging, then roll over and sit up when I see that it's Jay. I greet him softly, squeezing Gretchen's hand before taking the conversation into one of the latrines. I sit down in a stall and ask Jay if he's calling to rescue me from the rigors of basic training. Silence on the line for a moment, perhaps Jay weighing the seriousness of my comment. I chuckle. Mo said he'd go easy on me, but I think there's going to be some fighting, I tell him.

"That's good," Jay says, without enthusiasm. "This is how you learn; even if you don't have to take a fall, pay attention. Ask Mo to explain the *bagua*, the trigrams." I don't know what he's talking about and say so, but he only advises me to be patient, to listen, and learn. "Don't worry about it right now," he says. "I have important information for you, bad news, more bad news." He pauses just a moment. "Your friend Chaz Logan is dead."

What? I'm stammering. I just saw Chaz. "Yes, listen," Jay says sternly, laying out the news in a nugget: Officially, Chaz fell off the 31st floor balcony of his Bellagio penthouse suite. But it's suspicious, and some think he was pushed, that it was a hit by one of the many Las Vegas criminal syndicates. Then, the kicker: "If Chaz is Master Whiz, and I think he is, there's a good chance the hit was directed by someone at your poker table. And if so, you may be in danger."

"What!" Forgetting my potty perch in a sleeping bunkhouse, I've bolted to my feet, looking around above the stall. Then "shit!" quietly as I sit back down. How could that be? Chaz was just a facilitator for a friendly game. Everybody was friendly; we even talked it over, the

206

ground rules and all. Didn't I send a copy of the column to Chaz for his review? I'm wracking my brain. I don't remember a conversation or editing changes. I was in the hospital, in a fog. It's what I intended to do, how I wrote it. I didn't even know they'd printed it.

"This is just my suspicion, and Zhou's," Jay says, "based on chatter picked up by intelligence. Could you have caused problems, with your column?" Jay asks, not waiting for a response. "I thought it was genius, myself, looking at Trump through the eyes of the Illuminati, this secret society of rich kingpins and money launderers, but I thought they also could be dangerous. Maybe they think you fingered them."

They agreed to play; I mutter a protest, but now have the sinking certainty that I didn't fully vet it. I thought I sent Chaz a copy, but I was on the run. I didn't hear from him, and so I assumed it was all good. Did he even receive the call? The more I protest, the more uncertain I am. I seem to be losing control of my narrative, this story about myself, and I'm careening down the highway toward who knows where. Is someone after me?

"Don't use this phone again," Jay says before hanging up. "Marcel will bring another device." I climb to the top bunk and stare at the ceiling.

24. *The Vibe:* Is This Game Poker?

By Raymond James, San Francisco Chronicle, April 18, 2017

LAS VEGAS – It's Tax Day, and millions of Americans are scrambling to meet tonight's midnight deadline to file their returns. More people put off filing until the last minute this year, hanging on promises of tax reductions by President Trump and the Republican Congress. Nothing has come of these promises to date, but rich and well-connected individuals and corporations are already taking their tax breaks to the bank – stashed or laundered offshore.

That's a nugget I pocketed during a high-stakes poker game with some of the richest men in the world – me as the interloping poor journalist willing to accept a handout to buy into the game and them as the self-described misunderstood and much-maligned benefactors of the global economic engine, who just want me to set the record straight. How they came to place such faith in your humble scribe, I cannot say, although I did agree to disguise their identities and to allow a review of the column. I've always been guided by the facts, as I see them, in writing *The Vibe*. It's the truth as best I know it.

My fellow poker players may be anonymous, but symbolically they represented a select few in a global class. In fact, they only half-jokingly referred to themselves as "Masters of the Universe," the superheroes winning in the global marketplace. That moniker came from the player we shall call Message Master, a U.S.-based communications guru who guided political and public relations campaigns in the United States and abroad. Message Master directed the table chatter in his disarming drawl, trying to assure that *The Vibe* was in tune with the narrative he was spinning.

208

We will come back to the omnipresent Message, but let's go around the table, and get a sense of the players and their games. With this group, it's appropriate to start with Money Master, a European of no national identity or loyalty. As a corporate lawyer, he has studied how to manipulate laws in most First and Third World nations, delivering tax havens for his clients, including the players in this game. In tending to the sheltering of the fortunes of the world, Money contributed to losses to national coffers estimated by the International Monetary Fund at hundreds of billions of dollars each year. But governments get plenty, Money argued as he played a bit more haphazardly than others, staying in with a pair of 10s in one hand, bluffing in his self-assured style, seeming intent to stay in every hand, for the conversation if nothing else. Money is talking:

"Everybody wants to be rich, and they can. You just have to be smart, keep your head up, and look for opportunities. Invest, that's the secret; it's not hard work. Just learn the law, play the angles, and be smart. Remember what Trump said when Hillary said he didn't pay taxes? 'That makes me smart,' he said. And he's right." What about the needs of nations, or the cities and states where corporations make their profit, then hide it in tax shelters? I want to know. Aren't the rich starving the governments that provide the services that keep communities running? Not so, Money said. "Business pumps up the economies, creates jobs. Employees pay a portion of their wages in taxes, but owners make it happen by donating time and money. They need incentives to invest, or it doesn't work. All society benefits from entrepreneurs."

Entrepreneurship is a relatively new phenomenon in Russia, but with several small and well-placed bets in Boris Yeltsin's wild and woolly Moscow in the early 1990s, Chess Master made a fortune, rising to the informal rank of oligarch in league with other rich friends, including those in the Kremlin. He may be the richest man at the table, with investments all over the world, but he played his cards more cautiously than most, tossing in his hands with regularity when a gamble presented itself. I asked Chess if caution is the key to his success, and he agreed, to a point. He was actually responding to the faces and body language of the other players.

"I play by feel, you know, with my gut, like Trump," Chess said. "He seems stupid, right? Stupid like a fox. I know him; I met him in Moscow when he was running Miss Universe. He likes to impress people, always Mr. Cool. I know that game. You don't play the cards; you play the players," he gestured around the table. "I watch, I listen, I look for the end game, not just one hand. That is the benefit of an old country with a long history, not like the U.S. It is ebb and flow, not go-go-go. Be patient, and bide your time. Not everything is win-win."

Chess was interrupted by the boisterous Master Whiz, an American high-tech innovator who made a small fortune with social media tools and is working to expand it by gambling in Las Vegas and on Wall Street. "What's wrong with go-go-go, win-win-win?" he asked. "Nothing ventured, nothing gained, I say. Especially now, with Trump priming the pump, you got to move. You talk about timing. The time is now!"

Around the table, wary chuckles and raised eyebrows at the interjection by the brash American Whiz, who had been raking in chips since the game began. Whiz was the guy who organized the games, arranged the hosting and entertainment, as well as security – the poker ringleader, although these players were unlikely to follow him anywhere. They responded to his braggadocio by wondering aloud what happens when the luck runs out. Will Whiz continue to double-down? "You will have to watch and see," Whiz said, "but why not? You have to play to win. Every time you miss, the odds are better for you. You win if you manage your risk with smarts."

"But you must also manage your attitude; you can be too smart," said Master Dharma, sharing his ancient wisdom. "Karma is real. The greedy lose." His remarks drew hearty laughter from the other players, seemingly pleased that the taciturn Chinese businessman, the group's newest member, upbraided Whiz. Money helped him broker lucrative real estate deals in Las Vegas and elsewhere. Dharma was a natural for a regular seat at Whiz's poker table and provided a unique Chinese perspective, not so inscrutable as is claimed. Specifically, he offered a different take on Trump, elaborated in a conversation before our game.

"Your president likes to play games, make his own rules, Tweets whatever he wants," Dharma said. "No filter, no thought, just talk. So we learn there is no meaning in his words. Why rise to empty insults? Just smile, nod, and wait until time to act. Then, he will act in his own interests, which is good relations with China. More money for him and Trump family. And for his friends. We learn over many years from American businessmen. Trump is like all these."

In other words, Trump is just fine with the Chinese, is what I hear. He is a devil they know. In fact, he is the America they know. They are learning a lot from us, at least in the crass art of business profiteering, which is precisely the game the Masters engage in at the table and around the world. Message rushed to assure me, in a phone conversation after our game, that these players are all dedicated to peace and prosperity in the world.

"What you've witnessed, playing in our game, is a microcosm of a big moment in history when people of all backgrounds and nationalities are able to play well together to create prosperity for humankind. You hear so much criticism in the media of the so-called 'one percent,' but these are the 'makers,' the creators," Message hammers on his talking points. "These are the people making history and building the future. Some people may criticize the game we play, but entrepreneurs are feeding the kitty, pumping livelihood into the neighborhoods. So we're not just feeding the kitty at our poker table here; we're putting food on kitchen tables around the world."

Among the "makers" at this poker table, Chinese real estate mogul Dharma proved to be an especially astute player, smiling, nodding, and waiting patiently before striking like a cobra, winning nearly $3 million in the end. Whiz never broke a sweat in winning $1.5 million, minus the $15,000 your reporter lost for him. Chess cautiously walked away with about $500,000, and Message broke even. Money Master contributed to everyone's bottom line, happily. "I never really lose," he said with a dismissive wave of his hand and a laugh. "It always comes back to me – in spades."

25. Mind Over Body

I learn that Mona wants to see me virtually, just days after springing me from the hospital, because the latest CAT scan reveals nodules in my lower left lung, suspicious enough to require a biopsy, which I should schedule immediately, she says, showing me photos via Skype. She also presses me on my meds' regularity and prescribes a new round of each. I get a new ointment for my face, the opportunity to shed bandages, and a plea from my daughter to pull it all together. Liver, lungs, heart, blood, and skin. The evidence of decay is mounting as the systems begin to flare up or shut down. I need an overhaul, but I'm not eager to undergo a biopsy using a needle to puncture a lung to retrieve a sample. But I tell Mona I will.

Gretchen is sweet and warm when we wake up and start the day, a return to the bouncy, self-assured young businesswoman with a passing fancy for me, maybe. We talk quietly about her plans to move, probably to Monterey, as we ride to the airport in the Diamond M-branded pickup truck driven by Carlos. We share a lingering kiss and embrace before she climbs into her plane, with promises to stay close, even as we drift. Her curvaceous departure evokes my first memories of her, the threesome with Cherry Fine, and then the group excitement that put me on the floor. That's when all the tests began, when I started falling apart. At least, that's when the evidence became apparent. I've been a mess for a while, I must admit.

Neither the melancholy of sweet parting nor the anxiety of deteriorating health takes my mind off the sudden death of Chaz and Jay's warnings that my life may be in danger. In my mind, I'm looking around that poker table, reexamining the expressions and exchanges of the "Masters" at play. Who would come after me? Who did I offend, or expose? Are they pissed I took off on their "Masters of the Universe" line? Nobody said it was off-limits. I gave them all credit for their positions, and they had the megaphone they wanted to broadcast their rose-colored, Ayn Rand scenarios showing how unfettered capitalism saves the world, and who better to unfetter it than Trump, the capitalist show horse. I quoted truthfully, maintaining a matter-of-fact tone, maybe with some cynical reflection of the crazy ideas, like always. They had to know I wasn't buying their line.

Maybe Jay is misreading the tea leaves. I still have my phone, at least for the time being, monitoring my messages. That's how I know that Marcel will be waiting at the ranch when I return. He arrives about mid-morning, while I'm at the medical center. It's odd that he's sending a text message if he's carrying a "new device" to replace my phone, which apparently is compromised. If anyone is listening, it's Zhou, who has eyes and ears all over.

Marcel pleads ignorance. "Why do you need a new phone?" he asks. We're touching hands in a preliminary "sensing" drill, and he doesn't like my form. "Relax the shoulders," he says. "sink and search for my center." All I know is what I'm told, I tell him.

Mo's martial arts training hall, with a big hand-lettered sign "Fight Club" above the door, is in a shaded grove down the hill beyond the main house, nearly identical in style to our bunkhouse, but without the bunks. The wood floors have been buffed, and mirrors hang on facing walls. At one end, mats are placed on the floor against the wall, which is itself padded. That's the place to fall. A heavy bag hangs in one corner. Marcel and I are pushing between the mirrors, and I'm watching Marcel's form as a model of my own, a fine model with muscles and blond good looks, and me struggling to keep the structure upright, muscles relaxed. I try mightily to sense Marcel's center of gravity but am easily distracted by his penetrating, blue eyes.

Mo has paired me with Marcel while he works with Doug near the padded end of the hall on an exercise I don't recognize. They are walking in circles, stopping and posing in different postures, lower to the ground than in the Tai Chi form. Bagua Zhang, Marcel tells me, is "different movements, but the internal energy principles are the same. Still circular motion and postures, but strikes with palms, and weapons." I pause to watch the instruction, which Mo is focusing specifically on self-defense applications.

"Each movement anticipates a movement by your opponent," Mo says as he crouches to face Doug. "The form puts you in counter positions as you move and circle out of the way of his strike; you counter, coiled, balanced, and ready to release full-body power." He stops talking, noticing that Marcel and I are watching. He motions for everyone to gather around him. "We need to backtrack a bit to give Ray the basics."

Mo wants me to understand that Bagua is more similar to than is different from Tai Chi, despite the more aggressive action and faster motion. "You focus the internal energy differently, but it's the same source of power. You still exercise your intention, focus, sink qi and draw energy from inside, from the earth," he says, demonstrating a circular walk. "Each step, turn, and palm change is balanced against an opponent." The pace of the movements is varied because you are training to adjust to change, Mo says, adding, "you must do the internal work, or it doesn't work."

That translates, for me, into an hour and a half of mostly standing $qigong$ exercises, similar to "the Bear" that Jay taught at Big Sur but with more intensely uncomfortable circle holding – maybe not as difficult as the over-the-head circles held by Falun Gong practitioners, but what Mo calls "tree-hugging," arms circling forward. Relaxing my shoulders and elbows helps me to sink down while maintaining an upright structure, and I project myself as a tree spirit, rooted in the earth, standing against the force of nature. From this position, I passively observe Bagua's steps and palm change training at the other end of the room, rooted in this space. I've come to appreciate this standing exercise, using my breath to focus my intention, to sink into the earth, to relax, and balance.

Over lunch of soup and sandwiches, I learn that "*bagua*" translates as "eight diagrams," specifically the eight trigrams that make up the 64 hexagrams in the Book of Changes, the *I Ching* oracle I consulted with Jay's help. The "Limitation" guidance seems even more auspicious after Las Vegas. With my drugs and alcohol confiscated, I feel a surge of new commitment to limitation, inspired by the invigoration of *qigong* exercises and the testimony of true believers in the powers of internal mind-body practice.

Marcel offers an animated commentary on the history of *bagua*, as he understands from a book about *fengshui* that Jay gave him. The *bagua* symbol includes the eight trigrams arranged octagonally around the conjoined *yin* and *yang*, the Tai Chi symbol, the underpinning of Taoist philosophy. "The trigrams represent different aspects of the five elements – earth, wind, fire, water, and metal," he says. "Diviners use the *bagua* to figure out relationships of things and spaces."

"That's all hocus-pocus bullshit," interjects Mo, who has been listening quietly to Marcel's rap. "The important thing to know is there are eight points around the circle for defense, eight different palm plays you use when you are walking the circle." When we return to the Fight Club, Mo walks me through the basic circle walk, demonstrating the importance of balance and internal centering with each step and palm change. Just when I think I've got the basics, he changes course. "We're going to move on to Xing-Yi to give Doug his money's worth," Mo says. "It's final exam time."

Doug smiles broadly and bows to Mo, fist to palm. He moves toward the mats and the suspended heavy bag, apparently knowing the drill. Mo turns to me and explains that Xing-Yi is the most useful internal martial art for police or others who may have to fight in close quarters. "Xing-Yi is straight-ahead, no retreat, bring down the bad guy," he says, demonstrating the five fist strikes, corresponding to the five elements, meant to overwhelm the opponent. "There are also 12 animals to match your attack, but we'll save those for another day."

Doug has paused, facing away from us and assuming a stance with his right hand extended by his side, the other in front of him. At Mo's signal, he leaps forward with a series of rapid-fire punches, finishing with a volley through the heavy bag, which swings wildly from the impact. "Good!" Mo says. "We're going to work on the defensive applications, with Marcel's help. But first, let's get Ray set up." I groan, anticipating another standing exercise, and it's much worse than I think.

Santi, the basic Xing-Yi stance that Doug began his attack, is also the first stage of training, Mo explains. Translated as "three body," *santi* helps build internal power, the full-body force that can overwhelm an opponent. Unlike the double-weighted standing positions, however, training *santi* requires me to put all my weight on the rear leg. I am instructed to will away the discomfort, and to maintain the posture even as my muscles grow taut and intensely painful. "You must 'eat bitter,' the ancient Chinese saying, before you can enjoy the fruit," Mo says.

The *santi* standing exercise proves to be a bitter pill indeed, with 15-minute intervals per leg, but I endure by applying the "mind-over-muscle" strategy that Mo suggests – concentrate on aligning my structure and let the bones and ligaments support me as I send mental balm to the muscles. After a few minutes, my mind has moved past the pain as I sink *qi* to my foot and feel a reciprocal flow of *qi* rising from the ground. I practice "pulsing," as Mo says, activating the internal power from my lower *dantian*. Whether the energy is real or not, I am exercising my mind to intend it, a good feeling that easily supplants the soreness in my legs.

Meanwhile, Marcel is clearly giving Doug a workout, judging by the smacks and thuds and Mo's instruction from the padded corner. I hear about it later from Marcel, whose face is flushed with excitement, having moved from fake action in movies to grappling with an honest-to-god Texas Ranger – and a big guy at that, "maybe 6-5," Marcel says. "He's still using too much muscle, not enough *pengjin*, but he's gonna be hell on Texas criminals."

We're at the stables saddling two quarter horses – I get an assist from Carlos. It's a couple of hours before the dinner bell, and we've got Mo's approval to ride off into the sunset – or at least to the lake.

218

Marcel has picked out his favorite steed, Graceland, and I introduce myself to Steady, a horse with a name I can trust. I've had a few trail rides, but the idea of saddling up with a bona fide cowboy stuntman is intimidating. Marcel certainly looks the part, with his black Stetson, faded brown leather jacket, and leather boots. I'm lucky to find a pair of jeans and a denim jacket, and my Giants ballcap to shield the fading sun.

Lucky for me, Marcel doesn't plan to race me to the lake, which sits about two miles away at the edge of the ranch, a little farther than we thought because of the lower water level. Mo warned the lake dries up periodically and never gets more than 10 feet deep. We dismount and lead the horses to the water, then take a seat on a bank. I ask Marcel if he brought anything to drink. "Just water, partner," he says with a slow smile. "You know, Mo, don't let us party." I shrug, figuring it was worth a try. I'm on the naltrexone, or I'd be climbing the walls. I have to concentrate, and give it a chance.

Marcel's natural touch with the horses is homegrown, I learn, a product of his work in a stable growing up in Denver, not far from where George teaches in Boulder. "I dropped out of school so I could spend more time with the horses," he says. "They take to me, too." Marcel pulls out his phone, takes a quick look, and tells me we've got to go. "We need to stop at the Lodge up the road before we head back."

Our destination is across the road from the restaurant and gift shop known as the Lodge, where cabins are available for relaxation and seclusion. Marcel knows exactly where we're going, guiding Graceland past the Lodge and up a wooded lane to a single cabin, We hitch the horses to the rough-hewn wooden porch, and I follow Marcel up the steps where he raps loudly on the door of the cabin. I hear a scuffling inside, a chair being pushed back, and then the door being pulled open. Standing there, looking furtively to our right and left, and then quickly ushering us in without a word, is Zhou. He's dressed all in black, like a ninja without the mask, but still hiding his face behind a brusque manner. I offer my hand; he takes it with a nod and soft grip, a thin smile, then guides us to seats at the table in the middle of the room.

"Did you bring your phone?" he asks, the first words out of his mouth. I nod and retrieve my device as Zhou reaches into his bag and pulls out a box with a new iPhone and accessories. He instructs me to unlock my phone and then connects the two to transfer my contacts. I now have a new number with all the old numbers in the address book, but I shouldn't call anyone from this phone for a while, particularly close friends and relatives, Zhou says, offering up Jay as a message carrier, if necessary. "You are being watched," he says matter-of-factly. "They're tracking your phone."

"Who?" I want to know, but Zhou holds up his hand. "We've detected the surveillance activity, but from different sources. I'll take your phone back to LA with me tonight, move it around a bit, and make some bogus calls. Maybe we get a fix on who's tracking you, or maybe not. But you should move soon." Zhou disables the location finder on the new iPhone and tells me to limit Internet searches, particularly map directions. "Go to a gas station and get a hard map if you need one."

Without the old phone, I should be able to fly under the radar for a while, if I don't announce myself, Zhou says. But he wants me to identify the players at the poker table, my sources for the Vibe column, "to help us protect you." I can't do that, I tell him. I've promised to keep their identities secret. It's part of the journalist's creed: Thou shalt not identify those who provide information on the condition of anonymity. It's the cost of gathering news in a society that values free speech.

Zhou snorts. "It's a license to lie," he says. "You protect them, but they put you in danger." I shake my head and shrug. No sense debating unidentified sources with a fed whose job involves invading private silos to gain information. "Listen," Zhou says, touching my arm with a gentle pat of conciliation, "I'm really sorry about Frank. We should have given him protection. I didn't think ..." I cut him off, insisting he couldn't know. Frank took risks; it wasn't Zhou's fault. But I don't understand why I'm in danger? What does he know that I don't?

"We're watching your back, and we see others watching you too; it's that simple," Zhou says. Also simple, apparently, is figuring out who was at the poker table in *The Vibe* column – Zhou knows the identities of more than half of the players. "Han is on our radar," he says. "He's posing as a businessman, but he is working for the Chinese government. He's been getting a lot of traffic about the arrest of young Miss Xu, and the way you wrote about her arrest." I'm disturbed by this revelation, and I protest to Zhou, who led me into the story. He takes responsibility, saying his intention, not approved by any higher-up, was to expose the Chinese connection to the fentanyl traffic. "You wrote an important story," he said.

I could also be a target of a Russian oligarch, unnamed by Zhou. "There're dozens of these crooked Russians," he says. "They're laundering money by the boatload." Leonhardt is a known associate of Chaz and Han, the likely suspect covering up the movement of fortunes, so Zhou has identified him as the "Money Master." He doesn't know Loving, the communications guru who apparently has been keeping a low profile in his overseas work, nor has he fingered Bredkoff, although he's surely on a short list of possible suspects.

"Han is my prime suspect as the person tracking you," Zhou says, "but I don't think he's responsible for Chaz Logan's death. Logan had plenty of enemies, apparently, not just guys at your poker table." Chaz wouldn't go down easy, I say, telling him about pushing hands at Jay's retreat. I don't tell him that one of the players, Bredkoff, also was a martial arts player, maybe an expert. But Chaz probably was already incapacitated, if he was thrown off the balcony. I'm sure he didn't jump on his own. He was having too much fun.

"You will have to move soon," Zhou says. "The phone diversion may work for a while, but the track leads back to Flagstaff." I like the idea of getting out of Mo's Army quickly; also happy to hear I'll get to keep my sidekick for the next leg of my journey. Marcel is assigned to stick with me for a while, until the coast is clear. "Jay will call you on your new number, probably tomorrow," Zhou says.

Back at the ranch, Mo hasn't heard of my plan to escape, so he's busy erecting a gauntlet for me to run through to toughen up. "I can teach you to fight, but the most important thing you need to do is to get your body right," he says, and I know it's true. Not just the injuries, and the symptoms of cancer and heart disease. The physical gnawing of the missing intoxicants also is clouding my focus, scattered further by lost love and the missing anchor, the newspaper job. It's not easy to concentrate. I have to fortify my mind if I'm going to save my body. That's the lesson from Jay's retreat, and I repeat it back to him when he calls that evening.

"Right," Jay says. "You're in control." I snort, knowing I fall well short of that ideal. He says I should take a couple of days to train

222

intensively with Mo while Zhou clears an escape route – or at least to put me on the road clear of any tails. I admit it's a relief to have the opportunity to regain my footing, take a deep breath, and relax into my being, self-possess. Get my mind off the possibility that I'm a target of ill will, and get my body ready to defend myself if I am.

My more positive frame of mind fits with the program as my martial taskmaster Mo Williams abruptly turns the Fight Club into a reserved temple for Tai Chi form and standing post, for slow, balanced movements and breathing exercises – not to mention the sensation of "listening" to your partners. Without his Texas ranger, Mo has gone back to basics. I don't have to fight to generate internal energy, even if understanding the martial aspects is important, Mo says. I must have the spirit of a warrior, whether it's my purpose or not.

After a few days, I'm beginning to see a little light. The sensing skill I need with a push-hands partner has been elusive, but I have a breakthrough working with Sparrow, who is athletic and powerful, compact and well balanced, and a warrior herself. "I was the point guard on my high school basketball team," she says. I like her expressiveness, and soft brown eyes that smile beyond her taut lips. And she has a sensitive touch that seems to come from deep inside her. In push hands, you aim to sense your partners' center, and their root. With Sparrow, her "listening" *(tingjin)* skills are keen, and I feel I'm drawing from her *qi,* which she yields gently, like a healer. Sparrow is sharing her center with me even as she commands mine, and I'm getting the rhythm as we move through the four directions, feeling *peng, lu, ji, an.* For the moment, I'm in a zone.

Later, as we break for dinner, Sparrow pulls me aside and tells me that I'm "waking up inside," and that I'm on the right path. "But I also

feel you are worried, and sad. Your intention is ... um, not ... steady."
Yeah, I have a lot to learn before I become sure of myself, I confess.
She lifts her hand and places it, palm down, against my chest. "Your
spirit must rise and harmonize here, with your intention. I feel you.
Keep working."

26. The Chief and the Rail Runner

Sparrow is our trail guide when we get Zhou's "go" sign in May, and I'm eating dust trying to keep up with her and Marcel on a daylong horseback ride to the train station in Winslow. We stop for walking and stretching to salve my aching butt along the way, and I can't complain about the open air and beautiful spaces. My body is feeling more in tune than it has in many years, just with a few weeks of Mo's drills. Early this morning, Marcel and Sparrow led me through an invigorating set of *qigong* and Tai Chi forms, and I felt the power coursing through me as we flowed through 37 postures, like lithe cats in a circular parade, defending the ranch. I transfer the well-balanced and powerful movements of my companions onto myself, even if I may stumble around a bit. I feel the energy in me. The mind is the controller, after all.

I haven't completely forgiven Mo for the cavalier way he chased away Gretchen the first day. And he "lost" the drugs he seized from us, except for a tiny bag of pot I reclaimed. The bennies and the coke are gone, maybe with Gretchen. But Mo is quick to offer Sparrow as a guide when we ask to rent horses for the ride to Winslow. That works out perfectly for him, since Sparrow plans to bring back two seasonal hands from the Navajo reservation, her younger brother and his friend, along with the horses. She wants to "rescue" them all, she says as we skirt the lake and lowing pastures, our horses plodding along trails through the pines and eventually galloping along the border of the reservation, land held "in trust" for the tribe.

"Trust!" Sparrow snorts. "No trust." She likens the forced settlements to herds of animals rounded up and isolated. "They rob

225

you of your dreams." She feels lucky to be rescued by Mo, who proposed to her the first time they met in a Flagstaff bar. It was an indecent proposal, she laughs, but she turned it into a steady gig. Mo trained her in martial arts; she trained him in horse husbandry. For all intents and purposes, except for legal documentation, they're partners, I tell her.

Sparrow leads us across open plains without landmarks that I can see, her eyes on the horizon, and the bearings she knows by heart. I'm getting the rhythm of Steady, the gentle quarter horse I adopted for my rides, getting more comfortable as we go. But I know precious little about our destination, other than the Winslow train station, where we'll catch the Southwest Chief, Amtrak's service to Albuquerque and beyond. This is a route I figured out months ago, plotting a course to Colorado from LA, but I thought I'd be on the road and not the rails – certainly not on horseback.

The Chief also runs through Flagstaff, but Zhou insists on evasive actions, warning of lurking danger. My old phone is no longer being tracked, he says, but Gretchen is in San Francisco talking about me, saying she hasn't been able to contact me. I'm to avoid both the Flagstaff airport and train station, which Zhou says are under surveillance. Nothing is private anymore, leastwise conversations around and about me. Which of these prying ears should I be most concerned about? All I can see is Zhou in the middle of it.

It's late afternoon when we approach La Posada, the great railroad hotel built in the 1930s by the Santa Fe Railroad, back when Winslow was a main attraction. The city itself has faded along with the famous Route 66 that passes through, with fewer than 10,000 people, but the Chief still stops on the way between Los Angeles and Chicago. So La Posada was restored as a handsome hacienda-style inn. Sparrow is planning to move along to the reservation, where she's spending the night, but I persuade her to join us for dinner. We check in and grab a table in the restaurant.

This is where my mouth starts watering, and I have a dull ache in the pit of my stomach, a gnawing desire for a cocktail, something from the U-shaped martini bar at the far end of the room. But I order the sparkling water favored by Marcel and Sparrow and double up on the naltrexone dose. The drug supposedly lessens the cravings for alcohol, but my mind still wanders off to drink. Even if the naltrexone turns out to be a placebo, I'm counting on it to buy me time if I can bide it. The demon rummaging in my brain will not force itself on my dinner dates, I vow, smiling agreeably to hide my discomfort, my weakness.

Sparrow is talking about her initiation into Tai Chi practice with Mo, who makes a big deal about the first few postures, for *peng, lu, ji,* and *an,* known collectively in the English translation as Grasp the Sparrow's Tail. "The first few weeks, we couldn't get past that beginning part, because Mo kept talking about the name and my tail, and he can't keep his hands away." Marcel and I roar with laughter at the image of Mo trailing Sparrow and trying to grab her tail, and she is pleased we enjoy her story, which she no doubt has practiced a few times. We order enchiladas and tacos, and I ask her about Navajo life.

"It's not easy for Navajo to live here," Sparrow says, looking around the restaurant and lowering her voice against townsfolk ears, relating an incident last year when a Winslow police officer gunned down a young Navajo mother in the street, apparently because she didn't respond quickly enough to his order. "He says he's afraid she would attack him," Sparrow says. "She had a little pocket knife and a smile for everyone. He shot her four times."

Sparrow's dark eyes flash with anger as she tells the story of the young mother's death, a woman she knew, her voice quavering with emotion. I reach over and squeeze her hand reassuringly. I feel an affinity for this sensitive Navajo woman, a kinship. Later, when we are saying our goodbyes, she hugs my neck and presses her other hand against my chest, as she did after push hands, summoning the spirit I must harmonize with my mind. She whispers in my ear, "If you go to Colorado, you should see my brother, Curly Wolf. He will help you."

I can't move, paralyzed by her hand against my chest, feeling the warm urgency in her touch, which reaches to my heart. She quickly produces a card headlined, "Curly Wolf, Shaman," with an address and telephone number in Pueblo, Colorado. "Spiritual Healing," is the legend at the bottom, big and bold. Having loosened her hold on me, Sparrow grasps my hands and squeezes a goodbye. "I hope you will come back this way," she says.

Marcel is amused by my lingering goodbye with Sparrow, which extends to a long look at her behind as she sashays away toward the horses and the reservation. "She's sweet on you," he says with a big grin. I laugh his comment off, pointing out that I wouldn't cross Mo for any woman. And besides, Sparrow is sweet to everyone. Marcel agrees. "And Mo has no claim on Sparrow, except for the business. She's come to me when I visited before. She's her own woman."

I admit that Sparrow has an unusual hold on me; just a touch, and I'm proverbial putty. "You get over that after a while," Marcel says, "after you figure out what she's doing." What's she doing? "She's feeling you, tapping into your emotional center," he says. "She's an

228

empath." I pooh-pooh this notion – science fiction, I say. But Marcel argues that Sparrow has the power. "I think she's just naturally blessed, or maybe cursed."

I suppose it can be taxing to be so exposed to other people's emotions, but Sparrow seems at peace with her gift, if that's what it is. I remember how I connected with her during push hands, and how she counseled me later about my feelings. Now I'm feeling remorse for having to leave just when I might be able to learn about these deep feelings. I play back our conversations in my head. She may have reached out to oblivious me more than I know.

I talk Marcel into sharing my last blast of weed, rolling up the sativa in a tight joint and leading him on a walk away from the inn. Only a shimmering light remains from the faded sun, and the spotlights are on the La Posada entrance, so we wander around the hotel toward the platform in the back, where the train is due to arrive for boarding at 5 a.m. "Maybe a little nightcap," Marcel says, "goose my dreams." I'm enjoying Marcel's company, the charm beneath the tough-guy veneer. I also appreciate the tough guy underneath, a guy whose quiet confidence puts me at ease walking in a dimly lit area similar to the Caesars Palace gardens, except less grand and with railroad tracks. That fateful night again flashes before my eyes, the violent and frightening last chapter in Frank's life.

The pot slowly loosens Marcel's tongue, starting with a widening of his eyes and smile. It's been a long time, he allows. I prod him about growing up in Denver, generally my destination. "I always wanted to get away from Denver," he says. "First chance I got, I took off, less than $100 to my name, hidden in my shoe. Hitched some rides, and even jumped a freight train into LA. I don't want to go back to Colorado."

229

Thus, I learn Marcel isn't accompanying me to Boulder. He's not sure how far he'll go, but he assures me I will not be alone. Jay and Zhou, definitely working together, apparently have taken control of the schedule – for good or ill, I can't say. If I'm in danger, as they say, I am most grateful. If the risk is overblown, I'm still happy just to hitch a ride. You need friends on the road, especially in times like these.

That night I dream of pushing hands in the surf with Marcel in Santa Monica, and we're waving and smiling at Serena, who's standing on the beach with her arms folded. I touch Marcel and feel the root at his back foot, but I can't feel my own. Instead, I feel a wave smashing against my ass, pushing me past Marcel head-first into the surf, and then the sucking ocean pulling me out, partially submerged, then fully covered and dragged along the sandy bottom. I hear muffled shouts and feel a hand on my arm, but I'm slipping and wake up, gasping for breath. Marcel is shaking me, trying to wake me.

It's time to get ready for the train. Marcel is dressed and prods me up and out toward the platform in the faintest light of a new day. There's little for me to pack, living out of a backpack and a small duffel bag, having shipped most of my clothes to George's address near Boulder. "The Chief stopped in Flagstaff at 4 o'clock, 30 miles from the ranch, so we're lucky to be right here at the Winslow station at 5," he says. "We can get breakfast on the train." We're the only riders on the platform this morning, so we take advantage of the space and quiet as Marcel orchestrates a series of joint-stretching and *qigong* exercises to wake up and focus our energy. As usual, I follow along closely, imagining my body performing as magnificently as his.

These moments of concentrated mind-body coordination give me a sense of wellbeing, finding calm and comfort in measured breath and gentle movement, pushing my mind from the top of my head to the tips of my toes, touching each organ on the way down, then back up, mental floss. We are waving our hands in the clouds, tapping into *qi* energy from the chill morning air and stirring it along the body meridians, flowing through blood and nerve ends, massaging the connective tissue, sinking, rooting. Working inside the body. *Neigong*. Bliss.

The train whistle cuts through the moving meditation. The Chief is on the horizon, beginning to decelerate toward the station. As it approaches, I see the double-decker sleeper cars where Los Angelenos, boarding last night, are sound asleep. With about six hours to Albuquerque, riding into the rising sun, we figure to spend our time between the dining car and the observation deck, the best seats for the view as we skirt the Navajo reservation and roll through the naturally wonderful Painted Desert and Petrified Forest.

Checking in with the conductor, we head directly to the dining car for coffee. It's another hour before the kitchen opens, enough time to pump Marcel for more information about our itinerary. Not being in control of my journey goes against my journalistic instincts. What happens in Albuquerque, our ticketed destination, I want to know. Marcel is more circumspect now, having slept off the truth serum, but allows that we will have a few hours layover before catching the local rail transit to Santa Fe, the Rail Runner. What's in Santa Fe? Marcel shrugs, "Don't you know?" he asks. I only know it's generally going in the right direction, and I'm along for the ride. I ask a few more questions, getting nowhere. Marcel is full of shrugs, apparently knowing nothing beyond Albuquerque.

The dining car staff, perhaps responding to our dawdling, gets the kitchen ready early, and we get breakfast ahead of the rush. I'm enjoying my omelet and toast when I feel a light tap on my shoulder, turning to see a familiar smiling face. "Wei-Lin!" I greet her excitedly, rising to embrace her. She introduces a tall, elegant Chinese woman called Tee-Wan, a choreographer for the Shen Yun troupe. "I am learning from her," Wei-Lin tells us, "for when I leave the stage." Tee-Wan is leading an advance team heading to Chicago to prepare a new troupe performance later in the month. "New dancers, more work," Tee-Wan says.

They join us for breakfast, Wei-Lin sitting beside Marcel so we can watch each other, by my reckoning. Even without her usual makeup, she is radiant, with sparkling eyes and a bright smile freshly offered to me, or so I will suppose. Yes, I'm boldly flirting with her, and she's returning the interest. Meanwhile, Tee-Wan, sitting quietly beside me, asks if I'm going to Chicago for the show. No, and I confess I've missed two performances in less than a month, briefly describing the latest incident, and how Wei-Lin was my sunshine when I was cooped up in the hospital. An embarrassed laugh and mild protest from Wei-Lin, who is clearly pleased, beaming at me. "You look much better now," she says. "No bandages, and sun shining on your nose."

I launch into an expansive description of Mo's boot camp, sparring with Marcel and a Texas Ranger, then the daylong horseback ride to catch the train. I can tell from Marcel's grin that he thinks I'm laying it on a bit thick, playing a Kungfu cowboy for the pretty dancer, and maybe I am – even fantasizing about going to Chicago, postponing my trip to Colorado. That's against Marcel's marching orders, but he is obliging enough to give me space to be alone with Wei-Lin. After breakfast, he invites Tee-Wan to join him in the observation car, and a stirring display of sunrise. I slip into the seat beside Wei-Lin, asking about her plans.

"I may travel the world with Shen Yun; I think they want me," she says. "Or maybe back with Jay and May-Lee. I love practicing internal arts, *tuina*, *qi* healing, and Tai Chi. Maybe I train to be a movie fighter like Lou Guy." I tell her she has a gift, transmitting energy through her touch. "I can feel it when you touch me, with *tuina*," I say. "You have healing power."

Wei-Lin responds by hugging my arm, laying her head on my shoulder, softly protesting that she is just a novice, and that May-Lee is the skilled one. Then, playfully, she says, "Maybe with more practice with you." Yes, please, I say, and she obliges on the spot, leading me to her bedroom car with its reclining seats and privacy lock.

Wei-Lin asks me to take off my jeans, which are too tight for massage, and retrieves a sheet to cover my legs and underwear. I lie down on my back, just as before. She starts where she left off that morning in Los Angeles, with my neck and shoulders, first spreading a cool ointment, her face close to mine, and then leaning into the push-pull of the massage. Slowly she works her way down to my feet, and then back up the other side. I know that the pressure she is applying to my body is salving my internal organs and should be calming my mind. But my heart is racing, and my mind is lost to the rising heat in my loins, excited by her touch.

Wei-Lin is working around my erection, which must be visible to her as it throbs under the sheet, but she appears to be giving it no notice. She is pressing and pulsing along the acupressure points at my wrist, then up my arm to my shoulder and neck when I reach up and gently pull her head down, kissing her lightly on the lips, then hungrily as she responds. She is rubbing my chest and abdomen, then stops suddenly, pulling back from me. "We cannot," she says. I let out a slow breath that whistles through my teeth, and moan my disappointment, telling her I may have to go to Chicago with her. "No need," she says. "I will go with you."

Wei-Lin was never going to Chicago; it turns out. She joined her friends from the Shen Yun troupe on a regular run because she knew I'd be on the train. She might still join them later, but her plan is to get off in Albuquerque with Marcel and me. I learn this over the course of the next several hours as we sit with Marcel and Tee-Wan in the observation car, watching the rugged geological show, the fabulously weathered terrain of the Great Plains as it shimmers in the morning sun. We are joined by other senior members of the L.A. Shen Yun group, dancers, and musicians, about a dozen in all. They mostly speak Chinese, and I enjoy trying to understand the passing conversation, and reading the body language if not getting the words.

It's almost noon as we near the downtown Albuquerque train station, when Marcel and Tee-Wan reappear. She is carrying a small suitcase for Wei-Lin and gives Marcel a lingering hug, while insisting that I must come and see the show. I agree, thinking about finally seeing the lovely Wei-Lin on the stage. For all our differences, I feel a commonality of interests and purpose, both of us traveling the same road to discovery, becoming friends, maybe lovers. But first, companions.

Marcel steps off the train first, reaching back to give Wei-Lin a hand. As I alight on the platform, Marcel and Wei-Lin already are walking toward the station, waving at two men who are hurrying toward us. I follow them, squinting in the noon-day sunlight and seeing the beaming face of Jay Lee as he strides our way. Behind him, a short, stocky man, not smiling, wearing sunglasses and scanning the platform. The body language gives him away before I see his face. It's Lou Guy. Apparently, the team is huddling.

27. Jay Lee: The Dharma Wheel

Lou Guy was in Flagstaff for a week, stealthily taking video of comings and goings at the airport and train station, searching for trouble from Sinaloa cartel toughs or suspected Chinese agents. Those were Jay's instructions, in that order, but Lou Guy only had eyes for Chinese spies. He saw nothing suspicious. His final trip to the airport was to meet Jay, then drive to Albuquerque in Marcel's car, which they retrieved from Mo's ranch. "I think we can relax a bit," Jay assured Lou Guy. "We're going to retreat, rescue our friend, and make time to meditate and practice *qigong*."

But Jay's first task at the station was to calm down a visibly agitated Ray James, who hadn't responded well to Jay's efforts to protect him. "Listen," Ray said, "I just learned I'm going to Santa Fe, and I want to know why. What the hell is in Santa Fe? And why am I being steered blindly along this route?" Jay was amused and sympathetic about this "unfortunate situation," but assured Ray he'd reveal all tonight over dinner. "It's friends, of course. You're surrounded by friends," he said. "I hope you'll accept our hospitality while we help you avoid potential dangers. I have information for you."

They piled into the car, Jay upfront with Marcel, who was beaming back in the driver's seat of his streamlined baby. Wei-Lin sat between Ray and Lou Guy in the backseat as Marcel wheeled into traffic. "We'll get you back to the station in the morning to catch the Rail Runner to Santa Fe," Jay said. "We have rooms and an eight-course meal waiting for us at the Inn, one of my favorite retreats. We have much to talk about."

Marcel steered onto a two-lane road lined with towering cottonwood trees, the shaded drive into the Inn. Jay rolled down his window and invited everyone to do the same. "Smell that?" he asked. The air was thick with a fragrance that was at once familiar and rare. "Smells like *tuina*," said Wei-Lin. Jay nodded. "The Los Poblanos lavender fields produce a line of oils and lotions we stock and promote at Way of *Qi*," he said. "Lavender is one of our herbal remedies, a rare treat, but you get it free here, in your room."

The sales connection made Jay a special guest at the Inn, and he and his entourage got the executive treatment when they arrived at the desk. Jay was afforded a suite, and the others got cozy rooms in the main section of the inn. "Finally," Ray said. "It's the first private room I've had since the hospital – which wasn't so private." As the clerk checked them in, Ray picked up the *Albuquerque Journal* from the counter and studied a story headlined: *Trump abruptly axes FBI's Comey in midst of Russia probe.* "Holy shit!" he exclaimed. "It's gotten worse." Jay Lee grabbed Ray's arm and shook it.

"Let it go," Jay Lee commanded, meeting Ray's startled expression with an intense gaze. "You need to relax, and focus on yourself for a while. You're almost there." Ray objected, sputtering that he is far from "there, wherever it is, I need to be with my physical, mental, and emotional wellbeing." Jay laughed. "No, I mean you're close to your geographic destination. The other road will continue for a lifetime, I hope. You take one step at a time, correct course, and keep going."

Ray acknowledged that he was "less than 500 miles from Boulder, and I could drive up in a day if I had a car, and a driver's license." But he was content to take the time to synch his body and mind with the Chinese medicine and magic being held out to him. "I'm just not happy about this cloak-and-dagger secrecy," he said. "I'm not even allowed to contact my daughter." Jay offered a smiling apology and a one-word response, "Tomorrow."

Ray frowned and shook his head, obediently folding the newspaper and stuffing it into his bag for bedtime reading. "She's not just my daughter; she's my doctor," he said. "And she's worried about me. It's been weeks since we had a video chat about my condition, or conditions. She's trying to help me, just like you are. She'll want to know about my medicine, for sure."

"Tonight you get the best medicine of all – good food, well-cooked and with the best herbs, good-for-you herbs," Jay said. "Chinese medicine starts in the kitchen. I told you this before. Now we explore. Special meal prepared at Chef's Table here at the Inn." Ray nodded, remembering Jay's rap from the Esalen workshop on nutrition and digestion. "Ah, yes, we must eat," he said.

Jay Lee dismissed the sullen response, confident that Ray's spirits would rise as he learned more about his situation. The opportunity to offer a happy glimpse came as they gathered for dinner, when Ray arrived with Wei-Lin on his arm. "Good! You'll make a fine couple traveling to Santa Fe on the Rail Runner," he said. "Did Wei-Lin tell you? She'll be your companion for the trip and will introduce you to her friends." Ray absorbed this news with a slow smile that eventually grew abeam, seeing more promise in Santa Fe.

"I was telling Marcel about the Chinese herbs and vegetables they grow here, with my help," Jay said. "Now they've also cultivated wood ear on the cottonwood trees ..." he stopped, smiling at Ray's bewildered expression. "Wood ear. It's a type of fungus, a mushroom, jelly-like in the wild, and you dry and chop it up for different dishes. A good herb for your health. You'll get a taste this evening."

More than a taste, in fact. Wood ear was in the flavorful and stimulating tea served at the start of the meal, along with red dates, reishi mushrooms, ginseng, wolfberry, and the omnipresent ginger, "spice of digestion." Jay introduced everyone to Chef Lin, who specialized in Asian dishes but deferred to Jay on spice selection. White wood ear mushrooms were in our soup, along with pears, red dates, and figs. Then came bok choy, with wood ear and shiitake mushrooms, adding flavor and healthful juju. "Gotta love wood ear," Ray said.

"Delicious but also very effective against anemia, hypertension, heart disease, constipation, diabetes, even cancer," Jay said, pointing to his gut. "We are feeding the spleen, a big part of digestion. The stomach breaks down the waste, and the spleen sends *qi* energy to the heart and lungs," he added, raising his hands in a burst of expression.

Because the spleen is a cold yin organ, it works best when food is warm, Jay said, explaining why they weren't eating cold salads with their meal. "Cooking is like pre-digestion, a little cooking for the vegetables, not too much," he said. With the arrival of the next course, "Enhance the *Qi* Mountain Yam Congee," Jay turned to Ray with the news he'd been waiting for. "Zhou says you are probably in the clear," he said. "The U.S. is negotiating with China over Miss Xu, so Han won't mess with you, at least for now. It's a good time to move on, to slip away." Any chance the Sinaloa smugglers were on his trail faded with every mile he retreated from Las Vegas, he added.

Ray is visibly relieved by these developments, sitting back in his chair and smiling with the arrival of Chrysanthemum Broccoli, with dried white wood ear fungus and ginger, of course, and lemon juice and sesame oil balanced by honey and maple syrup. Chef Lin brought it with a round of vegetarian spring rolls, and the news that this round is good for dry skin, acne, and high blood pressure.

"You will meet John and Sherry Wong in Santa Fe," Jay said as they shared the vegetable dish. "My good friends," Wei-Lin added. "They are artists, very creative. You will like them." Ray nodded, pleased by the news that came with the appetizers. Jay explained that the Wongs worked on stage sets for Shen Yun in LA, and now sell their paintings and ceramics at the artists' market in Santa Fe. "I have a John Wong painting of the Falun Dafa, the Dharma Wheel, on the wall at my studio."

"You mean the graphic with the swastika in the middle of it?" Ray asked. "We ran that with my article in the *Chronicle*, and readers were really upset. It definitely doesn't help a movement outlawed in China to brandish a Nazi symbol."

"Swastika is a German word and German concept," Jay said. "In China, it's *wan*, meaning 'good fortune', and is connected with the Buddha. It goes back thousands of years, the Dharma Wheel of Buddhism, and the *yin-yang* symbols of Taoism. They're all turning together, in harmony."

"I tried to explain it to readers, how the symbol represents the universe, the cosmic order – circling and moving like the planets in a solar system, or the spinning molecules of life," Ray said. "But people only saw swastikas." The main course, Champion Chicken with Goji, cooked with olive oil, garlic, ginger, and green onions, arrived. "Good for whatever ails you," Jay declared.

Lou Guy had become agitated, trying to follow the conversation about symbols. "Falun Gong teach be happy, have success, follow Dharma Wheel law, practice *zhen-shan-ren* ..." he said, looking to Jay for help with the translation. "That's being truthful, compassionate, and tolerant – forbearance," Jay interjected. "Yes," Lou Guy continued, "we meditate on 'Way' of peace, practice *qigong*, stand, sit. Is like rising to heaven." He extended his arms in a circular embrace of the universe, in Falun Gong fashion.

Chef Lin returned with two finishing dishes, Sticky Sesame and Walnut Balls, with honey – for insomnia, Jay said – and chocolate candies made without sugar, except for the fructose in strawberries, with a boost from stevia and coconut butter. "Will curb your diabetes," Jay said with a wry smile as they enjoyed their semi-sweets. "Digestion, the most important thing. Right, Chef Lin?" Jay asked as the host, and his assistants cleared away the final dishes, bringing more tea. "You know it so, Master Lee," the chef said, and

Jay nodded. "We must stand and help the flow," Jay said. "When we finish our tea, we will adjourn to the courtyard for *qigong*.

The evening air was clear and cold in the high plains, and Jay encouraged the party to grab their wraps. The Sangre de Cristo range loomed in majestic splendor above as they took positions in front of Jay, relaxing into a standard standing posture, back straight, head erect, knees slightly bent, breathing deeply into their stomachs. "Good!" Jay exclaimed. "I can feel your energy. We will do the first exercise of Falun Gong, 'Buddha Showing a Thousand Hands,' in honor of Lou Guy's journey, and we will follow Wei-Lin, our graceful expert."

The four men pivoted to face the beaming Wei-Lin, who bowed to each of them in turn. As they began the movement, Ray was the hesitant one, being unfamiliar with the Falun Gong exercises. Watching him closely, Wei-Lin slowed it down, explaining how her hand positions, as a woman, are opposite the men's. She cupped her left hand under her right; they put their right hand below – *yin* and *yang* reflecting each other.

There are eight distinct hand movements in this one exercise, with colorful names like Two Dragons Diving Into the Sea and Bodhisattva Placing Hands on the Lotus Flower. Wei-Lin narrated each one and repeated an admonition each time to extend arms and straighten knees as they reached high. "We are stretching the entire body each time," she said. "Feel it?"

The breathing exercises were completed in less than 30 minutes, even if digestion was not, as Jay gathered the group into a small huddle warming against the wind whipping through the courtyard.

"I've learned much here," Ray said. "Thank you for the hospitality and for letting Wei-Lin show us how to move."

Marcel put his arm around Ray's shoulder and leaned into a hug. "I hope you come back our way," he said. "You never say goodbye to your friends," Ray said, a statement that drew amens around the tight circle.

28. Cultivating the *Yin-Yang*

As we retreat from the evening air, walking to the building entrance, I pull Wei-Lin aside, asking her quietly but bluntly if she will stay with me tonight. She puts her hands against my chest and, peering up at me, whispers, "I will visit, and we will talk." Not a wholehearted acceptance, but an opening. Her lips yield to a quick kiss. "I'm happy we travel together," she says as we turn and walk into the Inn, where Jay is waiting in the lobby, making sure we'll be ready for early transit in the morning.

In my room, Wei-Lin excuses herself to the bathroom. Kicking off my shoes and plopping down on the bed, I study the door and imagine, in the best scenario, how my beautiful Asian girlfriend will emerge naked and aroused, ready to finally consummate a relationship that's been building inside my head and loins. My whimsy is scuttled as she emerges fully clothed, although with a bright smile and a bottle of lavender lotion. She walks to the chair beside the bed and sits on the edge of the seat, placing the lotion on the table.

"I want to talk to you about Falun Gong, about love ... and making love," she says sweetly, and I swing my legs off the bed, sitting up straight to face her, still excited but not liking the sound of this opening. "I don't know your feelings, but I feel you're very excited." She puts up her hand as I stammer to reply, continuing. "If you do not know, I will tell you: In Falun Dafa, sex outside marriage is bad. It is part of human failing, a distraction from the path true to our spiritual nature, *xinxing*." I shake my head, not hiding my pained expression.

She hurries to add that it's good to seek virtue, to feel love, and push away human desires that make love less than it is. "In Falun Dafa, we let the human spirit guide what we do with our bodies," she says. "In our exercises, we look within ourselves, connect to the universe, to the Tao. We cultivate for a higher purpose than just being. We must overcome karma by doing good, for *zhen shan ren*," the Chinese terms Jay translated as honesty, compassion, and tolerance, the Falun Gong Golden Rule.

Leaning my arms back on the bed, I stare glumly at Wei-Lin and consider the implications of her statement. I can't argue religion with a devotee; I know this. How do I prevent her beliefs from coming between us, from me getting closer to her? She genuinely cares about me, and I feel it, but I don't understand her terms, or how they translate into a relationship I can accept. The prospect of physical love denied outside marriage is so devastating I'm briefly tempted to ask her to marry me. Is this a trap? "So you're a virgin?" I ask instead.

She responds with a small laugh and dismissive shrug. "No. I make mistakes, and I was married before. He went away." Again she shrugs as I offer condolences. "A boy I met in LA, he wasn't good for me." She rises and comes to sit on the bed, leaning against me. "I have a desire too, but I fear it would be the end of us, the end of love ... unless ..." she trails off, then stands in front of me, taking both my hands. Unless what? I ask.

"If we were to join as we meditate, as we cultivate our spirits, if we can do that together with our bodies," she says, "we could raise ourselves higher, experience pure love." Wei-Lin's breathing is racing with her words as she moves in front of me, grips my hands, and presses against the bed between my legs, agitating me further. I lean in, look into her intense eyes, and agree. "Yes, teach me."

Wei-Lin pulls me up and begins unbuttoning my shirt. "First, we shower," she says, and I eagerly help with the undressing, hands trembling as I free her lean, athletic body from her loose, silk Kungfu blouse and pants, black as night, and her delicate panties, also black. I grasp for the spiritual view of our naked frolic, a ceremony of water, thinking back to Jay's sermon on the Taoist water tradition as we all held hands and vibrated in a rhythmic breath. And again, I have an erection, which Wei-Lin appears to ignore. This is part of the test, I decide, gritting my teeth and following her into the bathroom and the shower.

"Close your eyes," she commands as she turns me to face the shower spray and away from her. I feel her soapy hands trace circles from my neck and shoulders down my back, pinching and pulling against my skin in *tuina* fashion as she presses her firm breasts and stomach against me. One arm circles my waist and presses against my stomach for leverage as she kneads and drums her fingers down my spine to my buttocks, which she smacks with a vigor I'm not expecting. She soaps her hands again, and I feel her fingers kneading the muscles and ligaments along the backs of my thighs and calves, one arm circling my knees.

"Turn around," she says, and I obey, looking down to watch as she washes my feet before pressing firmly on the pressure points behind my toes, working her way up the instep to the ankles and then to my knees. Rising, she rubs along my hips and up my abdomen and, leaning in, folds my stiff penis back toward me, circling my waist with a hug. "Now do me," she commands.

Trading places, the water now flowing against her front, me behind, soaping up my hands and slowly working her neck and shoulders the best I know how, trying to reciprocate her magic touch,

246

encouraged as I hear her moan softly. I wash and stroke slowly down her back, lingering along the lower back and buttocks, venturing a small smack that elicits a giggle, then working down her legs to the ridges behind her ankles, the point Jay pressed to relieve my pain a few months back. She turns her body to face me, as I crouch on one knee below, following her guidance, soaping her feet and pressing against the points behind her toes, stealing a glance at the peeking morsel above. Her eyes are closed as I move slowly up her legs, soaping and kneading reciprocal points on her body where her fingers worked on me moments earlier, along her hips, then more gently against the abdomen and between her breasts to her shoulders, wrapping my arms around her and holding her close. She pushes away.

"Come," she says, taking my hand. We towel off each other, "don't rub," she says as we dab in silence, my heart racing. She leads me to the bedroom, but not to the bed. Instead, we make room on the floor, in front of the couch and shuttered window. We move a table and a chair, and Wei-Lin guides me to face the window, telling me to relax, "stand *qigong*." I obey, arms extended out and down in the "Bear" position, releasing the tension in my neck and shoulders, focusing *qi* to my lower *dantian* as I breathe, willing my erection to relax along with the rest of my body, with only slight success.

Even as I focus my mind inward, I'm mindful of Wei-Lin piling pillows on the floor around us. I smell the lavender lotion before I feel her firm application on my shoulders and neck, slowly working the lotion down my back along the meridians to my hips. I close my eyes and breathe in the fragrance and serenity of the moment. Wei-Lin is facing me now and continuing to apply the lotion to my chest and arms and down my legs, again ignoring the penis, in semi-repose.

247

I feel her standing beside me now, assuming a Falun Gong posture. I don't look, just breathe, feeling her presence. We stand for maybe 10 more minutes, enough time for my heart to settle into a normal rhythm, my desire abated for the moment. She steps in front of me and grasps both hands, facing me. "Sit," she commands, and I follow her lead down to the pillows, legs crossed in front of me, not nearly so flexibly lotus as the agile dancer, hands folded above my genitals.

"When we meditate, we leave the animal behind, the urges and attachments we have," Wei-Lin says. "The heat below clouds the vision above. Our minds should rule our bodies, so we don't lose sight." I nod slowly as I gaze into her eyes. She asks me to focus on the unity of the universe, "which is inside us and all around us."

Wei-Lin commands me to close my eyes and visualize *yin* and *yang* together in *taiji*, the integration of all things, the "supreme ultimate." We all have *yin* and *yang* inside us, male and female, sharing the same component energy, she explains. "Even as *yin* is my true nature, and you are truly *yang*, we share both male and female," she says. "In dual cultivation, we share energy, and grow ..."

Suddenly, I feel Wei-Lin's hand cupped beneath my scrotum, rubbing gently and encouraging a re-erection. With her other hand, she guides my fingers to her vulva, warm and dewy to my touch, then climbs onto my lap. I slide easily into her, and she rests her arms loosely around my neck; my hands land firmly on her hips, and I thrust, moaning. *Yabyum*, I'm thinking. *Yabyum*. I've been here before. I'm panting with excitement.

"Slow, slow," she commands, squeezing and circling on my lap. "Close your eyes. We're on a trip, riding together ... Breathe with me." Eyes closed, I settle into the rhythm of our singular breathing, relaxing into my partner, *yin* to my *yang*, conjoined, reaching for a cosmic mind meld while simultaneously probing the walls of her vagina. The physical sensation immediately overwhelms my mental gymnastics trying to elevate the *taiji* symbol; my chest heaves as I gasp to calm myself.

I open my eyes. Wei-Lin is gazing dreamily at me, commanding my attention unblinkingly, beckoning with her eyes to love her on a plane above the carnal, to some aesthetic pleasure I can only imagine. I try to rise above my sexual ardor and regain my equilibrium, only to be agitated by her words. "Don't come," she says. "Save *jing*, save energy." I gasp, not understanding, not believing my ears. She continues in a soft, even voice: "We join energy, increase life force, increase *qi*, don't waste *jing*." I stammer a breathy reply and question: We're making love. What's to waste? "Save it for your spirit, for your mind. I will help."

After all the stimulation, now deep inside her, I'm not sure I can hold my orgasm much longer. Perhaps she feels it, reaching down below my scrotum again, and I feel her fingers pushing against the area behind my balls, the perineum, pressing her breasts into my chest, her face nuzzling my neck, her hips still circling on my lap, pulling and pushing my penis across her labia. The feeling is both rapturous and frightening as I struggle to resist coming.

Slowly I realize Wei-Lin's persistent pressure behind my scrotum is beginning to override the yearning for release, creating a sensation of heightened sexual awareness without the urgency of imminent orgasm. I run my hands up and down her back, feeling her warm breath against my neck, her fingers still pushing into my perineum. We stay in this position for at least 10 minutes, maybe longer. I've lost any sense of time in the cauldron of this steaming love, unrequited – or is it? Wei-Lin's body is heaving and shuddering against mine, perhaps enjoying her own orgasm, her hand manipulating a joystick from below. Is she saving her *jing*? I ask her later after we've retreated to the bed, lying side by side, holding hands.

"Chinese tradition says women are not important," she says, "that we are simply here to make men stronger and healthier. But *yin* is essence too. Women are vessels of life, and we are excited when stirred by sex. You excite me, yes." She rolls over and kisses me squarely on the lips, rubbing my chest and abdomen. "We create *jing* together, and I feel it move through my body. I save it. I don't let it go."

I accept her explanation because I'm moved to do so, even if it seems like a cover story. I'm no expert on female orgasm, but it seems to me that Wei-Lin's bodily fluids, while stirred and flowing, are not necessarily released. How do I send my jism to my brain? As Wei-Lin describes it, this tantric sex allows men to gain power by suppressing their ejaculations, sending *jing*, the life essence, to their heads.

This is not the *yabyum* experience I remember from college, with George and our casual girlfriends, searching for deep male-female understanding through exquisite orgasms. At least, that seemed the point to me. Now I'm asked to consider the act of love without the release. What is the benefit? I'm pondering, in my cynical fashion, how this gender inequity may be an ancient Chinese ruse to keep women on top as I drift off to sleep, my arm around Wei-Lin, her warm breath on my neck.

When I awaken, she's gone, a few hours short of dawn. I crawl under the covers and sink easily back into the dreamworld; this time, I'm writing a newspaper article, working to finish it with Bradbury standing behind me, peering over my shoulder. I try to get away, but he follows me out the door and into the street, and suddenly I'm at the Crazy Horse, and Cherry Fine is on stage, naked and beckoning to me. I'm sitting close to the stage but with my laptop on the table, my editor still studying the screen, leaning into my line of sight. As Bradbury gets in my face, Cherry fades out, and I see his stunned expression, a look of sheer horror. What is it? What's wrong with me? I'm startled awake, groggily studying the thin first light of day filtered through the window shade. I roll out of bed.

Awake, the only dream on my mind is the evening of dual cultivation, with Wei-Lin riding on my lap, dreamy eyes and dancer's grace, sending me to the point of ecstasy that dares not release, that roils and rises somewhere in my mind but still tugs at my genitals, even as I pull on my clothes. Opening the shades, I'm greeted by the morning glory of lavender fields splayed in brilliant purple blooms, not yet ready for harvest, we're told. I relax into my standing Bear position and breathe deeply, the lavender lotion scent still with me this morning, the memory of Wei-Lin's soothing touch calming me. I move into the opening postures of Tai Chi, flowing into "grasping the sparrow's tail," remembering Sparrow, then letting her go, letting all thoughts go, even of Wei-Lin. Relaxing, breathing, finding my center, at peace, revitalized. Good for now.

Marcel is pacing, and Jay is on the phone when I arrive in the lobby. Wei-Lin and Lou Guy are huddled over a table in the corner, and he appears to be doing all the talking, my beautiful dancer listening intently and nodding, oblivious to anyone else, including me. Marcel spots me first and practically runs over with a big smile and greeting, grabbing my hand and pulling me in. "Gotta get rolling," he says of the day-long drive to reach LA. Jay waves as he continues his conversation. Wei-Lin is now walking toward me, greeting me with a quick embrace before giving me the news.

"Lou Guy is going with us to Santa Fe," she says softly but loud enough for Marcel to hear. "What!?" he exclaims, shaking his head and marching over to Jay, who has just ended his phone conversation. He raises his hand to acknowledge Marcel's complaint, motioning for us to all approach. "We'll talk," he says. "They're cooking up a fine breakfast to send us on our way, so let's enjoy it. New plan, Marcel; it'll all work out."

Marcel is visibly disappointed by the delay, naturally eager to get back home after nearly two months on the road. But he manages a tight smile as we walk toward the dining room. "You shouldn't miss auditions for that new Warner Kungfu movie," he says to Lou Guy, who nods without a comment. I want to speak up for the Kungfu movie and discourage Lou Guy from joining us on the trip, but bite my tongue. Jay is the engineer on this train.

Breakfast doesn't come with a running description of how the food cures ailments, but the choices all include fresh organic produce and seasonings whipped together into splendid culinary treats – a spring omelet with mushroom, garlic, and onion; "forbidden rice" that's actually prickly pear rolled oats, coconut fluff, and almonds, with fruit; something called a "Shakshuka" with tomatoes, poblano peppers, mint, feta, and poached egg. I pick the kale and quinoa poached egg, with avocado, dates, and beet chips. But the food is the last thing on my mind this morning.

We're still placing our orders when Jay breaks the news: Mo got two visitors yesterday, looking for horseback rides, but asking questions about "people who were here before," making him suspicious. "Mo thinks they're Russians, based on their accents. You still may have a tail, he said. So no phone yet." Russians! That can't be true. I'm incredulous as I quiz Jay, who says that's all he knows. It doesn't make sense, I say. "All I know is what Mo's CIA sense tells him, and what Zhou suspects," Jay says.

But there's more. Zhou says his Oakland agents found two men in a van parked near Mona and Maddie's condo monitoring their phone messages and Internet, using both wiretap and Bluetooth intercept. "They were local guys, and they were getting paid by people they didn't know," Jay says. "We don't know yet, but you shouldn't call Mona – or anyone right now."

Is Bredkoff coming after me? If anyone at the poker table was menacing, it was the cagy Russian, watching everyone, taking our pulses from across the way. I feel my throat constrict as I think about his eyes watching, hard and cold, dispassionate, patiently playing the long game. Why would he come after me? As I stew over my predicament, Lou Guy comes over and pats me on the arm. "No worries," he says. "I go with you, protect." I manage a worried smile.

Now driving solo and leaving later, Marcel agrees to stop off at Mo's ranch for a little reconnaissance, to spend the night, and report any developments to Lou Guy. I wish someone would report to me directly. Every bit of news nowadays is roundabout to me; I sulk, grabbing a *New York Times* from the newsstand at the downtown rail station, where we've got 15 minutes until the last morning train to Santa Fe. I bury my head in the newspaper to ponder this new predicament.

My current status seems to be encapsulated in a *Times* report on the FBI investigation into Russian influence in the 2016 election, the probe that got James Comey fired, it says. Could Bredkoff be involved in the Russian influence campaign? Influence means money in the USA, and Bredkoff's billions are especially attractive to Trump, who regards himself as a master of the "Big Deal." Maybe Bredkoff sees me as a threat now that I've written about him; maybe he's not as well-disguised as I think. He knows Trump, and he brags about it.

Have I been swept up in this news story, without a clue? Russia is implicated in the WikiLeak dump of emails from the DNC and the Clinton campaign, and the FBI is investigating Russia for other interference in the election. And how does that connect with the evidence that Bredkoff may have planted two men in a van to eavesdrop on Mona's communication? It's ridiculous. All they'll learn is how to treat a sick child. Why would I be a target? Yeah, so I made a mistake in not talking with Chaz before I sent the column to Bradbury. Even getting knocked silly doesn't excuse that. But it's not a capital offense.

29. Along for the Ride

The cragged rock formations loom as majestic sentries along the high desert floor of the Turquoise Trail, named for its rich deposits of the precious stone, mined to death. The hills are dotted with juniper and sagebrush, but the overwhelming aroma of lavender stays in my head as we wind along aboard the Rail Runner. Wei-Lin appears to have nodded off, rocked to sleep by the train's vibrations, her breath steady against my arm. Quaint small towns come and go; we slow down but don't stop as my mind wanders to my current predicament.

I'm on the run, not of my own direction, but probably in my best interest if the intelligence coming from Zhou and Jay is reliable, and I have no reason to believe otherwise. The journalistic mission to explain the bizarre election of Donald Trump has led not to the nonvoter as the culprit, but to a tableful of global influence peddlers who may have it in for me for my account of our poker game and table talk. I got a good view from the backroom, where fabulously wealthy players with no national loyalty scheme to prop up a man in their own image, the image-obsessed hospitality magnate Donald Trump. This is the most likely story, the empire builders throwing down their money to a greedy developer so as to tighten their grip on the system. Voters are just dupes in this scenario.

I'm missing something – maybe in the poker game, a clue about why Bredkoff or any of the players would come after me? I can wrack my brain but can't look it up; I'm a primitive journalist unable to communicate via phone or computer, lost in someone else's story. I feel a need to regain control of my narrative – not just the stories I'm paid to write, but the life story I've been trying to amend since I left San Francisco. I'm better now; I can feel it, not depending on booze and drugs, eating well, and having an experience with tantric sex – a mind-bending stunted orgasm to the brain. Is that healthy? Maybe I needed a wake-up call about the inconsequential nature of my orgasm. Do I believe that?

Wei-Lin rouses with the announcement we're approaching the Santa Fe station, and I squeeze her reassuringly. The ever-vigilant Lou Guy appears at my side, quietly slipping from the seat behind. I'm sure he wasn't napping. "Not this stop," Wei-Lin says, sitting up straight and stretching, sending Lou Guy back to his seat. "We go to the plaza by the Palace of Governors." She points to the modern State Capitol as we approach our stop, then takes my hand to lead us off the train. "You'll like my friends John and Sherry," she says. "They sponsored us, and helped me settle in LA."

John and Sherry Wong have staked out a section on the city plaza, a bustling hub of Santa Fe society and street commerce, art and craft tables with browsing tourists and regulars alike. Wei-Lin pulls me along when she spots her friends. John Wong is a big man from northern China, where people typically grow larger than those in the south. Sherry, greeting us with a wave from behind the table, is diminutive by comparison, shorter than Wei-Lin, and Caucasian. I'm guessing they're in their 50s based on Sherry's streaks of gray hair. John has the jet black hair of a man who dyes it regularly, a not-unusual Chinese conceit.

"So glad to meet you, Mr. James," Sherry says, extending her hand. "We loved your articles about Falun Gong. Thank you!" This declaration surprises me, since it had been nearly a decade since my series ran in the *Chronicle*. Wei-Lin has already introduced me, apparently. Also surprising to me is their embrace of Lou Guy, whom I learn worked with them to build the Shen Yun sets in LA.

"Everybody knows Lou Guy; he's a famous Kungfu fighter," Sherry says. Lou Guy shakes his head and smiles. "Kungfu acting," he says.

I look past Sherry to see a riot of color and energy in the paintings behind her, in surreal tones of light and shadows, the Wongs' work for sale – or at least on display. Falun Gong devotees are portrayed sitting or standing in meditative poses, hands facing one another top and bottom in front of them, as if they're holding a big ball, the light illuminating them from above, shadows and agitation below. The Dharma Wheel symbol, Falun Dafa, is featured in paintings or stands alone in desktop-sized frames. I ask John about the inspiration behind the artwork.

"This is the art of *zhen shan ren*, the meaning of Falun Dafa," Wong says. It's also the art of Shen Yun, he adds, noting that this collection began as stage sets for performances. "The paintings help tell the stories, more than scenery for the dancers, actors, and musicians." The story, Wei-Lin interjects, "is about the gods who gave us China and the men who try to take it away from us. In our art, we reach out to heaven. In our shows, we dance with the gods."

The classic struggle between good and evil is portrayed in images that straddle heaven and earth, the good being transcendent Falun Gongers, of course, conveying power in meditation as an awakening to light. I'm no art critic, but to me, these paintings are comparable to the European Renaissance works with the saintly biblical heroes, the images of church paintings and statuary of my lost Catholic days, showered with light and reaching for the finger of God. The signature of religious art is hope, the promise of redemption and peace in the face of war and death. And Falun Gong, with its mixture of Taoism and Buddhism, follows this spiritual tradition, aligned against an evil that seeks to wipe it out, a Communist Devil.

257

Our arrival prompts Wong to declare business done for the day. We are abandoning the makeshift market and heading to their home in Taos, about an hour-and-a-half north. I help them pack up Wong's SUV for the drive through the picturesque hills, then get out my notepad and turn on the recorder. First, the still nagging question: Why is the Chinese regime so frightened of Falun Dafa that it would ban the practice and throw its followers into labor camps?

"You can't be a good Communist and follow Falun Dafa at the same time," John Wong says. "The Party rejects spiritualism, even traditional religions like Taoism and Buddhism." But the regime draws power from the traditional Confucian philosophy, which encourages people to fit into society, and to get along, Wong adds. The Taoist philosophy, which developed concurrently with Confucianism, is shunned because it focuses internally rather than socially, and on a power higher than the state.

Falun Gong goes further than Taoism, Wang says. "It teaches moral values – truthfulness, compassion and tolerance – *zhen, shan, ren*. These are not of the modern Chinese state. That's why Li Hongzhi was banished and his teaching outlawed. Teaching morality threatens state control."

As Wong skirts the Sangre de Cristo Mountains navigating the "low road" to Taos, it becomes clear that his take on the history and mission of Shen Yun suggests he's more than an artist who signed up for a creative gig. He's describing an artistic vision of the aspirations and struggle of a movement he's been involved in from the beginning – at least since Li Hongzhi fled to New York.

Wong is a second-generation Chinese-American, a New York City stage actor and playwright who harbored some early Falun Gong refugees fleeing China. He became a devotee after meeting Li, who asked him to help create the Falun Dafa story for the stage.

"I scripted some of the early performances, then recruited Sherry to help with set designs," he says. "She's the real artist." Sherry was exhibiting her paintings and photography at a New York gallery when he stumbled onto the display and was smitten immediately. His first proposal to her was to work with him on the Shen Yun project, before he eventually proposed marriage. "It turned out we work well together," he says.

"And play well," Sherry adds playfully from the back seat, where she and Wei-Lin have stopped talking to listen to Wong's account. "With Falun Gong, we are connected in all things." She was skeptical at first, being a nonpracticing Jew who had become a secular humanist. But practicing the *qigong* movements and meditating led to a religious experience. "John opened my eyes to a spiritualism I'd never known, showing me how the art of *zhen shan ren* is in my art … and in my heart."

As I listen to my companions talk about their experiences with Falun Gong while we wind our way toward Taos, it occurs to me the philosophy has insinuated itself into my life, courtesy of these believers who surround me – and has since Los Angeles, when Jay introduced me to the connection between Falun Gong and Shen Yun. Somehow I've cashed in the performance ticket Jay gave me into a virtual ticket to ride with the artists who create the illusions of the Falun Dafa story, and especially the exotic dancer who extended our sexual encounter onto a spiritual plane.

Wei-Lin says Taos is one of her favorite places. "I try to come in summers for the big pow-wows, the Pueblo dancers, the beautiful costumes. Native tribes from all over New Mexico come to celebrate. I buy their jewelry when I come. It's beautiful." The Taos Pueblo inspired other artists to come here, creating an artists' colony, Wang adds.

"They arrive from all over the world to paint the pueblos and the local people at work, along with the deep blue sky here in the high mountains," he says. "It's colorful, yes, but it's also spiritual. This is a sacred place." The Pueblo religious tradition draws power from kachina spirits, mostly practiced privately, in kiva rooms inside the pueblo. "They bring out the spirits for the pow-wows," Wong says.

While Sherry was the driving force in their decision to move to Taos from LA, and to market their work in Santa Fe, John was equally excited, for different reasons. "To me, Taos is connected to the Tao, to the Way of Taoism," he says. "The kachina spirits are personal, representing people and things in the natural world – and Taoists also see the spiritual world in their surroundings."

John Wong steers his vehicle into the drive of a sprawling ranch-style structure, with an adobe-fenced courtyard and garden on one side and a second-story balcony overlooking the high plains on the other. "This is Ranchos de Taos, the old Spanish section south of downtown," he says as he parks. "We have electricity and plumbing here, unlike the Taos Pueblo north of town, but we still have to re-mud the adobe every few years."

"It's part of the magic of this land, the sorcery," says Sherry, who directs us as we begin unloading her artwork. "The Taos Pueblo are inside conjuring their spirits; they won't talk about it. But I see them all around, in their pottery and jewelry, their clothing. The spirits are here." She waves toward a man hurrying from the courtyard with a cart. "Hey, Billy!" she calls, then an aside to me, "My son, the curator, he'll store the art."

Billy, maybe mid-20s, is slight of build with shoulder-length hair, wire-rimmed glasses, and a wispy goatee – not Asian, and I assume from an earlier marriage, or affair. He assures us he'll take care of everything, and that lunch is waiting.

Lunch is a potpourri of Pueblo goodies (rabbit stew, sweet corn chicos, and tamales), courtesy of Nina, a young Tewa Pueblo cook who lives with the Wongs – or more precisely, she lives with Billy, who gives her a hug when he enters the dining room and announces they are engaged to be married. As we prepare to take a seat at the table, John Wong enters the room with a tall, thin Asian man of indistinguishable age, who smiles and motions toward Lou Guy.

"*Wu shifu, ni hao,*" Lou Guy says, rushing to meet him but stopping to bow to "Shifu (Master) Wu," right hand in his left fist. Wu returns the greeting while gazing around the table, bowing his head to Wei-Lin, who moves toward him. Then he smiles pleasantly at me. "You must be Mr. James; so happy to meet you," he says; I join the crowd and shake hands with Gaosan Wu, introduced to me by Wong as "our guru," a Falun Gong elder. So elder, in fact, that he is a childhood friend of Li Hongzhi, now a confidant as well as his disciple. As I get his story over lunch, I'm considering how Wu probably was looking for me, the American journalist who writes about Falun Dafa, even as he clearly was expecting Lou Guy when he entered the room. I ask how they know each other.

"Lou Guy, as you call him, is son of old friend, brother of Yang Sanfu," Wu says, looking fondly at Lou Guy as he responds. "Very good man. He is going with me to New York. Falun Gong need him."

I'm surprised to hear this news, and I say so to Lou Guy, who is squirming in his seat. "The Master calls," he says simply. Apparently, Lou Guy's martial artistry will be applied to protect Li Hongzhi, instead of me, and I'm relieved.

My phone rings – the new, nearly virgin smart phone is buzzing inside my pocket, and I quickly excuse myself and walk out of the dining room and into the courtyard. I don't recognize the number, but 510, Oakland-Berkeley, news from outside my travel bubble is welcome. I answer. Mona's voice both shocks and thrills, but I'm surprised to hear the always assertive young lady doctor speak with a little girl's voice I faintly remember. Not so self-assured now, a little sad and frightened, coming in short and anxious bursts. "Oh, Dad … it *is* you … I didn't know … Jay Lee gave me this number … Where are you? When are you coming home?"

I rush to assure her I'm fine, that I've been worried about her. I want to know where she is, if she's calling from a "secure" phone. Mona is confused; she's not the one lost on the road. She's calling from her office in Oakland. "I don't know about it being 'secure,'" she says. "Do you mean because of the wiretaps on Maddie?"

And so I learn it was the nurses' union and not me targeted by eavesdroppers outside their apartment. The union suspects a hospital chain playing hardball during negotiations, but the feds haven't tracked the source, Mona says. All the arrested are "rent-a-cops" or street hustlers working through intermediaries they don't know, people they figured were feds.

But the feds weren't listening very closely, only watching and thinking I'm the target. I'm not sure the coast is clear, but Jay felt at ease enough to give Mona my new phone number. I'm losing my bodyguard, and I'm gaining a driver's license. "I can bring it to you," Mona says, her big-girl composure back as she tells me she's flying to Denver next week, on a trip with Maddie, nurses' union business. "I'm taking a vacation; I want to make sure you're okay."

I'm fine, I assure her; my wounds are healed. I've become a wise and healthy consumer of food and drink, still taking my meds, and practicing Tai Chi and meditation. Mona is not impressed. "I've talked with Jay about your holistic health program, and my professional opinion is that it's fine as far as it goes," she says. "It will reduce stress and give you peace of mind, maybe, but you have evidence of disease that requires drugs and maybe surgical treatment."

I agree to meet at her Denver hotel the next Tuesday. She's determined to run me through a series of tests, including a lung biopsy. I bow to her best wishes, if that's what it takes to recover my driver's license. I sign off and call Jay for an update on my Russian problem. What about the Russian horseback riders poking around the Diamond M?

"Zhou doesn't think you're in the clear just yet," Jay says cheerily, but the visitors to Mo's ranch weren't Russians after all. They were Ukrainian tourists who were looking to channel their inner Cossack with an adventure on horseback. "Mo quizzed them, and said they didn't like the Russian oligarchs any more than we do. Zhou says you can use your phone, and he'll keep his ear to the ground, or wherever he gets his information. Just be careful."

The Wongs and their guests are filing out into the courtyard, so I say a quick goodbye to Jay and find Wei-Lin. "Falun Gong," she announces reverentially. "Master Wu will lead us." I fall in the semicircle beside her, Wu taking a stance in the center. Again, we breathe in, stretch, breathe out, relax, and repeat with different positions, keeping the dharma wheel in front of us, over our heads, on both sides of our heads. Like all the *qigong* exercises I've learned, the Falun Gong sets focus on looking inside, calming the mind, and centering breath as we move energy through the body. I may be oblivious to *zhen, shan, and ren*, but I feel my anxieties melting away with the breathing exercises.

As we break, I ask Wu for time to talk, and we agree to an extended interview in the morning, after breakfast. I hurry to catch up with Wei-Lin, but she's huddled with Sherry, "preparing the guest rooms," John Wong says. Sadly, we each have our own room, leaving me only the sweet memory of my near-orgasmic lovemaking the night before. Tonight, without Wei-Lin, I will be released.

30. Catching up to Karma

After my now-routine morning stretch-stand-breathe-relax *qigong* meditation, I call Bradbury, presenting the prodigal reporter still recovering from a savage bop on the head. It's time to re-emerge. I'm on my way to Denver for a series of health tests, I tell him, and will be recuperating in Boulder for a few more weeks before returning to San Francisco. In the meantime, I've got a column for him – following up on the Falun Gong story.

"That's old news," Bradbury snorts gruffly. "What's that got to do with the new Trump world?" I assure him that the political connection, just one month after the Trump-Xi meeting in Florida, is solid, starting with a Kungfu champion who fought his way out of a Chinese labor camp, and is now part of a large cast of Chinese ex-pat dissidents at war with China's communist government, using art, music, and theater to draw millions of people around the world to the dramatizations of their persecution.

I rush on, explaining that today I interview an elder in the movement, a close friend of founder Li Hongzhi, and I expect him to elaborate on the situation in China, and how he and members of the performing troupe Shen Yun are being shadowed and harassed in the United States. Bradbury has stopped grumbling, listening in the silence until I wrap up. "I trust you'll bring it around to U.S.-China policy, and Trump," he says finally. "Listen: I'm not sure how you got off on this track, but finish it up and move on."

Bradbury is clearly agitated by the daily news and frustrated that I'm out of the loop on the nascent Trump administration. "He met with the damned Russians, the day after he fired the FBI director who

265

was investigating his connections with the Russians," he says, his voice exasperated as well as angry. It's not just the meeting in the Oval Office with Russian Prime Minister Sergei Lavrov and Ambassador Sergey Kislyak that is irritating Bradbury, but that "the media was not invited. We got the photo from Russia's official mouthpiece, *Tass*." This is astounding news, American journalists shut out of official government business, a development that increases my angst about Russians following me, another meddling media target. I tell Bradbury I'll follow the story by tracking down the Russian contact I met in Vegas, which, obviously, I'm not going to do. But it effectively ends our conversation.

My immediate task is to figure out the logistics of getting to Denver without a driver's license, and the delicate dance I must prepare with my sweet Wei-Lin. I will ask her to continue the journey with me – at least to Denver for now, and plan for future engagements. I can't get her out of my mind. She was in my dreams last night and my first thoughts this morning. Wei-Lin has become an obsession, maybe the most important person in my life, in a remarkably short journey of space and time.

Swiping through the months on my calendar, I reconstruct dates of events, amazed it's been just over two months since I left San Francisco with a new paramour, Annamarie Scott. I've traveled nearly 1,500 miles but even further in my head, leaving Annamarie and another life behind – aside from the employer who still takes my calls. I'm not sure where the Wei-Lin adventure will take me, if anywhere, and I'm no closer to understanding what George has in store for me, if anything. I call him, but he doesn't respond, probably leery of the unfamiliar number. I leave a voice message: I'm on my way; we need to talk.

A soft rap on the bedroom door; it's Wei-Lin, inviting me to breakfast. She is again dressed in dark workout pants but also in a pale pink sweatshirt with three Chinese characters above her left breast. I take a guess: *zhen, shan, ren?* I ask, pointing to the characters. She beams. "Yes!" she exclaims. "You're learning the language of Falun Gong!" Truthfulness. Compassion. Tolerance. It's a typical set of commandments, all focused on getting along with other people.

My phone rings, George calling back, and I hold up my index finger to Wei-Lin, signaling, "one minute," nod and close the door. "I'd given up looking for you," George says, "but I thought you'd be at my doorstep by now." I don't try to explain how my phone silence was part of a subterfuge to dodge Russian and Chinese agents, and Las Vegas drug dealers; too complicated even if I understood it. I give him the quick roundabout, still recovering from losing my phone and getting hit on the head, but maybe falling in love with a beautiful, sensual Chinese dancer who wants me to convert to Falun Gong.

"Whoa!" George exclaims, chortling at my exuberance. "Slow down," he says. "Are you okay?" I'm not sure, but I'm excited about being on the final leg of my trip, I tell him. I'm seeing Mona in Denver next week and should be in Boulder before the week is out. This news pleases George, who eagerly suggests he'll come to Denver, to meet Mona and guide me to his hilltop abode. Perfect, except for the details. I promise to call him once I've got a fix on the timing.

Arriving at the breakfast table, I apologize for my delay and take a seat across from Wei-Lin, who is flanked by Wu and Lou Guy, apparently still guarding the body as he watches me intently. Wu is nodding and listening to Billy, who is commanding the table with his news. "It's an opportunity, more than a job," he is saying. "I know

267

the pay isn't much, but it's a step up. And I get paid to do what I love to do."

Wu is being asked his opinion, as the family guru, if Billy, still grounded at home with his mother after two years at the Taos campus of the University of New Mexico, should interview for a job in Colorado, a nearly three-hour drive to Pueblo. A children's museum at the Sangre de Cristo Arts Center is looking for a stage manager for its theater, Billy's passion. He's self-confidently explaining how he built sets and helped stage Taos theater group productions at Kit Carson Museum. "If I get the job, I'll get a place and come back for Nina," he says, turning to Sherry. "First, we get married here, Mom, and celebrate."

Sherry is nodding and appears to have been expecting this morning news, saying "Good news!" to Nina, who at that moment is entering from the kitchen carrying a steaming egg concoction laced with vegetables. "Tortillas coming," she says sweetly, placing the dish on the table. She is well aware of the conversation. "I am very happy for Billy … and me …us," she beams before turning to retrieve the blue corn tortillas.

"You should follow your heart always," Wu says, nodding solemnly at Sherry. "Pueblo is not so far away. The young people know their hearts' desires, so I say do it." He addresses Nina, who has settled into the chair on the other side of Billy: "You have many talents, Miss Nina. The Wongs will miss your cooking, but you are also a good daughter."

The marriage is blessed, and I gradually realize as we celebrate over breakfast that Billy's opportunity may be my good fortune, a ride to Colorado – to Pueblo, in fact, where I promised Sparrow I would stop and visit her brother, a witch doctor, a shaman. What was his name? I will have to find his card. Meanwhile, I try to catch Wei-Lin's eyes as I calculate how I ask her to come with me to Denver, to meet my daughter. Do I mention Mona? No, too soon.

And too fast. Billy is ready to go. The interview in Pueblo is tomorrow afternoon, and he's got the pickup truck gassed and tuned for an early morning departure. He's amenable, maybe even excited, for a hitchhiking companion, and the Wongs welcome the news. I'm pleased but nonplussed by the lack of reaction from Wei-Lin, who shows no surprise or concern that I'm leaving. I'll need a good opening and an ardent pitch to get her to run away with me, but not now. Wu signals he's ready for the interview, and soon is guiding me toward the courtyard, confiding, "Master Li sends his greetings. He says you are U.S. expert on Falun Dafa."

I can't help but laugh and protest: I only report on what experts say; I'm no expert. But I'm interested in Falun Gong, I tell him. I still don't understand how a *qigong* exercise, breathing, and meditation, can inspire such hostility from China's communist regime. What do they have to fear from a moral code – *zhen shan ren*, truthfulness, compassion, and tolerance – that teaches respect for other people?

"The Chinese government is none of these things," Wu says as he takes a seat at a table under the bald cypress tree. The late-morning sun is ideal light for my smartphone photography, and I circle Wu, slowly clicking shots before taking a seat opposite him, and turning on my recorder. He leans forward, spreading his hands for emphasis, "Falun Gong teaches we must cultivate the spirit, free ourselves of human notions. No more desires for things, for fame, or any selfish thoughts. Or be a slave to things, to a state that tries to control what we think and do."

As Wu explains it, the goal of Falun Dafa is to elevate *xinxing*, human nature, to a higher plane, to be one with the universe. That's a place greater than the state. For China's autocratic leaders, this is apostasy. The communist ideology is paramount, and any belief system that challenges it is dangerous – particularly if 100 million people flock to it. "To cultivate *xinxing*," Wu says, pressing his hand to his chest and shaking his head, "we reject ideas like communism."

Wu's mention of "cultivation" reminds me of how Wei-Lin used the term to describe our union – "dual cultivation," she said. I ask Wu what that term means to him. "Not good," he says, shaking his head. "Master Li write about this. It is false, not real cultivation of true nature. This is not the way to virtue, just more human failing. Master Li say, 'do not fool yourself.'"

I was fooled, apparently, if this is true. Wei-Lin presented our meditative love-making as a lesson from Falun Gong, a religious experience. Would she knowingly violate a stricture of the Falun Dafa? I stand and walk away from Wu, taking a breath and clearing my head, turn to snap another photo, and then walk slowly back to my seat. I can't shake the image of Wei-Lin naked, straddling my lap. What does Falun Dafa teach about sex and sexual activity? I ask.

Wu considers me for a moment without answering, quietly disapproving of this departure from his lesson. "If you mean we don't allow homosexuals, that is not true," he says finally, although that's not what I mean. "Maybe you hear people who criticize us, but they are wrong. We welcome gay people." Here Wu pauses and stands up, wringing his hands gently in front of him as he continues. "Too much interest in sex in U.S.," he says, extending his arms and turning his hands palm down. "It is proper in marriage, families. That is all. More distraction from *zhen, shan, ren*. It is lust, not love."

I can't help but see a puritanical view of sex akin to evangelical Christianity, with a strict-constructionist view of the Bible, or whatever holy book. Li Hongzhi has written more than 50 publications or lectures, including the introductory text, "Falun Gong," which I've read. Wu slowly brings me up to speed on the philosophy behind the movement, citing Li's "Zhuan Falun." Believers must continually work to rid themselves of the mundane attachments of their lives, he says, to elevate their nature, *xinxing*, to the nature of the universe. According to Falun Dafa, our spirits are on a path of continual rebirth, and we control that path through our actions. We must overcome karma to elevate ourselves, he says.

Wu uses "karma" to mean a constant negative force, without a redeeming quality, a departure from the meaning I understand – the result of any action, good or bad. Is there no good karma? Wu's description of karma reminds me of how Christians describe "original sin," something you are born with and must work off with good deeds. Wu confirms this view: You inherit karma from previous lives, and if you don't shed it, you pass it along in future lives. The only path is to rid yourself of human attachments, he says, by adhering to *zhen shan ren*.

As Wu explains it, acting according to these principles of Falun Dafa lessens the karmic weight on your spirit and improves your chances of being reborn to a higher order. Christians don't believe in reincarnation, of course, although it's a staple of many Eastern religions. As Wu explains it, Falun Gong is, at heart, a religious belief system similar to Buddhism, while incorporating traditional Taoist principles and practices, such as *qigong*.

Wu is becoming impatient with my ignorance of Falun Dafa, so I try to guide the conversation away from the philosophical weeds I've

271

stumbled into. I tell him I'd like to know more about the politics of the spiritual movement in the United States, and its ongoing persecution from Chinese agents who follow the Shen Yun performers from city to city. What does Falun Gong expect to achieve with Shen Yun?

"We tell story, expose lie of China, communism evil rule," Wu says. "Not just Shen Yun and art of *zhen shan ren*. We have newspaper, *Epoch Times*, video, Internet shows. We are heard." He acknowledges that he serves as the liaison for Li Hongzhi to editors of *The Epoch Times*, and an instigator for new media content. "We have new ways to talk to world on Internet," he says. "We see numbers, people watch and listen, and learn."

Wu won't name specific websites, except for *Epoch Times*, saying, "we just start social media, but many see us." I grab my phone and google *Epoch Times*, begging Wu's pardon. I see a different newspaper than the one I read a decade ago, which was focused heavily on criticizing China's leadership and communist doctrine. Instead, I'm looking at a banner headline heralding Trump on his trip to Jerusalem – "a new savior for the Mideast," it announces. Jesus!

How is it that Falun Gong is such a big fan of Donald Trump? I ask. "He will help China return to people," Wu answers quickly. "He challenge China rulers. He is for freedom." I suggest, diplomatically, that many believe Trump's trade war with China is driven by self-interested economics. He's not interested in the Falun Gong movement or the people being held in Chinese labor camps. The intent is to get a more favorable trade advantage for U.S. businesses.

Wu objects to my analysis but keeps his smile and manner at ease while he insists that Trump is an important ally of their movement, someone who will fight for freedom everywhere. I quickly retreat to nodding, surprised by this rapturous view of the 45th president of the United States, the self-aggrandizing and still untested Donald J. Trump. As Wu tells it, the Falun Dafa movement is fully in Trump's camp. "We have office in D.C., we tell our story there, and President invite us to news conference."

How is Falun Gong using the Internet to promote this vision of Donald Trump? I ask, getting a generalized statement about social media and viral posts on Facebook and YouTube, nothing specific. I will need to do more research, bookmarking the *Epoch News* site. That evening I discover something called "Beauty of Life," an international organization connected to *Epoch News* and its parent New Tang Dynasty, as well as to numerous pro-Trump Facebook pages and Twitter accounts.

Who's *not* engaged in manipulating the U.S. political system? The Russians apparently meddled in the election, and the FBI director was fired for investigating. Both the Chinese government and Chinese dissidents are creating social media platforms to influence public opinion. The Internet is a teeming hive of disparate messages and likely disinformation. And Falun Gong is part of the noise, maybe as dissonant as WikiLeaks. And now I feel like I'm being "guided" to a story they want me to tell. That's not going to work, no matter how compelling the philosophy or how sweet the lure.

31. Mind Games

Wei-Lin is away all afternoon, shopping for new clothes with Sherry. I'm reminded how ragged I've become on this journey, lugging a backpack and a small bag of personal effects and having neither the time nor the opportunity to replenish supplies. Denver provides an opportunity for rejuvenation, maybe even a haircut. But first, I must talk with Wei-Lin, to see where we stand in the light of the revelations from Wu, and her own reserve toward me. I'm leaving in the morning, and I don't know her intentions. Is this goodbye?

What's waiting for me in Pueblo, if anything? I retrieve the card that Sparrow gave me in Winslow: *Curly Wolf, Shaman.* I punch the number into my phone and hear one short ring before a woman's pleasant voice, "Doctor Wolf's office." Dr. Wolf? Curly Wolf is a doctor-shaman? A witch doctor? I learn he's with a patient. Would I like an appointment? I've been referred to Dr. Wolf by his sister, who gave me his card, I say. I will be in Pueblo tomorrow and would like to meet him. I leave my name and number, and within 10 minutes, Curly Wolf is on the phone.

"Hello, Mr. James," he says. "You have a message from my little bird?" No message, I tell him, but she says Curly Wolf, the shaman, can help me. He laughs. "She held on to that card? It's been years."

Curly Wolf, aka Carlos Wolf, explains that he's a clinical psychiatrist at the Colorado State Mental Health Institute in Pueblo, with enough autonomy to work me into his schedule the next day. He's not surprised that Sparrow is managing horseback rides at a ranch, but admits he hasn't seen her in several years. Curly got off the reservation early, with a scholarship to Arizona State University and the Mayo Clinic School of Medicine, then graduate studies at the University of New Mexico Health Research Center. He last saw Sparrow in 2014 on a visit to the reservation before moving to Pueblo to take his current position. That's when he was passing out the cards to his Navajo friends, as a joke, the young doctor making a bow to the old tradition.

I'm on doctor's orders to give up alcohol, I tell him, and Sparrow and her friends taught me how to cope using internal martial arts and meditation. But Sparrow doesn't think I was getting it, based on our push-hands exercises, and her keen senses. She put her hand on my chest and told me my heart wasn't into it, and I don't know what she meant. The doctor emits a low "hmmmmm," and tells me he's happy to meet me. We make an appointment for lunch the next day. "Are you still drinking?" he asks. I haven't had a chance to think about alcohol for more than a month, but eventually, I will, I admit.

With a few hours until dinner, I sit down with my laptop and take a first stab at drafting a Falun Gong story that has become more amorphous the more I learn about it. I turn on the tape recorder and let it run, Wu's halting English prodding my exposition. I'm less enamored with the philosophy now that I've heard the tenets, even if sympathetic to the plight of a persecuted group. There's only one villain here, even if the Falun Gong movement is idiosyncratic and absolutist. I can't overlook the fact that the Falun Dafa principle of *ren*, tolerance, or forbearance, doesn't appear to brook any deviation in behavior, which is not tolerant at all. There's always karma to pay.

And what about Wei-Lin's violation of the first Golden Rule, *zhen*, truthfulness? What am I to make of her conjugal dalliance with me, and especially the metaphysical, sexual ceremony that apparently runs counter to the teachings of Li Hongzhi. I'm not deluded enough

275

to believe she was succumbing to my charms. She was in charge of the encounter, teaching me, and leading me to fall for her. Was I being played?

This question gnaws into the narrative I'm trying to develop with my "Falun Gong story." Two hours later, I've got notes and fragments of a story, nothing I can write home about. Bradbury's stern dismissal of my adventures rings in my ears. I need to develop the Trump angle. Maybe Bradbury will buy the story of an Internet campaign by an outlawed Chinese interest group to woo the new president. I'll need to work it as the American political story of Falun Gong rather than the China political story of political persecution. I make a few quick notes on research. I flesh out the story before joining my hosts for dinner.

A revelation is served with dinner that further complicates the story – and my uncertain relationship with Wei-Lin. Once again, I arrive after everyone has claimed their seats. As I approach, it's John Wong who greets me – with a goodbye. "We're sorry to see you go so soon, Mr. James," he says. "Everyone is leaving us tomorrow, sadly for Sherry and me. We've enjoyed your visit."

I thank the Wongs for their hospitality and assure them I will be in touch. Wei-Lin is studying me with those smiling eyes as I take my seat. I ask her if she's going to Chicago to catch up with her troupe, and she shakes her head slowly, the smile broadening. It's Wu who answers: "Wei-Lin is going with me," he says. "Lou Guy, too. We all go to Dragon Springs."

Dragon Springs is the secretive, heavily guarded compound in New York state, where Li Hongzhi has built a small community around a Buddhist temple. For Wu, it's home, and he sees Wei-Lin fitting in along with Lou Guy. "We have two schools, one trains Shen Yun performers," he says. Wei-Lin will be teaching? "Yes! Yes, I hope," she says excitedly. That is not decided, apparently, because Wu is considering her for another job. I learn this news later as I walk with Wei-Lin to the Ranchos de Taos plaza, finally finding a chance to talk.

She explains how her dream of teaching dance at Dragon Springs may be foiled by Wu's scheme to install her in Washington to help lobby the new administration. "We fly tomorrow to D.C., first stop," she tells me. "I will meet the director of the Falun Dafa International office, maybe interview for a job." Wu's first priority is to beef up the D.C. office; and he sees her as "a diplomat, ha-ha," she says dismissively. I'm not surprised by his judgment, I tell her, given her obvious charm and fluency in English, her ability to persuade Americans about Falun Gong. This is my opening.

"You persuaded me that 'dual cultivation' is a teaching of Falun Dafa, and now I learn that's not true," I say. "I'm disappointed about that." Wei-Lin's reaction is swift and loud – a cry, "No!" She grabs my arm, alarm and pain in her eyes as we stop along the path, demanding to know what I said to Wu, assuming I had learned about her deception from him. No worries, I say. I didn't mention her at all in the interview. I only asked the question.

Tears quickly fill Wei-Lin's eyes, a soft blush on her cheeks. She takes my hands and looks pleadingly into my eyes. "I know I made a mistake; I wanted to please you," she says. "Eventually, I will pay." Tears are now streaming down her cheeks; I put my arms around her and assure her that our spiritual commingling should not be condemned, or denied. Her voice is calm in reply: "But I never said it was a teaching of Falun Dafa. I said it was a Taoist practice. Buddhist,

Hindu, Tibetan, Asian culture. Master Li says no, it is 'fooling yourself.' "

There's that term again, Wu's explanation to me, Li's dictum not to fool yourself. Wei-Lin knew exactly what she was doing; she says as much without speaking the lie. She yielded to the opportunity of seduction, to exercise her power over me, which I readily ceded to a lovely, desirable woman who apparently cares enough about me to risk the scourge of karma. I'm charmed that she melded her body and mind with mine, an unforgettable moment, more satisfying to me than any divine relationship based on *zhen, shan,* and *ren,* even without the orgasm.

But I'm not sure we have a relationship at all, given the circumstances and temporality, barely two months removed from that exquisite moment of *tuina* truth when she thrilled me with her soft, firm hands. Then reappearing to lead me to a sexual adventure, holding me in thrall nose-to-nose, engorged with heat and spunk. Wei-Lin is otherwise a stranger to me. I know her through my association with Jay Lee, and the friends he's gathered around me. He's the one who pointed to her as the way to continue my inquiry into Falun Gong.

I bid Wei-Lin adieu later that night, promising to call and write. She returns the promise with a hand-holding, tender yet Dafa-respectful goodbye, an all-too-brief parting hug. Now, as I return to my task considering how to recast the Falun Gong piece, I see an obvious stumbling block to telling the story. Can I tell a story about the object of my affection who may soon be in league with the object of my scorn, the 45th president of the United States? Of course not. I couldn't keep my balance dancing around that. Instead, she must be incidental, the artist and *qigong* devotee spreading the gospel of Falun

278

Gong through Shen Yun. If she becomes a lobbyist for the organization, I may learn more. For now, my focus is on Wu's commentary, and the trail of online nuggets and threads tying Falun Gong's mission and media to promoting Trump.

I google late into the night before nodding off, dreaming I'm flying across the plains astride a horse, wind whipping my hair and the horse's mane. Suddenly I see Sparrow beside me, signaling to follow her as she haws toward a rocky hill, slowing her horse as we climb. I bring my steed to a trot as I trail after the expert horsewoman, watching her guide her horse with arms and hips, her rear waddling in the saddle, her thighs caressing the animal's back. Admiring her technique and grace, I'm moving with the rhythm. Before long, we reach a ridge overlooking an immense expanse of the canyon and the outline of a river running far below. The stunning beauty of this majestic scene illuminates the glowing visage of my companion, who is dismounting. I join her, putting my arm around her shoulder, feeling her warmth against me. She turns to face me and puts her hand on my chest, as she'd done at the end of our last ride. She's still smiling as she pushes me backward, and I'm falling, falling into the void, kicking and flailing my arms.

As usual, I wake up before I hit the ground, but I toss and turn for the next hour, unable to shake the image of Sparrow's sardonic smile, until the light is peeking through the blinds, and I climb out of bed. It's going to be a big day. I begin the final leg of my trip with shaman analysis from Dr. Curly Wolf, and I'll need to work out the details to get to Denver. Mona has texted her schedule; she's arriving in Colorado later today. I'll call her from the road.

Breakfast is just for me, Billy, and Nina, who is preparing huevos rancheros when I arrive at the table. "Mom and John took Mr. Wu and your friends to the airport," Billy explains. "They have an early flight out." Wei-Lin had prepared me for missing her, so I'm not surprised, but I express regret for missing the chance to say goodbye. "You will just have to come back," Billy responds.

Behind the wheel of his pickup truck, Billy is talkative and forthcoming, describing how he had wandered across the country, "lost and loaded," before finally returning to his mother's side. He never knew his father, and Sherry apparently has been less than forthcoming about a man she never married. "I've always felt rootless, even after settling in with Mom and John ... and Nina, who is the best thing that ever happened to me," he says, part of a nonstop breeze through his vagabond years and settlement in New Mexico, then the discovery of community theater, his nuts-to-soup involvement with local productions, the excitement of taking his passion to the next level – all a prelude to his main point.

"I've never really interviewed for a job," he says finally. "I want to make a good impression, but I'm not sure how to act, what to expect." Yes, he needs my advice. I interview people for a living, but I'm not hiring any of my subjects, or sources. I give him the critical pieces: understand what they want, then explain how you fit in, and what makes you especially good for the job. Experience helps, if you've done similar work at a high level. Show that you collaborate well, and can both follow instructions and contribute suggestions. Keep an even temper. Smile. Be prepared for any question, but think before you answer. Ask a question yourself, to clarify, or just to think about your response. Have questions, take an interest. The interview goes both ways: You're finding out about them as they're finding out about you.

Billy admits he doesn't know much about the job, just the posting – creative stage manager for a children's theater. "Some personnel guy at the Sangre de Cristo art center called to set up the interview. They have my resume, but I have to show them more. Maybe I should put on a show." I laugh and warn him not to go overboard. But they're looking for creativity, so it won't hurt to spin a story. Imagine the staging of a nursery rhyme, for instance, something kids would enjoy. That's the audience, so he needs to think about the kids.

This suggestion pleases Billy, and he's beaming as he rattles off a few experimental pieces, based on productions he worked on at the Kit Carson theater. I excuse myself to make a few phone calls, leaving him to sort through childhood plays in silence, except for the soft humming to himself. I call George first, to tell him I'm on my way and to check his schedule. No answer, leave a message. Mona is at the San Francisco airport, waiting for her flight, and Maddie is already in Denver, in meetings. She says Denver Health has agreed to let her consult, and she will arrange an appointment for me, with 24-hour notice. I tell her I'll be there in a few days.

I automatically dial Bradbury's number, then end the call before it rings. I'm not ready to face an inquisition on my formative story of Falun Gong's embrace of Trump's presidency. I call Jay instead. He owes me a few answers. He is cheerful, and glad to hear I'm safe. Was I ever in danger, I want to know. "Zhou thinks so; he's been worried about you," Jay says. "But, you know, he's conflicted. He blames himself that your friend was killed. And he says there's still a lot of Chinese and Russian chatter around you."

I tell Jay that Wei-Lin and Lou Guy are on their way to the Falun Gang retreat in New York. Does he know Wu? A pause before Jay answers. "I've never met him. But he called me, on behalf of Lou

Guy. They're friends. I didn't know about Wei-Lin. I thought she was coming home to LA, maybe after Chicago. What is she going to do in New York?" That's not clear, I tell him, but Wu wants her to work for Falun Gong, maybe to teach Shen Yun performance.

Jay sounds genuinely disappointed that Wei-Lin won't be joining him and May-Lee at the studio, quietly dispelling a notion I entertained that he is in on a Falun Gong plot to cultivate a *San Francisco Chronicle* reporter. I've been suspicious that my Taos hosts are familiar with my articles, and how they've presented the practice and religious philosophy very artfully to me, for publication. But Jay has criticized the religious zealotry of the sect, even as he teaches the underlying Taoist theories and internal arts. Now he says, "I hope Wei-Lin doesn't get too caught up in the Falun Gong cult," which he compares to the esoteric Buddhist sect he walked away from in San Francisco, with its devotion to *feng shui*.

After saying goodbye to Jay, promising to be in touch, I quiz Billy about his connection to Falun Gong and the U.S.-based arts and religious movement challenging China's regime. His only connection, he tells me, is love for his mother and respect for Wong and his work. "I've learned a lot about creative expression from them," he says, "how to translate things from your heart. They encouraged me to pursue the theater work, even though it never paid much."

Billy says he knows nothing about the teachings of Li Hongzhi, or Chinese philosophy in general, but was impressed with Gaosan Wu, whom he'd never met. "He is an important man; you can tell by the way he carries himself, very self-assured," he says. "Mom was thrilled when she heard he was coming, and Lou Guy … she told me about him, how he fought his way out of a Chinese prison camp. So, it was a big occasion. And it all came together for me too."

Back on a roll, Billy continues his breathless monologue for the next 50 miles, until my phone rings. It's George, who says he's unable to meet me in Denver because he's been invited to speak at a retreat in the mountains – at Red Feather Lakes, about 100 miles north of Boulder. He wants me to meet him there. "This came up suddenly; I really couldn't pass it up," he says. "I think it's fortunate for us … a peaceful place to meditate and reconnect." The site is the Shambhala Mountain Center, a Tibetan Buddhist preserve founded by a Tibetan lama who also founded Naropa University, where George teaches. "You'll enjoy the Stupa, and the blue-eyed Buddha who presides. Many of my students are here," he says.

Why not? Travelling to see my guru has been a long and winding road to his point. Naturally, I have more mountains to climb before I find him.

32. On the Road with Curly Wolf

Billy drops me off at Burrito's Betty, near the mental institute, an entry to meet my doctor shaman. Billy is fidgety and nervous, so I encourage him to find a quiet place to sit and think since he's got time before his interview – to take notes about what he wants to say and what questions to ask. I reassure him he's the man for the job, and we trade phone numbers before I climb down out of the truck and grab my meager portable possessions. Wishing him luck in his new start-up life with Nina, I wave goodbye and look for a quiet place to sort things out for myself while I wait for Curly Wolf.

Around the side of the stone building, I find an old wooden bench to sit and stew, thinking about the story I will tell about Falun Gong. I want to believe Wei-Lin is still in my life, despite the evidence to the contrary, and her character in the article is slowly coming together in my head. I have to be honest with myself about this situation. She is part of a story that found me, and not vice versa. I wonder if I'm being cultivated in more ways than one.

Wu and his Master Li clearly see me as a sympathetic messenger who can help elevate Falun Gong as a political player in the United States. They'd like to see me portray the organization as a righteous force in league with the new American president, who is threatening a trade war with their archenemy, the Communist regime in China. Wei-Lin could end up driving the lobbying effort, given her intelligence and charm, even if she'd rather be teaching Shen Yun performance art. Jay and May-Lee would be her third choice, and then maybe she'd consider me.

Unlike with Annamarie, whose sudden flight left me anguished and blue, Wei-Lin's departure is bittersweet and sad, but not the end of the world. We will continue to talk and write, and maybe I'll get a scoop, if not a *tuina* massage. But I could never accept a restrictive religion like Falun Dafa. Truthfulness, compassion, and tolerance are all fine principles of behavior. But excessive adherence to anything is stifling and exhausting to me.

I may be faithless to a fault, but I'm not immune to karma. It's easy for me to see Wei-Lin's departure, like Annamarie's abandonment, as payback for casual and sometimes downright hostile attitudes toward women, those who've loved me or expected more from me than lovemaking. Karma is a bitch, no matter how you define it. Whether my behavior dissolves my life's bad karma or gives me a new lease on good karma is irrelevant. The fact is its lunchtime at a Mexican restaurant, and I'm not even thinking about a margarita, or even a cerveza. Karma can be a blessing, whether you believe in it or not.

As cars roll in and out of the restaurant parking lot, I'm looking for someone who might be a Navajo doctor named Curly Wolf – imagining a big, strapping brave with long wavy hair, maybe tied in a ponytail. Would he be wearing a tie or a neckerchief? I have no idea how old he is, and I will not be able to guess when I see him. The man who gets out of the Jeep and walks toward me looks nothing like the imaginary Wolf in my mind. I stand to greet a bald man, lean and well-built but not much taller than Sparrow, and sporting a short, scruffy beard, jeans, a light jacket over a white T-shirt, and carrying a Colorado Rockies baseball cap. The legend on the T-shirt: Head Case. He is walking briskly, smiling broadly, and extending his hand.

"Mister James," he says, giving me his firm grip as he places the cap on his head with the other hand, covering his non-curly head.

Dr. Carlos Wolf, perhaps interpreting the amusement in my eyes, remarks: "You're probably wondering how a bald man came to be called Curly, aside from a sound-alike name. I decided to take control of my identity; this is me." With this oblique introduction, Wolf asks if we can skip lunch and take a drive. He insists that my breakfast should hold me until we get to our destination, which he does not disclose. But we're driving out of town.

"I spoke to Sparrow about you last night," he says as we angle toward the highway, heading north. "You impressed her, and she's not easy to impress. She says you have a heart problem." I rush to assure Wolf that I'm over that. I had some blockage, got overexcited, and passed out, but I'm taking anticoagulants to keep the blood flowing. He nods as he checks his mirror and changes lanes, speeding around a semi-truck. "I don't think that's what she was talking about," he says.

I recount my Tai Chi push-hands play with Sparrow, how she helped me synch my body with hers as we tried to sense each other's center of gravity through the light contact, admitting that it felt very intimate with Sparrow because of her extrasensory touch. She said my intention was good as far as my head goes, but that I needed to feel it inside, and she placed her hand over my heart. I understood her to mean the heart as an emotional center, not a physical or health issue.

"I'm sure Sparrow wouldn't ask me to see you for a physical problem," Wolf says. "She worries about how you're feeling – and I don't think she meant your sensitivity in Tai Chi, something else." Wolf pauses a moment, perhaps waiting for me to respond, but I have no explanation for Sparrow's feelings, or any speculation about my own. She's very sensitive, I say, and Wolf nods. "I think she was sensitive to your dealing with substance abuse, especially alcohol addiction," he says. "I think that's why she gave you my card, because I deal with patients trying to quit."

Just like Professor Cross, who offered specific behavioral tools for me when Annamarie and I visited him in Carmel, this psychologist at a Colorado state mental hospital has a specific treatment program. I ask if he, like my former professor, recommends a "rational recovery" strategy for addicts, or does he follow the more conventional Alcoholics Anonymous approach. He laughs with a sidelong glance at me. "No, I'm much more unconventional from a psychologist's point of view, although more traditional as a Navajo shaman. You'll see. I'll explain more when we get to our retreat."

My goal on this trip is a retreat, I tell him, identifying Red Feather Lake, north of Boulder, the Shambhala Mountain Center. "I know that area; we're not going that far. We'll be near Colorado Springs, a good jumping-off point, near Cheyenne Mountain. I have a cabin – a hogan, we call it – we'll crash there tonight. I can drive you to Denver tomorrow, if you like." Yes, that's perfect. I like this Dr. Wolf. He wants to be helpful, even if we're not sure what that is. I owe Sparrow a letter, at least, maybe a visit.

I tell Wolf my recent medical story, basically running away from health scares – a mild heart attack, liver damage, suspicious lung X-ray, and my determination to rid myself of alcohol dependency. Then a concussion, a blow on the head that put me out of commission for weeks. Sparrow and her hard-driving rancher friend were trying to toughen me up, with some success. I feel like I understand my weaknesses, at least, if I haven't fully conquered them. I'm learning a new way of looking at my body and my health, like in Tai Chi, on the path of a warrior.

Wolf looks at me sharply, a smile playing on his lips. "A warrior, eh," more a statement than a question. "I would expect as much from what Sparrow said about you. She thinks you have a special power. She wants me to help you tap into your potential." That makes me laugh. I'm just trying to overcome addiction, I say. I have an addictive personality.

"That's not really a psychological profile, you know," Wolf says. "You may have personality traits that make you more likely to become addicted, but it's not like an albatross you always carry around your neck. Genes can be a factor, but also who you associate with, and how you grew up. There is no addictive personality that rules your life. You have the power to change, and I can help you. That's why we're taking this little trip."

The trip so far has been pleasant enough, even instructive. I always assumed I was prone to addiction because of a personality flaw. Doctor Curly Wolf tells me all personalities are complex, with different traits that develop over time, or via genetics. I may be predisposed to certain addictions because of these traits, but they don't define a personality. I suppose I feel better about this, although the bottom line is the same. My propensity to drink too much alcohol, to troll for sex in the Tenderloin, to pop Ecstasy or snort coke to get a rush, and even my morning java, become part of me over time, even if not technically defining my personality. I am what I consume.

"Do you have problems with psychedelic drugs?" Wolf asks, seemingly out of the blue. No problems, I say, but it's been years since my few LSD trips in college. George was my guide on a camping trip

– I still remember freaking out over the animal noises that night. We were being stalked by a black bear, I was sure. I like the mild psychotropic stuff – marijuana and hashish – not getting too far out. I'm no acid head.

"I'm asking because they are part of my treatment – for addiction, PTSD, depression," Wolf says. "Specifically, mescaline and psilocybin." That's peyote and magic mushrooms, in the natural world, I know. I admit to some youthful dalliance with these psychotropics – alcohol and young women also were involved, so the drug-taking was part of a head-spinning bacchanalia. There may have been fireworks. I remember it was fun, no bummers.

That's nothing like the trip we'll take, Curly assures me, although he promises "it will be fun enough, an experience to remember." He reaches past me to fish in his glove box and pulls out a small, tin container with an "aspirin" label. Not aspirin, "two tabs of pure mescaline, extracted from the peyote cactus." These are produced for clinical research and treatment, he explains, and easier on the stomach than eating peyote buttons – but skipping lunch was a precaution. With about 20 minutes to go before we reach our destination, we begin the trip, washing down the drug with bottled water Curly brought for the occasion, pulled from a cooler full of provisions. I offer to pay for all his out-of-pocket costs, as well as for the treatment itself, which I will simply expense as "mental health."

"No, no," he insists. "This is a treat for me, as well, an invite from my sister to get back to my shaman roots. I'm happy Sparrow brought us together." Wolf says he left the reservation before actually studying shamanism, "but I learned a lot about the sacraments, particularly peyote. It was a big part of my education growing up, the ceremonies … and the visions." The experiences pushed him to become a psychologist. "I became the expert on mescaline and psilocybin experiments in school, because I'm Navajo. I've written about it; I'll send you links."

If Dr. Wolf is living his dream, then maybe I am too. I'm being driven up a mountain pass by a Navajo shaman trained in science and potions, on a trip to find the inner me, lost somewhere on the road. I think the mescaline is slowly kicking in as I feel the comfort of this envelope, the drone of the engine, the rocky crags and patches of green that speed past the window. I try to assure him I've begun to find myself, forced to live a more spartan, disciplined life. And I've been fortunate to have guides like Sparrow to help me navigate the rocky terrain.

"I expect you'll get a better sense of where you are and where you're going over the next 24 hours," Curly says. "We'll try to make this a good point of reference for you, but everything changes, all the time. You meet up with turning points; you have choices." He describes one such time for him, when he decided to lose his braids and shave his head. It happened when he was an undergraduate at Arizona State, fresh off the reservation and struggling to connect with students of other backgrounds who teased him because of his long hair, and the braids that got him the Curly nickname.

"I lured a small group of boys I knew into the desert for what I said would be an adventure, and gave them peyote," he says. It was a select and diverse group – a black and an Asian, both from California, a Latino from Tucson, a gangly white kid from Dallas, and an athletic multiracial boy from Las Vegas. They were all eager to take the peyote, several admitting it was their first time. "I wanted them to understand me better, but it became a big window on me. I was the only one in the group that was truly outside the community I was

290

trying to join," he says. "They saw me differently. I was the stranger in my own land."

Curly says he had a revelation that the traditions he proudly cultivated on the reservation, and things that were part of his identity, including his long hair, were unnecessary barriers in the social circles he hoped to enter. "I decided then; I made a big speech, I was cutting my long hair, and asked them to help. I had a hatchet in my backpack; they took turns whacking at my braids – not too close," he says with a laugh. A few years later, when he was going off to medical school in New Mexico, he shaved it all off. "I reclaimed myself, took control of my identity. But I kept the nickname, Curly. People remember me."

I laugh at the subterfuge – turning the mocking of his classmates into an entry to their clique, or to the academic and social world he desired, the next step for young Carlos Wolf, Curly. I can feel the happy glow of the mescaline and a warmth toward my new friend, but I'm troubled by the ease with which he abandons the traditions of his tribe, as an escape mechanism. I ask him if this sacrificial scalping was worth it. Has he gained the acceptance that he sought?

"Oh yeah. It was what I needed to do to move on," he says. "We all move on, and we have choices. I'm satisfied with mine. We'll take a look at yours. We will have time to explore." Wolf turns onto a gravel road that winds up the hill, and I take a deep breath as I feel the Jeep absorb the shock of the new terrain. All my choices are suspect, I think. I don't know where to begin. But this looks like the place: We pull into a space in front of what appears to be a giant adobe wigwam, except it has five sides -- pentangular – and a rounded roof topped by a chimney vent, awaiting stoking of wood into embers. A safe place.

291

33. Déjà vu Do

Curly's hogan, with specific dimensions and orientation toward the sun, has creature comforts like a hardwood floor and an abundance of cushions for sitting and sleeping, along with the woodstove in the center of the structure. Before we get comfortable, he needs my help to haul a propane tank out back where a small shed houses a generator "for minor electrical use – charge your phone, maybe," Wolf says. "I also brought music, for later."

Most importantly, the generator provides juice for the light in the privy, which is set away from the hogan, but not too far. I explore it with much trepidation as the landscape begins to move around me, advancing creepy, crawly creatures I dodge gingerly. Inside, I find a hanging cord attached to the light switch that illuminates the pungent, faded brown interior and the plastic toilet seat. I push it up, open my fly, and point a stream of urine into the dark hole, thinking I'll want to avoid grains or other diuretics that may move my bowels tonight. I'll take my chances that psychedelic plants won't cause a purge.

The biggest chore at the moment is navigating through the lizards and crocodiles. So much teeming life in the brush and in my mind – not a total freak-out since I've been in these weeds before, and I've got a competent guide, even a certified one. Curly seems almost reverential as he describes how Colorado set aside this teeming property, part of the Cheyenne Mountain State Park, as a base for treatments, and retreats, conducted by the mental hospital. "These mountains were a refuge for Cheyenne and Arapaho, and you'll see why," Curly says. "We'll follow the trail up this ridge, down into the valley where the Rock Creek flows."

I register a small protest about the galloping hallucinations I'm experiencing: I'm not sure I can climb on rocks. Curly sympathizes, telling me that he himself is seeing visions, "but I recognize they're not dangerous. They're helpful. We'll sort 'em out." He retrieves two walking sticks for bracing ourselves in the uneven terrain and packs bottled water into a small gunny sack that he slings over his shoulder. "We'll go slow," he says. "It's not far. We can use these sticks to ward off the demons."

I follow Curly up a trail past jagged rocks right and left, poking the terrain ahead with my stick – gingerly at first, then with more authority as I gain my explorer stride, faithfully following in the footsteps of the natives and their worthy descendent, my scout Wolf. Curly has the easy outdoor manner of a man who has spent his life wandering the Colorado River plateau, which extends from the base of these Rocky Mountains to the Grand Canyon, encompassing the homes of many tribes. He turns to make sure I'm keeping up and points to a thatch of shimmering shrubs.

"Juniper," he says. "Rocky Mountain juniper. We'll collect the dry brush on the way back. Good for kindling, chasing away evil spirits." This statement, presented as a basic campfire lesson, is hilarious to me, and I burst into a hearty laugh that I contain awkwardly as Curly waves his hand and turns to wade further up the hill. "The seed cones add flavor to our mushroom tea," Curly talking over his shoulder as he moves ahead. Mushroom tea, yes. I'm feeling buoyant as I two-step around a huge toad, it's sandstone camouflage betrayed by the bulging of its neck and eyes. Mescal vision, I assure myself. The creature shrinks before my eyes.

I hear the gurgle and splash before we top the rise. We look down to a rolling stream pushed along by a waterfall at the top of the next rise. "That's where we're going," Curly says, pointing to the distant waterfall. "It's not too far. We follow the creek." The kaleidoscopic beauty of the scene in front of me overpowers any fearful image, bright greens and reds sparkling in a sea of elegant blues and grays, a palette balanced in the radiant sunshine and the clear mountain air. Cheerful birdsong fills the air, and gnarly tree limbs appear to be waving to us, beckoning to me. I'm filled with a sense of well-being and vitality, part of a bright verdant scene, in step with all the life in front of me. The world is incredible from this lofty altered perspective, and I'm glorying in it, striding gleefully into the journey, punching the ground with my walking stick as I match Curly's sure-footed pace.

We make our way along the cleared creek bank, a state park preservation project apparently, along with the restored creekbed that is framed by large stones seemingly perfectly placed, splattering water playfully as it gurgles through the canyon, running all the way. My head spins, suddenly overwhelmed with the wondrous possibilities of human engineering. I call out to Curly as I stop, bending over, hands on knees, studying the ground. Wow! Another piece of nature harnessed, another mind-blowing vision. "Where are we going?" I ask myself aloud.

"Just around this bend up here, Mr. James," says Curly, providing a partial answer. I shake my head. I seem to be entering into a microcosmic relationship with the environment. "The mesc is working its magic. Just up here," he says, pointing the way. "We can sit and enjoy it." I follow him, sheepishly now, keenly aware of the lurking Mescalito, Don Juan's god of this Otherworld, looking over my shoulder. The water is falling through a rainbow of sunlight, the shimmery spray leaping from the pool below. I join Curly on a rocky perch beside the pool.

"The waterfall is a powerful spiritual symbol for Navajo, a place where the Great Spirit can appear, and reveal yourself," Curly says, inviting me to breathe deep from air splashing our way, "like the breath of the almighty," he says. "Do you feel it?" Sure, in my condition, it's easy to conjure the vision suggested by my guide. The sparkly fresh spray is borne through the air; I can feel it, whether it's a natural or supernatural effect. I enjoy a shiver down my spine.

Navajo philosophy and religious tradition, handed down through the ages, is grounded in the natural world, Curly says. "*Nilch'i*. That's our word for air, or the wind, one of the four elements – water, fire, air, and earth. *Nilch'i*, listen. You can hear the sound of the wind rushing by in the word, *nilch'i*." The Navajo learn that *nilch'i* also is everywhere, including inside you, he says. "It's a cosmic energy that the shaman can tap into, and can use to heal."

I'm blown away by the coincidence, and I tell Curly: Your concept of air or wind representing cosmic energy is similar to the Chinese concept of *qi*, and even has the same sound, the aspirated "ch'ee." And the four elements of the Navaho also hold symbolic meaning in the Chinese Taoist philosophy. He nods vigorously.

"Many similar traditions across cultures," he says. "That's what I learned from Carl Jung, studying at the university, the 'collective unconscious' that informs human myths and social interactions." Also, Native American ancestors come from Asia, he adds, citing archeological information based on genetic testing. He's excited enough about the kinship that he's read, *Tao De Ching*. "The Chinese *tao* is like *hózhó* for the Navajo, a spiritual path," he says. "The work of the shaman is to help people find this way to balance their *nilch'i* with the energy around them, to find harmony and beauty, the way, *hózhó.*"

Curly holds up his index finger, points at me, and asks, "What's the one most important thing in your life?" I don't have a ready answer; not sure I've ever thought about it in those terms. I shrug. I suppose it's my work, I tell him. It's my station in life, my job: reporting about current events, and giving my perspective on the news. I'm not just working for the paycheck; it feels like a mission. "What do you hope to accomplish?" I don't know. Save the world? That's what my friend George said, mocking me. It's a noble cause, journalism. And I like to write. It's what I do: communicate.

"What about your friends and family? How do they fit in?" Curly probes. Aside and after the fact, I say. I'm a lone wolf, just my daughter who's waiting for me in Denver and an old, best friend I'll see at Red Feather Lakes. I just lost a good friend, killed in Las Vegas, and long ago, a brother who died too young. Then my associates – including Jay, who's become a friend, perhaps a teacher, too. I have regular playmates, and very few close relationships, but I'm looking for someone, a soul mate. I tell him about Annamarie and Wei-Lin, admitting that Sparrow also gave me heart palpitations. My love life is fallow, but I want to cultivate it for a late bloom, hope springing eternal.

Curly listens quietly and impassively as I condense the story of my life – as I imagine it, a journalist free to travel the world to cover people and events that touch the lives of hundreds of thousands of readers each day, meeting new people and polishing his prose. Not just a newshound, but an erudite cultural and political critic, with a human touch. I'm pretty high, obviously, laying it on thick, but Curly

296

is facilitating as he hears me out. He finally interrupts to ask, "How have your alcohol and other substance abuses affected your work or your relationships?" Ah, yes, the shaman is focused like a laser on the head case before him.

"You don't need to answer now, but think about it," Curly suggests, instructing me to gaze into the water, the sunlit spray falling and splattering in a dancing rainbow of hues made increasingly vivid by the mescaline, and the conjuring of a shaman. "Your life isn't too far removed from what you see there, the collision of water and air," he says. At Curly's suggestion, the refracted image of the waterfall now seems to reflect billions of molecules circulating in the spray, energized by the fireball above, dancing and skittering in the late afternoon sun, and I'm conscious of being grounded here on the fourth element, this rock, which supports the bundle of spinning molecules that is me, flesh and blood bubbling in Mother's magic cauldron.

The natural order of things is moving and evolving all around me, and I'm feeling in tune with an elegant string of causality, reacting predictably to stimuli, moving inexorably toward … some place. Wherever I'm going is connected to my actions and the actions of others, however it fits me. I see this clearly. I've taken many roads to this excellent wonderland. I'm thrilled and comforted by it, not thinking much about what I might do to mess it up. It seems just fine. What are we looking for? I ask Curly.

"It's a beautiful world, isn't it?" he chuckles, perhaps seeing the wonder in my eyes. "You can even see further than your eyes can see. Close them for a few minutes." I oblige, and a kaleidoscope opens behind my eyes, shifting shapes and colors filling my head; I can feel the rhythm of the spinning wheels, and taste colors in flavors from citrus to chocolate. Wow, I say aloud. Curley prompts me further.

"Go inside your body, take a fantastic voyage through the blood vessels to your organs, your heart, lungs, liver, kidneys," he instructs, and I follow the anatomical graphic in my head, down the neck into the chest cavity, finding my heart thumping excitedly, happy to see myself, I suppose, then I see the patch, the stent implanted after my episode at the sex club to prop open the clogged artery. As I pass through, I see the fleshy blood vessel pulsing against the wire mesh, looking like a harnessed pimple ready to pop. I slip through my diaphragm, riding a wave of fresh air into a lung, another marvel of genetic engineering that defines the rhythm of life, in and out, expelling the byproducts of the vital exchange of gases. Skittering along the air sac, I see the delicate tissue now turning hard and bumpy, seeing what Mona warned me about, suspicious spots, the wear and tear of abuse. I slip into a blood vessel and exit into the liver, a thoroughly dark and dismal place. I feel it laboring as it sucks bile in and out, wrinkled and old, exhausted. Down I sink into my stomach, where the enzyme juices roil and tumble with huevos rancheros and bits of other smelly debris that swirls around me, drawing me down, down … I open my eyes with a start and issue a soft curse, "Shit!"

Curly is watching me with a look both curious and amused. "Was it too dark?" he asks, a smile playing on his lips. Dark and ugly, I didn't make it to the kidneys, I tell him. I took all my fears into my body cavities, and they scared the crap out of me. Curly nods and sympathizes. "You're worried about your health; it's natural," he says. "Healing comes from connecting what's inside with what's outside, and vice versa. It's all the same beautiful world."

My head is still spinning, the colors and shapes of the waterfall wonderland slowly coming back into focus as I'm talked down by my shaman, whose language again conjures the practices of *qigong* and

298

Taoist meditation. How do I connect my sickly insides to this teeming, vibrant outside world? How will I be healed? I ask.

Curly nods and reaches into the gunnysack, pulling out two bottles of water and a plastic bag. "It's a process, Mr. James. You're already on a road to recovery, based on what you've told me. You want to change, and you are. Now we're just looking at all the possibilities." Curly is loading a small glass pipe he's retrieved from the gunnysack, a fine granular substance I guess is a local strain of grass. "It's *psilocybin mexicana*, with a little kush for flavor," he says. Should I get any higher, I wonder, particularly by smoking? I've seen my lungs, and they're not pretty. But he reassures me. "It's a one-hitter, a microdose. It will calm the fears, probably even soothe the lungs."

I take the proffered pipe, and Curly lights it as I inhale gently, filling my lungs with a sweet and musty flavor that's not unpleasant as I think the best thoughts, pushing the drugs into my mainstream, flowing with the *nilch'i*, the *qi*, and the blood, the substantive fluid of life. After only a few minutes, I can see that everything is beautiful again. Curly is virtually beaming, rays of light emanating from his body, beatific, and I'm feeling increasingly close to my therapist. "We'll let it settle for a while. No words needed," he says, motioning toward the waterfall. "Enjoy." Curly turns to face the waterfall, pulls his legs under him in a modified lotus position, and closes his eyes.

I'm not ready to close my eyes, still unsettled by the disturbing images of my insides, but the falling water and whoosh of the spray relaxes my mind, and I settle into a meditative state that allows the commingling of sounds and aromas around me with my senses within. Eyelids droop, and the mind wanders through the stimulation inside, colorful patterns and geometric designs waltzing along the ebony ballroom floor, shooting stars spiraling above as the sunlight flickers just outside the corona dome. My mind is dazzled, my mood ebullient. I can't remember when I felt so content.

"Tell me about your daughter, Ramona," Curly asks softly, amid the wowie pyrotechnics between my ears. Ah, Mona. I get a warm feeling thinking about my baby and her loving reach to wherever I am, always on call even though I call too seldom. I missed her early years, I tell Curly, but I helped her follow her dream, to become a doctor – and to keep tabs on me. She's the only family I have, and I love her more than anything. Acknowledging this filial fealty brings a lump to my throat, a rush of emotion to my chest – tears welling in my eyes.

"What about her mother?" Curly asks, and I flinch. Deep breath. Memories of Patricia flood my brain, none tender, many raw. I stammer her name, and dismiss her as a fling. The baby was a mistake, even if she did grow to be a treasure, my darling girl. I don't want to think about her mother.

"Sometimes the greatest treasure comes by accident," Curly says. "She has left you rich beyond measure, this Patricia. Why do you hate her?" I don't hate her, I object. I just didn't want to stay with her – or the baby. She presented the pregnancy as her claim on me; that's how I felt. She wanted to possess me, and I rejected it, rejected her and the paternity until she eventually proved it. Maybe I was a cad. But I took responsibility for my daughter, and provided all the financial assistance I could. When she was finishing high school, I took her in. We said goodbye to Patricia. I know Mona stays in touch, but I have no use for her.

"You pushed her away," he says. "How does your Mona feel about it?" The magic of the moment is going poof under the weight of this conversation, I object. My therapist is ruining my buzz, a prospect that amuses Curly. "We'll talk more tonight," he says. "No rush. We have much to see." I'm relieved to get back to the supernatural splendors of this place and away from the petty relations of feeble minds and hearts.

34. A Question of Identity

With the sun angling toward the western ridge, casting brilliance to the billowing clouds above and shade along the crags below, Curly announces it's time to return to his cabin. The scary walk to our sanctuary now is a path to glory – even the plants are murmuring to me, trees whistling in the breeze. "*Nilch'i*," I say aloud in response, drawing out the *cheee* sound of the rustling wind. "That's right," Curly responds, turning and nodding his approval. "The energy is all around us. Do you feel it?"

Something, whether imagined or real, stirs my senses and emotions, and I'm aware enough to credit the heady brew of mescaline and psilocybin, herbal inspiration for Native American tribe visions. Whatever the origin, I'm blissfully communing with nature, feeling awash in cosmic energy. The woodpecker's rat-a-tat-tat is a coded message, the mournful cooing of the mourning dove a serenade, the kingfisher swooping stealthily along the creek a performing artist. Mushrooms glow like ornaments beneath the spruce trees. Are these magic, I wonder as I detour off the trail to get a closer look.

"No, don't try those," says my guide as he follows me to the glistening 'shrooms. "It could be a psychedelic mushroom, or its evil cousin. Same toxins, but one thrills you, and one can kill you." Enough said. No unprescribed experiments. I retreat and follow him back on the trail.

Gathering juniper kindling and berries on our way back is more adventure, and no chore at all. Curly retrieves a small tin container from his bag for me to collect the berries while he gathers the wood.

The juniper berries look like blueberries at first but, up close, are revealed to be tiny seed cones with fleshy scales. I sniff the pungent berries as I pick them, inhaling the peppery, pine-like aroma, very pleasant, "spice for our brew," Curly says, tucking the half-full tin back into his bag and handing me an armload of wood to carry.

Curly directs me to take the wood beyond the cabin, past the driveway, to a clearing where three large logs are arranged in a triangle. At the center is a shallow pit circled by a dozen or so stones, with the charred remains of camp fires past at the center. I drop the wood beside the pit and head to the Jeep, where Curly is unpacking more gear, including a sack of groceries. My mind is too busy to think about food, as Curly suspected. "Just some easy-on-the-stomach snacks for later," he says, "and lots of water."

Water is the ingredient Curly is intent on turning into an elixir, emptying a bottle into a kettle and placing it on a hotplate, which he plugs into a power cord and turns to high. Using a fork, he smashes juniper berries in a wood bowl, then adds bits of fleshy brown fungus he identifies as "primo magic mushrooms, laboratory grade." He places the concoction into a strainer that he lowers into the kettle as the water begins to bubble gently from the bottom. Curly turns the heat down and claps his hands once, sharply, then raising both arms as if celebrating victory, a Navajo shaman gleefully practicing his ancient craft.

"Relax anywhere in our circle," he says, gesturing broadly to the expanse of cushions spread along the outer contours of the pentagonal structure. I take a seat against the wall facing the entrance, which is open to the bright reflection of the retreating sun. Curly lights a kerosene lamp atop the woodstove, which is filled with kindling but unlit. The sun emits its dying rays, abandoning a mountain chill as it settles atop the mountain behind us.

The flickering light illuminates three large pieces of artwork – sand paintings, Curly explains as he pulls out two large mugs and tends the tea. Geometric patterns and deep colors are created from natural minerals in the earth, representing the natural world. He hands me a mug half-filled with the mushroom-juniper concoction, murmuring an incantation, I suspect, something in another tongue. I sip tenuously, then more fully as I study the sand painting nearest me, a circle of browns and ochers merging into crimsons and forest greens, and I smell the pungency of the forest floor, hear the golden baying of a coyote, the violet buzzing of the insects, the dripping scarlet ascension of the birds. My senses are acute, but my mind is a jumble of mixed sensations, and metaphors. I take another sip, inviting the virtual lift into the sensual cosmos enshrined in the sacred Navajo mandala.

"The mushrooms we saw on the trail, mushrooms you see growing everywhere, are part of a vast network of fungi connecting with other plants, and affecting humans too," Curly says. "The psilocybin is a connection to it all, why nature seems to be talking to you. You're feeling the nerves of the planet, tapping into the life you share with all of Earth's organisms." I'm wowed by this notion, the vision of the interconnected world, a universal fungi nervous system. But Curly pushes the conversation back to my little node of the system.

"How will you greet your friend George?" he asks, again seemingly out of the blue. "You say it's been many years?" Memories of George flood my receptors, streaming through the deep greens and blues of my inner vision. I will greet him like a long-lost brother, I say, surprised to hear my voice so soft and halting. I take a deep breath and plunge into tales of the wilderness hikes with George, not unlike this trip. He would enjoy this view, these sensations. We drank wine, dropped acid, smoked hash, and tried peyote and mushrooms, but without direction, just enjoying wild and crazy college experiences, discovering life willy-nilly. I describe how George informed my Falun Gong articles and the trip to China, his teaching of Chinese philosophies and spiritualism, deepened for me during this trip to his mountain retreat.

"What do you hope to accomplish when you get there?" This question confounds me further, and I complain that I'm too taken with exquisite visions before me, the signs and sounds of the now, to ponder the future, whatever will be. Curly laughs and agrees, with a slight apology. "We have time, no sweat. I only want to help. How do you feel?" I try to describe the intensity of the sensations, the connection I'm feeling with everything around me, and with my past and future. My existence is logical, natural, consistent, in tune. Life is good.

Curly rolls off his cushion to his knees, reaching to retrieve his bag. He pulls out a small boom box and plugs it into the floor outlet. "Music will help us celebrate the harmony you feel," he says, turning it on. From another bag, he pulls out a small bongo drum for him and a tambourine for me. I take and shake, the rattle jarring at first, then soothing, as I catch the beat of the chant, three male voices singing gently in ragged harmony. The words are foreign to me, as essentially native as they are, and the syllables are repeated over and over. I hear: *Hama holo go ayoo jimi go hama holo go ayoo jimi go* with a recurring *yowie nay hay* sung sweetly and melodically.

Curly, who is singing along, pauses the music to explain. "It's a healing song, sung by the Navajo for hundreds of years," he says, translating it as, "When you love your mother, you will gain strength, from now on into the future. Great Spirit, please protect and bless our mother. We thank you for keeping our mother safe each and every day."

The Mother is the nurturer in the Navajo matriarchal society, and the chant bows to Earth as the giver of life, Curly explains. Healing is a byproduct of Mother Earth, whether from sacred medicines like peyote and mushrooms, or from basic sustenance. The mushroom-cactus potion keeps my mind firmly planted in the Earth, even as my head orbits with heightened sensations and grand visions. I've never felt so anchored. I suggest we go outside and enjoy the end of the day.

"Excellent idea," Curly says, rising spryly to his feet. "Bring the tambourine. We'll get in tune with Mother's rhythms." By now, in the shadow of the mountain, our campground is cool and ready for the spark to the juniper kindling. Curly lights it up, and the crackling of the wood merges into the panoply of natural sounds – the insect clicking, birdsinging, and wind rustling foremost – to rival the healing songs from within the cabin. I begin swaying with the rhythm of Mother's concert, tapping the tambourine against my leg to complete the music in my head. "Hi-ay yo …," Curly starts a chant as he thumps on his drum, and I jump in and follow him as we dance around the fire, tripping along with nature's evening serenade in the foothills of the Rocky Mountains.

This is how humans celebrate, moving to the music of their tribes, playing the instruments in tune and time with fellow musicians, the band, and the community. Curly and I are in synch with a tribe of our own, I've decided, neither Navajo nor Anglo nor any cultural link.

We are Mushroom People. We have a common denominator multiplied by an exponential accelerant. I rattle the tambourine joyously, tripping beyond physical limitations, out-of-body experiencing infinite something; I can't put my finger on it. Godliness? Delusion?

Curly slows the chant, and my mood adjusts to the new rhythm, keeping time with the gentle sounds of creatures settling in for the evening – the steady chirp of the western chorus frogs punctuated by the blackbird's call, "whooorrrippp, chkachkachka." I jingle the tambourine in response, feeling the languid movement of evening possessing my body, then drop the instrument and settle into a standing *qigong* position, the Bear, closing my eyes and turning away from the crackling fire, breathing in the cool evening air. Curly stops chanting, and I only hear the ambient sounds of nature as I sink into a meditative state, calming my mind and silencing the inner voice, allowing the hallucinations to fade into my eyelids.

I lose time, standing there, breathing, and absorbing the energy of this place, which stirs my internal *qi* energy and brings images of mingling molecules, rotating in the cosmos, finding peace in this steady good grace of existence. When I open my eyes, after an unmeasured time of contemplation, the evening is a deep purple sparked from the fire behind me. I turn to find Curly sitting on a log, watching me, curiously, without expression. He motions me to take a seat beside him. He wants to know what I'm doing.

Technically, I'm "standing post," or *zhanzhuang* as the Chinese call it, building internal energy for Tai Chi or other martial arts. But personally, I'm meditating, using *qigong* breath exercises to tap into the energy around me that is so powerful, so accessible. I try to explain to Curly how I've broken through, with his magic potion, feeling like I've never felt before. I'm reminded of Sparrow, who brought us together, who feels so deeply and communicates so well, verbally and psychologically – an empath, right?

"Nothing magic," Curly says. "Sparrow opened up to you; she likes you. She can have sharp elbows, too, if you cross her." I laugh, recalling Sparrow's quick elbow shot at Mo when he struck her accidentally during dinner at the ranch. Curly enjoys the anecdote, typical of his sister, he says. "She played basketball at school, very good, sharp elbows, as I said. People were naturally drawn to Sparrow."

Like a magnet. I'm thinking of the push-hands technique Sparrow used so well on me, "sticking and adhering," teaching me how to root and balance myself enough to feel her center, to sense her as she was sensing me. Looking back on it now, through this psychedelic lens, the exchange was intensely intimate – almost like sex, I tell her brother, who nods understandingly. "I'm not surprised," he says. "Sparrow's not a fighter, but she will fight if pushed. She was playing with you."

I recalled again how Sparrow put her hand on my chest, measuring what she told her brother was a "heart problem." Was she playing with me, then? "I think she was telling you something, maybe that you should look inside yourself. When I watch you with your standing post, the meditation, I think I understand what she sees. She thinks you're looking for something, and I can help you find it."

What am I looking for? This trip started as a lark to see an old friend, under constraints determined by my job and worries associated with my declining health. George sounded eager to see me, to tell me … what? He wants to catch up, and talk about "something we missed" in our early adventures. What were we even looking for? We've been pen pals for years, sharing letters and then emails, and occasional telephone calls. His thoughts often came in verse, snippets of thoughts, really, with rhythm and occasional rhyme. The poet plays with words artfully to tickle your emotions, to make you feel their substance. Words on a page have always been like music, to me and George alike, my efforts seeming so pedestrian by contrast.

"You were telling me about your job, the most important thing to you," Curly says. "How does it look from this vantage point?" From this placid harbor, I admit I can't see the political story I'm covering, don't even want to think about politics and a nation ruled by Donald Trump. "Does it really matter?" he asks, reminding me of George's dismissive "business as usual," nothing to worry about. But I think it does matter; it's my job to help people sort it out, to explain current events, and to sound people out about what they think. But from this altered state, I'm not sure who I am to play this role. How did I get here? Dame Fortune smiled on me, lifted me up, or hung me out to dry.

This question suddenly seems critically important to me, or not important at all, compared with all the stuff of the universe, this sensation of being lifted out of my natural environment to explain events but maybe ignoring "bigger things," as George said. In this state, Ray James seems like a made-up persona, a player in a game that's totally irrelevant to the structure of this world, to the reality of this existence. I've been telling Curly I'm fulfilling a critical role in my community, opening a window on the world around us, but is that even the world we're in? I'm sure my confusion about what's real is torturing my rush of words about my work's effect on other people, reflected in the bemused look I'm getting from Curly.

"So you're on a mission," he says matter-of-factly, and I can't help but laugh out loud. It's true, I say; it's a crusade, a sanctified path anointed in journalism schools and confirmed by media outlets and their fraternal organizations. I am a defender of the First Amendment; speaking for many, I like to think, and not just for myself. I've worked for decades to bring my mission to this mobile platform, but suddenly I'm not sure I know my way.

The shadows lengthen toward darkness, and the chill rushes off the mountain. Curly pokes the embers to dust, and we retire to the cabin, where he quickly stokes the stove. I find my cushion opposite the door and sit cross-legged, close my eyes, and consider the case of Ray James, a journeyman writer at twilight in search of a story and himself. Putting the story aside, I'm beside the point. The dancing light show on the inside of my eyelids illuminates nothing. I open my eyes and see Curly, who has his eye on me.

"Is it still a dark and ugly place inside you?" he asks. Not at all. My worries have faded into wonder. Who am I? I wonder. I can't figure out the basic thing: Beyond the role I play in workaday life, the intrepid newspaper columnist, what is the meaning of my life? Or does it mean anything at all?

35. Getting Somewhere

As I help Curly load the Jeep and we get back on the road, I try to reconstruct the meandering conversation that faded into sleep early this morning. I remember I never pinned down who I am, at least beyond what I already know. The mystery of consciousness and concerted action, or serendipity, in the course of events in my passion play remain elusive, including the passion part.

Curly got personal, in his gently persistent way, drawing me out about my relationships, or lack thereof. He wanted to talk about Mona, "the only family you allow yourself to have," he said pointedly. I protested mildly, without much defense. I admit I've long since abandoned the tree of James that took root in New England and then branched away. I'm part of the migration. No James has come looking for me, even with a byline that travels across the country. My mom and dad are long gone, and I have the elusive spirit of a sick brother to nag at my memories.

But floods of memories of Mona rushed through my mind when I told Curly about her, trying to explain the singular position she holds in my orbit. My dear Mona, my treasure, so proud of her accomplishments and promise. She is even carrying our name forward in marriage, and a child! For the first time in months, I think of my fetal granddaughter, soon to spring from my daughter, barely three months away from emerging. Mona will be swollen with motherhood when I see her in Denver. I'm overwhelmed with a rush of emotion – love, certainly, and a sense of wonder at the cycle of life and regeneration. A new generation.

Curly wanted to know about my mother, Mary Catherine Agnes James, nee Burke, a saint as far as I'm concerned. She pushed me to excel at everything I did, especially schoolwork, and took a special interest in my fledging writing. Then she got pneumonia and died soon after I went away to college, and my dad drank himself to death the next year. Two sad homecomings to Lynn, bittersweet moments of memory and morbidity. The local bank settled the small estate and consolidated the proceeds into a trust I managed to mostly squander while still at Stanford. I never returned to Massachusetts.

Haltingly relating these old times to Curly left me cold, and he saw it. I admit my emotion from those events is long since spent, a stark contrast to the deep emotional response I feel with Mona, the next generation, and my connection to the future. Curly tells me that psilocybin may be partially responsible for my feelings. "You are feeling more deeply, and apparently, you're not feeling deeply, too," he said, referring to the farewells to my parents. "Has anyone ever loved you as much as Mona loves you?"

I wasn't sure how to answer this question, and I took it to sleep with me when our conversation finally wore me out. I hardly ever think about how other people feel about me, not even Mona. But certainly, no one loves me as much as does Mona, and I admit as much now, in the light of day with autos whizzing by on I-25. Looking back now, I recognize how shallow my relationships have been over time. I haven't endeared myself to many people – at least, not for long.

Curly listens to this confession quietly as he navigates the Jeep around Colorado Springs, heading north to Denver. I ask him if Sparrow's concern about my "heart problem" has anything to do with my lack of lovability. He doesn't respond immediately, except for an almost imperceptible nod of his head. "Maybe … something like

312

that," he says eventually. "She was sensing something – maybe that you weren't connecting to the moment you're in, you weren't 'present' with others, including her. What do you think it means? Why did she send you to me?"

Again, I don't know what Sparrow sees in me, her perceptions. But she knew her brother would provide organic substances, Navajo sacraments, that would make me hallucinate, would force me toward introspection. From here, I've considered my place in the universe, my infinitesimally small station, my drip into the ocean. The meditation on mushrooms has clarified for me the kinship of life on this planet, animals and plants, and how we all exist within the collective consciousness of Earth-kind. From this perch, I sense the force Navajo call Great Spirit, the deity that roams the fields and mountain ranges, providing bounty for those who dance for it. I think Sparrow wants me to see how the Navajo way connects the human spirit to the planet, and the universe. She wanted me to feel how we are united under the sun. Now I have this overwhelming desire to return to Sparrow, to see what she feels in me now.

I see things clearly today, coming down from my out-of-body mushroom experience, but how does that affect my behavior? It remains to be seen. Certain behavior is unavoidable, even imperative – telephone calls, for example. I need to check in with Mona – and with Bradbury, who has been peppering me with emails since we last talked, before I met with Wu and learned about the Falun Gong-Trump connection. I excuse myself to make the calls, and Curly cheerfully turns on the radio, where announcers are setting the lineups for the baseball game, his Colorado Rockies versus the Los Angeles Dodgers.

The conversation with Mona is short; she's in a meeting and can't talk. I have a room waiting for me at the TownePlace Suites near the hospital, where she and Maddie are staying, and she'll make reservations for dinner this evening. Tomorrow I walk the gauntlet of hospital tests – blood work, a stress test, and a CT scan of my chest. She's still pushing the lung biopsy, but I resist. I exaggerate a dry cough. I'm not smoking, see? Nothing to worry about. I don't want to further delay my rendezvous with George.

Bradbury is less demanding, probably figuring I'm out of the loop and inconsequential. "OK, so when will you be done with your holiday?" he asks when I tell him my location. Don't count me out, I tell him. I've got a hell of a story brewing about foreign activity on the Internet, and campaigns to court President Trump. Not just the Russians and the Chinese, but also the dissident group I've been following along with its performing arts group. Wu, the Li Hongzhi confidant, was forthcoming about their plans to establish a Washington office to lobby the administration. I promise a draft – at least an outline – before leaving Denver for the wilds of Red Feather Lake.

The hometown Rockies just scored, but I see that Curly has tuned out the game, as he studies me peripherally while I sign off with Bradbury. "You've got a big story," he says, turning the radio off. "It's a scoop!" I laugh, assuring him it's just my sales pitch to the boss. I haven't even figured out the story yet, chasing blind leads over the Internet. That's my job today, before dinner. The Denver skyline is rising slowly on the horizon, like the city of Oz to my still mildly hallucinogenic mind. And I'm here not to see the Wizard, but Dorothy, who will protect me from the Witch lurking inside me. I'm daydreaming about my Mona, who certainly loves me more than anyone ever would.

Curly drives directly to the hotel, conveniently located near Denver Health, his own primary healthcare facility. I can't thank him enough for the mystical experience, his expertise and advice, and the mushrooms and peyote, for sharing the sacraments. I tell him I feel uplifted, more understanding and sensitive to feelings, mine and those of others. Sparrow should be happy, and I want to thank her personally, on the return trip. "It's a beginning," Curly says, "and it's easy to get sidetracked. Remember, meditation will help more than any medication. Stay true to yourself, and those you care about."

Words of wisdom from my psycho-pharmacologist: Avoid drugs. Breathe deep and be kind. The key to good health and long life. It sounds impossibly simple, and of course, it is. The fallible human gene is in play, the urge for immediate gratification. But the logic of meditation is evident in the afterglow of psilocybin revelations, and I assure Curly that everything will be all right for me, that he's helped me see the way.

I'm feeling even better than all right as I check into the hotel and set up my workstation – more like a superhero, the powerful and invincible journalist Clark Kent. I'm in my element, on deadline. I've got maybe five hours to write before dinner and unlimited wi-fi. There's much to research. I dig in.

First, looking back to the election, *The Epoch Times* has been beating the Trump drum for quite a while, and praising the new administration's agenda, including the travel ban against Islamic countries and his claims of a "witch hunt" into his relationship with Russia. There are photos of Falun Dafa protesters outside Trump's

Mar-A-Lago resort when President Xi was visiting, with a story praising Trump's get-tough stance on trade with China. No mention of Trump meeting with the Russian ambassador after he fired the FBI director, but there's a lengthy article about how the international Falun Gong campaign may be having the effect of loosening restrictions against the practice in mainland China.

While still condemning the repression in China, the newspaper has taken a more optimistic tone, hailing a movement by young Chinese to quit the Communist Party, linking to a website that promotes the campaign in China and abroad. Reporting overall seems to reflect a new spirit about an evolving "new China," connected directly to the rise of the new president of the United States, portrayed as an ally in the fight for their liberty.

My googling has created a steady advertising drumbeat on my Facebook feed from Shen Yun, now joined by ads from *The Epoch Times*, and from *The Beauty of Life*, which appears to be the newspaper's social media outlet. "The BL" has an assortment of links across social media that preach truthfulness with an assortment of lies and half-truths, well-populated groups, and pages connected to pro-Trump sites with similar dubious claims. The cross-pollination cuts across media, with sources parroting the same tropes and memes on Twitter, too. Plenty of "news" from different "anon" posters, including the ridiculous QAnon that inspired an assault on a pizza parlor in D.C. The BL is still promoting the QAnon attacks against Democrats, described as a satanic cult of pedophiles bent on destroying the social fabric of a nation. Seriously, and with millions of followers.

The Internet's promise of global resources at your fingertips has become a brave new world of disinformation and hyperbole, a cesspool of conspiracy theories and crazy talk. The BL may bring a calmer tone to the noisy hive, in the spirit of the Falun Gong meditation, but it keeps its parentage secret, not even a link to *The Epoch Times* nor a mention of Falun Dafa, even as it swears by the tenets of truthfulness, compassion, and tolerance – *zhen, shan,* and *ren* – while hyping Trump. The irony of applying these moral principles to support a leader whose behavior is antithetical to such high-minded ideals is glaring.

I begin writing:

"President Trump's tough stance on trade with China is cheering not only American workers who've lost jobs to global trade, but also Chinese dissidents living in the United States, who see Trump as an ally in the fight against China's Communist regime. The Falun Gong religious movement, banned by China in 1999, has mounted an international Internet-based campaign to support Trump, flooding Facebook, Twitter, and other social media with paid ads, and using multiple anonymous posters, pages, and links with pro-Trump messages, much of it untrue.

"'We have good newspaper, Epoch Times, *videos, Internet shows. And we know we are heard,' " said Gaosan Wu, senior advisor to Falun Gong founder Li Hongzhi, who now lives in exile in New York. Wu recently helped set up an office in Washington with both news and lobbying operations. But he is especially proud of the influence of the organization's Internet networks. 'We learn new ways to talk to world,' he says. 'We see numbers, people watching and listening, and learning.' "*

I plug in background on the organization and its decades-long growth outside of China, and the influence of its cultural program,

317

Shen Yun. Then a section on the beliefs and practices of the religion, its connection to *qigong* and ancient Chinese philosophies, and bring it back to the political realm – Trump's meeting with Xi in Mar-A-Lago, with the Falun Dafa "educational displays" and quiet protests against the Chinese dictator. A final graph about the talented Shen Yun dancer, the beautiful Wei-Lin, heading to Washington to interview for the job as Falun Gong emissary. It's a first draft, good enough to send along to Bradbury for review. I've got 45 minutes to freshen up to meet Mona. I jump into the shower.

36. Mona: What We Leave Behind

Parting with her mother was excruciating for Mona, although she came to agree with Patricia's assurances that "this is the best thing for both of us." At the time, being a 16-year-old junior in high school, she didn't understand – especially with all the teenage confusion. She hadn't figured out boys, and never would. She needed her mother; she was sure of that. But Patricia stayed in constant contact – phone, text, letters, Skype, then Facebook, Twitter, and Instagram. They were never closer than in their absence, reaching out to each other as never before.

More trying was adjusting to a father she barely knew. He was the sad, awkward man with unruly hair and a scraggly face that prickled when he hugged her on those rare visits. Mona would curl her nose at his distinctive odor, which she eventually came to realize was the result of bad food and excessive drinking. Her high school friend, Heather, gave her the first clue, asking after meeting her dad if he might buy booze for them. Mona was horrified.

Still, she knew he cared about her – whether from some sense of duty or maybe from shame, having disappeared as a father for much of her young life. He worked hard to win her trust, not smoking or drinking around her, and being attentive to her needs. Mona believed she was reforming him, the daughter being the mother of the man, saving her father from himself. She was kidding herself, of course, but it gave her a sense of mission, an impetus to become a doctor.

Eventually, the parting with Patricia made perfect sense, as Ray threw himself into his responsibilities as a dad. He may not have set a fine example for his daughter, but he gave her the means, encouraging her curiosity and exploration. He met her material needs as well as giving her a shoulder to lean on. The condo was transferred to Mona at minimal cost post-graduation, and then bought back with a lump sum payment that helped her get started in San Francisco. He also supported her in her personal life, not just accepting but loving Maddie. She felt the bond, and so did Maddie. "We've got a good dad," Maddie told her.

Mona never lost hope Ray would reconcile the relationship with her mother. He refused to talk about her and resisted every overture for a conversation until he finally snapped at her, "Patricia went through a lot of men before she got to me. It was not a loving relationship then, and we have little chance of being friends now." Mona never believed it. She was sure she could make them agree to be agreeable, to be friends. After all, they both had her. If they could share, they could care.

So Mona arranged for her mother to meet her in Denver at the same time her father was coming up from New Mexico. Patricia had moved back home to Indiana, got married, and then quickly divorced. She finished the degree she abandoned at San Jose State as she followed Ray around the bar circuit, and now teaches American history at an Indianapolis high school. Mona liked to think her mom's teaching pursuit was driven by a desire to pick up where she left off with her, with kids her age when her mother split. She never held it against her. Patricia was right: It was for the best. It's not like Mona lost her mother; she'd always been there to listen. And she seemed much happier, having flown away from her sad state of affairs.

Although Patricia knew they were meeting Ray for dinner, Mona didn't tell her father – worried he wouldn't come, remembering the times he avoided her mother when he came to pick her up. She and her mother arrived first at the restaurant, taking a table where Mona could watch the door for Ray and Maddie, who had been in union meetings all day. Patricia was nervous, not sure why Mona was bringing them together, insisting that she had moved on, glad Ray was out of her life. But she knew it was important to Mona that they all get along. "I need for my parents to be civil, to have a relationship even if it's not close," Mona told her.

Mona needn't have worried. Ray was in a buoyant mood, and his face lit up when he saw them together. He greeted Mona first, patting her swollen belly with delight, then turned to Patricia and gave her a brief hug. "You look great, Granny," he said. "Time away from me seems to have done you a world of good." Patricia led the chorus of laughter at the obvious truth. "You seem to have turned out all right yourself, grandpa," she responded. The bad feelings seemed to have dissolved over the nearly 20 years since they parted, probably a surprise to them both. Ray seemed genuinely intrigued to learn Patricia's story, especially the history teaching.

"What do your students think about the course of American history now that it has led to this moment, to President Trump?" he asked her, evoking a lively discussion in which they agreed with each other on point after point. Patricia said: "Sometimes I think I need to bring their parents in for a few civics lessons, and maybe they would stop corrupting the minds of their kids," a comment that Ray actually applauded with three soft claps.

So engrossing was their conversation that they didn't notice Maddie until she was standing beside Mona, clearing her throat to announce her presence. Patricia was the first to rise, rushing to embrace her, excited to meet in person after phone and Skype chats, whispering sweet mother-in-law nothings into her ear as Maddie beamed. She'd had a busy week and was eager to get back to Oakland. Mona was sticking around to monitor her father's hospital tests, and to ensure he didn't duck out with his new driver's license and rental car, already arranged for pickup. "You have to slow down, Dad," she told him. "We know how stress hurts you."

"I'm good," Ray said. "I move at the pace of life, and I'm getting more relaxed about it, with the breathing exercises and meditation. I'm sure the medical results will show it. Plus, I'm taking all the meds you gave me." He reached over and squeezed her hand. "I've also got the best doctor in the world, my sweet daughter."

Mona offered an affectionate smile at her father's bravado, placing her other hand on top of his. "We're all pulling for you, Dad," she said. Indeed, Ray's good mood was infectious as he offered tales of his travels – most recently with the Navajo "witch doctor," and the insight he said he gained through the psychedelic treatment. Mona maintained her usual skepticism without criticizing his unconventional holistic approach, pleased that her father had warmed up to her mother, which was at the heart of this evening.

To celebrate, Mona had ordered a bottle of wine for the table, but Ray insisted on sparkling water and iced tea, then ordered a cup of coffee with dessert. "It's best I don't slow down my brain right now," he explained. "I haven't gotten much sleep lately, and I still have a lot of work to do." He didn't begrudge spirits for the others, however. "As long as you don't get hooked, you'll be okay," he said, pleased with the irony of his little joke. Mona was getting the sense that her father, for the first time, was out of crisis and in control of his own destiny without chemical interference. She felt exhilarated. She had succeeded.

But it remained to be seen empirically. She wanted to see data from the Denver Health medical tests scheduled the next day, and she made sure her father showed up for them all, meeting him in the hotel lobby and walking him to the hospital. She greeted the receptionist, nurses, and technicians on duty, introducing the patient. She had a letter from the hospital administrator approving her access, but it wasn't necessary. Everyone was expecting them.

Ray was playful but respectful of everyone's time and goodwill, cheerful but focused, and eager to get the tests behind him and be on the road. Mona had never met George, but had heard plenty of stories. Ray wouldn't stop talking about him now. "I feel like George and I are having a grand summit meeting," he said. "He's like my guru at the top of the mountain, and I expect a revelation."

Mona laughed, amused by Ray's enthusiasm and depiction of his friend, the poet and Asian scholar, as a "guru," obviously a metaphor, even if he looked sincere at the moment and smirked at her reaction. "Not everything is in the bloodstream, doctor," he said, breaking into a grin. "Everything I need to diagnose and prescribe treatment to bring your body back in balance is in your blood," she retorted.

The test of that proposition would come later, but it wasn't drugs alone that accounted for Ray's excellent test results at Denver Health. Mona was shocked, given the short time since she saw him in Las Vegas, how good his vital signs were – normal, strong heartbeat, low blood pressure, good breathing rate. His labs also were good, with no abnormalities in the blood; cholesterol levels good, liver and kidney function stable, and sugars and other dietary poisons were under control. More surprises with the chest scan, which no longer showed a nodule in his lung. What appeared in Las Vegas to be a potential tumor now looked like congestion that was breaking up, and dispersing.

Like many Western physicians, Mona recognized the value of Asian meditative arts, and didn't discount the positive effect on her father's general well-being. But having watched the steady deterioration of her father's health and mental acuity over more than 20 years, she saw his sudden turn toward eating healthy foods and avoiding alcohol as the determining factor. Better habits rejuvenated his body, however, he came to them. He had a change of heart, reinforced at various stops along the road to the top of the mountain. He was sure he would find enlightenment at the Shambhala Mountain Center, communing with his guru, old friend George.

But he never got to the top of the mountain, to the Stupa of the Blue-Eyed Buddha, as George Bayer called it. George tracked Mona down, calling to ask why Ray didn't follow through on their plan to meet at the retreat. That was a week later, and Mona had already returned to Oakland, certain that her father was enjoying a meditative reunion with George. She called the Colorado State Patrol, and flew back to Denver. But the police investigation was fruitless. Ray James was nowhere to be found.

They knew Ray had mechanical trouble with his rental car and called for roadside service. The tow-truck driver found the car along the road near Rustic, Colorado. The hood was up, and Ray apparently had set out on foot. He'd left a duffle bag filled with a few changes of clothes, but took his backpack with his primary accoutrement, a laptop computer, also missing. Mona wouldn't give up, pushing the police via phone and emails from Oakland over the next few months, and lobbying reporters to conduct their own investigations. Maddie even hired a private detective to sniff around the cold trail, to no avail.

Jay Lee called Mona when he heard the news, reassuring her that Ray would be okay. "I think he was kidnapped," he said, "being held, but not in danger. Have you heard anything?" No, Mona had received no evidence or encouragement her father was alive. But she prayed to whatever power could intervene on behalf of Ray James, a good man on the brink of finding himself, who had yet to meet his namesake, granddaughter Rae James. Mona was gratified a month later when Jay arranged a Taoist memorial service at the Ma Tzu Temple in San Francisco, packing the intimate Chinatown hall.

Annamarie, who sat beside Mona and Maddie, was sad and stoic throughout the service. She introduced Gretchen, whose doleful, hollow eyes reflected the pain of losing two men she loved. Jay brought his assistant Mei-Lee, who explained that her sister, Wei-Lin, was unable to attend, distraught and in retreat in New York. Many *Chronicle* staffers sought out Mona, including managing editor Jim Bradbury, who said the newspaper would end *The Vibe*. "That was Ray's work," he said. "We retire the title until he returns to reclaim it."

The *Chronicle* published Ray's final column, along with a companion article that Bradbury said is the first in an ongoing series about the growing use of social media by foreign and domestic organizations to manipulate public opinion, politicians, and the American political system. "Your dad was just beginning to glimpse the story with his focus on Falun Gong's *Epoch Times* and The Beauty of Life," Bradbury said. "The story is bigger even than WikiLeaks. There's a complex web of disinformation out there. A new era of cyber-warfare is underway, with platforms all over the world. We're all plugged into it one way or another, and Ray helped us see it."

Mona was consoled by so many people sharing their grief with her, so many people who loved her Dad, who saw through the bluster to the good heart and best intentions of the man. He had more friends than she ever knew. In brief remarks to the gathering, Mona expressed her gratitude for the memories her father's friends had shared with her, and confided in them her fervent wish for him. "My dad was driven by his reporting and writing, getting 'the story,'" she said, using air quotes for emphasis. "I was looking forward to him slowing down and spending time with the people who loved him – and now I see his family was bigger than I ever knew.

"Dad would have loved this gathering," she continued, "and I'm so sorry he's not here to experience all the love I feel in this room. I haven't given up hope that he'll return, and even now, thinking he could come waltzing through the door with a sideways grin like a latter-day Tom Sawyer, crashing a premature wake." Ray James' friends laughed appreciatively, thinking that would be just like Ray, if he could pull it off. They, too, earnestly wished that he would.

37. Annamarie: Chasing the Blues

The mellow blue notes pouring through the open door of Fitzel's European Jazz Pub drew a steady stream of patrons to the wooden benches and chairs lining the wall and fronting the cool-blowing Quartet. The singer floating the sweet melody across the bar and onto Bourbon Street was New Orleans newcomer Annamarie Scott, who was gently tickling the keyboard while she warbled the old Hoagie torch song, longingly, touching more than a few in the audience: *It's not the pale moon that excites me/ That thrills and delights me/ Oh no, it's just the nearness of you …*

Annamarie was pouring her heart into the song, as usual, her voice caressing the notes playfully and sensually, feeling her way to connect her musical expressions to the jazz devotees who haunted this venue, the first place she looked for work, when she finally decided to flee the legal and administrative straitjacket her job in Oakland had become. She exchanged emails and recordings with musicians and agents in New Orleans, and soon had three open invitations and no hesitation in boarding a jet to fly away. Thank you, Ray, she thought as the plane settled into a cruising altitude high above the clouds, nothing but blue skies ahead. He was right. She had to take that first step to move ahead. Up, up and away.

The memorial for Ray in Chinatown was excruciating, but Annamarie was determined to stay composed – especially for Gretchen, who was an emotional mess. Losing Frank was hard enough – for both of them. Annamarie suspected Frank was dealing drugs, even when she represented him in the PTSD case. And he contributed to Ray's substance abuse problems, more than she cared to know. But they were good men at heart, easy to love. Sweet memories. She had little hope Ray survived, her worst fears supported by Gretchen's claim of foul play. "The Mexican drug cartel got Frank, and they came back to finish the job on Ray," she said. Believing this, the two women clung to each other while consoling Mona, hopeful for her and baby Rae, at least.

Annamarie credited Ray with the idea of trying the music circuit in New Orleans. "It's the perfect environment for your jazz singing," he said. "You'll be the toast of the town." He offered to quit his job and focus on promoting her musical career, but she dismissed it as a joke, just stroking his new love interest. When the time came to follow her heart, however, she followed his advice. She rented a time-share for a month, stowing her household goods until she could settle in and get a place.

Fitzel's could be noisy and rowdy, like most joints on Bourbon Street, but jazz was the main course, and Annamarie felt appreciated – not only by the customers but also by the band. They had a brilliant pianist, Joey Connelly, so she could spend most of her time up front with the microphone – the voice and the face of the Hank Strand Quartet. Hank was the cornetist, a local legend, and bassist Eddie Collins was young and hip – also actively seeking to lure Annamarie into his bed. She wasn't ready for a fling, especially with a bandmate. She discouraged him sweetly, but firmly.

Annamarie lingered on the final phrases of the song, taking the message to the front of the audience, holding out her arms to couples up front as she sang earnestly: *I need no soft lights to enchant me/ If you would only grant me/ The right/ To hold you ever so tight/ And to feel in the night/ The nearness of you.* Hank provided a fanciful cornet outro, then moved into the band's break song. Annamarie bowed to the ovation, waving and smiling to her new fans before retreating to the back room with the band to celebrate and freshen up for the next set. "You're like Ella when she was young," Hank beamed as he shook both her hands. Eddie was at her side, planting a kiss on her cheek. "Magnificent," he whispered.

Annamarie excused herself to visit the bathroom – just a toilet and sink but also serving as a dressing room and escape hatch. She scanned her phone for email and private messages. Bay Area friends were worried about her sudden exit, and she's tried to assure them that she's fine, and just needed time away. She got a leave of absence from the Oakland mayor's office, cashing in a month of vacation and comp pay. She's certain she won't return to that job, and maybe not even the legal profession, as long as the music opportunities are here, or anywhere. The possible run for office became a pipedream for an attorney defending bad cops and government neglect. Maybe she would perform in front of juries again someday, but not until the applause stopped. She felt at home in this house of jazz.

Her phone rang, a New Orleans number she didn't recognize, maybe another job prospect. She picked up and offered a pleasant "hello." The voice on the phone was equally friendly, a man who addressed her as "Ms. Scott," and then said, "You may not remember me. We met in Big Sur, at Jay Lee's *qigong* workshop. I was one of the Tai Chi experts, standing right beside you."

"Oh, my! Yes!" How could she forget the hunky guy with the graceful movement – "the actor, right?" He chuckled. "More a stuntman," he said. "Action hero double. Keeps me in shape. Can you come upstairs and talk? I'm on the balcony. I have something for you."

With 20 minutes before the next set, Annamarie powdered her nose and quickly walked the gauntlet of cheering fans, smiling and waving her appreciation as she headed to the stairway, where the attendant waved her up. The upstairs was called Potions, private rooms with soft music and exotic drinks, a place for lovers, out of bounds for Annamarie at this time of her life. But she liked to sit in the open balcony overlooking Bourbon Street, waving to the revelers and regulars, absorbing the intoxicating aura of this city. Tonight only a few of the balcony tables were occupied, and it was easy to spot Marcel, sporting a Panama hat and shades, utterly cool and balanced on his perch in the corner, like a big cat serenely surveying his domain. He rose as she walked to him and extended her hand.

"Ms. Scott, that was amazing," Marcel said, taking her hand and flashing his all-American smile. "I stopped in to hear you sing before coming up here – you have an angel's voice, the way you express yourself. Ray told me you were a great singer, but I had no idea."

At the mention of Ray's name, Annamarie's smile disappeared, and she sighed, "Poor Ray. There were so many things I wanted to say to him, and didn't get a chance." She took the seat Marcel held for her and put her hands to her cheeks, shaking her head. "His daughter, Mona, is torn up, but keeping a brave front. I saw her at a memorial service for Ray in Chinatown last month. And now she's got a baby, Ray's granddaughter. It's so sad." Marcel took her hand, stroking it gently.

"What happened to Ray, do you know?" he asked. Annamarie shrugged. "He just disappeared. I've heard he may have been taken out by a Mexican drug cartel, because of his connection to his friend, Frank O'Connor, a drug dealer killed in Las Vegas. I just don't know."

330

Marcel sat back in his chair and studied Annamarie silently for a while, nodding his head in understanding. Then he leaned forward and pulled her closer, speaking in a hushed tone. "Close, but not quite right," he said. "I'm going to tell you more, but you must promise to keep it secret, okay?" She eagerly nodded her assent.

"Ray was targeted by a gang, all right, but it wasn't the Mexican drug cartel," Marcel said quietly, matter-of-factly. "It was an international syndicate, run by the Russian mob, with illegal operations all over the world. They got him, but he got away."

"He's alive?" Annamarie exclaimed, excitedly, and Marcel shushed her softly, looking around to ensure the Bourbon Street revelers weren't paying attention. "Listen," he said. "Ray's hurt, not bad, but he's also in hiding. The feds are trying to bring in the leaders of the gang, and it's complicated. The ringleader, a guy Ray played cards with in Las Vegas, is holed up in Russia. Ray's not safe until he's neutralized."

"Neutralized!" Annamarie raised her hands, sat back in her chair, and sighed, shaking her head. "I don't understand. Where's Ray? Is he okay?" She studied Marcel's face for answers before leaning forward to hear more. Marcel laid out the story deliberately as if it was dictated to him. Ray was being watched by federal agents as well as foreign gangsters, but they were a couple of steps behind when Ray was beaten and hauled off in a van. They intercepted the bad guys, arrested them, and rescued Ray. "He's under a doctor's care, with a security detail," he said. "I've seen him. He asked about you."

Annamarie's face had broken into a huge smile, relief mixed with excitement and awe. Could this be true? Marcel hurried on. "They were after Ray because his columns in LA and Las Vegas caused problems with their drug-running and money-laundering operations," he explained. "And this guy Bredkoff really hates Western reporters, and thinks Ray double-crossed him."

"What did Ray say about me?" Annamarie wants to know. "Did he send you here?" Marcel nodded and leaned toward her to whisper conspiratorially. "He wants to talk to you, but he can't come, not now." Marcel sat back, smiled, and patted her hand. Reaching into his inside coat pocket, he pulled out a phone and put it in her hand. "He'll call you tonight. You tell me what time."

"I want to talk with him now!" she exclaimed, hushed but excited. "After this next set. 10:30." Marcel stood and took Annamarie's hands, gently pulling her to her feet. "It will be done," he said. "I hope to see you soon." She kissed his cheek and whispered her thanks, then turned to descend into the raucous party below. She's got five minutes to compose herself and sing. It's a psychic jolt, Ray back from "dead," not quite risen. He can't be seen, his name not heard. He wants to talk to her. What about his daughter? Does Mona know? So many questions, no time to think. She can't go automatically through 10 songs and play for the audience; she's got to concentrate. But her head is spinning past New Orleans and all this jazz. Ray needs her. He's alive! And he needs her.

She closed with "Unforgettable" in the style of Natalie Cole, trying to curb her excitement as she intoned, "... *darling, it's incredible/That someone so unforgettable/Thinks that I am unforgettable too*," literally dropping the mike as she hurried through the back room and out the door. She shuffled quickly down the three blocks to her rental, dodging the merry revelers. Her mind now was racing back to the last time she saw Ray, before she wrote to break off their brief but eventful affair. She got a helicopter ride out of Big

332

Sur, and Ray was standing there at the edge of the clearing, waving to her as she retreated over the ocean, abandoning her to another nightmare of dangling in the air, hanging on for dear life. She promised herself she'd forget him, but he didn't forget.

Annamarie hardly recognized Ray's voice when he called, promptly at 10:30. He sounded restrained, softer, maybe weaker. "Are you okay?" she asked, a plaintive plea as much as a question. "Yes, yes," he rushed to assure her, then sighed. "I was blindsided. They beat me up; I got shot when the feds came to bail me out. Just my shoulder; it could have been worse. They meant to kill me, that's what I'm told, and I believe it.

"Listen, I sent word to Mona, and she's promised not to say anything, to wait until it cools down," Ray said. "That's how I found out you were in New Orleans, running away from the political spotlight and all that legal mess. The nurses' union was disappointed. What are your plans?"

"I plan to take root here, to follow this dream, to sing the songs I love in a place where they're appreciated," Annamarie said. "This is fun, Ray. You were right. I wish you were here with me." A pause on the line before Ray responds, "That's not possible right now. I have to stay in this bubble for a while."

Annamarie was wrestling with her conflicted feelings about Ray, and her confusion about her own journey. She took a huge risk abandoning a promising, if aggravating, career to chase a dream in New Orleans. Ray encouraged her, but she wasn't sure how he fit into the dream. "What do you want me to do?" she asked.

"Just keep singing," he said. "I'll be listening, and finding others to listen, pitching you to music agents and record companies. But don't sign anything until you talk with me. Okay?"

"Oh, my God! Are you serious?" Annamarie had jumped from her seat, startled by this surprising proposition. Ray assured her he wasn't joking. "I told you before that promoting your singing career was a perfect job for me," he said. "I meant it. Especially now. It's my only job."

That night, Annamarie couldn't sleep, giddy with the prospect of real success, a star turn, and supported by someone who believed in her. Who said he loved her. Could it be real? She took a deep breath. She was afraid before, but not anymore. She was ready to fly. Softly, she sang: *"Though it's just dreaming I make your love true And I trade in this real world for one dream of you...."*

Epilogue

The excitement in Annamarie's voice thrilled me; it was a magic elixir for my gloomy disposition, even if only a momentary respite. I'm quickly back to reality, realizing I'm in no shape to give Annamarie the career boost I promised. I'm relying on Jay Lee, who says he'll pitch her to talent agents he knows in Hollywood, always on the lookout for budding stars. We've got audio recordings, and Marcel shot video in New Orleans. I have great hope Annamarie will be a star, but little hope of rekindling the spark that animated my relationship with the brilliant jazz diva who now comes to me in my dreams. I credit her for forcing me to face my dishonesty and hypocrisy in our relationship, and with others, willfully "fooling myself." But that's little consolation for me now.

Yeah, I fucked up. I wasn't thinking straight after I was attacked in Las Vegas, working my way back to reality as I recovered in the hospital. I should have sent the poker-game draft to Chaz, but I'm not sure it would have changed anything. I was bound and determined to write my cheeky parable for Tax Day – that's how it was presented, a bunch of global tax cheats playing with their hidden wealth, promoting themselves. Not exactly a murderers row, but certainly a gang of white-collar criminals. I'm not sure what Chaz was thinking, inviting me to the poker table, or why a bunch of global mega-dealers agreed to talk to me. But I owed Chaz a chance to read the story, to bitch, and maybe I'd change something if he had a reasonable objection. If I had any idea my life depended on that story …, what the hell! It's done.

Now I'm even more dependent on Jay Lee and his well-connected friends, including Mo, who set up medical facilities for me in the backroom of the Diamond M Ranch house, where I'm recuperating from wounds much more substantial than I let on to Annamarie and Mona. Jay has visited several times, bringing intelligence reports from Zhou and updates on Wei-Lin, who's teaching dance at the Falun Gong school. "I'm trying to get her to come back to LA," he said. Lou Guy has become Li Hongzhi's primary security guard, and Wu has been deposed, banished to the Dragon Springs Buddhist temple to meditate on his karmic sins.

"Your article really shook up Falun Dafa; you must have expected how it would hurt them," Jay said sternly, reflecting his displeasure with my reporting on Falun Gong's stealth lobbying efforts promoting the Trump administration. Had he fallen in with the Falun Gong cult? Jay shrugged off my suggestion. "I agree with many other Chinese-Americans and ex-pats," he said. "We should help the Chinese people get rid of the cruel Xi dictatorship. "Falun Dafa is a victim but also a heroic movement inspiring people to resist. I want them to succeed."

I'm reminded again how my road to recovery, guided by my Chinese doctor with his mystical philosophy and integrative health practices, is entangled with the stories I'm trying to tell about the nascent Trump administration – and assisted by the administration's drug enforcement and intelligence operatives, Zhou and Mo. And Jay with his own beautiful and brawny assistants. Am I being too cynical? Paranoid?

I can't help but think the worst while lying here alone, largely immobile, my life reduced to a bed with a lever I can use to prop myself up to eat and write on my laptop, or lower myself down to sleep. Sparrow brings me food on a tray. Sweet Sparrow, my comfort.

She knocks and enters now to announce I have a visitor, a friend. Behind her, a man steps out of the shadow, thinning gray hair pulled back in a ponytail, a scraggle of gray beard on his face. I raise the lever to pull myself up. "George?"

George Bayer rushes over to my side, placing his hand on my cheek as he grabs my hand, squeezing and stroking as he speaks hoarsely, "Ray, I'm so sorry. I came as soon as I knew where you were, that you're alive! I've been so worried." His greeting came in a burst of emotion, words rushing out, eyes moist with both concern and relief. He hugs my neck, and I pull him close. "So good to finally catch up with you, George, or I suppose it's the other way around."

George pulls a chair close to me, still holding my hand, looking pleadingly at me. "I'm so sorry," he repeated. "I feel like I'm responsible for this, for what happened to you. How are you doing?" I'll survive, I tell him, but I'll never walk again – short of a medical miracle or technological revolution. The bullet wasn't a glancing blow; I was hit in the lower back. It severed my spinal cord, tore my spleen, perforated my gastric system. I'm a mess, mostly healing, except for mobility. I've lost the use of my legs, paralyzed from the waist down.

George gasps with this news, and tears flow as he sobs. "I didn't know. Jay said I should come to see you, that you needed me." I pat George's hand and tell him not to worry. I'll get through this and eventually join him in Colorado, to complete the trip. I won't be able to go hiking with him again like in the old days, so he'll have to slow down so I can keep up. The doctors stabilized my bladder, but they told me I'll need more operations before I could start the recovery. But don't count me out as a driver and wheelchair operator, I tell him. I'll be back on the road eventually.

"But, George, tell me: What is it we missed those many years ago?" I ask. "There was something very important you had to tell me. Now we can talk."

George sighs. "It really wasn't important, especially now after all that's happened," he says. "I just wanted to walk and meditate with you, like we used to do, take stock of the dreams we shared. Where do we go from here? You always inspired me, the way you think. When I heard you were seeing Jay Lee, following the *qigong* story, I figured your journey would be the main thing, that you would bring important lessons from your trip."

I groan at the thought; the lessons in front of me are painfully clear, of little use to anyone else except perhaps as warning. There's nothing to share except the misery of immobility and dim vision of what lies ahead. I bite my lip to squelch the anguish and apologize to George. He doesn't need to know the extent of the indignities I'm enduring as I work myself back to life. There have been valuable lessons. I won't be discouraged by this cruel twist of fate; I'll rise above it, even if I can't land on my feet.

The dull throb at the base of my neck reminds me I need rest and medication, so I make a date to see George in the morning. He's staying in the bunkhouse for a week, and I'm sure he'll get a full briefing from his old CIA buddy Mo and *qigong* master Jay – at least, briefed as much as he needs to know. I won't complain about my friends rallying to my side in my distress, even if I have this sinking feeling that I've been a useful idiot in the larger scheme of things, another journalist used by sources for political ends. It happens, even among friends.

338

Sparrow knocks on the door and enters with a tray filled with drugs and paraphernalia. I'm going for a nice long sleep, but first, she's got to tend to the accumulated waste and change my diaper, not a fun event with all the tubes and mess. The woman who touched my heart is now wiping my butt. And when she's done, Sparrow smiles and hugs my neck as I settle back in the bed, take a deep breath and relax my mind. Perhaps there is another person who loves me as much as does my dear Mona. I'm still not worthy, but I can work on it. Every day is new. I follow the next dream.

Down to Earth

Mountain mist feeding grey green ferment, freshens a breeze

Bantering boys being boys becoming men find Meaning

On the way to high adventure, with wonder and wander

Lust, embracing the newest way to see and believe

The farther you go, the further you may see

Merrily then we run, no fear, no chance we fall, so high

On licorice mint, manic motion mingling emotion

Our human burden, scuffing the ocher earth

With Purple Passion blowing in the wind

Rustling memories, birthing dreams.

The Poet plays on these dubious heights grasping straws

Searching for natural Truth in haphazard tripping

Uphill, lying obscured amid thorns and bristles

Distraction, inaction, confusion, illusion

Just breathe away this monkey mind

Clarity lies not along this road but back where it began

The source, looking inside, inner-venture, let Solitude

Strip away points of reference: I am therefore I am

A Poet not wasting words in lyrical nonsense

Searching for Sanity in a clutter of ideas.

Man with mighty Mouth so grandly tells the story

Visions of glory and pomp weigh in every word

Vainly speaking in symbols, reeking of hubris

Daring to ask what and not caring why

We're still going round and round

So we race past the myopic images, the daily items.

A sphere of constant change with and without us

Go with it, flow with it, grow with it, and know

The inevitable triumph of Earth churning

Through our petty human story.

■ George Bayer,
October 2017

Printed in the USA
CPSIA information can be obtained
at www.ICGtesting.com
LVHW050221090923
757426LV00021B/1606